MW01074634

Marion Ettlinger

Roxana Robinson is the author of three earlier novels, three collections of short stories, and the biography *Georgia O'Keeffe: A Life*. Her work has appeared in *The New Yorker*, *Harper's Magazine*, *The Atlantic*, *The New York Times*, *The Washington Post*, *The Wall Steet Journal*, *More*, and *Vogue*, among other publications. Her writing has also been published in *Best American Short Stories*, widely anthologized, and broadcast on National Public Radio. She has received fellowships from the National Endowment for the Arts, The MacDowell Colony, and the Guggenheim Foundation, and has taught creative writing at the University of Houston and Wesleyan University. She now teaches at the New School in New York.

"Robinson's fourth novel is an engrossing tale of a patrician family's unraveling during a summer in Maine. . . . Robinson moves nimbly among the numerous characters' mind-sets."   —*The New Yorker*

"This is simply one of the most heart-wrenching and powerful novels I have ever read. . . . Impossible to put down, its bleakness relieved by Robinson's elegant, restrained prose and breakneck pacing. . . . Beautiful and terrifying."   —*Down East*

"In her forceful and gripping new novel, *Cost*, Roxana Robinson creates a psychologically mesmerizing family dynamic in the vortex of one son's drug addiction. . . . Robinson gives a nuanced emotional and physical account of an addict's life."   —*South Florida Sun-Sentinel*

"Robinson has always been a sensitive and revelatory writer, but she attains new degrees of intensity here in her scorching depictions of the nightmare world of addiction. Her illuminations of the churning inner lives of her smart and deep-feeling characters depict good people facing brutal forces beyond the reach of reason and love."   —*Booklist*

"A strikingly realistic, psychologically astute study of family relations in modern America's educated class . . . Robinson gracefully launches and bolsters her psychological insights with the concrete details of her settings. As always, she writes with impressive polish."—*The Atlantic*

"[A] brilliant and devastating novel . . . some of the most harrowing passages this reviewer has ever read."   —*Bookpage*

"*Cost* is a gritty portrait of the havoc wreaked upon a family by one member's drug addiction. Roxana Robinson's vivid, sensuous prose moves effortlessly among relationships and points of view, evoking a brutal war between familial love—in its infinite power and mystery—and the mechanical devastations of pathology."

—Jennifer Egan, author of *The Keep*

"*Cost* is stunning. Each of the characters is so perfectly realized, each is made known to us with such heart and intelligence. This is a very big book: the territory of family is more fragile and dangerous than any geography we know, and Roxana Robinson has made life of that. I loved, admired, and was frankly undone by every minute of it."

—Susan Richards Shreve, author of *A Student of Living Things*

"With passion, feeling, and a keen eye for detail, Roxana Robinson brings chillingly to life a family and a family tragedy, showing us how—like a luminous yet ominous landscape—their tangible visible world can coincide with the invisible tumultuous world of their emotions."

—Lily Tuck, author of *The News from Paraguay*

"Roxana Robinson is surely one of the most graceful stylists and psychologically perceptive writers working. . . . *Cost* approaches the subject of drugs' impact from an original and very significant angle. This book shows further the extent of Robinson's insights into the whirl, the generational ironies at work, and the desperate indulgences to which we turn in our confusion. *Cost* is an important, timely book that furthers insight into our preset fortunes and dilemmas."

—Robert Stone, author of *Prime Green: Remembering the Sixties*

COST

COST

ROXANA ROBINSON

PICADOR

SARAH CRICHTON BOOKS
FARRAR, STRAUS AND GIROUX
NEW YORK

www.picadorusa.com

Picador® is a U.S. registered trademark and is used by
Farrar, Straus and Giroux under license from Pan Books Limited.

For information on Picador Reading Group Guides, please contact Picador.
E-mail: readinggroupguides@picadorusa.com

A portion of this work appeared in slightly different form in *Epiphany*.

Designed by Michelle McMillian

Library of Congress Cataloging-in-Publication Data
Robinson, Roxana.
Cost / Roxana Robinson.—1st Picador ed.
   p.   cm.
ISBN-13: 978-0-312-42846-4
ISBN-10: 0-312-42846-4
1. Middle-aged women—Fiction. 2. Sandwich generation—Fiction. 3. Parent and adult
child—Fiction. 4. Alzheimer's disease—Patients—Fiction. 5. Heroin abuse—Fiction.
6. Family—Fiction. I. Title.
PS3568.O3152C67   2009b
   813'.54—dc22   2009001785

First published in the United States by Sarah Crichton Books,
a division of Farrar, Straus and Giroux

First Picador Edition: June 2009

In memory of
Henry Ward Scoville
1909–1924

PART I

ONE

Her memory was gone.

It came to Katharine like a soft shock, like a blow inside the head. She was in the yellow bedroom at her daughter's house in Maine, standing at the bureau, getting ready for lunch. She'd just finished doing her hair, smoothing it back to her modest bun, tucking in the small combs to hold it in place. The combs were hardly necessary now, her long, fine hair—still mostly black—had turned wispy and weightless, and no longer needed restraint. But vanity, like beauty, is partly habit, and Katharine still put the combs carefully into her thinning hair, though now they slipped easily out, then vanished, beneath the furniture, against the patterns of the rugs.

Hair done, combs briefly and precariously in place, Katharine looked around for her scarf. It was an old soft cotton one, a blue paisley square. She'd worn it once at a birthday party, and now, for a moment, in her daughter's guest room with its faded yellow walls, the sunlight slanting onto the worn wooden floors, the idea of the scarf and the party seemed confusingly to merge. She had a sudden sense of the party blooming around her—a blur of voices, laughter, a fireplace—a sense of pleasure at being with these people, whoever they were. Green demitasse cups, those tiny tinkling spoons, a tall brass lamp by the fireplace—or was that somewhere else?

She tried to remember herself further into it, but could not. She could not mentally arrive at the event. She stood at the bureau, her mind groping. Everything else about the party—whom it was for, when it had happened, where—had vanished. The small, hard, bright facts, like nails that should connect it to the rest of her life, were missing. The place where her memory had been was gone, blurrily erased, like a window grayed by mist. Beyond it was unknown space.

Other things, besides that party, were vanishing—the names and places she depended on, the familiar links that made up her past. This was happening gradually, as though pieces of her mind were breaking off and floating away, like ice in a river. She couldn't stop it, she didn't want to think about it.

But now, standing at the bureau, this realization rose up around her, closing in on her like a high breaking wave. She felt as though she were being held helpless and still, while the rest of her awareness slid past her, increasingly fast. Who were you if you had no past? If you existed nowhere but in this room, right now? If your life were being swept away from you?

Katharine stood still, disoriented by the thought. She held on to the bureau with both hands, bracing herself, as though this were a fast current she might be able to resist. She looked down at the hands before her: they did not seem to be hers. They were mottled and swollen, slow with arthritis, the knuckles thick. She'd always had graceful hands, pale, with long narrow fingers. Hadn't she?

She stood without moving in her daughter's yellow guest room, gripping the bureau and looking down at her things as though they might keep her steady: the blue cotton scarf, which was right in front of her; the spray bottle of lavender cologne—the scent reminding her of her mother—missing its cap; a round silver pin etched with leaves—a birthday present, years ago, but from whom? One of the children, she thought: it still held a strong charge of affection. She saw all these things in front of her, whole, present, while that thought ranged greedily through her mind—radical, bewildering, calamitous—her memory was gone.

Julia, in the kitchen, was making lunch, moving quickly, her movements hurried, slightly inept: having her parents in the house put her on high alert, her pulse thrumming. When they were here, there was not enough of her. She should be everywhere, all the time—in the bedroom, helping her mother find a lost comb; in the cellar, looking for a tool for her father; out on the porch, quickly sweeping it before lunch; in the kitchen, fixing meals.

Julia wanted her parents here—she loved them—but their presence altered her gravity. She had to struggle to stay upright. As she swung open the door of the refrigerator, leaning into its chilly radiance, taking out the wrapped packet of ham, the mayonnaise, she could feel the beat of anxiety, the hurrying of her pulse. Down the hall, in the yellow room, were her parents, breathing, speaking, about to need something.

What she felt when her parents were here was something large and unsayable, confusing, nearly unbearable. Affection, anxiety, resentment— although she was an adult, with her own children, nearly grown, and she should long ago have moved beyond this confusion. But her parents' presence still unsettled her. When they were here, the house seemed small and ill equipped, the doors put on backward, the light switches unconnected, a troubling dreamscape where nothing was right.

Deliberately, Julia slowed herself down. She drew a long breath. *Relax.* Deliberately she took down the blue-and-white-striped plates, set them down on the counter. You can't do everything, she told herself sensibly. (Why did good advice come in platitudes?) Her parents enjoyed it here. The visit itself, that was what she was giving them. Julia liked having them here, liked offering them all this, the summer day, the house, with its faintly spicy, cedary smell. The early-morning twittering of finches in the lilacs. The sun on the tall ferns that crowded the back porch. The long pink grass of the meadow, rippling down to the cove. These were the things her parents were here for. *And herself. Her parents were here to see her. They loved her.*

She drew another long, calming breath, releasing the clutch of anxiety. She picked up the jar of mayonnaise. Twisting the top, she felt its hidden threads turn smoothly beneath her hands, unlocking the grip of metal on glass, and felt sudden pleasure at the way things worked, at the way one neat circular motion did exactly what it should. A ripple of admiration for the whole mechanized world of gears, cogs, ratchets, levers, pulleys—the physical systems that made things work. *It was brilliant, the way people—men, really, engineers were mostly men, despite feminism—had established such ingenious control over the world of objects.*

What she wanted was to make her parents happy. It didn't matter when they had lunch, or if the porch had been swept. She unwrapped the damp translucent packet of meat. (There was something indecent about sliced ham, about the look of it, that pink succulence, its clinging moistness.)

Julia sliced a tomato, opening its juicy scarlet core, then lapping the slices in a neat circle on a plate. She opened the jar of mustard, for her mother and herself. Her father's sandwich would not have mustard or lettuce. The list of things her father did not like was legion: Edward viewed the world as a student project offered up to him for correction.

Edward's presence flooded through the house, powerful, demanding, judgmental. At any moment he might appear in the doorway, offering criticism, finding fault. The day before, while Julia was fixing dinner, Edward had arrived in the kitchen with a peremptory request for a flashlight to check beneath the sink in his bathroom.

"Water's dripping onto the floor," he announced. "I want to see what's going on."

"It's probably only condensation on the pipes," said Julia, her heart sinking. "Not a leak." *Surely she'd know if there were a leak? Surely this wasn't a leak?*

"I'd like to have a look at it," he told her, as though she hadn't spoken. "Could I have a flashlight?"

He'd stood in the doorway, waiting, while Julia stopped chopping carrots to root through the kitchen drawer. She found a flashlight, but it was dead, and there seemed to be only one new battery—a mystery, since they came in pairs.

"Sorry," she said, irritated at herself. Her father turned without a word and went back down the hall.

It was a fact that the house was shabby, and that many aspects of it were primitive or provisional. Julia and her ex-husband Wendell—both underpaid university professors—had always had less money than her parents, and now that she was single again, Julia had even less than before. Her father, who'd been a brilliant and successful neurosurgeon, had offered her no financial help during the divorce, believing that beds should be made and then lain in. He'd always seemed to take a stern relish in reminding her of her impecuniousness, pointing out the flaws in her house, her life, and the way she ran them. Now that she was poorer it seemed to Julia that he did this more often, as though being poor were merely an oversight on her part, and, if offered enough convincing evidence from him, she would change her mind and decide to be rich.

It was the constant threat of her father's appearance, his criticisms and demands, that made Julia feel harried. ("Rattled," her mother would say. "Nettled." She used those old-fashioned expressions. No one nowadays would know what a nettle felt like, the faint silvery irritation made by the leaves against your bare leg.)

She must relax, Julia told herself. *Though why was he so rude about her house? And so casually rude, as though finding fault were his right. As though he had some special entitlement to criticism.*

She drew another deep breath and laid out the slices of bread on the counter in rows, like bread solitaire. She spread the mayonnaise, smoothing it creamily out to the edges. The tangible world: she admired the rich surface of the mayonnaise. Opaque, succulent. How would you paint it, she wondered, and get both the glitter and opacity? Who used that heavy, creamy brushstroke? Chase? Sargent? It all looked like a painting already.

Her father was eighty-eight, her mother eighty-six. Julia loved them, and they were getting old. She didn't think of them as actually old, but as *getting* old. They were nearing that country, their bodies were less present in the world, they were losing height and weight and bulk. Her parents were being diminished. She could feel them moving away, withdrawing, sweeping out like the tide toward the distant horizon.

Her father appeared now in the doorway.

How is it, she thought, *that when we see someone, all the disembodied thoughts and emotions of that person coalesce in that figure, that presence? How does the body carry that dense weight of being?*

Her father's body held him, his character within it. If the body was lost, all his thoughts and feelings, his opinions, his irascibility, his surgical skills would be lost, swept into deep space. He would be intact then only in memory—a system so flawed and arbitrary, so unreliable, so wanting. The thought made her panicky. She looked at her father and was struck by her deep knowledge of him, by the way their lives were wrapped around each other's, the many times she'd seen him walk into a room. How she'd longed, she supposed, for his approval.

Her father was now shockingly small, nearly her own height. In her childhood, when she'd first learned him, her father had been immense, massive-chested, towering over her like a cliff. His head was in the upper regions of the air; she'd had to call up to his great height, her own voice tossed and tiny. Even when she'd grown up, her father had been tall. At her wedding, walking down the long aisle of the church, her father remote and distant beside her, in his dark suit, she'd felt his looming, powerful presence.

But now her father's eyes were nearly level with hers, and his movements slow. Now his forehead rose to the top of his head, and fine white hair ringed his bare pate like a tonsure. His hair was too fine and weightless to lie down, and it stood up wildly, as though blown by a small personal wind. His nose had become bulbous; on his pouched yellowy cheeks were faint brown stains. His small piercing eyes were faded blue, and deep disapproving lines were etched from nose to mouth.

He wore old khaki pants, ponderous white running shoes, and a stained blue windbreaker, zipped up to his chin. He wore the jacket every day, indoors and out, as though it were the only thing he owned.

This was not the way he'd used to dress. Julia remembered him leaving for the hospital each morning wearing elegant suits, dull silk ties, soft leather shoes. Now he looked like a poor person, homeless. *Which was what age did to you, it stripped you of what you'd had, of your presence in the world.* The sight of him like this, shuffling, heavy-footed, in his stained windbreaker, made Julia feel helpless with tenderness.

Her father frowned at her. "Do you have an atlas?" he demanded. "I want to look up where we are."

At once Julia forgot her tenderness, her anxiety. He had restored himself to despot. His manner—autocratic, imperious—never ceased to exasperate her.

"We do have an atlas," Julia said. "I'll get it for you."

She strode into the living room, bare heels thudding confidently on the floor. Crouching by the bottom shelf, where the big books lay flat, she ran her fingers briskly and uselessly down the spines: the atlas, she could see at once, was gone.

She looked further, her gaze ranging back and forth across the shelves, lunch unfinished on the counter, her father standing ponderously behind her, judgment gathering in the silence. *The atlas had its own place on the bottom shelf, everyone knew it. Why, right now, her father's frown embedding itself on his forehead, was the atlas elsewhere? More evidence of her inability to run a household. Where could it possibly be, that big ungainly volume?*

Julia sat back on her heels. "It's not here, Daddy. Sorry." She made her voice brisk and offhand.

"It's not there?"

"Someone's taken it and not put it back." She stood and headed for the kitchen, head high.

"I wanted to see just where we are on the coast." Her father shook his head. "You don't have an atlas."

"I do have an atlas," Julia corrected him. "Someone's taken it."

There was a pause.

Edward said, "I don't see how you can say you have an atlas if you don't have it."

"I do have an atlas," Julia repeated. "I just can't find it right now."

Edward shook his head. "I'd call that not having one," he said, almost to himself. "Do you have a map of the region? A local map? I want to see where we are on the coast."

"We're Down East," Julia said. "That's what you say up here. You don't say north or south, you say Down East. Because of the schooners, and the prevailing winds."

"*I know that*," Edward said. "I know about being Down East. What I want to know is *where*. I want to look at a map and see exactly where we are on the coast."

"There might be a map in the car," Julia said, though right now she doubted it, "but I'm in the middle of making lunch. Can it wait until afterward?"

What her father made her feel was incompetent: the missing atlas, the absent husband, the shabby house. *Don't say anything more*, she silently commanded.

She peeled off a translucent slice of ham and laid it carefully onto the bread. Her father waited for a moment, but she did not look up. Frustrated, he turned away. She heard him heading slowly down the hall, the floor creaking beneath his steps.

At once she was ashamed.

Why did this happen? Why did she snap at her father like an adolescent? Why did he unsettle her? She was an adult. She had two wonderful sons, an ex-husband, and a possible new boyfriend; she taught at a distinguished university, she was a working artist, she showed her work regularly at a good gallery. She should be far beyond the reach of her father. But her father, though he himself was diminishing, still cast a long shadow over her life.

Julia and Wendell had bought this house years ago, when the boys were small. It was supremely inconvenient—an eight-hour drive from Manhattan—but supremely cheap. Even so, the upkeep and taxes had always been a struggle, and many times they'd almost sold it. The house would never be worth much, though; it was not on a fashionable part of the coast: no presidents or Wyeths or Rockefellers lived in this small stretch of bays and coves and wild islands.

The clapboard house stood at a little distance from the weathered barn. This was unusual here: during the old, bitter winters it had been too dangerous to venture outside. The old farmhouses were connected to their barns by a telescoping series of constructions. Bighouse, little-house, backhouse, barn, they were called. Julia liked the notion of continuous shelter, and she liked the rhythm of the phrase. Sometimes she said it silently to herself as she passed an old farmstead.

This house—now entirely hers—was lapped by meadows. In the upper field, above the house, were ancient apple trees gone exuberantly wild, their branches tangled into a sweet green net. The lower field was only grass, soft and silky, sloping mildly down to a sheltered tidal cove. Now, in late summer, the grass had turned a tawny pink, and glowed mysteriously at sunset. Julia's studio was in the barn overlooking the meadow. Through the big picture window she had painted this many times, the rich rippling grass, the moving water beyond it, the glittering sea-bright light. It was a symphony; she had never come to the end of it.

Julia and Wendell had always planned to fix up the house properly, but they could never afford it, and the house had stayed shabby. The white paint peeled in the scouring Maine weather, the shingles turned mossy, the shutters drooped at the windows. "Look on the bright side," Wendell said. "No one would break into a house that looks like this."

Every summer Wendell and Julia had worked together on the house. Since the divorce, it was Julia and the boys, Steven and Jack. Julia tried to paint one outside wall every other year. It was peaceful work. She liked sitting high on the stepladder, scraping at the worn paint in the bright sun, no sound but the wind sifting through the grass.

Inside, she'd learned basic maintenance—fuse boxes, simple plumbing. How the window sashes worked, the hidden weights plummeting inside the wall. She liked knowing the house in this intimate way, the dim earthy spaces of the damp cellar, the cool touch of the pipes, the tiny beads of moisture on the singing metal. The hot motionless air of the attic, the sloping eaves, the faint desultory hum of wasps. She liked using the solid-headed hammer, the long gleaming nails. She liked the screwdriver, the firm twists sending the grooved shaft spiraling deep into the wood. She liked responding to the old house, earning her ownership.

Wendell had loved the house, too. It had been the biggest issue in their divorce, but Julia had been obdurate. At first Wendell had been furious, but then he'd married a woman who didn't like Maine. It was too far away, pronounced Sandra, too cold. They went to Bridgehampton. If Wendell had kept the house, he'd have sold it when he married Sandra, and that would have killed Julia.

Julia liked Sandra, despite her wrong-headed views on Maine. Sandra was small and smart and friendly, like a terrier. Wendell was lucky to have her. *As he'd been lucky to have her, Julia. Men were lucky to have any women, any women at all*, she thought, laying down the top slices of bread. Her father would never realize how fortunate he'd been to have her mother at his side, patient, merry, forgiving. *Men shuffled and stomped their way through life, women smoothed out the rucked-up mess they made with their big boots.*

To be fair, Julia remembered the smooth slide of the mayonnaise jar in her hands, engineers, the way men understood the physicality of the world, and their readiness to take risks, their reckless courage; she forgave them the boots.

To be fair, there were men who were wonderful, too, and women who were not. She herself was not so wonderful. She was often impatient, often ungenerous: look at the way she behaved toward her father—but she would do better. She would make it up, with her father.

There was the awful woman Wendell had left her for, ghastly and dead-eyed from drink or drugs. She'd been arrested once on the Mass Pike, Wendell had told her, DUI. *So unseemly!* Julia had been delighted. That was a woman who had not been wonderful in any way, except possibly in bed.

No, Wendell was luckier than God to have sane, comforting Sandra now in his life, a family therapist, and very kind. Kind to Wendell, kind even to Julia, and, most wonderfully, kind to Steven and Jack. And Simon, the man Julia had started seeing just before the summer began (a mathematician, and how unlikely was that?), was lucky to have her, Julia, in his life, too. Wasn't he? Though this was precipitate. She wasn't sure yet if she were in his life, or he in hers. He had become a presence—thoughtful, quiet, sympathetic—but things between them were in the early stages. She was cautious, he was reserved. It was too soon to say if either of them were lucky.

Julia leaned over the bowl of peaches, inhaling the rich sunny scent, inspecting them for ripeness. Two were dark tawny pink, gently yielding; one was darker, suspiciously soft. She took the bad one for herself, as penance for her behavior to her father.

She carried the lunch tray out the back door, to the porch overlooking the meadow. As she stepped onto it, the porch floor yielded slightly beneath her weight: it was rotting. Fungus and mold and many-legged creatures were burrowing furiously and constantly into its boards, slowly turning the wood into crumbling humus. It was a kind of alchemy, this continual mindless urge on the part of everything in the material world to return to an earlier, more primitive form: wood to soil, metal to rust, plaster to dust.

Julia imagined prizing up the soft wood with a crowbar, ripping up everything, revealing the damp splinters, the damp scuttling creatures. Banishing them, sweeping everything out, setting out the heavy new boards. Lining them up, measuring, sawing—though this was real, serious carpentry, electric saws, unwieldly lumber. It was beyond her. She'd take it up in some other life. The one in which she got along with her father.

She set down the tray and went back inside. In the front hall she called to her parents, still in the guest room: "Lunch is ready."

"All right." Her mother's voice was high and sweet and frail, like an old woman's. "I'm just putting on my scarf."

Her father did not answer. He would be standing beside her mother, his awful windbreaker zipped up to his chin, waiting, proud of his patience.

Julia waited, too. For this moment—the lunch tray out on the porch, the water pitcher coated with fine cold droplets, the sandwiches neatly cut—she was idle.

On the hall floor lay an ancient, threadbare Persian rug, its fringe ragged and meager. On the wall an old etching hung over a small, ponderous mahogany table. Beside it was a black Windsor chair. Sunlight irradiated the plaster walls, slanting past the etching. It was a picture of Paris at twilight, black roofs and chimneypots against a crepuscular sky. Julia liked the idea of Paris—its narrow streets and gilded salons, its worldliness and complexity—set here in the bare old house with its painted wooden floors, in the empty windswept countryside. She liked the sense it gave of the great reach and swing of the world. She liked the house itself, its simplicity, its worn surfaces, its offer of comfort and shelter. Its dry cedary smells, and its deep, deep silences.

The Windsor chair's narrow spindles fanned gracefully out, the lines set in rhythmic intervals, like a dark chord against the pale wall. The chair, the table, the picture of Paris, the wash of sunlight all seemed to form some mysterious balance. The house was soundless. Shafts of sunlight struck through the rooms, across the walls, the old rugs, the rickety furniture. The day was suspended, the earth paused. In this moment it seemed that a celestial order ruled. The sun flooded through her, she felt herself dissolving into luminous silence. She was here, in this moment, in the old house. Nothing was more luxurious than this deep soundlessness and light. Her parents, whom she loved, and who loved her—who were the great high cliffs of her world, still towering over her, though beginning to dissolve into the radiant dusk—were nearby. They were alive, they were here, and about to emerge into the sunlit hall.

Suspended, invisible, Julia waited for her parents to appear. She wondered what their life was like, their private life, when they were alone together in a room. Their shared silences. Who were you when you were unobserved? What were the things they kept from her? What were the things you kept from your children?

What did she keep from her own children? Very little now. When your children were small you tried to conceal your doubts and fears, your pettiness and failures. You tried to be what they needed—strong and certain, pure and loving. Of course they learned quite soon who you were—weak, uncertain, impatient, ungenerous. There was nothing of your character they did not know.

Though there were parts of your life you kept to yourself. There were things Julia would never tell them, things that should stay un-shared, unconfessed. There were secrets that should die with people.

When Julia was alone, her personality unbound, drifting, she had no idea what she was like. Would her children recognize her? Didn't she twist herself, quickly, instinctively, into the shape she always wore for her children? Was it different from the shapes she wore for other people? For her parents?

The guest-room door opened, and Katharine stood in the doorway, leaning on her cane. Over her hair was a blue paisley scarf, tied dashingly at the nape of her neck, like a Gypsy's. She smiled at her daughter.

As a young woman, Katharine had been beautiful, with high cheek-bones, liquid brown eyes, a square Gallic face and aquiline nose. She was still a beauty; the soft skin was weathered, but the cheekbones and profile were still firm. Her loveliness lay now in her warm luminous eyes, her inclusive smile: Katharine had always enjoyed her days.

Julia saw her mother's younger face beneath this one, as though a steadily thickening net, a veil of age, were being set over it. The earlier face was still present, but dissolving into this one, soft, lined, mottled.

Katharine made her way slowly down the hall. She wore baggy blue pants, a loose flowered shirt. Her small body was now shapeless—thick and bulky at its middle, slack and gaunt elsewhere. The womanly landmarks—waist, breasts, hips—had slid into insignificance.

Katharine walked unevenly, her torso dipping with each step. Her hip had been injured long ago, before she'd been married. It was part of the family history. An accident: icy roads, a skidding milk truck. Before it, Katharine had swum, skied, danced, played tennis. She'd famously climbed to the top of Mount Washington with her older brothers. Afterward, for a while she'd seemed to recover, but over the years everything had steadily worsened. Her spine had shifted, compensating for the damaged hip. An ankle had given way and had been fused. The other ankle weakened, a shoulder froze. In spite of operations and therapy, her body had become increasingly twisted. Now she leaned heavily on a cane, her movements slow and awkward.

What was her mother like, alone in a room?

Alone with her pain. Pain was the thing that was never mentioned. Katharine never spoke of it, nor did Edward, though they all knew it was present. There was nothing to be done; it was to be endured. To talk about it, even to admit it existed, was somehow shameful.

Her mother's life swam around Julia, a dense transparent layer of existence, like the veil of atmosphere surrounding her planet. Julia held in herself the sunny stretch of her mother's childhood as the darling of the family, the youngest child, the only girl. The Depression, when she'd nearly had to drop out of college. The accident, then the dark stretch of the war. Her domestic world, her husband, her three children. The ebbs and flows of Katharine's marriage—would Julia ever know about these things? Did she want to? Could she bear knowing them? She did not want to know her mother's pain, it was unbearable to consider. The intimate knowledge of her mother's life was charged, dangerous, too powerful and frightening to approach. Though in some way she did know these things, she knew them by breathing in her mother's life with her own. Julia was encased by her mother's life; she saw her own life through it, it was her air. We think back through our mothers, if we are women, Virginia Woolf had said. But it was alarming to think back, to venture into the closed and secret chambers of the mother's life.

Now Katharine smiled up at her. "I love those yellow walls in the guest room," she said. "It's such a pretty color. And thank you for the flowers. You know rugosas are my favorites."

"Oh, you're very welcome," Julia said lightly.

Her tone—airy, noncommittal—implied that the walls just happened to be that shade, that the flowers had somehow gotten into the room by themselves, that she didn't know her mother loved rugosas. Julia would not admit to trying to please her mother, though she did. She would not accept her mother's gratitude or praise. She resisted her mother, held her at a tiny stubborn distance. Some subterranean line had been drawn between them, sealing Julia off.

Edward appeared now, behind Katharine. "I wanted to look up where we are," he complained, "but Julia doesn't have an atlas."

"I do have an atlas," Julia corrected him. "I just can't find it right now."

"Well, I don't know how you can say you have it if you can't find it," said Edward to himself.

"*Edward*," Katharine said humorously. She caught Julia's eye and shook her head. She was used to this, distracting attention from Edward's bad manners, making him seem charming and funny. Julia saw her father smile to himself, pleased, like a naughty boy.

Julia turned away from them both, from their collusion, her father's irritating manner. "I thought we'd eat out on the porch."

They sat in a row in the bright shade. The air was hot and dry, with a whiff of cinnamon from the ferns. Before them the long pink grass rippled down to the cove.

Katharine sighed. "This is awfully nice. You have such a lovely place."

"It's a pretty nice view," Julia said.

"But the house," Katharine insisted, "the house is lovely."

"Falling to bits," Julia said cheerfully.

"But in such a charming way," Katharine said, smiling.

"I wish I'd found that leak in the bathroom," Edward mused. "I'd have fixed it for you."

Julia said nothing. Having her parents here roused something in her. She felt she was holding something at bay. She was patrolling the border. She was never not patrolling the border. It was a peacekeeping mission, she would not provoke an incident, but she would patrol, with

17

armed guards. She picked up her sandwich and squinted into the bright light. *For the meadow, for that smoky pink grass, first an undercoat of dead green, for depth. Or maybe yellow, deep yellow, for vitality.*

The sky was brilliantly clear and blue, but the sun had moved around behind the house, and the shadows—still short and black—were beginning to lean toward sunset.

TWO

Edward followed his wife as she made her way to the back door and carefully onto the porch. As Edward stepped down, he felt the floorboards yield springily beneath him.

Rotten, Edward thought, pleased. He liked discovering flaws, it made him feel successful. Through some arcane law of psychophysics, every flaw that Edward discovered elsewhere increased his own sense of well-being.

He knew what should be done to this, the rotten boards ripped out, the punky orange shards piled on the lawn. New dry wood, the snapping of the chalked string against it, the blurred shadow flawlessly straight. The boxy, blunt-tipped pencil, the dull iron shine of the nails. Everything set in place.

Edward once would have done it himself, though now it was beyond him. Still, he'd have liked to watch it. He enjoyed watching construction—carpentry, wiring, plumbing—anything with mechanical complexity. He liked this larger, inanimate counterpart to his own world of cutting and clamping and reconnecting. He liked knowing how systems worked, all of them; he used to read instruction books on wiring and plumbing. He'd once done those things. He liked having the tools laid out on his bench, clean and ready. He liked making things function properly, correcting flaws. And there was a dark, subversive thrill about using hammers, awls, saws. Power tools: the spinning disk of silver teeth turned smooth by speed. The high whine of danger as his hands approached it, feeding the wood steadily into the lethal cut. Putting at risk his own irreplaceable tools, his hands.

He'd always been proud of his hands. They were small, with strong, supple fingers; he'd kept them clean and well-tended, the nails short, the skin pink. The harsh surgical scrub soap was abrasive, you used lotion to keep the skin from drying and cracking. They all did. At first it seemed girlish and sissy, but later it seemed normal.

All that was over. Edward could risk his hands however he liked, though he could now only do minor handiwork, nothing difficult. He had become clumsy, his agile hands were paws, the fingers thickened, joints stiff. One hand would not entirely open, because of Dupuytren's contracture, a spontaneous scarring of the fascia. The other hand opened and closed, but with difficulty: Edward was being slowly hobbled by his own body.

Worse than clumsiness, though, was the ebbing of his energy. Things he'd once have done in a moment, before breakfast, without thinking, now took him all morning. Everything was slow and hard to manage, even talking. There were moments when he could not produce a simple, common word, one he'd known his whole life. It frustrated him. He'd always been in control of things; his limbs, his mind, his life. How had he been so quietly, so irrevocably, deposed from power? He was helpless before this. All he could do was keep his secret from the world.

Part of the pleasure Edward took in discovering flaws had always lain in his ability to correct them. He'd have liked to fix the leak beneath the sink, the rotting floor. He'd have liked to fix all these things, he liked to make contributions, but offering anything to Julia was risky. He hadn't dared suggest help when Wendell left her. She'd always been touchy, and whenever he made suggestions she turned antagonistic.

She was like that, his older daughter, challenging, argumentative. Something in her was abrasive. There was a gritty vein that would not rub smooth, that ran all the way through her.

Her younger sister, Harriet, was easier in that way; Harriet didn't argue. She didn't get angry with him; she said what she meant. But she was cold, somehow. Both his daughters were difficult. For some reason, he'd gotten stiff-necked, cantankerous ones. It was too bad; he'd have liked soft, winsome daughters, that kissed and petted him.

Julia helped Katharine into a chair, and Edward lowered himself beside her. The springy metal chair sank disconcertingly.

"Oh," said Katharine, as the chair dropped beneath her. "What a nice surprise!" She bounced gently. "I think this is lovely." She crossed her wrists primly in her lap. "How do you *do*, Mrs. Astor?" She nodded to them as though she were at a tea party, rising and falling decorously.

Julia laughed. They had the same sense of humor; Edward did not. He gave a bemused smile and looked into the distance. He didn't share Katharine's penchant for the absurd. He tolerated it, but did not approve.

Katharine looked out over the meadow, still smiling.

She took pleasure in the world, it was her great gift, though Edward would admit this only to himself. It was his policy not to admit anything publicly: neither flaws in himself nor strengths in other people. He gave compliments sparingly. Praise made people soft, he'd never looked for it himself. Success at the task was its own reward. Successful surgery was a serious achievement.

To himself, he admitted to admiring this about Katharine—the way she took pleasure in the world. Now that his days were quieter, now that they were alone together so much, he was more aware of what she did. He could see that it had given him—all of them in the family—pleasure. He was beginning to admire other things about her, too. She'd stood up to him. He could not now remember why, but there had been times when he'd nearly crushed her. She wouldn't let him do it, she'd resisted him. He admired that, though it wasn't something you talked about. Paying compliments made him uncomfortable, so did talking about emotions.

What you felt you should keep to yourself. The current rage for telling everyone how you felt, talking about your parents to a stranger, was ill-advised. You could talk to a therapist for the rest of your life and all that would change was your bank balance. It was self-indulgence. People should take responsibility for their own lives, get on with things.

Julia offered him a plate. "This is yours, Daddy. No mustard."

Edward looked at the sandwich. "Thank you."

He was looked after now. Other people chose what he would eat. It was a strange way of living. He looked out across the meadow and took a bite.

Take responsibility for your own life, your own actions: it was a favorite theme of Edward's. He was now alone, much of the time; in his mind, and he'd begun thinking more and more about these things. How his life had gone, how he felt about it.

Therapy was pointless, he agreed with himself once more. Subjective, irrational, unquantifiable, it was directly opposed to the fundamental premise of science. Therapy was for whiners, neurosis was self-indulgence, though it was unfashionable to say so. Serious mental disorders were different: psychosis, schizophrenia, severe dementia, those were all organic. They were caused by physical pathology and should be treated physically. At one time Edward had been involved in that kind of treatment. It was called somatic. Then those disorders had been treated surgically, though now the treatments were mostly chemical.

When Edward had done his training, the treatment of mental illness was almost entirely physical. Little had changed since the Middle Ages, though during the twentieth century there were experiments with insulin, horse serum, electric shock. One surgeon took out women's reproductive organs, claiming he'd eliminate madness in the next generation. Nothing had really been successful, and by the late forties the public hospitals were still using isolation and restraint. Locked wards and straitjackets were pretty much all they'd had.

After the war, thousands of soldiers came home traumatized by battle, psychologically incapacitated. The country was unprepared and the health-care system swamped. Mental patients occupied one out of two hospital beds in the country. Hospitals were overwhelmed, under-staffed, and underfunded. In the V.A.s, the ration was one staff member for every two hundred patients. Mental health was a national crisis.

It was a crisis and became a scandal. There were exposés, grim photographs in *Life* magazine. Images of hell: crowds of naked patients in straitjackets sitting on the floor in bare rooms. These were our brave boys come home, and this was how we treated them. The government called for investigations, medical science called for a cure. Edward's field was galvanized with urgency.

Psychosurgery was the answer. Edward remembered the first time he'd heard the term "leucotomy"—at a staff meeting, everyone's face solemn. It was a new procedure, the severing of connections between the frontal lobe and the rest of the brain. A Portuguese doctor, Moniz, had invented it, and an American, Walter Freeman, brought it here. It seemed to be the answer to mental illness.

Freeman's operation was simple and swift, and the V.A. embraced it. This was the answer to those hordes of desperate, hopeless patients. This was the silver bullet, modern, scientific, and humane. There were federal grants and public funding, a health initiative. Forty or fifty thousand operations were performed across the country. The symptoms were gone, and the brave boys went home to their families. It wasn't just soldiers: the procedure seemed to work on all mental patients. It was a miracle. The national emergency had been resolved. It was a triumph for his field. Edward had been right in the middle of it.

A few years later, when psychotropic drugs emerged, treatment shifted toward medication, psychopharmacology. Edward shifted, too, away from mental illness, toward other pathologies. He wanted to perform surgery, not write prescriptions. For the next forty years he addressed neurological disorders, physical malfunctions within the nervous system. He became an expert on certain procedures.

The sunlight here was dazzlingly bright, and the long grass hissed mildly in the wind. It reminded Edward of Cape Cod, his parents' house, the old saltbox on a low rise among the cranberry bogs. Those runty scrub pines, stunted by the wind. The air there smelled of the pines, and of the sweet, tangy bayberry; even, faintly, of salt, though the house was several miles from the beach.

Here, salt was heavy in the air, drifting up from the shore. The tides were high—he liked that about Maine, the great sweeping shifts of its waters, the brimming heights, the draining lows. The brutal iciness of the sea, closing like a fist around your heart. You couldn't swim here, there was no thought of it.

He'd never see the Cape house again. When Katharine could no longer manage the steep slope of the lawn, they'd stopped going there. Rather than leave it in his estate to be taxed, he'd asked Harriet if she'd like it, she'd always used it the most. He'd never thought to ask her to keep it, and two years after he gave it to her, she sold it to a developer.

It still made him angry, he felt it now in his throat. When he found out about it, Harriet told him coldly that she'd had no choice. She couldn't afford the taxes and the maintenance. She wasn't using it much, and she needed the money to start her practice. But if she'd only told him, of course he'd have paid the taxes.

Edward didn't want to see it now, crowded by other buildings, the bogs drained. He wanted to hold it in his mind as he'd known it, on its small hill, the old silvery-barked cedar trees on the front lawn, the high thick tangle of wild sweet pea and honeysuckle cascading down the hill behind it.

In the pond were snapping turtles. Once, when he was rowing across it, a turtle had clamped itself invisibly onto the oar, hanging on. He'd been small, only eight or nine. He remembered the sudden inexplicable weight, like a spell cast on the left oar. The smell of the flat green water, the stand of pines on the far hillside: mornings in that house had been pure and blue, silent and untouched. His father, in white duck trousers and faded blue sneakers, walking back and forth on the wiry grass, spreading the sails out to dry. Edward helped, tugging the heavy canvas from its damp folds.

No, he didn't want to see the place again. It was safe in his memory. Did it matter if it existed nowhere but in his mind? His memory seemed a better and better place to live. As he grew older, what was stored there grew more and more different from the world around him. The worlds diverged—*did it matter?* He wondered how Julia's sons were doing.

"Now, tell us, how are the children?" Katharine asked.

Edward thought, confused, that she'd just asked that question. Or had he just asked it? He looked sideways at Julia, to see if Katharine had repeated herself. Julia wouldn't say so, but her voice would be slow and patient. Edward hated people being patient with him, it was so patronizing.

"The boys are both fine," Julia said, frowning, looking out over the pink grass.

Julia wouldn't say if they weren't. She never did, though Edward knew things had been pretty bad at times. Both with the children and her divorce: she led a chaotic life, as far as he could tell. She never talked about it. *I'm fine,* she always said forbiddingly. She wanted privacy, he understood that. He didn't want to know everything, either. Hearing about other people's lives was either tedious or frustrating, they made so many mistakes. Katharine, of course, heard all those things; she was interested.

Edward had disapproved of Julia's divorce. He didn't know why Wendell had left Julia, and he supposed no one would ever tell him. Wendell was married now to someone else, so it had probably been woman trouble. Of course you had these urges, everyone did, but you didn't leave your wife. People were so ready now to give up, throw everything away, but divorce was the solution to nothing. It made everything worse, usually. Look at Wendell, off with some inferior woman, Julia on her own now. For good, probably, her face turning lined and leathery.

He'd never wanted to divorce Katharine, though he'd been interested in other women. He'd had flings. But he'd never have left her. His marriage was part of himself, like being a surgeon. Each day he had waked up married to Katharine, and a surgeon.

Surgery had been the thing, the center of everything. The operations he'd performed were still part of his consciousness. He could go through each step of each one. They were like the house on the Cape—still there, still real, ready for him to inhabit.

Surgery had been his life. He'd done thousands of operations, over nearly four decades. It had engaged him utterly, it had given him his greatest pleasure. There was nothing more serious, more crucial, more delicate. He'd welcomed the challenges. He'd welcomed risk—he liked it—and often taking a risk was the right thing to do. He'd been good and he'd been lucky, and he'd been rewarded for both. Young doctors came to train with him, he'd been twice head of the National Association of Neurosurgeons, which he'd helped found. Surgery had been his life, a continuing challenge, one he always rose to. It had been intoxicating: the excitement, the urgency, the thrill of commencement.

Pushing through the swinging doors into the operating theater he entered a separate world, self-contained, professional, purposeful. The clean, cold, invigorating room. The bold, caustic smell of antiseptic, and the draped motionless body, stark and shadowless beneath the bright lamp. The pale, exposed, shaved skin, brilliant in its glowing pallor, vulnerable and still. The body was now defenseless, its mind absent. The body was no longer the house of the soul but the site of the performance. All of them drew near, the nurses, the assisting surgeons, the anesthesiologist. All of them ready.

Gowned, masked, gloved, costumed as his professional self. That first moment of infinite possibility: making the first incision, the bright metal edge sliding easily into the elastic skin, as he entered his world. Once the opening incision was made, everything else fell away. Then everything was in his grasp.

The crimson interior of the body was his landscape. Cutting through the dense carapace of bone, removing its protective helmet, exposing the secret tissues of the brain: soft, intricate, pulsing, full of their own mysterious life. Here was the true center of the organism, this rosy, glistening, underground labyrinth, coiled, folded, furled, lobed, branched, and connecting, each a part of the quick, mysterious response to life.

Standing under the lamp, leaning into the terrible exposure of the wound he had made, Edward was focused and intent, drawn into himself, to a place without connection to the rest of his life. He felt utterly aware, calm, capable. Masked people stood silently by, all of them part of it, ready to suction out blood, hand him instruments, take them away, raise or lower the level of consciousness. The thudding heartbeat steady on the monitor, a bass line of reassurance. Edward heard the sound without attending to it, aware only when it changed. His own breathing was muffled and magnified by his mask. He probed delicately among the glistening tissues; he took a narrow-bladed instrument.

All this was present for him still, but gone now, vanished from the real world like the house on the Cape. He had saved people's lives, their senses, their movement—but it was now like a movie about someone else.

His skills were gone, his hands were mitts. Edward could no longer even shave himself properly. It still looked all right, or at least he hoped it did, but his cheeks were unevenly smooth, rough in places, though he drew the razor carefully across them every day. He passed his hand across his jaw. It was worse on the left, the stubble coarser there. That was the side away from the window. He turned his head slightly, offering the others the smoother side of his jaw. It was humiliating. The flesh had no business betraying him.

"What are they doing right now?" Katharine asked.

For a moment he was confused, but it was the children again, Julia's children.

"Well, Steven's been in Seattle," Julia said. "You know, he's been working for a conservation group there."

"Oh, that's right," Katharine said. "I can never remember what a conservation group is. Is it people who are conservative?"

"The opposite," Julia said. "Very liberal."

"That's right," Katharine said. "And what's he doing for them?"

"Trying to save the forests."

"Good for him," Katharine said stoutly. "Somebody should save them." She took a bite of sandwich. "From what?"

"Logging companies, mostly," Julia said.

"I bet that's tough," Edward said. "How's he doing?"

"He's kind of burning out. He's thinking of moving back East and doing something different. He's coming up here to talk about it."

"Well good for him," Katharine said again. "I'd love to see him. Will we get to?"

Julia shrugged. "I don't know. It's impossible to pin him down. My children come and go as the breezes of the air. They answer to no woman."

"I think he should come up here," Edward announced.

"I hope he will," Julia said.

"And dear Jack?" Katharine asked. "Where is he?"

Julia frowned. "Jack's in Brooklyn."

Julia offered no further information. She didn't like to talk about him, Edward could see. He couldn't blame her. Jack had always been a problem.

"Dear Jack," Katharine said again. "Does he have a job? Or what is he doing?"

"He doesn't seem to have a job," Julia said carefully. "It's not exactly clear what he's doing."

"He must be liying on something," Edward pointed out.

"He must be," Julia agreed, "but it's impossible to say on what. He's still playing music, but there's no visible means of support."

There was silence for a moment. Far out on the horizon, the line between sea and sky was becoming indistinct.

"Well, I'm very fond of Jack," Katharine said loyally. "Give him my love."

"I will," Julia said, smiling at her.

"I'm very fond of him," Katharine said. "And what is Steven doing?"

Julia looked at her for a moment.

"That's fog, out along the horizon," Edward announced. His voice was flat, absolute, as though he dared anyone to contradict him. "That gray line."

THREE

Steven shifted again, his seat entirely numb. He had been traveling for years, it seemed, for most of his life. These last two hundred miles would take as long as the first three thousand, and were the longest.

The bus roared steadily northward, the engine playing without pause its single plangent chord. Steven leaned, bored, against the window. Along the unfolding ribbon of the highway ran a high wooden wall topped by a dense mass of trees. Foliage foamed over the wall, as though from a container.

Next to Steven was another young man, his raised knees crammed against the seat in front. His head had fallen sideways, and he was snoring faintly on the indrawn breaths. The sound was mild and childlike. It was oddly intimate, listening to the soft exhalations of a stranger. Steven wondered if his girlfriend complained—though who would mind this faint high whistle?

Anything might tip the balance, though. Anything might make you recoil from certain flesh. The body had its own life. He thought of the dark line of damp clay beneath Eliza's nails, her moist pink fingertips.

And maybe this guy didn't snore in bed, maybe he did it only on long bus trips, sitting upright, head lolling. He was younger than Steven, in a grimy T-shirt, pocketed cargo pants, grubby running shoes. He and Steven were the only people their age on the bus. Of course he'd sat here, next to Steven: age was the great divider. You understood only your own cohort; shared experience was the essential thing. Older people's lives were wholly different. They had no idea what Steven and his friends were like.

Nor could Steven imagine his parents' world, that dim twilight epoch before his birth. People standing in the sun beside old cars, eating pre-historic food, their long hair and weird hippie clothes. Who knew what it had been like? All you knew of your parents came from them. There were no unmediated moments, you were handed history as your parents had written it. The material was theirs.

His father's childhood had been like this: the memory of *his* father coming home to the house in New Canaan, letting in a rush of cold air. Taking off his overcoat in the front hall, his first words a greeting to the dog. His mother, growing up in the stone house in Villanova, hiding in the forsythia bushes. The stories of his parents' childhoods made Steven feel strange. It was weird, thinking of them younger than he, still small and vulnerable, their adult lives ahead of them.

He picked up his paperback, wrapping the cover punishingly around its back. The book was bad, but he had nothing else to read. The video, played on the bus's tiny screens—a thriller, with pretentious dialogue and slow-motion gunplay—was over.

The roadside fence ended abruptly, and a string of chain stores ran smoothly past, their signs bright and urban. He wondered how the mall employees up here felt. Proud to be part of a national network? Angry at the exploitative wages? Glad to have a job, most likely. Steven shifted again, jamming himself into the corner, resting his head against the hard, humming window.

He wondered what his mother would say about graduate school. It would be the opposite of whatever his father said. One of them would ask, "Are you certain you need a law degree, Steven? Have you thought carefully about this?" The other would say, "Education is the highest privilege, of course you should go." Probably Wendell would be in favor of it; Julia, more cautious, would have reservations. "What do you want to do next? What does it mean for your future? I want you to think ahead," she'd say.

Both his parents had gone to graduate school, but when they were planning their futures, things had been different. People spent years at one place, their whole working lives. Loyalty was rewarded. You worked your way first to the outside wall, then the corner office. All that was over now, there was no such thing as job security. The idea of it seemed foolish and old-fashioned, like those big-brimmed brown hats men wore. A lifetime spent at one place, a gold watch at retirement: bizarre. Now no one stayed anywhere longer than five years; you worked somewhere until the next downsizing. There were no offices, people worked in cubicles without doors, with walls that didn't reach the ceilings. Or you worked at home, sitting before the screen in your sweats and a T-shirt, coffee rings on your papers, bagel crumbs colonizing the keyboard. Work was fluid now, a ribbon running through your life, not a box which contained you.

Everything was fluid now. The Internet, cell phones, communication, everyone was in touch all the time. On the sidewalk, people around you staring straight ahead, looking through you as they spoke into unseen ears. In a bookstore in Seattle he'd been ranging through the shelves while a woman nearby talked loudly to a friend. "You're going to have to get rid of her, Richard," she said. "Her needs are not in alignment with yours. She's very, very demanding, and you're going to have to recognize this. You like to keep these women hanging around, but it's not healthy. Remember that time in the sauna?" He wondered who Richard was, and if he wanted an assessment of his private life broadcast so clearly and specifically in the Travel section of Elliott Bay Books.

But people talked to each other all the time, everywhere, loudly, in public; there was no privacy protocol. It was while you were traveling that you most wanted to connect. Everyone in airports had phones clamped to their heads, talking, talking, talking to make sure their lives at home were intact, that their places in the world were still held, that they were still connected to something. On 9/11, all those doomed people on the airplanes, calling home, as though the connection itself could keep them alive.

Steven gazed out the vibrating window and felt the humming of the bus through his body. He'd read somewhere that all engines hummed in the note of E. He wondered if it were true and, if so, why? Was it metallurgical—was all metal intrinsically tuned to the same key? Or to do with the way engines worked? Engines all over the world—mopeds in the Philippines, vacuum cleaners in Edinburgh (DC current), hairdryers in India, trucks in Detroit—all humming a jubilant, unheard, universal chorus.

Outside, the trees were in place again, foaming thickly over the fence. Behind him, unimaginably distant now, was Seattle: the low friendly city, with its glittering waterside, the peaceful rhythm of the streets.

He thought of Eliza at the café on the last day. Her silky blond hair, short and thick as suede. Her hands curved around her coffee mug: her stubby, bitten fingers, like a child's. The clay rimming the bitten nails, she was a potter.

"I might come back after Christmas," Steven said, his words audibly untrue. They were sitting outside, on a cobblestone pedestrian mall. Behind Eliza he could see a street singer approaching them, with a battered guitar and a wide professional smile.

Eliza nodded, behind her mug.

"That'd be good." She understood he didn't mean it. She looked at him steadily. "It's too bad there aren't any law schools out here." This—gentle sarcasm—was the closest she would come to accusation.

Steven looked into his own mug, stirring it with the flimsy plastic stick. He could not explain exactly what had happened, how it had become clear that his time here was over.

The singer stood beside their table, already strumming. His guitar was held around his neck by a band of red hand-woven cloth. Steven looked up, the singer gave him a folksy grin. Steven's own face was stiff. "No, thanks," he said.

Steven's arrival here, a year earlier, had seemed like the discovery of a new country—glittering water, amiable people, the unknown Western birds. That sense of being on the very edge of the continent, on the shore of the raging misnamed Pacific, with its towering storms and plunging surf. Beyond it all were the great reaches of Asia. The Northeast looked toward Europe, but here in the Northwest it was Asia you looked to, wide, ancient, and mysterious. Stretching above you was Canada's cool green wilderness.

Steven had wanted to leave the East for somewhere less known. He wanted to do something serious and positive, and in Seattle it was easy to find a project. Nature was nearby, and important; idealism was current.

He joined an environmental NGO set up to protect a stretch of old-growth Douglas firs from clear-cut logging. Everyone in NOCUT was cheerful and energetic. They went hiking together on weekends, they all loved the wilderness. Jim Cusack, the head of it, was in his mid-thirties, older than the others. He was bearded and friendly, and wore work boots and plaid flannel shirts. He knew how to get funding, organize, draft petitions.

Things went well at first. They raised money, collected signatures, were written up in the paper. They set up a meeting with a congressman who sat behind his desk in his shirtsleeves, frowning intently, listening, nodding at each point. He shook everyone's hand when they left. They felt exhilarated then, but later things began to stall. There were no more articles, and the logging company refused to take their calls. The congressman's schedule was now crowded. When it became clear that logging was imminent, Jim suggested guerrilla tactics. He said they should chain themselves to the threatened trees.

There was a collective thrill at the idea of action. This was more than making phone calls and collecting signatures. The idea of using themselves, their own bodies, aroused them. They knew they would succeed. They were invincible. This was a holy war, and they were on God's side.

The day of the chaining started early—the middle of the night, really. Steven got up while it was still dark, moving quietly through his apartment. He felt the night outside, the sleeping people all around him.

He felt a sense of urgency and purpose. His apartment was on the third floor, and when he left it, he kept his footsteps light on the stairs, nearly soundless. They were meeting in the office parking lot, where he parked among the cluster of pickup trucks. Dim figures stood around them. Everyone spoke in low voices. There were meant to be twenty of them, but only twelve had showed up: eight men and four women. They waited until Cusack said they should go. He said this happened, people changed their minds. He didn't say anything about people getting scared.

They'd kept their plan quiet, not wanting to alert the logging company, but they'd told a reporter, swearing him to secrecy and hoping for coverage. It all felt serious—the strategy, the secrecy, the meeting in the chill predawn. There was the chance of danger; it seemed like war.

The reporter hadn't shown up, but they hoped he'd meet them there. Steven went with Cusack, heading out onto the dark roads. Once they were on the highway, Steven turned to Cusack. "So, have you done this a lot?" He was ready to hear the stories. But Cusack did not smile or look at him. Eyes on the road, he shook his head. "Never," he said. *Fuck*, thought Steven.

After the highway they took smaller, narrower roads, finally jouncing slowly over the dirt logging trail. The trail ended deep in the woods, in a rough open circle, the ground hugely torn and rutted. Around it towered the great Douglas firs. Their shadows shifted and fled from the beams of the flashlights. Faces, lit weirdly from below, became those of strangers. They stumbled on the uneven ground, the chains they carried clinking faintly. They felt the great shadows of the woods all around them.

They each took a tree, Cusack directing. Steven walked his chain twice around the huge trunk. Snugging the cold links up against his chest, snapping the padlock, gave Steven an odd flicker of excitement and fear. The bark against the back of his head was rough, and links of the chain dug in at his hip. There was no easy way to stand. The discomfort felt sacrificial, daring. They were at risk.

At first they called back and forth, laughing, but after a while the darkness and silence of the forest settled into them, and the voices stopped. The trees, reaching loftily overhead, became larger in the stillness. They could hear the high limbs shifting in the faint wind. It was still early, before daylight, and Steven began drifting in and out of a waking sleep. It was impossible really to sleep, standing up, chained against the trunk, but it was also impossible really to stay awake, in that lightless stillness. His mind drifted, freewheeling; he was not asleep, but he seemed to be dreaming. Great animals moved slowly around him, and something was not right, was there a storm in the offing? An eruption, an earthquake? The landscape was apocalyptic, full of dangerous lights and dread. He waked in darkness, confused, his neck stiff.

The light came imperceptibly, at first merely a shift to grayness instead of blackness. Silhouettes and outlines became visible—or did they? Nothing was certain. They vanished in the dimness, then reappeared, finally taking on substance. Slowly the scene took shape: the huge shaggy trunks, standing all around him. Tiny fir cones, scattered on the rough needle-carpeted floor of the forest, and on the rutted open ground. There were faint twitterings, high up. Woodland birds, maybe warblers. Colors came last: the needles were rusty brown, the torn earth dull ocher.

Like the light, the sound of the approaching trucks arrived so subtly that Steven heard it before he knew he was hearing it. When he realized what it was—the loggers were coming—Steven felt something shift in the pit of his stomach. He felt excitement, and something else.

The sounds grew slowly louder, and the trucks appeared. Four pickups, loaded with equipment, pulled into the open area and stopped in a semicircle. The drivers got out of the trucks and drew together into a group, all looking at Steven and the others. It was not quite daylight, the air was still dim and gray. The protesters had propped big signs up against their trees, with hand-painted slogans: CLEAR-CUT IS CLEAR MURDER, and THINK OF THIS TREE AS A CITY: YOU'RE COMMITTING A CAPITAL CRIME. None of the signs was as brilliant as they'd wanted. Steven's said TREES MAKE OXYGEN. PEOPLE BREATHE OXYGEN. ARE WE CRAZY?

The loggers wore battered hard hats and jeans. There were five of them, and they stood together, talking, looking at Steven and the others.

One, in a yellow helmet, set his hands on his hips and shook his head slowly. Their stances—belligerent arm-crossing, scornful hands on hips—suggested anger, and at that, pride reasserted itself. Steven was proud to be here, confronting an angry enemy, making a declaration. He felt excited and triumphant. His heart began to pound.

Yellow Helmet turned his back and began talking to the others. They all watched him. One of them laughed; Steven felt a small shock. *What could be funny?* This was serious. He wondered what they were saying. The back of the truck held chain saws.

Steven began to feel uneasy at their laughter, their casual stances, their saws. The loggers seemed to be in charge of this situation, whatever it was. They seemed practiced, experienced: they knew the forest. They ruled here.

The logic of the protest no longer seemed so clear. Was it foolish? Was it sensationalist, misguided? The back of Steven's head was chafed and raw against the bark. The chain now embarrassed him. It seemed silly and theatrical, with its evocations of imprisonment, religion, torture.

But if not now, when did you take a stand? All heroic gestures seemed foolish at the time, didn't they? It was afterward that they took on significance. Though this was only meant to be a gesture: it came to Steven very clearly now that he did not want to lose his life, or his leg. He wanted only to make a statement, not a sacrifice. But here he was, chained bizarrely to the rough bark of this tree.

It was, he understood now, absurd, a children's performance. But how else did you effect change? The company refused to talk, the congressman would do nothing. The forest—this huge natural engine, this silent, efficient factory of oxygen, soil, clean water, habitat—was at risk. No one else would protect it.

Behind him, someone began calling out, taunting and jeering: "Come and get us."

Steven, nearest the trucks, on the wide curve of his big tree, could not see the others.

"Chicken!" shouted someone. "What's the matter, you don't dare do anything?"

The taunts were idiotic. They hadn't discussed this at the meetings. *And where was the reporter? Who was going to record what happened? They shouldn't be yelling. Where was Cusack? Why didn't he say anything? This could get out of control.* He imagined the high, terrifying whine of the shredder, its stutter and catch when something was thrown into it.

Yellow Helmet left the circle and began to walk toward them. He carried a long shaft of rolled-up paper, like a blueprint. Steven watched him approach, his heartbeat rising. He braced himself: here he was, the enemy in the flesh. Here was the man who would bring down these towering giants, destroy this grove of silence and coolness, transform it into a churned-up wasteland.

The logger walked across the clearing. He was short, with a heavy chest and a thick middle. He wore jeans and a faded plaid workshirt. He reminded Steven of Jim Cusack, chained somewhere behind him. The same clothes, the same short, shaggy beards, the same ruddy cheekbones. Even the same bright blue forceful gaze.

We're the same, Steven thought, *we're the same.* He could feel the pounding of his heart. The idea seemed a revelation. The logger came closer, and Steven saw he was older than Cusack, his sunburnt skin thickened and lined. *He works in these woods,* Steven thought: this had the clarity and weight of crystal. The logger's life seemed suddenly immanent, a transparent fan of experience. *He lives near here,* Steven thought; *that's his truck. He has young kids, an ex-wife in a trailer somewhere.*

As the logger reached him, Steven felt a powerful bolt of kinship. He met the man's eyes, his own eyes eager. *I understand you,* he thought. He was ready to smile. *I'm like you.* The logger stopped before him and put his hands on his hips, a negligent, contemptuous gesture.

"You asshole," the logger said, and spat at him.

The impact was small but shocking. The saliva was heavy and clotted, and slid slowly down the side of Steven's nose. He tried to lift his hand to brush it off, but his arms were behind the chains. He felt it slip onto his cheek and stop.

"You think we want to fuck around with you guys?" asked the logger. "You know what it means to run an operation like this?" The man stared at him. "We know what you're up to. We know you freaks are trying to grow marijuana in here." He shook his head. "We should just cut these trees down with you assholes on them."

"Right," Steven said stiffly. He meant this to be cruelly cutting, conveying sarcasm and fortitude, but it came out like weak agreement. He felt like a fool. And what did the guy mean about marijuana?

NOCUT lost the battle, and the trees had come down.

The loggers had left that morning, but returned two days later with an injunction. This time Steven and the others stood by, unchained, while the sawblades whined sideways into the ancient trunks. The loggers wore ear mufflers, but the protesters did not, and their bodies vibrated with the roar. It drowned out the sound of their pulses, it echoed in their skulls. The big trees stood steady while they were cut, then went down fast and suddenly, toppling like mountains, thundering down like the end of the world. NOCUT held up signs and shouted slogans, but no one heard them in the din. The trees went down. This time the reporter was there, documenting their failure (he'd gotten the day wrong before). By the time the article came out, the forest was leveled. There were only splintered stumps and degraded earth left. Every bird, animal, and insect had been evicted from a densely populated thousand acres.

After that, Steven felt his time was over in the Northwest. He felt stranded, as though he'd been abandoned by some tidal movement. The day after the trees came down, Jim Cusack asked if he wanted to come hiking that weekend. They were all going, he said. Steven could see that for the rest of them nothing had changed, that they were all still carried along in that surge of energy, but for Steven it had stopped. He'd become separated from his life there.

On the bus, the snorer shifted, twisted, and settled his head on the other side. Steven wondered how old he was. When did you decide you were too old to wear dopey pants and Grateful Dead T-shirts? Was there a moment when it came to you, that you were too old for this now, or was the change unconscious, part of a sartorial drift that functioned throughout your life, moving you silently from one set of wardrobe options to another?

He looked out the window again: the fence was gone, and the mall. The bus was passing through thick woods now, conifers crowding up to the highway.

He knew his mother would ask if he'd seen Jack when he went through New York. He dreaded it. She'd wait until they were alone. Steven didn't know yet what he would tell her.

He had seen Jack.

He'd gone to see his new place, way out in Brooklyn, on a dingy street beyond Williamsburg. It was a crummy neighborhood, with trash littering the gutter. The tiny stretch of lawn was tired and beaten down. Jack's building was brick, low and blocky, newish, but already seedy and dilapidated. Its small windows were high and meanly spaced.

In the foyer was a row of buzzers. The slot for 3C held a torn-off strip of paper hand-lettered ANdorN. Steven pushed the button and was buzzed into a low-ceilinged hall. There was no elevator, and Steven climbed the uncarpeted stairs. Upstairs, the hall was narrow, the walls scuffed. There was a bad smell.

Steven rang at Jack's door and waited, trying not to breathe the smell. Inside the apartment there was no sound, though Jack had just buzzed him in, downstairs. After a while Steven pressed the button again, harder. Still silence. He waited again, then pressed the bell a third time. At once, as though he had released a spring, the door opened on his brother.

"Hey," Steven said.

"Stevo," Jack said, nodding. He looked terrible; pale, very thin. Dark stubble stood out against his white cheeks. He wore jeans and a long-sleeved shirt, the grimy cuffs unbuttoned and flapping. His feet were bare and dirty. "Good to see you. Come on in." He ran his hand self-consciously over his head. Steven had the feeling that Jack had just done something quick and furtive before coming to the door.

Steven followed him inside. A huge TV with a tangle of cords was on the floor. In front of it was a plaid sofa, its stained cushions flattened and sagging. There was nothing else, and the bare floor was scattered with CDs, empty cans, food wrappers. Jack stopped and stood awkwardly, with his hands in his back pockets.

"So, great," Jack said. He nodded and smiled again. "What's up? How long you here for?" His eyelids were heavy, and there was something wrong with his smile.

"Just the night." Steven looked around. The smell from the hall was in here, too. "Nice place."

Jack laughed. "Yeah. A palace." His eyes seemed unfocused. "It's not mine, it's a friend's. I'm just staying here while he's in LA. So. Want some coffee? Want to go out?"

"Sure," Steven said. "Let's go out." He understood that Jack didn't want him here in the apartment.

"Shoes," Jack said, and left the room. Steven followed him.

In the bedroom the shade was pulled down, and the window shut. The air was unpleasantly dense. The closet door was open, clothes heaped on its floor. A bureau stood beside the closet, one of its drawers pulled out. On a wooden chair lay an electric bass, its bright reflective surfaces gleaming dimly. The room felt claustrophobic, as though it were its own whole country, with its own secret laws, its own sinister climate. Entering it felt dangerous.

The bed had no headboard and stood slightly away from the wall. Jack sat down on the tangled sheets and scuffed his bare feet into shoes. His movements seemed labored. He stood up again and gave Steven the bad smile.

"Let's go," he said.

As they reached the sidewalk in front of Jack's building, a huge black man approached them. He was gray-haired and wore a knitted cap and a red hooded sweatshirt that said HOUSTON COUGARS. His enormous stomach strained against the shirt. He was talking loudly and making large swinging gestures with his fists. As they approached, he looked at Steven and said angrily, "Not once. *Not once!* Motherfuckers!" The brothers parted, passing on either side of him.

When they rejoined, Steven said, "Jesus. I thought he was going to take a swing at us."

"Nah, he's harmless," Jack said without interest. "I see him a lot. Turn here."

The next block was lined with dingy brownstones. This is Jack's neighborhood, thought Steven, these littered streets, run-down houses, weirdos swinging their fists. It was a shock, realizing how separate their lives now were.

Growing up, they'd shared everything. They'd gone to the same schools, known each other's friends, breathed each other's air. But now Steven saw how little he knew of his brother's life, how opaque it was to him. This was partly age, of course; Jack was still locked into that stupid college routine, all pot and no plans. Jack had always had dumb pot-soaked ideas, rock bands and big schemes, nothing that would ever work. But he'd been funny before, hilarious; he'd had a manic, luminous glow.

Now, in this seedy depressive neighborhood, in the sickening smell and strange silence of the apartment, things were no longer funny. Jack's presence seemed dead, flattened. No light came from him, the air around him was inert.

At the coffee shop they sat in the back. The waiters took orders in a normal voice, in accented English, then turned and shouted in Spanish at the top of their lungs. The other language flowed around them, soft and rapid. At the next table two girls were talking at top speed, like dueling machine guns.

The waiter came, and Steven ordered coffee and a bagel. The waiter looked at Jack.

"Coffee," Jack said.

"Nothing to eat?" Steven asked.

"Are you Mom?"

Steven shrugged. "I thought you'd want some breakfast."

Jack shook his head. He seemed not to be blinking.

The waiter filled their thick ceramic mugs and Steven took a sip. The coffee was thin and bitter.

"So," he said. "What's going on?"

"Nothing much," Jack said. He shrugged, frowning.

"You working, or what?" asked Steven.

"Is this an interview? Who sent you?"

"Come on," said Steven. "What's the deal?"

He was irritated by his brother's rudeness, his assumption of Steven's disloyalty, especially since it was justified. Jack always made him choose sides.

Jack shrugged. "I don't want breakfast, that's the deal." He sipped his coffee listlessly. "So, what's up with you?"

"I'm leaving Seattle. Left it," Steven said.

"Yeah? How come?"

Steven shook his head. "It's just finished," he said, "what I wanted to do there."

"D'jou save the trees?" Jack's tone was nearly mocking.

Steven shook his head again. "No," he said. "The trees came down." He looked at his brother, waiting for sarcasm.

"Too bad." Jack's eyes were opaque.

"So I'm coming back East. I'm thinking of law school."

"*Law* school," Jack said.

"Yeah," Steven said. "I don't know if they'll buy it."

"What if they don't?"

"I'll do it anyway, on my own. Student loans."

Jack raised his eyebrows again. "Long-term loans," he said. "Big-time debt. *Big*-time." He shook his head. "Might as well do *drugs*." He grinned: the idea seemed to cheer him.

Steven drank from his mug, looking at him. "Oh?"

Jack shrugged and glanced around the restaurant. He drummed a syncopated rhythm on the table with his dirty fingers. At the next table the girls hummed and buzzed like silvery bees.

"So," Steven said, "what are you doing?"

Jack looked at him, his eyes hooded. "Me! Nothing. What do you mean?"

"How're you paying the rent? How're you eating?"

Jack shook his head and rubbed his index finger on the tabletop, as though erasing something. "This and that," he said. "Got some things cooking."

"Like what?" Steven asked.

"My friend Mario is starting a record company." Jack looked at Steven. "It's gonna be big."

"What are you doing in it?"

"Different things," Jack said. "Producer, maybe. There are a lot of options. Plus the band's starting to cook." He leaned against the red plastic of the seat. His Adam's apple protruded: his neck was very thin.

Steven stared at him, Jack looked back, then away.

"So, you coming up to Maine?"

"Nah, don't think so," Jack said. "The band," he explained. He scratched suddenly, hard and fast, at the side of his neck. The skin reddened under the assault. The grimy cuff of his shirt fell back from his wrist; the inside of the cuff was spotted with dark blood.

Behind them the dark-haired girl spoke steadily and rapidly. Her voice rose and fell, waves of words.

"Jack," Steven said, "are you okay?"

Jack raised his eyebrows. "What," he said. "I'm okay. I'm okay. Might get a job in a video store," he added. "Need the cash."

Jack and Steven had sat in silence then, looking at each other, each waiting for the other to speak.

Steven, two years older, had always felt responsible for his brother. He couldn't remember a time when Jack hadn't been beside him, struggling to keep up, breathless, intrepid, making trouble. Once, when they were eight or nine, Steven had found Jack in their bedroom, crouched over the scrapbasket in the corner.

"Look." Jack had a book of matches. He was lighting them and dropping them one by one into crumpled paper in the bottom of the scrapbasket. The fire—oddly pallid in the daylight—had begun to creep along the edges of the paper, turning them brown, then black.

"Put it out," Steven said. Alarm pulsed through him.

"It's metal," Jack said, "it won't burn."

Steven reached for the scrapbasket. The flames were spreading briskly, he wasn't sure he could blow it out. Jack turned his back and shoulder against his brother, holding on to the basket, and they wrestled. Steven, heavier, stronger, weighted by the responsibility, was furious, grappling with his little brother.

"You stupid damn jerk," he whispered. "If you don't give me that, I'm telling."

It was the ultimate threat, the worst thing you could do. Loyalty was at the core of everything; telling their parents anything was forbidden. But then—often—Steven had *wanted* to tell on Jack. Either tell on him or kill him. Jack always went too far. His exploits were too perilous, the risks always too great. He tortured Steven, making him choose.

His little brother had always been Steven's responsibility. The time Jack fell out of the tree in Central Park: Steven had told him he was going too high. When he brought Jack back to the apartment, his arm dangling, Steven had felt as though he himself would be beaten, should be beaten, for failing to protect his brother, keep him safe. *Come down!* he had yelled at Jack, but Jack ignored him, clambering quickly from branch to branch. Steven had seen him fall, he had been right there. He heard the awful sound of body meeting earth. Now you've done it, he'd thought, now it's happened.

Steven looked out the window of the bus. He had not decided what to tell his mother about his younger brother. He didn't know, himself, whether the blaze was important, dangerous, whether it would extinguish itself, or whether they needed outside help: the fire department, men in boots, giant hoses. The siren of alarm.

FOUR

"I think I'll walk down to the cove," Edward announced.

They had finished lunch and were watching the afternoon light slant across the meadow. Edward stood, though he could not completely straighten. He was bent slightly at the hip, the joint stalled.

"Are you sure?" Julia asked. The path to the cove was uneven, the shoreline studded with sinkholes. Her father seemed both fragile and reckless.

"Yes." Edward took a step toward the edge of the porch, his legs apart for balance, his arms wide like outriggers.

"I'll come with you." Julia took his arm.

Edward shook off her hand. "I don't need help," he said. "This isn't Mount Everest." Did he look so fragile?

"Maybe I'll come, too," Katharine said.

"Mother, I don't think this is a good idea for you," Julia said.

"Maybe not, but it'll be fun," Katharine said cheerily.

Julia turned: her mother was up, too, smiling, leaning on her cane.

"I wish you wouldn't, either of you," Julia said, anxious.

Edward tottered toward the steps without answering.

"It's slippery and uneven, Daddy," Julia said. "I can't help both of you at once."

"I don't need help," Edward repeated. He turned sideways to go down the steps, and at the bottom he started jerkily down the slope.

"I haven't been in a meadow for years," Katharine said happily. She started forward, her hip rising and twisting.

"I really don't want you both to go down," Julia said helplessly.

As she spoke she felt the words dissolve into the breezy emptiness of the afternoon. What right did she have to tell her parents what to do? She wasn't in charge of their lives. And neither of them even answered.

Katharine swayed toward the steps. Edward, bent over, headed down toward the cove.

"I'll come with you," Julia said, giving up.

Why shouldn't they go down to the cove? This light, this view, the glittering air was why they were here. The light was beginning to redden toward sunset, flooding the landscape with carmine, as though beauty itself were a color. Her parents had nothing like this in Haverford, in their complex of big brick buildings, sidewalks, parking lots, Norway maples. Whatever lay ahead for them would be worse. Right now they should have the blowing pink grass, the shimmering blue water.

Edward moved steadily along, not looking back. He stepped carefully, feeling the ground as it sloped away. His feet were heavy and he had to lift them like objects. At the bottom of the meadow, the wind picked up, catching the water, and the surface began to fracture with tiny lapping waves, each catching the glinting light. Edward opened his mouth, to breathe more easily. He could feel this in his chest. He liked the struggle, the challenge, the salt breeze.

In college he had been a cross-country runner, and this, now, reminded him of that—the bright air, the openness and distance. During fall training, he used to run on a dirt road through the woods, scarlet leaves in great clouds overhead, the steady soft thudding of his feet. He remembered the exhilaration at being abroad in the country silence, drawing the cold air into his chest, his legs moving smoothly beneath him. The hushing sound of the leaves. He'd felt part of something large and golden and glowing.

Senior year, that was how he'd felt—as though he were running to meet the world. He couldn't wait for it: everything lay ahead. He remembered feeling certain of himself, and of how to do things. Feeling so capable physically: of running lightly and smoothly, the pleasure of springing off with each step against the dirt road. He'd felt he could run forever through that golden air, the hushing sound of the leaves.

Now, again, he was moving across the landscape, and again it was exhilarating, though this time he was only trying to stumble across an uneven meadow, his goal merely yards ahead, the irregular shoreline of this little cove. He was only struggling to stay ahead of his athletic, acerbic daughter. Still it was exhilarating.

He liked the challenge, and he liked knowing that here was his own hidden world at work: the neural pathways functioning, millions upon millions of axons flooding his system with signals, neurotransmitters galvanizing his muscles, the whole microscopic kingdom of circuitry working at unimaginable speed, coordinating everything—visual images, muscular memory, gyroscopic feats of balance, the control of temperature and breath and heartbeat, with the limbic system playing its mysterious harmonies on the emotions—here it was, the great neurological symphony, performed by the vast orchestral system of the body. Here was the world as we experience it through ourselves.

Edward paused in his headlong surge, negotiating a sudden dark opening in the meadow, a sinkhole, where the ground had been worn away underneath by the tides.

He didn't mind Julia's bossiness. He was actually rather proud of it, it gave him a feeling of kinship. He and Julia shared something, a stiff-necked, stubborn resistance to the world. He admired her refusal to submit, to placate. He admired it, though he wished it were not directed at him.

Katharine called him contentious, though this was not how Edward saw himself. He saw himself as helpful, offering assistance, trying to correct things. Other people were usually wrong, he found. He simply wanted to get things done, move forward. And he liked authority, liked being in charge: at the hospital he'd been head of neurosurgery for years. He'd always been in charge, it came naturally to him.

Later, the others had come to resent him, and there had been an uprising. It was painful, he didn't like thinking of it. They'd maneuvered him out of the department in a contemptible and underhanded way. They'd claimed he was losing his competence, that his eyesight was failing, his hands losing dexterity. Later, that had been true, but not then. They were wrong, Newt Preston, Lou Rosenberg, and the others. He remembered looking around the table and seeing the faces, all turned toward him. Newt Preston's peculiar expression—intent, contained—as he waited for Edward to understand. Edward's neck still swelled at the memory of that meeting. The door of the conference room had been partly open, and someone in a green dress stood just beyond it. His secretary, waiting: even she had known.

The blue water now stretched before him, Edward had reached the shoreline. He stood still, feeling the salt air in his chest. Down here, it was all different, the perspective low, the water vast and dominant. Along the far shore of the cove was a wall of firs, dense and dark. A motorboat, moored to a bright buoy, rocked on the running tide. To the right, around the point, was open water, the ocean. The swelling water pleated itself endlessly, glinting.

Satisfaction rose in him at the sight of the scarlet light, the golden water. He'd wanted to arrive first, unaided, and he had. He could hear his own breathing, deep and strong. He folded his arms on his chest. The wind blew against his bare head. He felt the spaciousness of the red-gold air, the soft lapping of the water against the ragged shore. Something rose in his throat, as though the spaciousness were entering him.

His life lay stretched behind him like a path, reaching neatly, like his shadow, exactly to his feet. Ahead of him lay the shifting blue water, cold and radiant.

"Almost there." He heard Julia behind him. "You're doing great, Mum."

"Just let me take it slowly," said Katharine. "You know I used to run up Mount Washington, with my brothers."

"We know that," Julia said. "We know you raced them."

"'And won, she said modestly,'" added Katharine.

She moved carefully, poking with the tip of her cane among the grasses. She leaned forward, one arm linked in Julia's. She took a slow step, Julia taking a half-step beside her.

"Great!" Julia said again. "We're here."

The three of them stood together at the shoreline. Katharine felt the sea breeze against her face. "Lovely." She turned her head, looking at the red sunset light, the running of the tide.

Katharine thought of Mount Washington and her brothers. She remembered climbing the rocky part, near the summit, the empty sky beyond the peak. Being out of breath, and her oldest brother behind her, laughing, pretending he couldn't keep up with her. She'd been the youngest and the only girl, much petted by her brothers, by the whole family.

Julia pointed across the cove. "Great blue heron," she said. "Do you see it?"

"Lovely," Katharine said, peering. She couldn't make it out, but she knew how it looked, those long, skinny, lordly legs, the coiled serpentine neck, the needlelike beak. The slow, meditative steps.

It was her father who'd taught her to know the birds. She remembered him taking her hand, walking across a field, early spring. He crouched down quietly to point out a bird's nest on the ground.

"Kill deer," he said in a low voice, and Katharine looked into his face, confused. She'd been young, four or five. "A killdeer's nest," he said, and then she understood: it was a name.

There was the neat clutch of tiny speckled eggs nestled in a shallow concavity in the furrow. The eggs, flecked with the same colors and patterns as the broken stubble, were nearly impossible to see, coming magically into focus only once you understood how to look. Nearby, the frantic mother ran back and forth, dragging her wing as if it were broken, crying her own name over and over, trying to lure them away from the eggs.

"We must leave," her father said quietly, in her ear. "We're causing the mother distress." He was almost whispering. Katharine had tiptoed out of the field, her hand still in her father's. She'd turned her head, discreetly, so as not to cause more distress, watching the tiny mother bird skimming along the furrows, her narrow legs flickering as she ran.

Now Julia spoke. "I love this view. It's one reason we bought the house."

"It's a good view," Edward said, not as though he were agreeing but as though he were pronouncing her correct.

"Do you remember my father?" Katharine asked Julia. *Had they just been talking about him?*

"A bit," Julia said. "He wore a waistcoat and gold-rimmed glasses. He took silver dollars out of my nose."

"Silver dollars? Out of your nose?" Katharine repeated.

"It was a magic trick. I kept the dollars for years. I still have some, in a little wooden box."

"Can that motorboat get out of here at low tide?" asked Edward.

"He knows every rock on this coast," Julia said. "He grew up here."

"Who is it?" Edward asked.

"Dan Ellsworth," Julia said.

"He a neighbor?" Edward asked.

"The local contractor," said Julia. "He built a house up the cove last year. He's a nice guy. He came over when I arrived this summer and offered any help I might need."

"Nice for you to have a neighbor," Katharine said. "I worry about you, all alone here."

"I'm all right," Julia said.

Though it was true she was alone. Last week, slicing cheese, she'd cut her finger. The bright blood had startled her. She'd thought of the Plath poem: *What a thrill! My thumb instead of an onion. Something*

something . . . then all that red plush. It was a shock that her body could do something so dangerous, gush with such arterial splendor. Dizzied by the sight, she'd been oddly slow to react. It had taken her long moments to remember what to do: hold the finger beneath cold running water, find something to bind it. There was no one to help her, she'd understood suddenly: she was alone now with her body. It was her task to protect it.

"Do you ever think of living here full-time?" asked Edward. "When you retire?"

"Oh, that's too far off to think of. And I don't even have tenure yet, I may have nothing to retire from," she said cheerfully. "I may have to go on working my whole life."

Julia had thought vaguely about her future, but only vaguely, and only up to a certain point. Everything was meant to get better, wasn't it? That was how you planned your life, looking ahead, toward improvement. It was easy to imagine yourself *older*: white-haired, spry, entertainingly outspoken, freed from convention. But not really *old*— incapacitated, mind gone, body failing, unable to care for yourself. How were you to plan for that? No one wanted to reach that place.

She didn't want to, and she didn't want her parents to, either. She wanted them to be no older than they were here, right now, on this sunset point of land, the three of them watching the reddening, waning light as it flooded across the liquid surge of the tide.

"Just don't put us in a nursing home," Katharine said, out of nowhere.

Turning back, Julia saw a man standing on the porch. He raised his arm, calling against the wind and stepping down into the meadow.

"Who is it?" Katharine asked.

What she feared was not recognizing someone she knew. Worse, someone in her own family. Would it come to that? How long would it go on, this slow tide eating at the edges of her mind? She felt the deep shame of illness, the need for secrecy; she wanted no one to know. "I can't see against the sun," she said.

"It's Stevo!" Julia said, her face alight. "He must have gotten a ride from the bus station."

Steven headed down the path toward them, his strides loose and long, his face ruddy and gilded in the setting sun. The others began the trek back, Edward shuffling determinedly in the lead, Katharine and Julia following, arm in arm. It's a procession, Julia thought. The elders, greeting the young monarch. She wondered if Steven saw himself as the future of the family.

Walking down through the meadow toward them, Steven was struck by the sight of his grandparents in the wide landscape. They seemed suddenly small and insubstantial against the billowing grass, the moving blue water. All three were smiling at him, irradiated by the raking light. His grandparents seemed suddenly, shockingly, old: Edward's pale face lined and papery, Katharine's thin hair blowing in wisps. And his mother's face, polished by the setting sun, looked worn—was she becoming old, too?

They met in the middle of the field; around them the long grass was blown in smooth flattening swaths by the evening wind. Steven leaned over to hug them. He was taller than his father, he was taller than everyone else in the family, and Julia liked this. Julia thought it proper that Steven should be so tall. She thought he should have whatever he wanted.

"You're back," Julia said.

"Hey, Ma," Steven said, putting his arms around her.

She hugged him, clasping his young man's body, strange and familiar. She patted his sweatered back: it was odd how much the body meant, how it reassured. And how odd—wonderful—to feel your son taller and stronger than you; to understand, in your own body, that he had passed beyond you in certain ways, that he was carrying himself forward into the world without your help. It was reassuring, too: this body would protect yours, care for it.

"Let me look at you," she said, standing back. "Have you changed into a West Coaster?" The question was only a pretext to hold him longer, to gaze into the beloved face. What she wanted was to eat him whole. "No," she announced, "you still seem like Stevo."

Steven waited, smiling, allowing himself to be hugged, gazed at, discussed. Adored. As a teenager, her embraces had embarrassed him and he'd resisted them, but after the divorce things changed. He became patient and indulgent, protective of his mother.

One night, up here, he'd wakened to hear Julia walking around in the room she had shared with his father. The house was silent—it was very late—and in that absence of sound the creak of the floorboards seemed loud. It was strange to think of his mother waking up alone in that double bed; he wondered what she was doing, in the middle of the night. His mother, in her worn white nightgown—was she getting a blanket? Was she cold? Steven lay in his own bed, listening. He could not hear separate footsteps, only the creak of the floorboards. Was she lonely? What was she thinking? When it was quiet again, he went on listening, imagining her alone in the room.

After that it was not possible to think of his mother as oppressive, her embrace intrusive. After that he thought of her as alone, vulnerable.

Now Steven moved close to Katharine and put his arm out for her, taking Julia's place.

"Why, thank you," Katharine said demurely. "I may be a little slow now, but I hope you know I climbed Mount Washington when I was younger."

"I know that," Steven said. "Katharine 'The Goat' Treadwell." Wasn't that what you were called?"

Katharine laughed with him, confused. The Goat?

He slowed his steps to match hers as they all made their way back through the blowing grass to the house. The sky was now wild, streaming with sunset.

Supper was in the dining room, where the wide floorboards had once been painted deep blue, but were worn in places down to bare wood. Against one wall stood a heavy mahogany sideboard, holding a white ironstone pitcher filled with daisies. Against another wall was an ancient daybed, beneath a faded Currier & Ives print of the celebrated trotter

Lucy. In a corner, on a rickety spool-legged table, was the only telephone in the house.

They carried in plates and sat down around the battered drop-leaf table.

"Well, Steven," said Edward, unfolding his napkin. "Tell us what you've been doing."

Steven told them about Seattle—the forest, the project, the loggers. When he began to describe the confrontation, Julia put down her fork.

"You chained yourself to a tree, in front of loggers with chain saws?" Julia asked. "You never told me that."

"No," said Steven, "I thought it more prudent not to." He grinned at her. "It wasn't 'in front of chain saws.' They weren't going to cut us in two."

"Goodness!" Katharine said. "It sounds pretty dangerous." She wasn't sure she understood this, why Steven had chained himself to a tree, if that was what he had done, and chained the saw there, too?

"It does sound dangerous," Julia said sternly.

"It wasn't," said Steven. "We weren't at risk. These were loggers, not gangsters. Everyone was very rational and calm."

"And what happened?"

But Steven would not tell them the rest, about the spitting, his pathetic epiphany, his moment of communion with the logger who despised him. The battered work boots, the muddy truck. The saliva, high on his cheek, warm from the logger's mouth. Instead of fading, the memory had actually become worse in retrospect, more disturbing.

"Nothing much," Steven answered. "The loggers got an injunction against us for trespassing. They came back with the police, and we had to stop. But we achieved something, we established a moral position. The papers wrote it up. We struck a small blow for the environment. The weird thing, though, was the loggers thought we were trying to grow marijuana."

"Marijuana?" Katharine looked from face to face. "While you were against the trees?" Marijuana wasn't something you could tie yourself to, was it? Things had gotten completely muddled.

"Marijuana," Steven said to her. "You know what marijuana is, Grandma." He mimed smoking a joint, sucking in his cheeks, inhaling loudly. She smiled uncertainly. To Julia he said, "They had the idea that that was our real reason for protesting. We wanted to grow pot back in the woods."

"Completely bizarre," said Julia. She couldn't, actually, think of this at all—the chain saws, the huge trees, Steven bound and helpless.

Edward shook his head. "Sounds like a damn fool scheme to me," he announced.

Steven looked at his grandfather. "Not everyone agreed with it as a plan," he said mildly.

"I'm glad to hear it." Edward shook his head again. "It sounds pretty silly."

Steven lifted his glass and drank.

"Daddy, don't jump on Steven," Julia told him. "There isn't only one solution for a problem. There are different approaches, you know."

"But not different *sensible* ones," Edward said. "Most problems have only one sensible solution." He leaned back in his chair. "You can tear down the chimney and lower the grand piano through the hole in the roof, but the *sensible* plan is to carry it in through the front door." Edward was enjoying himself. He liked helping younger people, having intellectual discussions with them, offering guidance.

"That's not a useful comparison." Julia could feel her father settling in for an argument.

"All I'm doing is telling the truth," Edward said. "Steven doesn't mind my telling him the truth. You don't mind, do you, Steve?"

"That's like asking me if I've stopped beating my wife." Steven smiled good-naturedly at his grandfather. "It sounds like you're asking, 'Do I mind or not mind your telling me that I'm wrong?'"

"What are you saying?" Edward asked, frowning.

"It's the premise I disagree with—your premise is that I'm wrong. Whether I mind being told it is another matter."

"Now hold on." Edward raised his forefinger. "I'm talking about facts. Chaining yourselves to trees that are about to be cut down is a cockamamie scheme: you know that."

"So was Gandhi's plan a cockamamie scheme," Steven said. "Sometimes unorthodox methods work better than conventional ones. You know it's true in science. Coming up with cockamamie schemes is the way scientists often make discoveries. You did experimental work, didn't you, Grandpa?"

"The experimental work I did was not reckless and haphazard," Edward said reprovingly. "What I did was based on clinical research."

"But still, it was experimental, you were taking risks," Steven said.

"Experiments in medicine are done responsibly, with great care," Edward said, looking thunderous.

"May I be allowed to speak?" Katharine asked demurely. She looked around with an expectant smile.

Everyone turned to her.

"When I was the president of the Debating Society at Miss Hall's School, we had rules about this." Her tone was amused and self-deprecating. "You didn't just argue back and forth. You stated your position, and then your opponent stated theirs. Then you each gave a rebuttal, and then it was over. And *I* was the president," she added, cocking her head, mirthful.

"Yes, and I'm sure you were a very good president," Edward said, "for one so small."

Delighted, Katharine bunched her napkin and threw it at him; it fluttered to the floor. "Take that," she said spiritedly.

Julia was silent, refusing to smile at the high jinks. She could feel heat in her face: her father infuriated her. He let nothing go by. He had to correct the world. And why were her parents acting like this? They had never done this while Julia was growing up. They had rarely shown affection; it was considered inappropriate to display it. At school there had been a sort of unofficial rule: No PDA, public display of affection. You kept your feelings to yourself. All this jocular sentimentality was new, and oddly discomfiting. It was embarrassing, watching her elderly parents flirt. Besides, those were the rules the family had lived by, now flouted. Were the years of restraint and discretion now to be dismissed, casually and completely? What other codes were about to be interdicted?

But maybe this was how it was, growing old. They were nearly ninety—maybe discretion had been merely a phase. It wasn't for her to say how her parents should act toward each other. But it was strange to see them like this, as though they'd become unmoored from their own characters, as though they now were drifting, aimlessly, somewhere else.

Julia glanced protectively at Steven, bent over his plate. She hoped he didn't feel attacked by his contentious grandfather, hoped he didn't feel offended or sorry he'd come. When Steven was a teenager he'd been moody, retreating often into silence and distance, resisting his parents, whatever they offered. It had been hard to know what might set him off, what it was they were doing wrong. Everything, it seemed sometimes.

But now Steven seemed unconcerned, and Edward seemed to have forgotten the argument, flirting with his wife. Right now Julia missed Wendell, who had liked her parents, even her outrageous father. Wendell had teased Edward, flirted with Katharine, and made everyone laugh.

Suddenly Julia missed her sister, too. It was odd to miss her here, since Harriet rarely came to Maine. But Julia wished she were here right now, sitting across the table, rolling her eyes at their father's comments and taking Julia's side. She missed their old alliance, the sister of her childhood. Though that was long ago. It had been years since Harriet had taken Julia's side.

Steven glanced up at her, and Julia smiled and shook her head slightly, to show Steven that he shouldn't mind his grandfather. Steven smiled back. He was older now, twenty-four, past the tumultuous stretch of adolescence. He had become calm and reliable. She could trust him now—couldn't she?—not to take offense, to judge his grandparents. Or her. His family were who they were, and he seemed old enough to accept them. It was a relief, this change.

It was she, Julia realized, who was having trouble with her parents: they were starting to seem like strangers. So old and frail. Watching them now, she was struck by the difference between these people and the parents she'd always known, the people who'd been in charge of her life.

On Sunday mornings her father used to get up first and make breakfast for everyone. He walked around in the kitchen in his pajamas and plaid bathrobe, singing from *South Pacific* in his high, sweet tenor. "Some Enchanted Evening," he sang, "Bali Ha'i." Sometimes he made scrambled eggs, sometimes pancakes or waffles, fancy treats. He stood at the stove in his bathrobe and slippers, singing. And her mother, Julia remembered her gardening, kneeling among the flowerbeds, the basket of tools beside her, a pile of weeds on the lawn. Looking up at Julia and smiling with pleasure: "Look at these white iris!"

Those people were gone. Her father was now barely able to walk, her mother was struggling to follow the conversation. Her parents were drifting away, locked in a losing struggle with their bodies, their minds. The tide was going out.

FIVE

During the spring, Julia had called Harriet one Sunday afternoon. Harriet was sitting at her kitchen table, wearing blue-and-white-striped flannel pajamas and a gray sweatshirt, extra large. Her bare feet were hooked over the chair rung, and she was frowning intently at her laptop. With one hand she was stroking a small seal-point Siamese that had draped his front end—he was paralyzed in his hind end—around her ankle.

Harriet's kitchen was small and full of too-bright light from the plate-glass windows. One side of her building faced the Schuylkill River, though not Harriet's side. Her apartment looked out over the low dark-red grid—brick and brownstone—of nineteenth-century Philadelphia. She was on the twelfth floor, high above the urban hum. The cars and people below her windows seemed small and remote, miniature copies of real life.

The kitchen was white and minimalist, but not stark: dirty dishes sat in the sink, and on the counter were pots, jars, an open jar of peanut butter, a loaf of bread, and a sprawl of mail. White metal chairs stood haphazardly at the table, which was piled with green folders. Over the plate-glass windows was a thin coat of grime, like a scrim.

In front of Harriet was a mug of tepid coffee and a stack of folders. One, marked "Biscuit Patterson," lay open. Harriet was scrolling through an article on canine lymphoma, and when the phone rang, she picked it up without looking at it, still scrolling, as though the aural and visual parts of her brain were unconnected.

"Hi," Julia said cautiously, "it's Jules."

They rarely called each other.

At the sound of her sister's voice, Harriet felt something tighten inside her. Impatience began its rapid drumbeat.

"Hi," Harriet said crisply. "What's up?"

At the sound of her sister's voice, Julia felt something clench inside her. Tension began its ratcheting twist.

"Not much," Julia said. "I just thought I'd see how you were doing."

"I'm fine," Harriet said without inflection. Her tone, the self she presented to her sister, was smooth and impenetrable.

"Any news?"

"No news. All day, sick animals. All night, grumpy boyfriend."

"What's wrong with Allan?" Julia asked, glad of the diversion.

"Permanent bad mood," Harriet said. "Projects are being canceled, budgets are being cut. It's not a good time to be an architect. What's up?" she said again, still scrolling.

"I'm actually calling about Mother and Daddy," Julia said.

"What about them?" Harriet's tone was slightly challenging.

"I think we should talk," Julia said. "About what's happening."

"'What's happening'?" Harriet repeated, irritatingly. She opened a new screen on blood chemistry.

"Just that they're having kind of a hard time," Julia said. "They won't be able to go on indefinitely where they are. I think we need to start thinking ahead."

"Why?" Harriet asked.

"They're getting older," Julia said. "At some point they won't be able to manage."

"I know they're getting older," Harriet said, "we all are. But they can manage now."

"Not very well," Julia said.

"I think they do fine," Harriet said, "and I see them all the time. They're perfectly chipper and happy. They go toodling around and see their friends—I think they're fine. They don't want to move out, you know."

"I know that." Julia disliked Harriet's proprietorial reminder that she lived so close—she didn't think, actually, that Harriet saw them much more than she did—and she disliked the patronizing "chipper" and "toodling." "But I just had a talk with their doctor."

"And?"

"He's doing some sort of neurological assessment. He thinks they should move into one of those places. A home."

"Oh, for God's sake," Harriet said. She looked up from her screen, leaned down, and scooped the cat, Paley, into her lap. He purred, closing his eyes and raising his head against her hand. "He has to say that so he won't get sued. They're just getting older. Of course they're forgetful. *I'm* forgetful. It doesn't mean we're all non compos mentis."

There was a pause. Paley began kneading his paws against Harriet's thigh, piercing the thin flannel, reaching her skin. Carefully she shifted him onto the heavy sweatshirt.

"No," Julia said reasonably, "but Mother keeps canceling her appointments, and saying she wants to change doctors."

"Because their old doctor retired. People are *always* nervous about choosing new doctors. They're afraid they'll make a bad decision. They're *always* anxious about it."

"Right. But Mother keeps changing her mind. She's mailed her medical records all over the Main Line. We don't even know where they are now."

"She told me about that," Harriet said. "I actually don't blame her. One doctor was only there on Tuesdays, so if she went in any other day she'd have to see a stranger. She tried another doctor, but he was away when she came for her first visit, so she saw someone else, and it kept happening, each time she went in he was away and she'd see someone else, and it finally turned out that his daughter in California was sick, and he left the practice completely and moved out there. So then she decided to go back to the person who'd bought her old doctor's practice, but once she saw him, she remembered why she didn't like him. I mean, she may be confused, but the situation wasn't exactly simple."

Paley was still lightly stabbing her thigh. She shifted him again, holding her legs together to give him stability.

"Yes," Julia said. "But it's other things, too."

"Like what?"

"Mother puts in the frozen dinners and they go in to watch the news and she forgets the dinners and they burn up in the oven."

"Big deal," said Harriet. "She's been burning food all her life. I never had a piece of unburnt toast until I got to college."

"Yes," Julia said again. "This is different. Daddy complained about it. Apparently they actually catch on fire. She might set the apartment on fire. Do we want to wait for that?"

"She might die in her bed before she does," Harriet said. "I have to say all this sounds alarmist." There was a pause. "What's your point, Julia? Are you saying we should move them out of where they live, quite happily, and into a 'facility,'"—she said this disdainfully—"which they have *always* said they did not want to do? For one thing, can you imagine moving Daddy somewhere he did not want to be moved? But even if we could, I think *that* would do them in. They're not animals, you know, or children, that we can just move around however we want."

It was presumptuous of Julia, thought Harriet, to act as though her point of view was the only one. And why did she think she was in charge of their parents when she, Harriet, was right here and saw them all the time? *And* was a practicing physician.

Julia fell silent, partly because in some ways she agreed with Harriet. This felt deeply disloyal, talking about their parents behind their backs, listing their failings.

"Harriet," she said finally, "I wish you'd stop treating me like an enemy. Please don't act as though everything I say is absurd. We're going to have to deal with this—whatever happens—together. I'd like to be able to talk to you about it. I'd like to be a team."

"Well, we could be a team if we felt the same way about it," Harriet said. "But honestly, Julia? I don't think you're considering their best interests. They've always said they didn't want to go into one of those places." She rubbed her knuckles hard against Paley's head. He purred loudly.

Again Julia didn't answer, partly because Harriet might be right. She wasn't certain that she *was* considering her parents' best interests. How could you tell? If you were planning something covert and revolutionary, a coup that would depose them, strip them of their powers—how was that in their best interests? But what if they were already being quietly and invisibly stripped of their powers by something else?

Also, Julia didn't answer because something in her sister's voice was fixed and stony. There seemed hardly any point in answering.

They waited, electronic silence between them, each listening for the other.

When they were children, Julia and Harriet had been close.

In those years they'd shared a bedroom in the house in Villanova. When Julia woke up each morning, the first thing she did was look over at Harriet's bed, to see if she was awake. If she was asleep, Julia whispered Harriet's name in the stillness—"*Hattie! Hattie!*"—until her sister opened her eyes. Then Julia could start her day. She felt only half-present without Harriet; together they were a partnership. She gauged the world around her according to its effect on her sister— whether she would be frightened by a dog, whether she could reach a water fountain. Their mother had depended on Julia for that: Julia was in charge of her sister. She showed Harriet how to eat an ice-cream cone, licking the drips off the sides before they reached her fingers; she taught Harriet how to button her sweater, from the bottom, to make sure it was even.

For Harriet, her older sister defined the world. It was Julia who taught her the difference between her right hand and her left, how to remember them. She looked at Julia's face to see how she should feel when something happened that confused her. It was Julia who was in charge of everything: their games, their conversations, how they spoke, and what they believed. "Friend-cynthia," Julia told Harriet, "that's the name of it." She pointed to the big shrub, with its riotous tangle of yellow flowers. "Friendcynthia." She said it fast and waited for Harriet to say it after her.

Once Julia told Harriet to stand with her before the long mirror in the front hall. They stood straight, their toes aligned. "That's me in the mirror," Julia said, pointing to Harriet's small intent face. "That's me, and the person next to me is me." She waved at their reflections. "They're both me."

After a moment Harriet asked, "Where am I?"

"You don't show in the mirror yet," Julia said. "You're too young."

Harriet didn't exactly believe her sister, but she didn't exactly not believe her. She trusted Julia. Her sister had a large and powerful understanding of the world that Harriet respected. Harriet was her disciple, her dependent.

When Julia went away to boarding school, at fourteen, she moved into another bedroom, and things between the sisters changed. At first Harriet was eager for Julia's visits, but Julia was turning strange. She had entered a new world that she could not share with her younger sister. Julia had become anxious and uncertain of herself, and she turned distant to Harriet. Harriet resented this, and felt abandoned. When Julia came home for vacation, Harriet no longer followed Julia to her room. Harriet went to her own room and shut the door. Julia, when she wanted to see her, had to stand outside and knock. "What do you want?" Harriet answered, instead of "Come in." Julia was hurt by Harriet's coolness. Distance settled between them, and they no longer depended on each other.

Julia went to Sarah Lawrence and studied art, and Harriet went on to Penn, where she took science and math. Everyone assumed she would go to medical school, but one Christmas Harriet announced her plan to go to veterinary school.

It was before dinner, and Katharine was out in the kitchen, the others in the living room. Julia was on the sofa, Harriet in an armchair. Edward, in his dark elegant suit, stood by the fireplace. It was empty, as usual: the fire was rarely lit, and the house was always cold. It was healthier, cold, Edward said. This embarrassed his children: their friends complained, and asked why their house wasn't heated.

Harriet sat very straight to tell him. "I don't want to be a doctor," she told Edward.

It was a shock to Julia; she felt a sharp pang of betrayal. How could her sister not have told her something so important?

"I see," Edward said. "What do you want to be?"

"A veterinarian," Harriet said boldly.

This was treason. Julia looked at Edward.

"A veterinarian?" Edward repeated, frowning. There was a pause. "Why would you rather treat animals than humans?"

"Because I'm really interested in them," Harriet said. "It's an interesting field."

Edward shook his head. "Not as interesting as human medicine."

"In your opinion," Harriet said.

Edward tilted his head. "I beg your pardon?"

"It's a very interesting field," Harriet said, losing her nerve. "Animal medicine. There's a lot going on in it."

"It's a lowering of standards," Edward informed her. "It's a disgrace."

"It's hardly a disgrace. It's actually extremely difficult to get into Penn Veterinary School," Harriet said, her voice rising. "It's one of the best schools in the country."

"Regardless," Edward said dismissively. "It's a lesser endeavor."

Katharine, sensing trouble, came in from the kitchen. She looked at their faces. "What is it?" she asked.

"Daddy thinks I'm a disgrace to the family," Harriet said.

"What is it?" Katharine asked again. "What's the matter?"

"I'm going to veterinary school," said Harriet. "I'm going to be removed from the family tree."

"Edward," Katharine said, distraught.

Edward shrugged his shoulders, as though he had nothing to do with this. "Anyone who can get into a good medical school should go," he said. "You have a responsibility to the world. You should use the talents you were given."

"Who are you to decide that?" Harriet asked.

Julia drew in her breath.

"Don't be rude," Katharine begged.

"Who I am is head of neurosurgery at Jefferson Hospital," Edward said coldly, "though I don't think I have to tell you that."

"No, I mean who appointed you to decide the hierarchy of human endeavor?" Harriet leaned back in the big armchair as if flattened there by the wind.

"I don't need to justify myself to you," Edward said. "Looking after animals is a lesser endeavor, just as animals are lesser creatures than human beings. I don't have to tell you that."

"You sound like someone from the Middle Ages," Harriet told him. *"And what I'm doing is not a disgrace."*

"Harriet—" said Katharine, anguished.

"Did your grades drop?" asked Edward. "Is that what happened?"

"My grades did not drop, Daddy," Harriet said. "I have a 3.9 average. The last two years, a 4.0. I happen to want to treat animals. I think they're really interesting, and I think the science is interesting. I like animals, and I like being around them. I respect them, which is more than you can say about your patients."

Edward drew breath, but Harriet went on.

"Why can't I decide what it is I want to do?" she asked. "And why are you such a snob?"

"Please," Katharine said, desperate. She was shaking her head back and forth. "Please stop this. Just stop it, both of you."

Edward shook his head, his face bleak. "I'm happy to stop. I have nothing more to say about this. Harriet, of course, may do as she wishes. It's her life."

He walked across the room to the small armchair by the window, where he sat down in silence. He did not look at them.

"Harriet," Katharine said, but Harriet shook her own head stubbornly and said nothing.

During dinner no one spoke. The air was frozen, they could hardly breathe. The only sound was knife, fork, plate. Julia heard everyone swallow. Katharine closed her eyes while she drank from her water glass, her face a mask of grief. Julia would not be drawn in. She would not come to Harriet's public defense, when she had been so carefully excluded from Harriet's private plans. Julia hardened herself against her mother and her sister.

That night, when Julia heard Harriet come upstairs, Julia didn't open her door. Why had Harriet not told her? She heard Harriet go into her own room. Julia lay on her bed, listening, as Harriet moved quietly about. It seemed as though Harriet had deliberately jumped overboard, off the family ship, and now was being carried far out to sea. She was too far away to be saved, and it had been her own choice to jump.

As she heard the small noises of her sister, Julia's heart felt tight, compressed. She was furious at her sister for being so stupid—she agreed with Edward, Julia told herself. It was stupid to go to veterinary school, it was lowering your sights. Harriet was flying in the face of everything, and why should Julia take her side?

She felt virtuous and sensible about what she was doing, keeping herself quiet, keeping this distance between herself and the miscreant. But really she was hurt: Julia felt utterly betrayed by Harriet. She did not let herself admit this, nor did she admit that there was something terrible about what she had done.

Edward paid for Harriet's tuition at veterinary school, but he disparaged it. He did this lightly, as though he were only teasing, and in a way he actually was only teasing, but in a way he was not, and Harriet grew increasingly acerbic in response. Disapproving, resentful, Julia watched her defiant younger sister and kept her distance from both her and Katharine. She had taken sides, it would be dishonorable to renege.

Edward had triumphed that night, standing by the cold fireplace, and Katharine had been reduced to misery and silence. In a way this was familiar: Katharine was always in pain, and this was not to be discussed or even acknowledged, since there was nothing to be done about it. They put it from them, they had always done this.

It seemed that Edward's rationality was the way of the world, the way life had to be lived. Allying herself with her mother, her mother's pain, her mother's feelings, had been a part of Julia's childhood, but now she was pushing herself into adulthood. She disclaimed her younger, weaker self. She was trying to become adult, not to allow herself to be held by these terrible, painful chains of emotion. She began to withhold herself from her family, to keep a cool distance from all of them.

Harriet began to use the same acerbic tone to her sister that she used to her father. Harriet seemed scornful of every aspect of Julia's life—marriage, children, New York, teaching, the art world. Harriet did not get married, though she had a series of long-term boyfriends. Julia did not understand Harriet, who was so brisk and dismissive, so ironic and cool, so disengaged.

Now the sisters seldom saw each other, and when they talked, animosity seeped into their conversation like moisture into felt. Julia had dreaded calling Harriet, and it had been just as bad as she'd feared. It was strange, now, to remember the time when they were children, when they'd trusted each other, when they'd hidden together under the covers from their parents, thick as thieves.

SIX

After dinner they all went out to the back porch. Julia put the chairs in a row, and they sat watching the sky for shooting stars.

At first they could see nothing. The night around them was opaque, a dense and uninflected black. It held them muffled and sightless. Slowly their stares softened into gazes, and the nocturnal world emerged. The watchers became aware of the dark openness above the meadow, with the quiet shushing of the invisible water beyond, and gradually they could see the revelation of the starlit sky overhead, black, transparent, scattered with glitter, endlessly deep.

It wasn't possible, thought Julia, to imagine the sky as endless, whatever science said. You couldn't conceive of infinity. The mind balked and slid sideways—toward beauty, for example. She thought of painting the night sky, the problems of rendering the velvet quality, the depth. The transparency, and the endlessness: there it was again.

The air coming off the water was cool and damp, and Julia, shivering, went inside to get blankets. She brought out the heavy Hudson's Bays, which were coarse white wool with broad bold stripes of color.

She liked these, liked them for both their actual substance and their romantic heritage.

The blankets had first been made in the eighteenth century by the English trading company. They'd been bartered for furs, in the northern reaches of Canada. Julia liked the picture: she imagined the Indians arriving at the trading post with their burden of supple, lustrous skins, and loading up with the heavy, handsome blankets, carrying them back into the silent forests. The green, glassy waters, the tall-masted ships dropping anchor in the wide bay. The stillness of that pristine landscape.

Now, of course, you were taught that any exchange between colonials and indigenous tribes was inequitable, but Julia chose to see the scene as benign. Blankets for furs was not a bad trade, and the blankets were heavy, warm, handsome. She chose to see the exchange through its beauty, and wasn't this the way you defined your vision of the world? In just such a private, fumbling, illogical way, freighted with emotion, dimmed by ignorance, fueled by conviction?

So Julia handed out the blankets, which came, not from a silent galleon on a silver lake, but from a mail-order company in Maine, and was reminded of an earlier sublime moment, which was possibly imaginary, but which gave her comfort.

She tucked striped blankets around her father and Steven. The best and the heaviest, with the rose-colored star in the center, she put around her mother. It was too heavy for Katharine's fragile shoulders, and Julia propped it around her like a tepee.

"Thank you, darling, that feels lovely." Katharine's smile glimmered up at Julia in the dimness. She smelled of lavender.

Her mother's gratitude was like a tiny blow, an offer of intimacy against which Julia hardened her heart, though she did not know why. She patted the frail shoulder beneath the blanket. "You're welcome," she said lightly.

Julia sat down between her mother and Steven. His body radiated warmth and maleness; she was surprised again by his size.

"You're nice and warm," she said, leaning toward him. She had a right to the heat he gave off: he was hers, in a way, as she was his. She thought of Simon, who was not hers, nor she his. Possession was not a part of their relationship, at least not yet, but he liked to wrap his arms around her, and she liked this very much. Body heat: why was it so powerful? She sat in the glow of Steven's, grateful that he hadn't stormed off to his room, that he was not judgmental and moody but patient and forgiving.

"I think I see one." Edward's head was tilted back, the blanket standing like a ruff around his face.

"Where?" Julia asked.

"Over there," Edward said. "Gone now."

"You can never show your shooting star to anyone else," Julia said. "It's always too late."

"But you can see one together," Katharine said.

They sat in silence, wrapped in their rough blankets, heads tipped back, gazing expectantly up into the darkness. The salt breeze moved past them.

"I don't dare blink. I don't want to miss one," Julia said. "My eyes are drying out."

"Age," Edward announced. "The older you get, the less fluid you produce."

"Wizening," Julia said. "We're all wizening. Even you, Stevo."'

"I can feel it already," Steven said. "Yaugh!"

"There's one," said Katharine. "Don't I see one? Over there."

"You've always had sharp eyes," Edward said proudly. "She finds four-leaf clovers, too."

Katharine was famous for this. She could sit down on any lawn, at any picnic, and casually pluck up the magic things. "Here's another," she'd say brightly, while her children, on their hands and knees, scrambled fruitlessly through the grass.

"'Thank you, she said modestly,'" said Katharine.

Actually, Julia thought, *they're charming.*

Affection flooded through her for her elderly, struggling parents, who were trying to make their way through each difficult day, who were beset and confused by the changing world, handicapped by their failing bodies, finding solace in humor and each other.

Julia, cocooned in the Hudson's Bay, felt the anxieties and irritations of the day falling away. The dinner and the argument were over, the kitchen was clean, the dishwasher rumbling and steaming. Above them rose the dark limitless sky, before them lay the deep benevolent mystery of sleep. The world seemed calm.

She couldn't protect Steven from his grandfather, who was complicated and demanding—as was she, as was everyone—and who loved him. In fact, Julia was suddenly proud of Edward and his absurd, infuriating antagonism. It was some essential thing. It was part of what he was, what charged and animated him.

The black sky stretched up into deep space. Julia wondered again how to paint it, how to capture its warm blue-blackness—not true black, but a velvety purply black. Maybe layers of transparent glazes, built up slowly like Jan van Eyck's soft, gauzy skies—though his were daytime ones. Few artists did the night sky: Whistler. Douanier Rousseau, *The Sleeping Gypsy*. O'Keeffe, the one of the sky and stars from underneath the tree. *How to manage that soft breathing mysterious quality of the nighttime air, the sense of expanding space?*

Julia thought of her handsome Jack, and felt the familiar flick of anxiety. She wondered where he was right now: not, presumably, sitting on a quiet porch overlooking the sea, waiting for the heavens to reveal themselves. Or maybe he was doing just that. Waiting for chemical stars to burst inside his brain. Handsome, bad-boy Jack, with his glinting, merry, sidelong glance. Jack, leaning back in his chair, throwing his head back to laugh. Jack's laugh.

She wanted to hear Steven's news of him; she was sure they'd seen each other in New York. She trusted Steven. He looked after his brother, and he knew Jack in ways she never would. Kids nowadays lived in another world, you'd never know what it was like. (What was it like?) They would never let you in. But Steven was reassuring about Jack. He's still a kid, Steven always said.

Jack played in a rock band; she'd watched him perform. Onstage, bathed in the exotic glow of the overhead lights, he was a star. She'd seen him up there, shifting his hips, giving that slow, knowing smile. Tossing his hair back from his eyes. He was so thin, that sexy, narrow torso, the flat stomach, the long elegant limbs. He was a hunk! It made her laugh. How did your own child become a hunk? It made her proud. What were you to think, his mother?

Whatever Steven had to say about Jack, she didn't want it said in front of her parents. She didn't want them to discuss Jack. Edward would turn authoritative and judgmental. It would be like her lack of money; he'd act as though Julia had deliberately chosen to have a son like Jack. Her father would have a list of reasons for Jack's situation: too much television, not enough discipline, the divorce. As though she'd had a choice about divorce, or as though she could go back now and do things differently.

Maybe they had been easier on Jack than on Steven, somehow things seemed to slacken with the second child. They'd done everything properly with Steven, the first time, but it seemed as though once they'd done it, it was done. It had seemed unnecessary to do it all again, and they were too tired. Had that been it? What were they thinking of? Now it made no sense.

It was a blur to her now, a patchwork mosaic, all those years of the children's growing up. There were scattered moments that stood out: coming in to find the entire bathroom soaked, including the towels hanging on the racks, the boys in the tub together, shrieking, bright-eyed, their bodies rosy. The time Jackie fell out of the tree in Central Park and came home holding his poor dangling arm, his face pinched with pain. It seemed as though their childhoods were the same, but they had turned out two such different people, Steven so earnest and responsible, and Jack—well, Jack was not so much. Not so earnest and responsible. What had happened?

Probably Jack *had* stayed up too late, watched too much television. Too many video games, with their flickering psychotic lights, their vertiginous vistas and violent tasks. His brain had certainly been fried, if that's what video games did. She and Wendell hadn't given him any—one or two, maybe—but in New York you couldn't keep your children from doing whatever it was they wanted to do. As soon as they were safe on the streets they were gone, and so was your authority. Jack had spent hours on video games at his friends' houses.

But Jack was a sweetheart, her heart's darling. His life was unsettled, but whose in their twenties was not? Steven was in flux, too. And if they were looking for blame, what about Wendell leaving his family for that awful nitwit, why mightn't that be the problem? Why wouldn't it be Wendell's fault? In any case, wherever the blame should be assigned, it was not for her father to assign it. Julia would not hear a single word from Edward about Jack.

Her father looked intently at the dark sky, scanning it for movement. He could still see perfectly well, though his feet were clumsy, and his hands—that had once tied off microscopic blood vessels and stitched filament-sized nerves—were now like paws. The thing was to keep going, never admit weakness or defeat. His eyes were still good, and his hearing. He didn't have a hearing aid. Carter Johnson, who was exactly his age, had a flesh-colored plastic snail curled behind each ear. You could hear them, that high insect whine, and he was always fiddling with them, looking troubled, turning them up and down. They didn't seem to help him at all.

All this was partly genetic, but it was also taking care of yourself. He'd never let himself run to flab. He got out every day and walked. He was fit and hale for eighty-eight.

He kept thinking he saw the flicker of a falling star, but as soon as he focused, it was gone. Staring made his sight unreliable, things glimmered mysteriously on the perimeter of his vision. He was vexed at missing Katharine's star, he didn't like missing things. Katharine's vision was good, too—they were both doing well, apart from her hip.

Her hip—but Edward couldn't bring himself to consider Katharine's hip. When he'd first met her it had seemed insignificant. She'd been lithe then, and active. Over the years, though, it had steadily worsened, and he'd been helpless, unable to stop its encroachment, despite the operations and therapy. Katharine never complained. Sometimes, at night, he'd rub her back, and sometimes she wept silently. They both pretended it wasn't happening. If she broke out into sobs she apologized. He knew it was from the pain, and from relief so sharp it felt like pain. He rubbed her shoulders and told her it was all right. He'd been helpless to help her.

There was one, a bright liquid streak in the darkness. He announced it, but by the time he spoke, it was gone. Staring at where it had been, he wondered if he'd really seen it. Was he beginning to imagine things? The thought made him fearful. Dementia: it lay ahead for most of them, humans. He was afraid of failing, his whole physical plant turning decrepit. This was why he walked daily, why he busied himself with Julia's plumbing. He was determined to stay vigorous. He was fighting off decay, resisting the pathetic downward slide into decrepitude. It happened against your will. Tom Lounsdale's children had banded together, like a mutinous crew, and taken away his car keys. Tom could do nothing, and his voice had cracked when he told Edward the story.

Edward would disinherit his children if they tried this. The idea of it set him into a boil. He would not let other people determine his life. (Though his body was turning to dust.)

Katharine looked up into the night sky.

The blanket was too heavy, really, but she did not want to hurt Julia's feelings and sat quietly beneath it. All this was beautiful, the quiet sounds of the water, the hissing of the grasses, the deep velvet of the sky. On Mount Washington, with her brothers, the skies had been open and wild, the constellations close. There were hundreds of falling stars. She'd fallen asleep watching them, then she'd waked in the night and seen them spread out above her. That had been before the accident.

She'd been fortunate, really. She'd had all that in her life, she'd done everything. Hiking, tennis, foot races—in eighth grade she'd won the fifty-yard dash. The coming-out parties, where they'd danced until the midnight breakfast, silver salvers full of steaming scrambled eggs; then they'd danced on again until dawn. Mary Rue's party in Virginia, the big white tent on the lawn, fireflies in the field beyond. The girls in long dresses, the boys in black tie. She'd had a dress with a

rose-colored sash, the skirt like petals. She'd had all that. She was sorry
for the people who'd been crippled since birth, who'd never known those
things. You lost things to age, there were things no one her age could
do. But she'd done those things—hopscotch on the sunny flagstone
walk at recess, skating on the frozen pond. It was odd that she could
call up all these distant things, when so many recent ones were gone.

Even after the accident, things had been all right for a while. Years.
Sometimes Edward rubbed her back at night, though this was never
mentioned to the children. She knew it would make him feel demeaned,
like a servant. She'd tried never to let her pain be known; she knew it
made him unhappy. He was used to pain, but during surgery the patient was anesthetized. (He'd used saws, she knew, electric drills, sta-
ples. Surgeons were used to it. The pain he inflicted was necessary,
a part of the cure.) There was nothing to be done about her pain, and
no point in discussing it. She tried never to talk about it.

Now she could see that Edward was beginning to fail. It saddened
her. He was stiff now, and ungainly. His feet were heavy. He tired easily,
and couldn't carry the groceries in from the car in one trip. He asked the
store to use several small bags, so he could carry them one at a time.
He didn't tell her, but she'd seen it. Since he'd retired, he'd been doing
the marketing, because her limp was worsening.

Katharine's body had been giving out for decades, it was in endless
decline. She was used to it, but Edward was not used to being in decline, and it was hard for him. He'd relied on his body all his life, it had
always done his bidding. She didn't know what would happen to him,
to them, if his body really did give out. She didn't think about the
future. Edward had always been the one to do that. Anything might
happen, they might both die in their sleep.

They had friends who had gone into those places, "facilities." As-
sisted living. The Medways had put their names down five years ago,
so when they needed it they'd have a place to go. Eleanor had sounded
so smug about it, as though it were laudable to plan for her own de-
struction. But shouldn't you struggle against it, resist? Wasn't the thing
not to give in? Katharine had resisted all her life. She'd never called

herself "disabled" or "handicapped," those words seemed like defeat. She didn't want now to put herself in another category. She didn't want to go into one of those places, nor did Edward. She'd rather die. In fact, she was secretly rather looking forward to dying: it would be another adventure. And a relief. She felt she'd earned it.

She wondered what Julia's thoughts were for the future. If she'd remarry. She'd had other men in her life, after the divorce, Katharine knew, but Julia never talked about them. Katharine hoped she'd remarry, it would be such a waste of beauty and possibility if she didn't. Julia's wide face, the lovely wings of hair, all that emotional vitality. Those long strong legs. Katharine loved her daughters' lean tanned legs, so straight and fine, their steps miraculously solid and even. They were her redemption.

How could Wendell have left Julia? Katharine had loved Wendell, his sense of humor, his warmth. How could he have done this? Broken something so lovely and intact.

"There's one," said Steven. "I saw it with my wizening eyes."

"I saw it, too," Julia said: a bright streak of falling light, a flare of hope. She thought of Simon.

"I did, too," Katharine said.

"So did I," said Edward, pleased.

There, thought Julia, as though something had been exquisitely proven. She felt a wave of pleasure. Her parents were fine. They were frail, but they were wholly present. Risks lay in the future, but they always did. Just now, Julia, wrapped in the striped blanket, sat between her mother and her son. They were all sitting on the vast, sloping, darkened side of the earth, looking into the limitless reaches of the sky and watching miracles of light and motion. Right now they were safe.

PART II

SEVEN

When Julia woke, the house was silent. Her room was flooded with the thin light of early morning, and the plaster walls were bright with sun. The big dormer windows stood open wide onto the front meadow, and the air was cool and sweet.

As she woke she found herself thinking of Jack, and wondered if she had been dreaming about him. The glint of his red-brown hair that grew straight downward, resisting the part; the way he raised his chin when he laughed. He was so handsome: really, with his straight brows and brilliant blue eyes. It made more difference than it should.

Julia was smiling, remembering the time they'd been at a diner somewhere—where? Outside, it had been winter. Sitting at the counter, drinking coffee. Wendell was there, so it was before the divorce, and Steven. They'd been talking, with Jackie at the end of their row, listening intently.

Too intently: there was something odd about his look. He was staring at them, and they turned, one by one, to look at him. He was humming quietly, stirring his coffee. As they turned he began to sing, that corny ballad about the logger who stirs his coffee with his thumb. It took them a moment—Jack's expression was so earnest—to see that he was doing it, stirring his coffee with his thumb, his finger buried deep in the inky liquid. It was his face, that manic, deadpan stare: it still made Julia laugh.

Jackie was always the star, the center of things. There was a glitter about him, the hypnotic gaze, the slow wide smile. The sense of wild possibility. He might do anything, and you wanted to be there when he did. He didn't care what happened. Risk appealed, you could sense it.

It had caused trouble for years. All those times Julia had been called in to meet with his teachers, his principals. But Jack was a sweetheart, not one of those sullen, hostile kids who hated their parents. (Julia knew kids like that: what would you do? Shoot yourself?) No, she was grateful for Jack, good-natured, warm, smart, creative. He'd always gone his own way, and why not? He was electrifying. You couldn't take your eyes off him.

She remembered the time they'd all been down at the dock, loading the boat for a picnic. Jack was carrying the hamper with all the food, sandwiches, fruit, potato chips, cookies, napkins, the works. Wendell stood in the Whaler, receiving things from the others, setting them in the bottom. Julia was walking down the ramp, carrying her own bundles, when it happened.

Wendell took a bag from Steven and set it down at his feet.

"Hold on," he said to Jack. "Let me move some of this. Everything's over on this side, let me balance it."

"That's okay, I'll take it around to the other side," Jack said. He walked along the dock beside the boat, up to the bow, then started to walk around it, stepping casually off the dock and into the air. Dropping, with the loaded basket in his hands, into ten feet of ocean at fifty degrees. His expression, as he went down, was mild and unconcerned, his body frozen in mid-step, hands locked on the hamper.

It was so absurd, and electrifying: they couldn't believe they'd seen it. She'd been furious, all those soaked sandwiches, the ruined food. He was outrageous, he dismissed everything the rest of them took seriously: warmth, dryness, order. He liked chaos, reveled in it. But it was impossible to stay mad at Jackie, he was so funny. So original, so bright and charming, so good-natured.

Though it was hard not to worry about him. His life was late in starting, or something. Was that it? He'd finally, barely, managed to graduate from college (an obliging one that no one had ever heard of, in northern New Hampshire), but at least he had a degree. Which had led him exactly nowhere, so far. He lived a Gypsyish downtown life of start-up bands, part-time jobs, optimistic schemes, and the very occasional unpaid musical gig. He was in a band, though not a rock band. It's not *rock* music, he'd told Julia, shaking his head and grinning with that generic rolling-eyed amazement at parental ignorance. As though she'd called it Latvian chanting. What it was, instead of rock, was a mystery to her. Mostly rhythm and electronic feedback, as far as she could tell.

But Jack loved it, and she loved watching him play, seeing him onstage in his skinny black jeans and black T-shirt, his head nodding in charmed obedience to the monstrous beat. That slow grin, the magnetic sideways glance. Who knew how he'd end up?

The bands he was in never actually seemed to progress. They seemed continually to be part of some emerging and dissolving process, like early life forms, and Julia wondered how long this ought to go on. At some point, didn't you accept the fact that the music wasn't succeeding? Move on? Though your child should decide this for himself; the parent's task was to be supportive. What Julia was determined never to be was like her father: judgmental. The world would always be the critic, her job was to be the fan.

Despite what seemed very ill-considered choices. There were things it was hard not to worry about. Drugs, of course, had always been a part of Jack's life. Certainly part of the downtown music scene, they were all around, she knew it. Julia rolled onto her stomach and burrowed her head into her flattened pillow.

During his adolescence, drugs had seeped into Jack's landscape like a toxic plume. All those things she kept finding in his bedroom, under the bed, among dirty clothes in his duffel—the grubby bags of pot, the bongs. And nothing seemed to stop Jack, not her and Wendell's serious talks, not their later anger and shouts and threats, not Jack's suspension from school, not even, once, his expulsion. They might as well have been ordering him to breathe a different kind of air.

She picked up the pillow, punched it, and laid her head down again.

That time they'd gone together—though by then they'd been separated—to visit him at college, when he was so weird all weekend, grinning, unfocused, completely stoned. Wendell was angry, but Julia was hurt to see he wouldn't face them without chemical protection. But it had been just after the divorce, maybe Jack had been angry at them for that. Acting out his rage.

For a moment Julia allowed herself the luxury of blaming all Jack's problems on Wendell's despicable behavior—why not? Wendell actually had been despicable—though this lasted for only a moment. It was a dangerous luxury. Considering Wendell's despicable behavior would lead to considering her own behavior, and to the (morally indefensible) fact that she did not know, absolutely, who Jack's father was.

It had been Julia's only affair, and brief.

For five months she'd been caught up in its runaway current. She'd been in thrall, powerless, it seemed. Each time she came home from seeing Eric, each time she stepped into her own apartment, into the safe domestic haven she'd created, the one which she now mocked so cruelly by her behavior, she felt remorse. Each time she opened the door onto its mute reproach, each time she saw the trusting faces of Wendell and Steven looking up with pleasure as she arrived, each time she saw them like this—innocent victims of her deceit—her heart smote her, and she determined in that instant to end it.

And the next day—the very next day!—hearing Eric's voice on the phone, she felt her heart quickening again in her chest, and nothing else was permitted entry into her mind. She thought of nothing else. She abandoned the rest of her life. She found herself rushing from the apartment, beds unmade, dirty dishes on the table, appointments ignored or forgotten. She lied to her husband, friends, babysitter, anyone who asked. She lied about a dentist's appointment, a seminar, a student conference, moving the car on the street. When challenged, she produced more lies. She'd been shocked and impressed at herself, she'd had no idea what she'd been capable of. She'd done things that she'd never have thought of doing. In the back of their own car one night, parked on the street, on their own block. At a party, standing up, in a bathroom, Wendell knocking at the door. She'd been insane.

She'd been helpless, willing, thrilled. The tautness and electricity of this sumptuous, illicit love, how your body yearned for it! How her skin, everywhere, had waited for Eric's touch, for his breath on the back of her neck, for the urgency of his gaze. How her blood quickened at his husky, intimate whisper in her ear. She'd been taken over by pleasure, by ecstasy; it had been her entire life for five months.

Wendell, though, had started it all.

Late one evening, after dinner, the two of them still at the kitchen table, they'd emptied a second bottle of wine. Wendell's eyelids grew heavy, his manner affectionate and confidential. He told Julia how very fond he was of her, very fond. Then he admitted, grinning, almost proud, that he'd taken the secretary from the Classics Department to a motel just across the George Washington Bridge. He'd told her all this as though she, Julia, were his accomplice. Just for the afternoon, he said, as though that made a difference. When Julia stared at him, furious, he seized her hand unsteadily.

"Don't get so mad," he said. "It doesn't mean anything. Anyway, it was in New Jersey."

"You think you're not married in New Jersey?" Julia asked. "How many other states are you not married in?"

"Come on," Wendell said, shaking her hand gently. "Don't be jealous. I thought of you the whole time. When we parked the car I just sat there. I wanted to call the whole thing off."

"But you didn't," Julia pointed out.

"Don't be cross. You're much better in bed than she is. I'm weak, that's all."

Julia said nothing, furious. What she thought was *Why am I bothering to be faithful?*

So when Eric Swenson, a sort of post-Expressionist with a long auburn ponytail, smelling of turpentine, whose studio was near hers, asked if she wanted to go for coffee, she said yes, and for five months she was swept up in that stream. Then one morning she'd waked up to nausea, and when she rolled over in bed she felt the tenderness of her breasts and knew she was pregnant, but with no idea by whom. At that moment the switch was turned off. After that, she felt exactly nothing at the sound of Eric's voice. His touch on her skin made her twitch, and she wanted to shake off his hand like an insect. It was over.

When Jackie was born—after nine months of fervent virtue, as though she could make the unborn child into Wendell's son simply by her own good behavior—she told herself he was Wendell's son. It could easily be true; she'd never know. Jackie had her blood type, A negative, and he'd grown up as Wendell's son. Julia had never told anyone.

But Jackie was the secret reminder of her scarlet season, those days spent swinging out into thin air, over the wild shadowed depths of the canyon. It was the thrill of it, the luxury of yielding to something so dangerous, so delicious, so irresistible, intoxicating. She'd been incapable of resistance, she'd had no thought of stopping. It was a madness, it was addiction. Remembering those days was like a soldier remembering the battlefield—the explosions around him matched by those in his thundering heart—in disbelief that this life and the earlier one could have been contained within the same body.

Jack was himself, of course, but he was secretly this as well, and sometimes when Julia looked at him she saw a double image—himself and his mother's secret stain. She loved him for this as well as for himself.

Long afterward, Eric asked her about Jack, at a crowded cocktail party in someone's apartment on Claremont Avenue. Eric was standing near her, too close. He held a cache of peanuts in one hand, a glass of wine in the other. His voice was low and confidential, and Julia drew away. His eyes were bloodshot, and the skin on his nose was tight and drawn.

"I wondered," Eric said, watching her, "about your son. The younger one." He raised his hand, opened his mouth, and tossed in a peanut. "Because of when he was born." He chewed, his jaws grinding steadily.

"He's not yours, Eric," Julia told him. "He's Wendell's. There's no question."

Eric said nothing. He closed his hand over the peanuts and shook them. They made a soft rattling sound inside his fist.

"It's true. I know the night it happened," Julia said, as though by persuading Eric she could make it so. "Women always know."

He waited, still chewing, watching her appraisingly.

Now Julia turned over in bed, gazing up at the plaster ceiling, with its deltas of fine hairline cracks. She'd have said anything, to anyone, to make Jack into Wendell's son. Partly out of loyalty to her marriage, partly for Jack's sake. It still mattered. She'd do anything to make Jack into Wendell's son. The force of her will would make it true.

Anyway, all Jack's problems might be unrelated to his parents (whoever they were), or to their own bad behavior, or their divorce. It was tempting to think you played a part in everything your child did, since, when he was small, you did. But your child grew into his own life, chose his own path. And you couldn't blame everything on divorce—look at Steven.

She might be overreacting, in any case. Maybe drugs were no longer a problem for Jack, maybe they had never really been. It seemed everyone took them now. Steven had, she knew. Julia had herself, in college. Taking drugs was a rite of passage, an initiation into an esoteric society, somewhere darker and cooler than childhood. The illicit thrill of the secret community, the coded phrases, the rituals.

Though her own druggie phase seemed unrelated to Jack's: whatever your children did was always a little too daring, a little too fast. How were you meant to deal with them and drugs? It was hard to tease out a line to follow among the tangle of illicit behavior, tacit consent, public obloquy. Was it a question of degree? Telling your children never to take any drugs seemed naïve, so should you say that it was all right to try marijuana but not cocaine? Both were illegal. Where did you draw the line?

By the time it was a problem you had no control, anyway. Your children had left home, or were spending so much time elsewhere that they might as well have. You might draw the line anywhere you wanted, your children could simply step over it. And fighting with your children was so horrible, all that shouting and misery.

Maybe they had been too lax. How did you know? And what did you do if you had been? She thought drugs must be in Jack's life. She was hoping for them to subside, as they had in Steven's, where they must also have been.

The cracks in the ceiling had always been there. Julia thought they showed merely the way the old house shifted and settled with the seasons, the wood frame swelling and shrinking, the plaster dampening and drying. Wendell's view had been more ominous: he thought they mapped the fault lines where the plaster, some apocalyptic day, would give way. Wendell used to lie in bed, gazing upward and predicting ruin. Only a matter of time, he would say.

Julia's thoughts had become too boisterous for her to stay in bed with any longer, and she got up. She took off her nightgown, hanging it inside the tiny slanting closet under the eaves. The air was cool and fresh, and she felt her skin tighten against it. She shivered slightly, but she liked this brief moment of nudity, the sense of swimming in the morning's clear river. She dressed and padded downstairs, barefoot. The worn wooden steps were soft beneath her feet.

The kitchen looked abandoned and untidy, strands of corn silk on the floor, dirty pans soaking in the sink. The air was close and stale, and Julia opened the porch door wide and put on the kettle. She took the broom from the closet and began to sweep, enjoying the brisk abrasive passage of the broom, the deep virtuous satisfaction of cleaning. *Next to godliness: there was a lofty claim.* Certainly it was an instinctive impulse; animals did it, grooming themselves, licking and biting, keeping themselves clean. Dogs licking each other's face, horses biting languidly along each other's back. A healthy animal was clean, a dirty one was ill or wounded. *And who was Hygeia, anyway?* She washed out the last pans, rinsed out the sink, and made coffee.

She took her mug onto the porch and sat down on the steps, lifting her face. The air was quiet and fresh, and the sky clear. The grass in the meadow was heavy with dew. There was no wind; it would be hot later.

She wished Jackie were here, right now, to see the meadow, still shimmering with dew, the cove beyond showing a cross-hatched glitter. Right now, in this pale candid light, it seemed impossible to think of being troubled, impossible not to feel the certainty of some kind of clarity and grace.

The screen door behind her creaked, and she looked up, apprehensive that it was Edward. But it was Steven, tousled and barefoot, in wrinkled jeans and a T-shirt.

"Hi," Julia half-whispered, smiling: the morning was still too quiet for talk. "You're up early. Want some coffee?"

"No, thanks." Steven sat down in a chair above her. He stretched out his legs, crossing his ankles. "Yeah, I am up early. Don't know why."

They sat in silence, looking out over the meadow.

"So," Julia said. "You're back. Any thoughts on what you want to do next?"

"Yeah," said Steven. "I'm thinking of law school."

Julia took a sip of coffee. "What does your father say?"

"Haven't told him yet."

"Why do you want to go?"

Listening to Steven's response, she thought, *My responsible child.* She felt a wave of helpless affection. She wanted to say yes to whatever he wanted. She wanted to make herself into a carpet, flatten the world beneath his foot.

"Of course we'll do what we can to help," she told him. "I hope you'll end up in New York."

"Thanks," said Steven soberly. "I'll see where I get in."

"You'll get in everywhere," Julia told him. Steven grinned and rolled his eyes.

They fell silent, Steven squinting out across the field, Julia sipping from her mug. She was trying to prepare herself for the next, the difficult, subject.

"So, how's your brother?" Julia asked finally. "You saw him in New York?"

Steven shrugged, frowning. "Yeah, I saw him."

Julia waited. "And? How's he doing?" Anxiety began to tick in her mind.

Steven shrugged again. "It's hard to say. I don't really know."

Steven wouldn't tell, she could see that. She hated asking him to inform on his brother.

"He's not working," Julia said tentatively, hoping to be corrected.

"He says he's getting a job."

"That's great," Julia said. "Doing what?"

"He said working at a video store," Steven said.

"A video store?" Julia repeated, dismayed.

Jackie, with his quick bright mind, his sense of humor, his reach and grasp of life? In a video store, with its sluggish air, the bored and affectless adolescents behind the counter, the endless loop of action movies on the overhead screen? How had his gaze fallen so low?

But of course any job was better than none, better than sitting around in someone's apartment getting stoned. Anything was better than that awful glazed-eye apathy. Any job was better than those empty claims about rock bands and music production, those sad, noncredible schemes. Any job meant getting up each morning, clean clothes, punctuality. Responsibility. Those small-minded quotidian things. Her own gaze had fallen as well.

"Do you think he has a plan?" she asked. "I mean, long-term?"

"I don't know what he's doing," Steven said again, not looking at her.

Julia watched him.

"What do you think's going on?"

Steven shook his head.

"Do you think he's taking drugs?" she asked.

Steven hesitated, still not looking at her. There were certain things he did not want to say to his mother—or to anyone—about Jack. There was the question of loyalty. He and Jack were connected. He could not step across the family space to stand with his parents, though in his mother's question he felt the covert pull to do so.

"Everyone takes drugs," Steven said flatly.

"Do you?"

After a moment he said, "Not really. Not anymore. A little pot now and then. Not much. But Jack's younger."

"You think it's a problem," Julia said.

Steven didn't answer.

"I suppose you don't want to say," Julia said.

She remembered the afternoon, a few months ago, when she'd come home to the apartment to find Jack in the living room. For some reason she'd felt oddly alarmed at the sight of him; for some reason he'd looked like a stranger.

He'd arrived unannounced, and that too was disturbing, though she couldn't say why. Didn't he often come home without telling her? Or not? She couldn't remember, but this seemed different. And he looked so filthy, his hair so greasy and unkempt, as though for days he hadn't even run his hands through it. He seemed dirty in some alarming way, as though his body no longer mattered. Or was she overreacting? Most of her students were grubby and unkempt. But this seemed different, more serious.

He was wearing blue jeans worn to a colorless gray, an old zippered sweatshirt over a white T-shirt. He turned toward her when she came in, and she was shocked by his face. His eyes were empty.

"Jack!" she said. "How nice to see you!"

She'd tried to act casual and motherly, but her words had frozen. There was a terrifying absence about him. Was he swaying slightly, standing there? Convention held her on its rails (what should she have done?) and she offered him coffee, a beer. No, he'd said to everything, no, thanks.

Finally she'd asked if anything were the matter. No, he'd said. Nothing was the matter.

He shook his greasy head, and Julia suddenly remembered him as a child, sitting in the bathtub, small and naked, pearly white, his legs stretched sturdily out in front of him.

Julia, fixing coffee anyway, talked as she moved about the kitchen. They sat down, and Julia slid a mug over to Jack. He slouched bonelessly against his chair. He looked at her, then away. His silence was blank and monumental, she felt it pressing on her.

His skin was pale, nearly translucent. His eyes seemed glazed and hooded, the lids heavy. Below them were dark rings, faintly glistening with oil or sweat. He looked down at his mug, his gaze interior. His fingers grasped it loosely; his fingernails were filthy. The zipper on his sweatshirt was broken, the fabric thin and worn. Why did he look like this? Where were his other clothes?

Jack sat still, then looked up, his gaze moving about the kitchen. There was something in him that excluded her. Finally he stood, shoving his hair from his face.

"Okay, I'm taking off," Jack said.

"Can I give you something?" she asked. She was frightened by his stillness and distance. "A little hay for your horse?" A family joke: it was what Katharine always said when they came to see her. Katharine would tuck a rolled-up bill into her daughter's hand, to pay for gas. It was a love token.

Jack shrugged again, not moving. It was as though he were waiting for a sound his mother could not hear. His eyes were dull.

"Let me give you something." Julia rummaged through her purse and found a twenty, two of them. "Here. Take a cab home."

Jack took it without looking at it. "Thanks."

There was a field of silence around him. She followed him to the door. In the hall he turned to close the door, and she saw his face, now shadowed, beyond her territory. It seemed feral, the dark eyes watchful. There was something wrong with them, his eyes.

"'Bye, Ma," he said. "Thanks for the hay."

He'd been like a stranger, terrible. Why had he come? There was something, too, that clicked in her memory, about the visit, some forgotten unease. What was it?

Now, on the porch, Julia put her arm around her bare knees, hugging herself.

"What do you think we should do?" she asked Steven.

Steven leaned back in his chair, his hands knitted together over his flat stomach. He didn't answer.

It was certainly drugs, Steven thought now, suddenly, allowing himself to know, *it was certainly serious*. The knowledge crowded in on him and, now it was clear, had been there all along. The stinking hall, the awful apartment, Jack's blank dead stare. The weird eyes, the wrong smile. The blood on his shirt cuff. The familiar request. Steven had given him money, as always. He felt sickened by all this: his brother's sinister affect, his mother's cautious questions. Her request for loyalty, the insidious "we."

"Steven?"

"I don't know what you should do."

Steven refused to be we. He didn't know what his parents should do. He only knew of cures—rehabs—from friends who'd gone through them. He didn't know about the other side, how the parents had done it. He knew kids who'd been handed plane tickets and taken, that minute, to the airport, muscled into seclusion like involuntary monks. He'd had friends who'd asked their parents to get them into programs. He'd heard of those creepy couples who burst into bedrooms in the middle of the night, taking some poor kid off to one of those sinister boarding-school boot camps. He didn't know about making the arrangements. He wasn't going to be part of some organized plan to hunt Jack down.

Julia sipped her coffee, aware of his distance.

"You know," she said tentatively, "I wish you'd help me. I'd like to know if you think it's serious, and if we should do something, or if you think it's just a phase he's going through, and if we should wait for it to pass. I'd appreciate your advice."

Julia had always believed that parents should not ask children for help, they should be capable of dealing with their own problems. But now she needed Steven: he knew more about this than she did.

After a moment, Steven answered. Saying nothing was also taking a position.

"Okay," he said reluctantly. "Okay. I think he's in trouble. I think it's bad."

The words echoed oddly in her head.

"What do you mean, bad?" Julia did not look at him. The air had taken on some kind of charge.

"I think he's on serious drugs."

"What kind?" Her chest felt constricted.

"Heroin," Steven said.

There was the word. He'd loosed it like a snake, quick, black, lethal, whiplashing fast and horribly into their world. But it wasn't his fault, was it? The word had already entered his brother's world, the long black shape sliding into the crevices of his brother's life, vanishing into the shadows, where it was coiling and expanding, gathering strength. Taking up more and more space, crowding out the life that had been there.

EIGHT

Heroin.

The word was too large for her to absorb; she felt its sickening impact. It had a dark, absorbent presence, lethal and endless. It became suddenly so large in her mind that she could not think exactly what it was. *Was it from poppies, or was that opium? Were they the same?*

"You inject heroin, right?" She was groping for balance, trying to keep herself upright with facts. Injection, addiction. She wanted something hard and substantial.

Steven nodded. "Or sniff it. Most addicts shoot it up."

Julia tried to focus. Nodding off, that was heroin, wasn't it? Wasn't it what you dissolved in a spoon? Or was that crack cocaine? The rubber hose tugged tight around the arm, the glinting needle, wasn't that heroin? She'd seen it in movies, but what she knew had turned incoherent and confused. None of it could have anything to do with her son.

"You don't know this for sure," she said.

"I don't know it for sure. It's what I think."

Something was swinging back and forth in her brain. "Why do you think it's heroin?" Julia asked.

"A lot of things. The way he acts," said Steven.

"Which is?"

"Different from the way he used to be."

"How?"

"Not like how he is on pot. Pot makes you goofy, it's kind of mindless and innocent. Everything's funny, and then you go to sleep. But on heroin, everything is slowed way, way down. It's heavier," said Steven. "People act like they're nearly asleep. You've been pulled into somewhere separate from the rest of the world."

It was like receiving a penal sentence, each word felt hammered into her skull. She did not believe it, though this very word was the one she'd dreaded. The word was killing, toxic. She'd heard it, but could not receive it into her mind.

"You might be mistaken," she said.

"Mom," Steven said soberly, "you should see him. He's living in this filthy place, everything's a mess. After he buzzed me in, it took him a really long time to answer the door. I had the feeling that he'd just done something. He acted weird, and his eyes were pinned. The pupils were like pinpoints. That's what happens with heroin."

She looked at Steven. He met her gaze.

"You could be wrong," Julia said. Her chest had grown larger, it had grown huge, and her heart was laboring to work inside its chasm. She could hear the blood pounding in her ears.

"I could be wrong," Steven agreed. "But you asked me what I thought. He had blood on his shirt cuffs, from shooting up. I think he's on heroin."

Julia put her face down on her knees and closed her eyes. *People died from this.* She could feel the sun on her hair. She saw sunspots in the darkness behind her eyes. There was a roaring in her ears. Without lifting her head she spoke.

"But wouldn't we know, if he was?" Julia asked. "Wouldn't it be obvious? I mean . . ."

She stopped. She didn't know what she meant.

She felt as though she'd been bargaining with someone, with something, for years. Over and over she'd yielded, reluctantly accepting facts she wanted to deny. She had agreed, reluctantly, to pot and drinking, lack of responsibility, failure to do this and that, yes, they were true. She'd accepted all those things, really, so she'd never have to accept this.

Not that this made any sense, she was raving. Who was she bargaining with?

But she'd had the notion that there'd be some sort of payoff later, some sort of reward. Not for herself but for all of them, for the family, a badge of merit for entering the crisis, accepting it. How could this be right? Over and over, all those crises over Jack; the family had gone through them and they'd done well, hadn't they? They should get badges, not this body blow. Jack, her beautiful pearly darling. *People died from this.*

Everything in her mind had been slowed down. Every thought was dragged from her.

"I think you're wrong, Steven," she said with great certainty. "I don't think this could be true."

Steven said nothing. Julia put her face down again on her knees. She felt the hot sun on her hair.

"If he is on heroin," she said, "what should we do?"

"Talk to him," Steven said. "You and Dad."

"Yes," she said. "Would it work?" She lifted her head.

"I don't know," Steven said. "You could start with that. Maybe he's ready to quit." Steven didn't think so.

"Yes."

"I think he needs help," Steven said.

Right. Of course, thought Julia, *he needs help.* She understood that. She'd get him help. She was a professor; if he were her student, she'd know what to do. She'd refer him to Mental Health, she'd walk him over there. She'd call Mental Health now, they'd know what to do. The university had systems to deal with this.

Heroin, she thought, *Jesus.*

She felt frozen. It was her child. Any decision might be the wrong one. The wrong program, the wrong therapist, errors could be fatal. It was her son.

She would call Mental Health and ask for advice. It occurred to her that they would ask her name, her social security number. These strangers would know that her son was on heroin, that this was how well they had succeeded as a family. She thought of her father, shaking his head with disapproval. She wondered if she could keep it from him. From her sister. Julia felt a sudden ferocious glow of resentment at her judgmental family.

"But are you sure?" Julia asked again. "This is speculation. You don't know about the blood, it might be from a cut. You could be wrong."

"*Stop it,*" Steven said. "This is what I think. If you don't want my opinion, don't ask for it, but don't keep asking me to change it. *I think Jack's a junkie.*"

Julia looked at him.

"Cocaine speeds you up. Heroin slows you down," Steven said. "Jack is slowed way down. There's something wrong. He's not there. He's gone."

He's gone. He's gone.

"So—" but Julia spoke out loud only in order to keep the words from repeating themselves in her mind. She couldn't find the next thought. What was the next thought? The landscape of her brain was shattered.

"So," Steven said, "if he's on heroin, he needs help."

Julia nodded. She could not focus. What was the matter with her? How could she know so little about something so important? She knew nothing about this, she realized, nothing.

"If you're on it, how often do you take it?" she asked. "I mean, once a day? Three times? What?"

Steven shrugged. "Depends on the habit. If you're really an addict, more than once a day. I mean lots. It can be really expensive."

Now it bloomed, chillingly, in her mind, the realization of what had bothered her, the day she found Jack in the living room. Now she un-

derstood what was wrong—it was not just his condition but his intention. *He hadn't been there to see her. He'd been there to steal.*

"Can you work if you're taking heroin?"

"Depends on the habit," Steven said. "A friend of one of my roommates was a high-functioning heroin addict. He worked on Wall Street.
He had all sorts of rules for himself, exercise, how much he took, when
he took it. He was on a strict maintenance level."

"Maintenance level?"

"Enough to keep the high steady and the craving quiet," Steven said.
"But he was unusual. I think most people just barely get along. I don't
know. I guess to a certain extent you can function."

"Maybe work at a video store," said Julia.

Steven nodded.

Julia looked out at the cove, where the water was beginning to
shimmer. On this bright airy morning her son might be a junkie, his
mind consumed by that one black hole of a thought.

"Have you ever taken it?" She wanted to fend this off with talk,
keep the conversation going, while her brain struggled to absorb it.

"No."

"Cocaine?"

"A few times," he said.

"At college?"

"Yeah."

"How far did you go?"

Anything to keep him talking.

She had never asked Steven these things. You were meant to talk to
your children about drugs, but it had seemed impossible. At the time
when the conversation was crucial your children became unreachable.
You understood you might not be told the truth; you didn't ask them questions they'd lie about. Over the issue of drugs you became enemies, or
at least diplomatic adversaries. Only covert information was available.

"Further than I should have," Steven said.

They were looking out toward the water.

"Which meant?"

"At one point I had my own dealer. I had his cell phone number, he'd deliver to my apartment. Once I was on my way home from class, about six o'clock at night. I had twenty dollars, and I couldn't decide whether to spend it on food or coke. I remember walking up Amsterdam Avenue, trying to decide, and then I just thought, This is bad. I have to quit."

"Steven," Julia said.

"I know," he said. "It was bad."

"And then what? How did you get off it?"

"I was seeing a girl who took it a lot, really a lot. The next time I called my dealer, he told me he'd just seen her. She was going home for the weekend, and she'd asked him to meet her at Penn Station, so she could take some stuff with her for the weekend. The thought of the two of them meeting on the platform kind of gave me the creeps, and so did the idea of hearing about my girlfriend from my drug dealer. I thought I'd gone too far. I broke off with them both. I just quit the whole thing."

"What girl was it?" asked Julia. Steven had big herds of friends, and roommates of both sexes. It was hard to tell who was a friend and who a girlfriend, they seemed to shift back and forth seamlessly.

"Tara," he said. "I don't think you knew her."

"Tara." Tall and thin, black clothes, lank dark hair? Lounging on Steven's sofa, barefoot, silent, smoking? "I think I met her."

"You might have," Steven said.

"Well," Julia said.

"It's over," Steven said. "I'm not going to marry Tara. And I'm not an addict."

"But Jack is." Julia's voice was tentative, hoping for disagreement. Steven was silent.

After a moment, Julia straightened her back, set down her mug. Somewhere in her mind there was still a layer of resistance, but now she was filled with urgency.

"Okay," she said. "Your father and I need to talk to Jack. I can't go down to see him right away because of my parents. I'll ask your father if he'll come up here; will you ask Jack?"

"Ma," Steven said, "whoa."

"I'll call Mental Health," Julia went on. "I'll get information. But we need to talk to Jack face to face."

"Don't ask me to call him," Steven said.

"Steven," Julia said. "You started this."

"I'm not saying—"

"You said 'heroin,'" Julia said. "You're the one who used that word. Once you say it, everything changes. Now we have to do everything we can. You too." She felt swollen with something, dictatorial. She felt terrified.

"*Fine.*" Steven stood, his hands in his pockets. "Pull out all the stops. But don't ask me to help, I'm not in on this."

"Don't say that," Julia said. "You can't start this and then just walk away, Steven. You can't leave now."

"Mom, *I can't do it.*" Steven's voice was tight, and he shook his head. "I can't do this to my brother."

"It's because he's your brother that you *have* to do it," Julia said angrily. How could he not see this? She felt rage flooding through her. This was not a matter for discussion, it was a necessity. She would not tolerate Steven's mutinous response.

Steven shook his head again. He could feel his mother's rising rage. All of this was terrible. He had betrayed his brother's confidence, he had unloosed the word into the world, he had spoken his suspicions, and he had set his parents onto his brother like hounds onto a rabbit, and now his mother was reviling him. He could feel the surge of her fury. He saw Jack's strange dead eyes, he remembered the long silence as he stood waiting in front of the door. His mother's anger, his brother's distance. He felt the air fracturing around him.

"Don't ask me," he said, and his voice was strange in his throat.

The sound of Steven's strange, choked voice silenced Julia. She was still filled by something urgent, powerful, but it was not rage. Steven's voice was so tight and so perilous—it held the risk of breaking, and she could not bear it if Steven's voice broke.

She put a hand over her eyes, closing off the world.

"It's *because* he's your brother," she said. Now her own voice was low, deep in her chest, and not solid. Her own voice might break. She could feel things starting to splinter. "You have to help him, Steven. None of us can choose, anymore, what we do. You have to call him. He won't come if I ask, I've tried. I'm sorry. It has to be you."

NINE

"Fly to Portland," Steven said. "I'll pick you up."

"Can't do it," Jack said.

"Come on."

It was early afternoon, after lunch. Steven sat at the rickety telephone table in the dining room. He was leaning over, the phone at his ear, elbows on his knees.

"Everyone's up here," he said. "Mom really wants you to come. She'll get you a ticket."

"Yeah," said Jack.

There was a pause.

"So, will you?"

"No," said Jack.

"Come on," Steven said again. "Why not?"

"Just can't, dude," Jack said.

"You working?"

"Yeah."

"The video store can spare you for a weekend."

"It's not the video store."

"What is it?"

"Different things. I can't come up there."

Another pause.

"What's going on?" Steven asked.

"Nothing! I told you! I just can't come up there."

Steven raised his head and looked out the window. The sky was full of high scudding clouds. "Mom'll be disappointed," he said. "Grandpa and Grandma are here."

"I told you," Jack said.

"What would it take?" Steven asked.

"What." Jack's voice was wary. "What does that mean?"

"What would it take to get you up here?"

There was a silence.

"I need some money," Jack said finally.

"How much?"

Another pause.

"Six hundred," he said, at once correcting himself. "Eight."

"Eight hundred bucks?" Steven said. "That's a lot. You're in debt?"

"Sort of," Jack said.

"Jacko, what's going on?" Steven asked. "You in trouble?"

"Not really," Jack said. "Just some money I owe. I can't go out of town and leave it."

Steven listened to his brother's breathing. "Jack." He could feel his presence. Something lay between them.

"What is it?" Jack asked, irritated. "What is all this shit? Why are you bugging me?"

"It doesn't sound good," Steven said. "Why do you owe so much money? What's going on?"

"You know what?" Jack said. "It's none of your business. Why do you care?" His voice was now cool.

"Oh, great," Steven said. "Really great. Give me a lot of shit."

"Okay, fine," Jack said. "It's still none of your business."

"If I get you the money, will you come up here?"

"Yeah," Jack said.

"What'll I tell Mom?"

"Tell her anything," Jack said. "I don't care. Tell her I want to invest in a blue-chip stock." He laughed.

"Great," Steven said again. "She'll jump at that. Did you lose the job at the video store?"

"Never actually started it, as a matter of fact."

"Bro," Steven said. "If I get you the money, how do I know you'll come up?" The connection between them was tenuous. He felt as though he were trying to lead a racehorse with sewing thread.

"I'm telling you I will." Jack's voice was languid. "What, you think I'm a liar? Don't you trust me?"

"What if you just spend it and don't come?"

"Well," Jack said, "that's just a chance you'll have to take, isn't it? But if you don't send it, you'll know for sure I'm not coming. So if you need to be sure, don't send it."

"Right," Steven said. "Thanks for clearing that up. Okay, look, we aren't getting anywhere. I'll talk to Mom and call you back."

"I'll be right here," Jack said.

Steven hung up. It was worse than he'd thought.

Julia stood at the kitchen sink, waiting for Steven, peeling potatoes for dinner. She held one of them in her hand, flicking off the brown skin, flake by flake. The potato was turning from muddy brown to a glittering white, and its moist sheen—*how would you paint that?*—made Julia think of her studio. The silent, shadowy barn, the smell of old wood and dust. The slow movement of a wasp at the window. It was now another country, the site of an earlier life. She'd painted at the beginning of the summer, before anyone else arrived, and she'd hoped to work more at the end of the month, when the house was empty again. Right now it was unimaginable; it was a place she yearned to reinhabit.

What she wanted was to show the convergence between the shimmering realm of the tangible and the invisible tumultuous one of the

emotions. How they overlapped and interwove. The extraordinary loveliness of the world, how it was infinite and generous in its reach, how
it could be soft and glistening, tangled and dense, velvety and bright.
These potatoes, their juicy flesh moist and glittering. Though now, standing in the kitchen—potatoes, dinner, Jack—the barn and her work
seemed very far away.

There was no sound from the dining room.

Beyond all this, at the end of the season, was departure, her return
to the city. It lay before her like an unseen waterfall, the sheer drop beyond the river of summer. After that was the roaring whirlpool of autumn, classes, meetings, the rush and plunge of college, the city. Simon
again (who was, right now, somewhere on the Snake River, with his
sons). Her campaign for tenure: another sheer drop. Judgment by her
peers. The odious Jo-Ann Bair, with her lipless mouth and militant crew
cut, who was the head of her committee and had always disliked her.
A shock to realize that there were people who actively, consciously, disliked you, who held against you forever stupid things you'd said, people who thought you were awful, who laughed at you behind your
back. But you understood that you, yourself, were not odious or foolish. You were you: normal, as likable as anyone. You hadn't meant to say
those stupid things; you could explain them. But Jo-Ann Bair disliked
her, her face went rigid at the sight of Julia. What would happen if she
failed to get tenure? Julia dropped the peeled potato into a bowl and
picked up another.

She thought of her studio in New York (which belonged to the university, and which she'd lose if she didn't get tenure), its big grid of
grimy windows. The paint-splashed wooden floor, the racks of canvases,
the long, empty, waiting wall. That first entry into the studio after the
summer, her slow footsteps on the bare floor, the air full of expectancy.
She would stand for a moment to listen, as though she might hear the
sound of it, whatever it was that let her paint. Beyond the walls was the
dense hum of the city, comforting in its energy, its limitlessness, like an
endless stream of electricity and vitality to tap into. New York hummed,
the silent studio vibrated, all of it waiting for her to begin.

Steven was taking a long time. What were they saying?

She scraped briskly. He could be wrong, he could be mistaken. That day at the apartment Jack could have been sick, or worried. He could have just been high on pot, God knows she had seen him like that often enough. It could have been anything. Her tilted blade dipped in and out of the potato's indentations, slicing off the mottled flecks.

Steven came into the kitchen. She looked up.

"So." Steven came and leaned beside her on the counter. "I talked to him."

"What did he say?"

"He won't come unless we give him some money."

Julia looked at Steven, then down. "How much does he want?"

"Eight hundred dollars."

Julia frowned. "Eight hundred dollars."

Steven said nothing.

"What does he want it for?"

"He won't say."

"What do you think he wants it for?" Julia was angry at Jack: he was making it hard for her not to believe Steven.

Steven looked at her without speaking.

Julia frowned again, scraping crossly at the rough skin. "Why do you think it's drugs?"

"What do you think it's for?"

She turned to him. "You don't know, Steven," she said reprovingly. "You just think he's on drugs, we don't know it. He could have borrowed the money for something. Rent or something. Anything."

"Rent," Steven said.

"I think we're being unfair," Julia said. "Just because Jack has taken drugs in the past, it's not fair to assume he takes them every time something comes up." She rubbed her nose with the back of her hand. "I *really think* that, if Jack had a serious drug problem, we'd know it."

"Ma," Steven said.

"What?"

Steven looked at her, waiting.

After a moment Julia said, "I hate this." She looked down into the sink. The brown scraps were everywhere, sticking to the damp white surface like dirty snow. "I hate it. I feel like a policeman. I don't want to spend my life being suspicious of my son, doubting every word he says."

"It sucks," agreed Steven.

"I don't want to believe this," Julia said.

"That sucks, too," Steven said.

There was a long silence. Julia shifted her hold. The potato was slippery, hard to grasp. She did not look at Steven. She made quick short flicks with the peeler. She felt him waiting.

"Are you going to do something?" he asked. "To help Jack?"

Julia dropped the scraped potato into the bowl of water. Clean and pale, it sank slowly, releasing silvery bubbles.

"I'll call him," she said, not looking up. "I want to talk to him. Eight hundred dollars?"

"I left his number by the phone." Steven pushed himself off the counter and stood. "I'm going out in the Whaler." He let the screen door bang.

Julia, drying her hands, watched him head for the dock. This was the moment to call Jack, while her parents were resting, the house silent.

In the dining room she dialed his number. It was another new one; Jack moved constantly. She stood looking down at the table, waiting. The phone rang, rang again. Had she dialed it right? No voice mail, no answering machine. She looked at the number—should she hang up and try again? Someone picked up.

"Hello?" The voice was odd and low, not quite familiar.

"Hello," she said, "I'm trying to reach Jack Lambert."

"Hi, Mom," Jack said.

"Oh, Jack," she said, relieved. "Do you have a cold?"

"No. Maybe I do. I don't know."

"You sounded funny," Julia said, her own voice bright. "I guess you just talked to Steven."

"Yeah," Jack said.

"We were hoping you'd be able to come up. Your grandparents would love to see you. Any chance?"

"Yeah, he said that," Jack said. "It's kind of inconvenient right now."

Julia closed her eyes, listening. "Because of your job?"

"Not exactly," Jack said.

There was a pause.

It was like feeling her way through a forest at night. She had to move slowly. She was afraid of asking direct questions. She was afraid he'd tell her something different from what he'd told Steven. She was afraid he'd lie. She was afraid he'd tell her something she could not bear to know. She was finding it hard to breathe.

"He said you needed some money," she said.

"That'd be good."

She frowned. "If we got it to you, would you come up?"

"Think so. Yeah."

"What do you need it for, Jackie?" She'd risk it.

"I owe it to somebody," Jack said.

"For what?"

There was a pause.

"I borrowed some amps, for a gig in the East Village," Jack said. "We rented a van for our stuff. Afterward it was too late to return the amps, so I parked the van outside my place. We brought our instruments inside, but somebody broke into the van and stole the amps."

This could be true, couldn't it?

"No one had any insurance?"

"No," Jack said.

"I thought you weren't playing with the band anymore," she said futilely.

"No, we broke up, but someone called and asked us to play this gig, so we came out of retirement."

"Well, Jackie—" Her voice was full of reluctance.

"I know, I know," he said, placatory. "I'm not asking you to pay. It's my responsibility, I know that. I don't expect you to pay for it. It's just that I can't go off and leave without taking care of it."

"But how will you get the money for it?" Julia asked.

"Get some more gigs, maybe. They're talking about asking us back. And there are other things."

"What about the video store?"

"Video store?"

Julia did not answer. What did she expect from this conversation? Steven must be right. Everything Jack said tightened her chest.

"Excuse me." Katharine's voice, behind her, was intimate and cheerful.

Julia looked up. Her mother stood poised in the doorway, leaning on her cane, beaming.

"May I come in?" Katharine started forward.

Julia, smiling distractedly, shook her head and flapped her hand. "If you could wait just a minute," she called, "I'm on kind of a private call."

"Hanh?" Katharine asked brightly, cocking her head. It was a family joke word, and she paused, expectantly, for laughter. "What did you say?" She had not stopped moving slowly forward. At the dining table she pulled out a chair. "I'll just wait till you're finished," she said, sitting down and settling her cane against her knee. "Don't mind me."

Julia turned her back on her mother and closed her eyes.

"Jack," she said, "I'm going to call your father. Eight hundred dollars is a lot of money. I want you to come up here, but first I want to talk to him about this. Is that the whole cost of the amps? That's it?"

Wouldn't a new set of them cost more than that?

"That's my share," Jack said. "I told Steve it was eight hundred, but it's really more like nine."

"I'd like to call your father to discuss it."

"Yeah," Jack said. "Why don't you."

Julia hesitated. *Was that as insolent as it sounded?* She couldn't quite believe it. "What did you say?"

"I said, 'Talk to Dad. It's a good idea,'" said Jack.

"What did you say?" asked Katharine brightly. "Did you ask what I said?"

"No," Julia said to her mother, shaking her head. "I will," she said to Jack.

"You are or you aren't?" Jack asked.

"I'm going to call your father," Julia said. "I'll call you back."

"You must mean *your* father," Katharine said comfortably. "*My* father's dead."

"Okay, 'bye, Jackie," Julia said, and turned to her mother.

Katharine smiled sociably. Edward was stretched out on the bed, dozing, and she'd set off alone, looking for company.

"What are you doing?" she asked Julia. "Can I help? Give me a job."

Julia smiled doubtfully.

"Shall I set the table?"

But her mother could barely get herself from the kitchen to the dining room, let alone carry china and cutlery. Was she strong enough to cut up the peeled potatoes? Those frail hands, the bones so close beneath the loosened skin.

"I hate doing nothing," Katharine declared. "I want to help."

"Good," Julia said. "Why don't you set the table? I'll bring things in and you set them. After that we'll have a cup of tea."

"I can bring things in," Katharine said, readying herself to stand. "No point in your doing half of it."

"I'll bring the things in to you," Julia repeated, leaving the room at speed. "Wait right there."

In the kitchen she moved quickly, opening cupboards and drawers, hoping her mother wasn't starting down the hall after her. She wondered what Wendell would say. What did she hope he'd say? Did she want him to believe their son was a drug addict, or deny it? It would be a difficult conversation: a vague net of antagonism overlay all their exchanges. Julia set a stack of folded napkins on the tray, then slid the silverware on with a quiet clatter.

Why had Jack been so flippant? *You do that*—is that what he'd said? She added the salt and pepper shakers. They were a pair of chipped china Dalmatians with wild eyes that Jack had given her, years ago, for

111

Christmas. *You do that.* It was more than flippant, it was insolent. She felt sickened.

Who could she talk to about this? Her friends in New York? She didn't want to tell anyone: it was so shameful. Should she go and see her old therapist? His long pale face, the creaking leather chair in the little airless room, the shade pulled discreetly down to the windowsill. The box of Kleenex on the table. Going back to Dr. Rifkin would be like opening a grave, feeling the cold dead air of her past flooding around her.

But who could she talk to? She needed advice, another voice. There was something—someone had told her recently about someone who'd had a child in rehab. Who had it been?

Katharine appeared in the doorway, leaning on her cane. "Here I am," she said. "Load me up." Katharine held out her free hand.

Katharine shifted her weight as she raised her free hand. This movement—all movement—was risky. She leaned heavily on her cane.

Her body sang to her. Her bones, her frame, her skeleton and joints, the damaged hip, the uneven ankles, lopsided pelvis, all of them sang to her, a song of brittleness and fragility. It was always there, this ethereal keening, sometimes so faint it was nearly inaudible, but always constant. She had only to pause and she could hear it, this high ecstatic harmony. It was a chord, a long sustained and blended note. Her bones were like glass, her muscles lax and withered, her joints clenched and frozen: this was the song. The song was the body in pain. She ignored it. She never paused to listen.

Yesterday, walking over the meadow through the long grass, she'd been ravished by it all: the wide light, the lovely crimsoning of the sky, the beauty of the inflooding evening. The hush of the mysterious expansion all around her, the ocean stretching on forever toward the sky, the long supple grass bending in the ceaseless wind. And while her spirit was enveloped and exalted, and buoyed by a kind of bliss, her body was on a different plane, transfixed in its own corporeal moment, swollen, tender, inflamed, aching, chanting that melody in a minor key. Her body was singing its song, as it sang it now.

Julia smiled at Katharine. The tray would be useless. She took down a basket, setting into it silverware, napkins, glasses. "Here you are," she said. "I'll bring the plates."

Betsy Waterston. That was the person with the friend with the child in rehab. Betsy Waterston. She was in the English Department: Critical Approaches to Twentieth-Century Poetics.

Katharine took the basket. "Perfect," she said. "Just like Little Wet Riding Hood." She started down the hall.

Was that right? Little Wet Riding Hood?

It sounded almost right. There were certain familiar patterns that ran easily off her tongue, and she used them without thinking, without considering each word, hoping they meant what she intended. You couldn't stop in a conversation to examine each word. Though it felt risky, what she was doing, as though she were skating along the edge of something, right along the lip of it. She liked this, the sense of risk.

Julia had said nothing, so it must have been all right. *Little Wet Riding Hood.* Though it sounded odd.

Down at the dock, Steven climbed into the Whaler. The tide was coming in, running hard. He lowered the outboard into the water, locked it into place, and yanked on the ignition cord. The engine spat, then chugged loudly, coughed, and settled into a noisy rhythm, giving off a small translucent cloud, a petroleum stink. Steven cast off and sat down in the stern, steering toward open water. The little Whaler bucked. Wind and tide were against him, waves slapped loudly against the bow.

What he didn't want was to take his parents' side against his brother. He refused. And he didn't want to hear any more about the divorce. It wasn't the reason Jack was on drugs—if it were, then why wouldn't he be on them?

Though maybe it was the reason. He didn't know why Jack had been caught up in that whirlpool; he had no idea why it had happened, though he'd watched it.

Steven had visited Jack one winter, at his college in New Hampshire. Jack had been high all weekend, blissful and euphoric. He smoked intermittently all day, offering the pot to Steven with that meaningless generosity that marijuana confers. *Have some, man, come on, take a hit! Come on!* Steven had smoked some with him, out of camaraderie and boredom—it was all there was to do. Finally he tried to say something about it. "You're smoking an awful lot," he said, and at once Jack became combative. "Lighten up, man," he said angrily, "lighten up." This was the way it was. There was no point in talking about drugs when Jack was high, and he was usually high.

On Sunday, when Steven left, Jack was still high. He came out to the car to say goodbye. It was very cold, and snow was plowed into icy stacks along the edge of the parking lot. Breath made steamy plumes in the frigid air. Jack had come out without a jacket, he wore only jeans and a sweater, but didn't seem to feel the cold.

After they said goodbye Jack walked along beside the car like a puppy as Steven started off, breaking into a jog as the car picked up speed. The road was snowy and slick, and Jack slipped and staggered, his arms windmilling. He almost fell. As the car pulled away, Jack stopped running and he stood in the middle of the road, waving a big, slow, stoned goodbye; on his face was a wide addled grin.

Steven waved back, watching in the rearview mirror. As he drove he kept looking, back and forth, ahead at the road and behind at his brother, until finally the road made a turn and Jack vanished. *As though by watching, by holding on to the image, he could keep his brother safe. As though he could keep his brother safe.*

Now the water was slapping lightly over the sides in brief rhythmic smacks. It felt like rage, these hard careless slaps. Steven turned the rudder, heading the Whaler directly into the approaching waves. The smacks grew harder. Rage was what he felt, rage and fear. *What the fuck was he supposed to do?* Water cascaded up into the air, exploding against the prow as he crossed the blue choppy bay.

TEN

Wendell's wife, Sandra, answered the phone on the first ring, her voice pleasant. When she heard Julia's name she became even pleasanter.

"Oh, hi," she said easily, as though Julia's calls were both frequent and welcome. "Let me get Wendell, he's right here."

"Thanks." *Thank God Sandra was so nice.*

The phone was set down with a slight clatter. There were footsteps, then Sandra's voice, indistinct, then muffled sounds. Julia had never seen the house in Bridgehampton, and as the unseen Sandra moved through it, Julia imagined it: an old bungalow with low ceilings, ragged cotton rugs, creaky wicker furniture. Limp flattened cushions covered in mattress ticking.

She found herself holding her breath: she was eavesdropping on Wendell's life. It was still strange to her, after six years, to think of him living another life. Strange that he occupied a house she had never seen, when her own places—the Maine house, the New York apartment— were so known to him. They still held him, really.

Listening for him, she felt that in some way she herself still held Wendell. There was something indivisible about them, their lives. She owned his experience, he owned hers. They owned nineteen years of each other. They'd shared that time, it belonged to them both. They'd belonged to each other.

Wendell's voice was suddenly in her ear.

"Hi." He sounded preoccupied.

"Hi," Julia said. "Sorry to bother you."

"What's up?"

"It's Jack."

"What's up?" he repeated, terse.

"Steven thinks he's doing drugs."

"Again?"

"Apparently." Julia wanted Wendell to stop sounding so cool and flippant.

"And?"

"This time it's bad."

"What."

"Steven thinks it's heroin."

"Jesus," said Wendell, serious. "Why does he think that?"

"Something about the way he acts. Steven says heroin does something to you, it's different from other drugs. Junkies are slow, kind of leaden. Apparently. And he had blood on his shirtsleeve. Steven thinks it's from shooting up."

"But lots of kids are like that," Wendell said. "Slow. Disaffected. It doesn't mean they're taking heroin. Half my students are like that. They slop around, half-asleep, they look like crap. They're all exhausted, they're doing too much. They're not junkies."

"What about the blood? And he wants eight hundred dollars," Julia said.

There was a silence.

"For what?" Wendell asked.

"Not clear. Steven asked him to come up here, and first he said no, and then he said he would if we gave him six hundred dollars. Then he changed it to eight. He wouldn't tell Steven what it was for. When I talked to him he said it was to pay for some amplifiers he'd borrowed, that were stolen. By then it was nine."

"Jesus," Wendell said again.

"I know," Julia said.

There was a pause.

"He's not even in a band anymore, is he?" asked Wendell.

"He says they were called out of retirement. He says they borrowed the amps for the gig, and afterward they were left in a van overnight and stolen."

"Could be true," Wendell said.

Julia said nothing.

"Christ," Wendell said.

Julia waited.

"Well, it's still speculation," Wendell said finally. He no longer sounded certain.

"Maybe you should talk to Steven," Julia said. "He's very persuasive." She knew Wendell wouldn't argue with Steven.

There was a pause.

"I don't need to talk to Steven about it," Wendell said.

"Okay," Julia said.

There was another pause.

"Well, so what should we do?" asked Wendell. "If this is true. Which we don't know, by the way."

"I want us to talk to him. You, Steven, and me. Before we do anything else."

"Where?"

"It'll have to be here."

"In Maine? Julia, I'm out on the eastern end of Long Island. You can't get to Maine from here."

"I know, I'm sorry," said Julia. "But I don't think we should wait three weeks until we're all back in New York. I think it's important. Our son is probably a heroin addict."

Wendell sighed. "So what's your plan?"

"He won't come up here if we send him the money, he'll just spend it. Someone has to hand it to him, or to whoever he owes it to, and then put him on the plane."

"How about you?"

"My parents are here and I can't leave them alone. Also, honestly, I'm not sure I could get Jack to do it. Or Steven either. I think you're the only one who can make him come. Would you take him the money—I'll split it with you—and bring him up, so we can talk to him?"

There was another pause.

"And what good will this do?" Wendell asked.

"I don't know. But we need to talk to him first, before anything else. Face to face. And it will be better to do it here, away from the city."

There was a pause.

"Did you ask him the name of the place where the band played?"

"I didn't think of it," Julia said. "Good question." She paused. "I've started thinking about the times Jack asks me for money. It's a lot. Does he ask you?"

"I guess he does," Wendell said. "Now that I think about it. I don't give him much, but it's pretty often."

Julia sighed. "I think we need to talk to him right away. Do you want to talk to Sandra and call me back? And you remember where the phone is here, so please don't call during dinner. It would be in front of everyone, and I haven't told my parents about this."

"I can't just walk out the door and do this. I know this is important, but it's kind of abrupt," Wendell said.

"I know. I'm really sorry, but we need you. It's serious."

She felt calmer, merely at having told him. At least now there were two of them taking this on.

She had stopped being angry at Wendell years ago; the odd thing was that they'd traded places. When she'd stopped being angry, he'd begun. When he first left her, she'd been furious and he'd been apologetic. Being so angry at him made her gradually stop wanting him back.

In that way it was useful: it weaned her away from him, and he was not coming back.

Then one day her anger simply dropped away from her. She'd been sitting at her laptop, reading notices from her department. Two members of it were, famously, conducting a long-running feud, and when she saw the name of one of them—William Schaefer, who disagreed absolutely and furiously with everything Miriam Waldbaum said on any subject—she felt suddenly tired at the idea of long-term enmity.

I can't be angry at Wendell anymore, she thought. I can't afford the energy. I quit. Her own rage sickened her, she didn't want it coursing through her like a toxic drug.

She'd given up wanting Wendell back, and she'd given up being angry at him. Now she hoped that someday Wendell would stop being angry at her and they could be friends. After a certain point, you couldn't go on losing people from your life. Wendell was important in her life, and she wanted him as a friend. Who else could she talk to about their sons? All the other things she'd once discussed with Wendell—who should be president, whether or not *A Thousand Acres* was the Great American Novel, whether or not to reroof the house—she could discuss in the future with other people. But not the children: Wendell was the only person with whom she shared Steven and Jack. She wanted to talk about them to him easily and directly, without his holding up the shield of his aggrievement, without his making it seem as though everything the boys did was somehow, indefinably, her fault.

But after she'd stopped being angry, Wendell had become more so, as though a rage vacuum had to be filled. He'd become furiously resentful, as though it were her fault that the marriage had ended, which, Julia was sure, was what he felt. To keep the peace Julia found herself turned into a supplicant, an apologist, as though she'd been the one to leave him.

He said now, "Well, it's a real screw-up."

"I know, I'm sorry," Julia said again. "Do you want to talk to Jack? Do you want his number?"

"Then what?" Wendell said. "What if he says yes, he's taking heroin? Or no, he's absolutely not? Do we have a plan?"

"I've started making calls," Julia said. "Mental Health is closed until Tuesday, but I found someone whose daughter was in rehab for cocaine. I'm going to call her."

"Rehab," said Wendell. "Jesus."

"I know," Julia said.

"Heroin," Wendell said.

"I know," Julia said. There was a silence. "You know, people—" Her throat did something odd, and she found herself unable to finish. She could not say the word "die." She managed to say "Jack," but her voice was strange.

"Look, I'll talk to Sandra and call you back," Wendell said loudly. "No cause for alarm, no cause for alarm."

He hung up.

"No," Julia said to the empty line. She heard herself say, "People die from this."

In the hall, Edward was heading for the living room, with his rapid sliding shuffle.

The whole house had somehow emptied without his knowing. It was strange the way people drifted about, everyone ending up in one room. A sort of human tidal movement, which apparently excluded him. He peered into the living room: empty. He turned to the kitchen.

Everyone had gone off somewhere. He'd been lying on the bed beside Katharine. He'd slept a little, he supposed, though it hadn't felt like sleep, just a sort of loose drifting through the afternoon. When he woke up, the room was empty: Katharine had left without a word. He'd set out to try to find his own family, and whatever was going on that he'd been left out of.

In his earlier life he would never have had to look to find out what was going on. He'd been at the center of things. He remembered walking through the long corridors of the hospital in his white lab coat, moving on to the next event. Nodding when he passed another doctor. All the doctors then were men; women were nurses and secretaries.

Now it was all mixed up, women did everything. It would be strange working with women doctors. It would be strange having to listen to women, pay attention to their opinions. He liked women, but he didn't want to have to pay attention to their opinions. An unfashionable view, he knew.

He'd always liked working with women, the nurses. They wanted to work with him: surgery was prestigious, and neurosurgery the most prestigious kind. Neurosurgery was the most complex, the most dangerous, the most significant sort of surgery. Edward believed it was the noblest.

All surgery was an invasion of the physical self, but brain surgery was the invasion of the consciousness. No one knew how it worked, human consciousness. Here was the supreme challenge, entering the secret arena of the mind. It still held him.

Edward's earlier life was always with him, like a record playing continually in the background. Sometimes now he went through an operation, step by step, his heart speeding up at the memory as it had at the time, during the difficult passages. Sometimes he went through the discussions, the debates over technique and theory. Psychosurgery: all the arguments there had been over that. At first it had seemed the answer to everything. There was a lot they didn't know, in those days.

Edward had been a part of that first wave, he'd performed those surgeries. He'd believed in them, they all had. Exploration was how science advanced. You had to go down an alley to learn whether or not it was blind. Each experiment delivered new information. You couldn't just crouch in a cave, repeating what you already knew.

New ideas were always challenged. Edward liked controversy. He'd always enjoyed risks. When he and Malcolm Whitworth were in college they had climbed along the sloping cables of the Brooklyn Bridge. He remembered the thrilling sense of height and distance, the cold unresponsive metal in his grip. The dark water glimmering below. The excitement of it, the sense of exultance.

Edward stood now in the kitchen doorway, scanning the nicked and scored wooden counters, the white ceramic canisters, the basket of onions shedding their papery skins. The floor, worn bare in front of the sink; the calendar, magneted lopsidedly onto the refrigerator. All this evidence of activity: why was no one there?

Where was Katharine? How could she vanish like this without a word? Edward paused, resting his weight on the doorframe. Beyond the back door, the unseen porch was silent. Maybe someone was in the dining room.

He began his slow shuffle back down the hall.

He could remember each of his surgeries. The memories still gave him a racing rush. It was intoxicating to confront the lovely symmetry and logic of the neural system, so rich, so unimaginably complex: fourteen billion cells, a hundred million neurons, a trillion glial cells. Microfine filaments stretching into the distant reaches of the body, sending charged and coded messages at unimaginable speeds.

It was a beautiful, miraculous system. He had been privileged to spend his career exploring it, trying to comprehend the mysterious construct that housed the consciousness, that connection between awareness and the body it inhabited. The transformation of experience into chemically transmitted codes, sent to the brain, and then made into memory, an intangible stored in a physical location, the trembling red corpus buried deep in the cerebellum. Why was consciousness itself so deeply indebted to, so entangled in, the physical world? How did solid matter, chemical reactions among the cells, influence perception? Or the life or death of consciousness? It was a mystery.

When he'd started out, they were still guessing about parts of the brain. The entire limbic system, seat of the emotions, was a riddle. The hippocampus, no one knew what it did. It had all been experimental, fumbling and guesswork. Much of medical knowledge was based on malfunction; you didn't know what something did until it stopped working, until it was diseased or damaged or removed. Then you knew. There were things you couldn't find out any other way.

Edward had performed physical intervention to restore the brain to health, when consciousness was compromised by impairment. Vertigo, double vision, delusions, hallucinations—the terrifying symptoms of madness—often they had purely physical causes. Often, those causes—

lesions, aneurysms, morbidity, tumors—could be surgically corrected. Then that less tangible presence, the mind, could be reclaimed. Miraculously the eyes would open and clear. Consciousness would return; the self, that precious commodity, was restored. It was like a miracle. It *was* a miracle.

Being responsible for that moment—the return of the self—was the great satisfaction of Edward's career. There was no greater gift. He was proud to be in a profession that made it possible.

Edward wasn't religious. He had no interest in the imponderable, the real world was infinitely more exciting than the theoretical one. Still, there were certain questions. He thought about them sometimes.

Edward paused again, in the front hall near a spindly wooden chair. He considered sitting down, just for a moment. He could, but it would be giving in, giving up. Edward stood, one hand braced against the wall, catching his breath.

It was as though he'd had two separate lives.

One of them took place within the interior, the throbbing, perilous landscape of surgery. That life seemed to have had no connection to his other one, the ordinary one where his wife and family lived, and everyone else in the world. The two appeared not to have intersected. He could remember almost nothing, now, from his life at home, though he knew he'd been a part of it in some way. The girls had gone to school, the family had moved, twice; they'd taken vacations and had birthdays. He could remember little of it. The life at the hospital was where his imagination lived.

He pushed off from the wall and set off again. If the dining room was empty it meant everyone had left on some mysterious mission without him. On the hall rug he had to lift his feet up instead of sliding them. Shuffling was slovenly, he disapproved of it, but it had become necessary. It was an effort now to raise his feet with each step. All these things you'd always done without thinking.

And there was Julia, sitting at the telephone table. She looked up, frowning, worried—there was some disturbance in her face—as he arrived in the doorway.

"*There* you are," Edward said.

"Hello, Daddy." Julia stood, her face smoothing out. "I was just making a phone call."

"I thought the house was deserted," Edward said. "Like that ship, what was it called? That sailed along empty. Where is everyone?"

"The *Marie-Celeste*," Julia said. "Steven's gone off in the boat, and Mother's on the porch having iced tea. Would you like some?" She smiled at him. "Did they ever find out what happened on it? The *Marie-Celeste*?"

"No," said Edward. He put his hand on the doorframe and began to reverse. "It was an unsolved mystery. There were theories, but nothing was ever proven." He started back again down the hall, getting ready to lift his feet for the rug. He wondered about the expression on Julia's face, the disturbance, but didn't ask. If she wanted to tell him, she would.

It was during dinner that Wendell called.

Julia got up and spoke to him, standing at the little table with her back to the others, leaning over the phone as though she were shielding it.

"Sandra and I have been looking into this," Wendell said.

"Good," said Julia. "This isn't really a good moment for me to talk, though. We're in the middle of dinner. I'm right here with everyone."

"We're just about to go out," Wendell said. "This is my only chance to call. I just got off the phone with someone who specializes in this. I thought you'd want to know about it."

"I do," Julia said. "It's just that right now my parents are here and we're all having dinner."

"What would you like me to do?" Wendell asked.

"Why don't you tell me briefly what you learned and we can talk more tomorrow." Behind her she heard Katharine making conversation politely with Steven, carefully not eavesdropping. Her father, she knew, was eavesdropping unabashedly.

"Okay," Wendell said. "I talked to a guy who runs a rehab program and is an interventionist. He says we shouldn't talk to Jack alone. He says it never works, the family can't do it by themselves."

"Can't do what by themselves?"

"Can't be effective. He's had a lot of experience. He says emotions run too high, codependency is too strong—"

"Who do you think is codependent here?" Julia interrupted.

"I didn't say anyone was codependent," Wendell said. "This guy says that codependency is a problem within families."

"I can't talk about it now." Julia felt everyone at the table behind her, silent and attentive. "But I feel really strongly about this. I want to talk to him here, just us. I want to do that before we do anything else."

"Julia," Wendell said, "he's an expert."

"I *can't talk* about it now, Wendell. Just please, please bring him up here. Let's talk this over together first. What's the risk? I want to hear from *Jack* what's going on. We don't know enough yet to do something so radical. We don't know what's going on."

"Your mother sounds upset," she heard Katharine say quietly to Steven. "I hope nothing's wrong."

"You're the one who convinced me we should do something right away," Wendell said.

"I do think we need to do something right away, but not that," Julia said. There was silence. "I want to talk to him, all of us together, and you're the only one who can make that happen." She waited for him to answer, the phone pressed against her cheek. "Please, let's just start out like this."

"Okay," Wendell said finally. "I'll bring him up."

"Thank you, Wendell," she said. "I really think that's the right thing. When do you think you'll come?"

"It'll take me a day or so to arrange everything. Say the day after tomorrow, maybe the day after that. I'll call you."

"I'll meet your flight," Julia said.

Julia sat down again at the table, glancing around at the others and trying to look cheerful.

"Any news?" Katharine asked politely.

Julia drew a deep breath.

"Yes, as a matter of fact," she said. "That was Wendell. He and Jack are coming up here in a day or so."

Did she sound normal? Pleasant?

"That's lovely," Katharine said. "And will we see them?"

Edward turned to Katharine. "Of course we'll see him. He's coming here. Where we already are."

"I *know* where we are. Dear," Katharine added, for comic effect. "But when are we leaving?"

"Not for another week," Julia said. Surely she had told them this? "You're not going back until the twenty-second. Didn't I tell you that?"

"Oh, so you did," Katharine said easily. "Now tell me about Jack. What's he doing now?"

"He's in Brooklyn," Julia said, dismayed. "I told you. Don't you remember?"

"You probably did." Katharine shook her head. "I don't remember every single thing anymore."

Katharine heard the dismay in Julia's voice but ignored it. It felt precarious but exciting to carry on like this, to engage, ask questions. She felt as though she were flying, out in the wind, tied to something below by a thread. There was a continuous risk that she'd be found out, the air currents might suddenly tip her to the earth. But right now there was the bright sky, a fluttering buoyancy. She'd say what she liked.

She smiled at Steven, who smiled back.

Katharine had always loved Steven. Boys were sweeter, really, than girls; there was something tender and vulnerable about them. Girls were born with a kind of armor, some kind of knowledge, some connectedness to the world, that boys never acquired.

Her mind felt like quicksilver now, moving back and forth between brightness and fog. She shifted slightly in her chair, moving away from the pain. She took a long drink of water, eyes cast down. She could feel Julia watching her.

"I'm so glad Jack's coming up," Katharine said. "And Wendell, too?"

The look on Julia's face told Katharine she'd said something startling, but what was it? Hadn't she just heard that Jack was coming? And Wendell—had he been there earlier, or not? Were they divorced? She thought they were. She wouldn't ask.

"Yes," Julia said, "Wendell's coming, too."

"Oh good," Katharine said, looking down at her plate. The thing was not to pause. It was like walking a tightrope: never think about falling, never stop moving.

After dinner, after the dishes were done, her parents in bed and the house finally quiet, Julia went in to make a phone call—she'd tracked down the mother of the girl in rehab. Steven stretched out to read on the rickety sofa in the living room. Head propped against one arm, Steven fit its length exactly. He could hear his mother's voice in the next room, murmuring, low, intent.

He was reading a paperback mystery from the shelves in the upstairs hall. The books, which had come with the house, were all from the forties and fifties, tattered, mildewed, sensational. Steven and Jack had read them all: *The Case of the Lonesome Locomotive*; *The Blonde Who Couldn't Swim*; *Never Say Never*. On the cover of this one was a pillowy blonde in a tight red strapless dress, her mouth open in an urgent scarlet oval, one bare white arm raised in alarm.

The pages in Steven's book were yellow and brittle. The glue on the spine had dried out, and the pages came loose in his hands. As Steven read each one, he set it carefully back against the spine, aligning the edges, listening to his mother's voice.

When Julia had finished, she hung up the phone and sat in the darkened dining room without moving. She held a yellow pad in her lap. It was barely illuminated by the small lamp on the table. At the top of the pad she'd written: *Intervention??* Below that was: *Programs*, underlined twice. *Hazelden, Renaissance, Betty Ford, Gulf Coast*.

She looked at the names. These were real places, with dining halls and dormitory rooms. Counselors. People were walking around in them right now, eating meals, having group sessions. One of them was a place she might visit. The people there—the staff, the director—would know her. She would talk to them about Jack. She would watch their faces closely. They would help.

The house was still. In the living room she heard the small dry sound of Steven turning pages.

Steven looked up as his mother came in. Seeing her face, he put the book down on his chest.

"So," he said, "what d'you find out from your friend?"

Julia sat down in the sagging armchair. She kicked off her shoes and stretched out her legs, putting her feet up on the wooden bench.

"Friend of a friend, Erica Atwater. She says we should get help. Just what your father's expert says," Julia told him. "She says a family conference won't do anything. We have to get him into a program."

"What else?"

"Horrible stuff." Julia shook her head, closing her eyes. "All bad. That if he's an addict, he's a liar. We can't believe anything he says. He only cares about one thing. He'll say anything. He's only thinking about drugs."

Julia's chest and shoulders were in a pool of yellow light from the lamp beside her; her face was in shadow. Julia pulled a pillow from the sofa onto her lap and held it against her chest. Outside, in the darkness, a moth beat furrily against the windowpane.

His mother's lowered head, her tone of voice—muted, chastened—alarmed Steven. He was afraid that she was about to cry. This interfered with his attention to what she was saying, like a radio station breaking into a transmission. Julia rarely cried, and this threat made what she was saying more grave.

"Erica says just talking to him will be useless," she said. "She says we should have an intervention."

"Greg Alden and his family did an intervention on his father."

"For drugs?" Julia knew the Aldens.

"Kind of for lifestyle. They all got together and told him he was being really unhealthy—eating and drinking and smoking too much, not doing any exercise. Said he was risking his life, and they loved him and didn't want him to have a heart attack at fifty-nine."

"Did it work?"

"Not perfectly. He told them it was none of their business, it was his life, and they could all go fuck themselves."

Julia snorted. "Great," she said. "That can be our model." She sighed. "It's probably just what Jack would say. Why wouldn't he? But Erica says you do it with a professional, it's all very peaceful. No blame, no confrontation, no accusation." Julia looked down again, plucking at the fringe. "Sounds hard to believe."

"'An intervention professional,'" said Steven.

"I know," Julia said. "All these terms, 'interventionists' and 'co-dependents.' I suppose that gives the whole thing stature, having its own language. Makes you feel sort of distinguished."

Steven nodded. "Great."

Julia looked down again, smoothing the pillow. "This woman I talked to walked in on her daughter," she said. "She suspected she was doing drugs, and she kept asking her, but her daughter just lied and lied, and she believed her. She says you always want to believe your child, the alternative is so awful. But she walked in one night and her daughter was sitting on her bed, shooting up on crack cocaine."

"Jesus," said Steven.

"On the flowered bedspread they'd just bought together at IKEA," Julia said. "She was sixteen."

They sat in silence. Outside the window the moth buzzed drily at the black pane.

"I hate this," Steven said.

Julia laughed shortly. "*You* hate it."

"Are we sure about it?" Steven asked.

"Of what? That he's an addict?"

"Well?"

"You're the one who persuaded me," Julia said. "Now you think he isn't?"

"I know." Steven moved restlessly. "All this seems really extreme."

"If Jack's an addict, that's what's extreme."

Steven nodded unhappily. This was now taking on its own momentum. A stranger telling his mother what to do, Jack brought up here, like a prisoner. They were spreading out, beating at the bushes, hounds were sniffing along the edge of the woods. Steven felt the beastly rise of expectation in his own chest, the unholy excitement of the chase, the ache of betrayal.

"Do you not want to have the family meeting?" he asked.

"No, I still want it," Julia said. "I don't care what the experts say. I still want to talk to Jack first. There may be things we don't know about. I don't want to just hand him over to strangers. We owe it to him to talk first." There was a silence. "This is taking on its own life, isn't it." Julia looked mournful. "Once we start, I guess we can't stop it."

Steven did not answer.

"Right?"

"I guess," Steven said. We: he understood they had become partners.

Steven watched her fingers smoothing the fringe on the edge of the pillow, her tanned arms gleaming in the dim light. She sat up straight, her head tilted over the pillow. Her air of abstraction and tenderness, the slow, meditative plucking of her hand, were familiar and unbearable to Steven.

Watching his mother, Steven wanted suddenly to be elsewhere: in a carrel, deep within a silent library, the world excluded. For how could he help his mother, her eyes cast down, her fingers plucking at the ragged fringe of the cushion? And what were they planning for Jack?

Who was right now, perhaps, sighing with unspeakable pleasure, leaning slowly back on filthy sheets, a piece of rubber tubing tight around his arm, the syringe falling loosely from his hand onto the floor. His eyes glazed, unmoving, their pupils becoming tiny, distant pinpoints, outposts of his receding consciousness.

ELEVEN

The arrival gates were on the second floor of the terminal. Julia jogged up the wide stairs to a long, open, hangarish room with big windows, carpeted in beige. In the center was a kiosk full of color photographs of rugged granite coastlines, sturdy lobster boats, stalwart lighthouses. Below the photographs were display cases holding weathered gray driftwood, woven Passamaquoddy baskets. A bright red plastic lobster, eerily realistic, looked both boiled and alive.

Rows of chairs, mostly empty, stood at random angles across the room. In one sat a man in loose blue jeans and a gray sweatshirt, frowning deeply into a magazine. Beside him was a woman with a mane of frizzy blondish hair, her bright pink shorts ridden up high on her substantial thighs. Near them stood a small boy, his legs spread wide, swinging his arms and twisting restlessly from side to side. In another row, a man in a rumpled business suit stared down into his open laptop.

The wall facing the runways was mostly glass. Julia stood near it to wait: the flight from LaGuardia was late. Just outside, at the next gate, an airplane stood by the companionway, nosed docilely against it like a great sea creature.

Airplanes had become neutral again, though the other memory was just below the surface—that deep blue uninflected sky, the lethal whine of engines, those blossoming orange flames, the pluming black smoke. What were Americans meant to do with that seething hatred, *jihad*? With the fact that radical Muslims hated them all? Even ordinary people who hadn't voted for Bush? Who themselves hated the president who'd hijacked the elections and then the entire country, taking off on a suicidal mission of his own, destroying the environment in the interests of greed.

America was already under siege to its own religious fanatics, wasn't that enough? And did the jihadists not notice that America had its own internal critics?

Julia crossed her arms on her chest. She slowly turned her head from side to side, stretching her neck muscles, dropping her shoulders. Relax, she told herself, relax.

Beyond the big window was a strip of tarmac, and beyond that was long grass, scoured by the wind. Beyond that was the runway, and beyond that was deep blue.

A small silver plane slid suddenly down out of the sky. Nose up, it settled lightly onto the runway. Moving fast and purposefully, it raced out of sight beyond the terminal. In a few moments it reappeared, now taxiing slowly back, twenty minutes late if it were the 2:49 from LaGuardia. Heat fumes rose from the tarmac, giving a liquid shimmer to the fuselage. The plane rolled to a stop and the propellers became suddenly visible. They slowed, in a powerful, controlled way, seemed confusingly to go backward for a moment, then stopped dead.

A high metal stairway was rolled out to the plane. The door to the plane was opened from inside and a stewardess in a navy dress stepped out onto the platform. She stood to one side of the open doorway, hands behind her back, her short hair blowing in the gusty air. Passengers emerged beside her, straightening and squinting in the sunlight. Disheveled, they clutched at bags and packages, descending the steep stairs. Julia moved closer to the window, watching each face.

After six or seven people had come out, she saw Jack appear in the doorway. His head was lowered, and he went down the steps in a rush. Wendell was behind him, moving more slowly. The passengers walked in a shifting stream across the tarmac toward the terminal. On the ground, Wendell caught up with Jack and walked beside him. The wind beat at everyone, flapping hair, collars, sleeves, papers, everything tossing wildly.

Jack was wearing jeans and a cotton sweater. His hands were jammed deep in his pockets. A paperback was stuck under one arm, and his duffel bag hung from his shoulder. His hair glinted reddish-brown in the sun—shades of Eric the Red, there was no red hair in Julia's family, nor Wendell's. Jack was watching the ground, but Wendell glanced up at the terminal. Julia waved, but his expression did not change; she thought the windows must be opaque in the sunlight.

Invisible, Julia studied her son. *But he looked normal. He looked, actually, fine.* Long-torsoed, lean and lanky, the same. There was the familiar sideways tilt of his head, the familiar cool, ambling walk. Handsome. It was Jack. She felt a little lift of pride. What if he were fine, if all this were not true?

Wendell, in khakis and tweed jacket, looked up again, still without seeing her. He smoothed his hair down, but it flew up at once in the wind. His hair was coarse and graying, and on the top of his skull Julia saw a paler spot where the hair was thinner, as though Wendell were slowly rising, emerging crown first, into some unlonged-for realm where the flesh made its own decisions. The wind blew the spot visible as the hair around it flattened, then another gust hid it.

Julia felt a sudden pang of tenderness for Wendell, who was going bald. She wondered if the bare spot were the reason he had looked up anxiously at the window. She bore Wendell no malice. Right then she felt nothing for him but gratitude: Wendell had brought Jack home.

Jack's duffel slid off his shoulder, and he paused to hike it back into place. For no reason she remembered the time Jack had sent her flowers. It was after the opening of one of her shows, when she'd gotten a review in the *Times* that had nearly killed her. The critic said that her work, disappointingly, had not progressed. She could still recite it word for word. Not progressed. It still nearly killed her. That evening the doorbell had rung. At the door was a deliveryman holding a white paper cone of daffodils from the Korean market. The card said: *To my favorite, least disappointing, and most progressive mother.* Jackie'd been—what? Fourteen? She could still recite that, too.

Jack and Wendell had now vanished below, entering into the terminal. In the upstairs doorway passengers from their flight began appearing, each travel-tousled face emerging for a brief solo moment, pausing to scan the room before entering it.

When Julia saw Jack come through the door, she felt a giddy rush. Here was her darling. This was the face she knew: smooth-skinned and wide, the blue eyes bright and narrow. The low square forehead, the broad jaw, the oddly pointed chin. He looked normal, he looked fine. Jeans, sweater, sneakers. He wasn't some filthy street person, he was *fine.* She stepped forward, smiling, her arms out. "Jacko."

"Hey." Jack's glance met hers for a second, flicked past, and returned. He leaned over for Julia's hug. He felt the same as always—patient, indulgent. They'd been wrong about this. Feeling his arms around her, Julia felt sure they'd been wrong. They could work this out, whatever it was.

Julia stepped back to greet Wendell. He stood nearby with his hands in his pockets, leaning slightly back. She reached out to hug him as well—it would be too strange just to nod, or, worse, shake hands—but Wendell drew back from her as if bitten. Her hands grazed his receding shoulders, and she made the hug into an awkward pat.

"Sorry," she said. "Didn't mean to scare you."

"No, no," Wendell said loudly, and gave a public smile. She was reminded that he used that phrase—"No, no"—as an all-purpose response, denial of any discomfort. "All set?"

Walking out through the parking lot, they did not speak. The sun beat down on them, dazzling, insistent. The wind caught at everything, flinging candy wrappers against the curb, bowling a paper cup across the pavement.

At the car, Julia felt in her purse for her keys, and as her fingers closed over the heavy metal cluster she remembered: she had given it to Wendell for his birthday, years ago. It was a silver chain, with a four-leaf clover, from Tiffany's. At the time, the car had belonged to them both. Since she'd gotten the car in the settlement, she'd kept the key chain. But it was his, really. She wondered if she should give it back, or anyway the silver clover leaf. It was his. But who would want a love token from an ex-wife? And wouldn't the offer seem poisonous, malicious? After a divorce, all actions were suspect. The ghost of irony lurked behind every gesture.

She opened the trunk, keeping the clover leaf hidden in her fist. Wendell and Jack threw their duffels inside. Jack suddenly yawned, stretching his arms out, opening his mouth pink and wide, like a hippopotamus.

No manners, Julia thought happily, he had no manners at all. How had he grown up listening to rules about courtesy all his life and end up with none? This was the smallest, least important lapse, and its triviality made Jack into an ordinary child. He seemed fine, Julia thought again, only a little sleepy-eyed. They would talk this out, whatever it was. She patted his shoulder.

"Glad you're here," she said, and he nodded. What she wanted was for him to be all right. She was willing this to be so.

In the car, Wendell sat in the front with Julia, Jack was alone in the back. Julia buckled her seat belt, snapping the metal hasp securely, and again she thanked engineers, people who made the world run so smoothly, who figured out locks and clasps and things that clicked into place, things that could withhold you from the current of death.

Beyond the airport, they drove through the outskirts of the city and a bleak residential neighborhood. The lawns were closely cropped, the shrubs tightly pruned, their woody legs exposed: bounty and lushness and color played no part in this notion of beauty. They were so grim, these bleak little plots, thought Julia. Such a spiritless, unrefreshing view of nature, painful to look at. Why was it, she wondered, that every English cottage, every Mediterranean window box, had a bright flowering presence, but American suburbia was all like this? Vast tracts, rigid and colorless, everything that grew soaked in chemicals and cut down brutally to the root. As she drove past, Julia mentally replanted everything, replacing the sad faded lawns and dull pachysandra with exuberant meadows, edging everything with flowering native plants, spreading shrubs.

"So," Julia said, "how was the flight?"

"Fine," answered Wendell. "Uneventful."

"Good," Julia said. "The best kind."

They'd agreed to wait until they were all together with Steven to talk about drugs—if they had to have that talk. Julia wondered what had happened that morning. Jack and Wendell seemed perfectly friendly. What if everything had gone perfectly smoothly? What if Wendell had handed over the check to the guy with the amps, and there really had been a robbery, and that was that? What if all this had been a misunderstanding? What if there were no real drug problem, or just the usual one— that is, more drugs than a parent would hope, but the normal amount for a young man living in downtown New York, playing in a rock band, or whatever it was called, anyway, at least not that other drug, the one Julia did not want to name to herself, not that black lethal shadow, coiling itself around its victim and squeezing the life from it, at least not that.

They'd have the talk, anyway; it was good Jack had come, generous of Wendell to bring him. It would be hard on Wendell to be at the house: he had no place there now. He'd have to stay in the tiny room off the kitchen, the borning room. More post-divorce irony. Julia wondered how Sandra felt about his coming; she sent another heartfelt blast of gratitude.

"So, how's Bridgehampton?" Julia asked. She headed up the curving ramp onto the highway.

"Fine, fine," Wendell said, nodding, not looking at her.

"Tell me what you do out there," Julia said. She slid the car smoothly sideways into the stream of traffic, settling down to the trip. Julia felt expansive and interested. "Now that you don't have to spend your summers fixing the roof." She meant for him to laugh at this, remembering the years of servitude.

"No, no," Wendell said, not trusting her, rejecting whatever it was she'd meant. "What do we do," he repeated, considering, as though he were being interviewed. "Well, we play a lot of tennis."

"Really? Tennis?" she asked. "Where do you play?"

Wendell had rarely played tennis while he'd been married to her, and he'd always scorned clubs. "Only assholes belong to clubs," he used to say. "You might as well wear a shirt saying, 'Fuck You! I belong and you don't!'" Since there was no club near them in Maine, and none that they could afford in New York, there had been little temptation, during those years, to become assholes.

"We play at a little club Sandra joined, years ago," Wendell said, looking out the window. "Nothing fancy. Just a few courts, no pool or anything." He cleared his throat. "Sandra has a lot of friends out there. Well, we both do."

Julia was silent, thinking of Wendell's new life, with his new wife, who had so many friends and who belonged to a little tennis club. She pictured Wendell standing in the sun, talking to people she'd never met. Smiling, bouncing the strings of his racquet lightly against a cocked knee.

"Do you wear whites?" she asked. The question suddenly seemed intimate.

He turned and looked at her. "Well, yes," he said, with a trace of emphasis. "It's a tennis club."

"I'm just trying to visualize it," Julia said. "I don't think I've ever seen you in tennis whites."

Wendell said nothing, staring ahead.

Stop it, Julia told herself. Nothing she said sounded friendly or authentic. This was like a parody of a conversation. What did normal people talk about, people who had never been married to each other? Jack must think they were both crazy.

Jack, behind them, was not listening.

The backseat of the car had been designed for the legless. He slouched down and raised his knees, jamming them against the front seat. He leaned his head back and closed his eyes. He tried to remember how long the drive would take. It was an hour. Was it an hour, or more than an hour? It was an hour. They'd already started, it was now less than an hour. It was less than an hour.

He scratched his neck, hard, though not hard enough. He should have kept his duffel here with him instead of putting it in the trunk. Have a discreet snort. *No, that was crazy, snorting in the backseat while his parents were in the front.* He had to remember not to do anything crazy. It was hard to know what was actually crazy. He was beginning to jones, he felt the craving welling up. His nerves were beginning to sing. Things were beginning to bleed from one part of his life to the other. He didn't want this, but he couldn't stop it. He could not control it. Things that were crazy in one part of his life would not be so in the other, and vice versa. It was hard to keep them separate, remember which part fit where. Things that seemed normal to him were not things his parents would think normal. He had to keep them clear in his mind.

He opened his eyes and looked up. Covering the car ceiling was a taut white synthetic fabric, like a sheet on an upside-down bed. What he hoped was that his mother would not turn on the radio and find some music. Right now he could not tolerate any music that his mother would find. He flexed his left hand and began to form phantom chords on his palm. He shifted his fingers on the neck of the guitar, going through the long, descending opening passage of "I Don't Know (How You Do It)."

He gripped the invisible neck of the guitar, going down in sevenths, each drop farther than you thought it could go, the notes sounding in his mind as he played them, grinding the metal strings against the frets for the final, echoing, resonating chord at the bottom. His neck itched suddenly again. The guitar evaporated and he scratched himself hard. *Not hard enough.* He could feel the elastic surface of the skin giving way. He could feel his blunt nails breaching the fragile defenses of the skin. He dug harder, deeper. *Not hard enough.* The itch blazed, the bloom of it tantalizing. He ached to satisfy it.

"Do you think, Jacko?"

His mother was asking him something.

"What?" He leaned forward, tucking his chin down and resting his forehead against the seat, as though to hear better. He didn't want her to see his eyes, which were certainly pinned, the pupils shrunk to tiny dots, irrefutable evidence of his condition. Though his mother was driving and couldn't see his eyes. *This might be junkie paranoia. Still.* He kept his head down. She might look in the mirror, his father might turn.

"I asked if you thought there's a tennis court up here somewhere," Julia said. She looked in the mirror, but Jack's head was lowered and she could see only the top of it. "Where you could play with your father."

"A tennis court," Jack said slowly, head still down, as though he were thinking carefully. He fought his way up from the depths, where his mind had been swimming. *A tennis court.* Was this a trick question? It was like being interrogated by the enemy. You had to keep your wits about you, every second, you had to try to remember what reality was for them, never to violate their understanding of it, never to acknowledge the other, his own. He tried to remember.

"I don't know. No. I don't think so. Is there one?"

Why was she asking him this?

He and Steven had never played tennis up here. Had they? They'd done other things. They'd had elaborate games: shipwreck, trappers, ambush, smugglers. They'd gone out in the Whaler. They'd spent a lot of time on the water, all their time, it seemed now, always heading out somewhere, then heading back home. He leaned against the seat.

It was his wrist. He scratched it hard and fast, as though his wrist held a burrowing insect to be found and destroyed. His wrist was on fire. It was like warrior ants, or whatever they were. Soldier ants. *Warrior or soldier?* His body was being invaded, his body was a battleground. He watched his wrist, under the attack of his furious fingers, turn dull red, the color spreading under the skin like water. *Not hard enough, never hard enough.*

It was now less than an hour more, a good bit less. Wasn't it? Maybe forty minutes. He looked out the window: they were still on I-95, still droning along the highway, nothing but woods on either side. The sun beat down on the highway ahead, the paved corridor between the ranks of pines. The road was full of glare, hard to look at. He squinted. They passed one of those dopey signs with the motto in cheery script: MAINE: THE WAY LIFE OUGHT TO BE.

What? Life should be like a geographical location?

In that case, his own life should be like Brooklyn. Which it was. His neighborhood was charged with electric urgency. In the morning, when he went jogging down the stained concrete steps to the sidewalk, heading out to cop, the streets were full of risk, tension, concealed urgency. The dull pallor of the sky, the sullen colors of the buildings, the random movement of the passersby—everything that lay between him and his dealer was an obstacle to be overcome or negotiated. People were to be pushed past, everything was to be gotten by, gotten beyond; it was like struggling through high grass.

On the way home from his dealer he walked fast, full of accomplishment and anticipation. The trip along his own block was interminable, the last yards, from the corner to his shabby building and the broken walkway, endless. The stained brick walls, the lowered blinds at the windows stood waiting, full of promise. The tiny battered foyer. Fumbling for his key.

Afterward, after using, everything was transformed. Then the landscape had a knowing fullness, it became benign, full of a languorous plenitude. Then there was nothing he needed to get past, get through. Then he no longer had to interact with the landscape, with anything. Then he was part of everything, with bliss.

But the landscape there was full of dope, before and after, dope was everywhere. Heroin—the great H, junk, smack, brown sugar, snow, horse, downtown—informed the landscape, spread its measureless presence across all of it. Dark and rich and deep, miles of black velvet lay just behind the visible world, just inside it, a secret universe.

Maine was empty of what he thought of as life.

He could not imagine living here, he could not imagine living anywhere but where he lived, or doing anything but what he was doing.

COST

Music, heroin. It was the music he was focused on, though, heroin was just a part of things. A part of everything, every day.

He wondered about his breathing. It seemed shallow. *Was it shallow?* As soon as he thought about it, it seemed strange. He took a deep breath, slowly let it out. Heroin was just something he was doing. He was thinking about only one thing. There was only one thing, there was only one thing he was doing.

He might nearly have run out, that was the thing. Unbelievably bad planning, not his fault. Last night, for some reason, he'd done an extra bag. It had made sense at the time. He had been walking around the room, listening to a recording they'd made the week before, the amps turned up. The music, echoing and pounding through him, opening him to the boundless distances of the universe, made it necessary to do more dope. It made sense at the time. It always made sense at the time to use more dope. Heroin was the seamless presence, like air, always at play, always a part of his consciousness.

What he'd thought was, since his father was coming the next day to pay off his debts, and he'd be able to get new stuff from Dana for his trip, that it would be better to get rid of what he had. He'd start tomorrow with a clean slate. Clean slate: that was an invigorating notion. Didn't that make sense? He'd felt a kind of pride and a sense of responsibility, as though he'd completed an onerous chore. It was community service, more or less.

Everything had urged him toward the opening of the little glassine envelope, smooth and pliable beneath his fingertips. His hands were shaking slightly. Once he was holding the envelope there was no stopping. Everything went on by itself, unfolding like a flower.

Afterward, stupid with bliss, he stood at the window looking out at the empty darkened street. The small motionless trees, the littered sidewalk, the hidden streetlight shedding its dim radiance over the scene: it was all secretly his. Rapture welled steadily inside him, and he stood for a long time at the window, held in that current.

Which meant this morning he'd had only two bags left, instead of three. He'd thought of taking only half, when he got up, as a precaution, because what if he couldn't get more from Dana? She'd already refused him credit until he paid what he owed, which was not even a lot, really. But right then his father called, practically right outside his fucking house, and the thought of his father there in Brooklyn was so unnerving he'd used the whole bag. Anyway, half a bag was nothing, he needed more, a whole lot more, which he'd have to get somehow.

The thing with his father and fucking Dana had been a complete fiasco, and now he had only one bag left for sure. Dana could have slipped him something—like she didn't know what he'd wanted—but she'd just wanted to be paid what he owed. She knew he was going out of town and she didn't trust him, the greedy bitch.

And his father had stuck to him like a leech, he couldn't even pack his stuff alone. He'd crammed his works into the duffel before his father got there, and a batch of empty bags. He was pretty sure there was an extra bag somewhere, either in with the empties or in his other jeans. He kept stashes for emergencies, always one or two somewhere on the premises, but with his father staring at him like that, he couldn't check. He'd brought everything, all the empty bags, so in case he ran out he could at least lick his finger and rub it on the glassine. *It was pathetic, licking off the dust from an empty. Or no, it was inventive.* Depended on your point of view. He was pretty sure he'd find a little stash. He might even have two bags, sometimes he put them away and forgot about them.

He'd be able to find stuff up here, there was stuff everywhere. You could always find it. West of Bangor, he'd heard, was a county with the highest heroin use anywhere in the country. This made him vaguely proud, as though he were part of some brave underground movement.

His eyes suddenly needed rubbing. He bore down on the sockets, pressing hard. Then his face, too. The bones were obdurate in their resistance. He could feel his skin, tender and ready to itch. All the skin, over his entire body, was in a state of exquisite readiness. He felt the shadow of itch hovering over his body like a cloud. His skin was alive with the possibility of itching. It was like madness. Madness was hovering over him.

Now it was his ankle. The itch struck, and he yanked up the leg of his jeans. He raked at the bared bony knob, feeling the skin flake. *Not hard enough.* He scraped with his nails, digging in. Gratifying to see the blood. The skin turned red, then raw, then oozed with bright reflective drops, deep crimson. Deep crimson was an achievement, a considerable achievement.

No, it was not considerable, that was the dope talking. It was only an achievement. This was the kind of wild thinking he had to suppress. He didn't want to sound like a junkie. He hated hearing his friends sound like junkies, ranting, making the same idiotic arguments over and over, getting more and more pissed off.

Once Russ had told him to get the fuck out of the apartment. He'd claimed Jack had taken his pastrami and onion sandwich, which Russ had actually finished, himself, on the way back from the deli, tossing the wrapper onto the strip of beat-up grass at the end of their block. Furious, Jack had gone out and retrieved the greasy balled-up paper, which by then had unfolded, spreading itself outward into the air like a trash-flower. He brought it back to the apartment and showed it to Russ, to prove his position. Russ balled up the paper and threw it at Jack's head.

"What the fuck does this mean?" he screamed.

Junkie thinking, the loop. Your mind went around and around. You couldn't have a conversation with anyone on dope, or coming off dope. Unless you were on dope yourself, then it became tolerable. Everything became tolerable, the sweet dark shawl pulled smoothly over your consciousness.

It was much less than an hour now, less than an hour to the house. He was hurting, jonesing, the tracks on his arms were burning and smarting. He needed to use. Much less than an hour, wasn't it? It was hard to look outside. He squinted. Any light hurt. He didn't want his parents to see his eyes. He'd meant to bring sunglasses, which he didn't own. He'd meant to buy some in the airport. He hadn't remembered, though. His father would have bought him a cheap pair, if he'd remembered to ask.

He had to focus. Steven would help him. Sunglasses, dope: the things he needed. A tennis court. One thing he couldn't do on smack was play tennis: dope slowed down the world to such a syrupy crawl that it was impossible to move fast, unimportant to do so. Things were starting to unravel, he needed to use. That was what the itching was about, he was strung out. Only one more bag, and then where was he going to get more? But he'd find the scene, he could do that. He wasn't some kid with a little chip from the suburbs, he was urban, he was part of the scene. He had a solid habit, and could score at two o'clock in the morning, anywhere. You just had to know what you were doing.

In New York there were policemen all over the place, ready to bust you. A greedy street dealer might kill you for your money. The drug itself might kill you, but that was something else: that drew you. You wanted the great high, the great, great high. The first high you ever had was the best, you were always looking for it again. The last one was even better, that was the word. Junkies who were brought back from unconsciousness in the emergency room swore and punched at the doctors for bringing them down. The OD high was the last, great, killer high. Everyone wanted to know what the OD dope was. Killer dope, everyone wanted it. It was dangerous, it was cool, it was irresistible.

All the dealers had their own brands, the logos stamped onto the little glassine bags. Catchy names: *Killer. Backdraft. Homicide. No Way Out.* Dana sold a Colombian kind called *Hellraiser.* Smooth and pure. It was very good. Jack knew exactly how much of it to take. Too much dope would kill you, but just enough would keep you healthy, make you happy. Heroin was actually good for you, most people didn't know this. There was an exquisite pleasure in skating along the edge. You were in control. Even during the moment of the hit, when you were drowning, drowning, drowning, you were in control, till you weren't.

Jack knew all this. He had everything down. If Dana were out of town, he knew where to go for China White and Colombian, though you couldn't count on anything for long. Things changed from day to day, you had to be ready. The place you copped last week was this week bulldozed into oblivion: the cops had marked it. He knew how it worked.

Now he had Dana, he didn't buy much on the street, but you never knew how long these things would last. One day Dana wouldn't be there. Sometimes she didn't answer her phone, and if he needed stuff badly, he went to the street.

Buying on the street was dangerous because of the cops and because of the stuff. Junk off the street might be beat—cut with anything: poison, baby powder. It was dangerous if it was too pure, too—you could take your usual dose and wake up dead. You never knew what you were buying.

Copping on the street usually took place at night. There were abandoned buildings. You waited on the stairs and passed your money through a slot in the door. At one place they made you show your tracks before they'd let you up the stairs. Jack tugged up his sleeve, baring his arm, his badge of honor. A man peered down from the doorway. *Holy shit*, he said.

Some places, upstairs were the dealers and downstairs were the shooting galleries. Lightless, stinking rooms where people sank down onto the floor with their new dope, shooting up right there and nodding off. The smell, piss and vomit. He'd never used a shooting gallery, he'd always made it home.

There was one pair of dealers on the street. A big Latino stood on the corner holding an extra-large bottle of Diet Coke. "C or D?" he'd ask. *Coke or dope.* You gave him the money, and then you kept on walking to where his partner stood, halfway down the block, wearing a red wool knitted hat. It was Red Hat who slipped the bag into your hand as you brushed against him. You didn't look at him. You never looked back over your shoulder either. That was a giveaway, it meant you were watching for the cops.

Jack was worried now about getting strung out. Was he starting to now, or was he just thinking about it? He wished he had his duffel bag with him so he could get his finger into a bag and lick the powder off. Even that would make him feel better. By this time of day he needed a second bag, but his father had stuck right on top of him, and there had been no bathroom in the tiny plane. He had one bag, and he was sure there was something stashed in his jeans for a rainy day. He put stuff in places where no one else would find it. In case one of his addict friends started sniffing around, or the cops.

Was that paranoid, or realistic? Cops were definitely around. He knew people who'd been arrested. It was realistic. And he had friends who stole stuff. He was pretty sure Hank had taken a bag that he'd left out on the sink, though Hank denied it. Jack told everyone, and after that he called him Hank the Skank. Hank got mad, but not as mad as he'd have been if he hadn't taken it.

Jack liked to stash stuff, hide it from himself. He'd found a half-bag, once, folded over and over, a rubber band holding it closed, inside the jar of instant coffee. He was sure he had extra stuff with him now. Maybe two secret bags. He'd do a little before dinner, just to put himself straight, save the rest for the morning, when he'd have to find a source. He might even have more than two extra bags. Maybe he had enough to last if he were careful. Maybe he'd start cutting down. He would start cutting down, anyway, he would do that soon. He didn't know how long he was going to be here. Tomorrow he was going to have to get out somehow, off the place, and find a source. Borrow the car for something.

His grandparents were at the house. His grandmother would make a fuss over him, his grandfather would ask if he had a fucking job. Now it was his ankle again, and he lunged down at it. His skin was bleeding freely now. It was a relief to scratch it, though not hard enough. He felt a longing to keep going, get further, to go on somehow. Something was rippling and black in his consciousness, and he was tunneling after it.

There was another silence in the car, and he became aware that he was at the center of it.

"What?" he asked.

He didn't know who he was talking to. He felt as though he were floating free of the car, as though his being there with his parents, his agreeing to talk to them, was a courtesy. He felt generous about it. He didn't mind doing it, he was happy doing it, but he was floating and it was hard to stay connected.

"I said, That's quite some place you've got there. Your bachelor pad."

His father was being ironic, he was mocking Jack's apartment.

"Yeah," Jack said.

He didn't remotely care what his father said about the apartment. It was a horrific piece of shit, but this was beside the point. There was no point in his even entering this conversation, no point in his agreeing, or taking the teasing, or explaining that the apartment wasn't his, that it belonged to Russ, who was in Los Angeles right now, blowing the advance from his new contract up his nose. Nor in telling his father that Russ was a good guy, very funny and incredibly brave. Scarily brave, actually. He'd do anything.

Jack had once been with Russ on the street, three in the morning, buying dope from a big Dominican guy, five inches taller and forty pounds heavier than he. Russ handed over his money, but instead of giving him the coke the Dominican asked for his watch. Didn't make a move, just held him still with his eyes. Figured since Russ was shorter and whiter he'd take off the watch and hand it over.

Russ lunged up and punched the guy in the face as hard as he could, then threw him down on the sidewalk and kicked him in the stomach. Then, while the guy was lying there, moaning and writhing, Russ asked for his coke. Russ was a tiger. Not a great landlord—the apartment sucked, plus you'd be evicted if he thought you'd eaten his sandwich—but a guy you wanted on your team. Also one of the best keyboard players around. Wild in a good way.

But this was not a conversation you could have with your father. Actually, there were fewer and fewer conversations you could have with your father.

The sun, gradually lowering, was taking on a sinister aspect. The roof of the car seemed to be catching fire. Heat and some kind of glow flickered uneasily around the edges of it. In fact, nothing seemed to be the way it should. There was the horrible glare of the sun on the highway ahead, and the strange way his parents were talking, some ambiguous tone to their conversation that made it incomprehensible to him. Now it was his shin. It was always places where the skin was a thin layer over the bone, the blood vessels. The blood vessels lay very close to the surface here. He dug his nails into the skin, *hard, hard, not hard enough.*

They had left the highway some time ago, and now Julia turned off the local road, slowing the car to a crawl as she hit the driveway. This was just a narrow farm track, really, curving faintly through the meadow. The grass on either side was high and brushed gently against the car as they drove through it. They bumped to the end of the drive, then stopped in the turnaround.

"We're here." Julia turned off the engine and looked at Wendell. She wondered how he felt.

Wendell was looking at the house. It stood before them in the sloping meadow, old, shabby, beautiful, its ruined shingles mottled with lichen, curled up at the ends by damp. Its peeling white walls were lapped by the rippling pink grass; beyond, the water glittered blue. All of it glowed in the raking light.

Wendell turned to Julia.

"Still needs a new roof," she said. She felt tender and protective toward Wendell, with his hidden bald spot, now in the presence of his beautiful lost kingdom. His house, his family: he had given them up.

"I see that," Wendell said, smiling back. "Among a thousand other things." He looked at the key chain dangling from the ignition. "You still have that," he said. "I'd forgotten it."

Behind them, Jack was unfolding his length, opening the door. Julia released the trunk lever. "Trunk's open," she said, and Jack climbed out. He shut the door and they were alone.

"I still do," she said to Wendell. "Want it? I gave it to you once."

Wendell shook his head, not looking at her. "Thanks," he said.

Behind them they heard Jack rummaging in the trunk. They didn't move. It could have been any of a million times when they'd sat here together, in this car, before this house.

TWELVE

"You're in here," Julia said, leading the way.

The borning room was small, barely big enough to hold the narrow bed and the blanket chest at its foot. The walls were covered with floor-to-ceiling bookshelves, crammed full. The room was little more than a storage closet for things that did not belong anywhere else—odd books, cardboard boxes, a bicycle pump, a broken lamp, its cord messily unfurling. Each time she went in, Julia planned to clean it out. The boys would never use that volleyball again, she'd think, with resolve. (*Though they might, actually, or someone else might want it. What if it were asked for and she'd thrown it out?*) In the end, everything stayed.

Going through the low doorway Wendell ducked his head. He moved to the end of the bed and stood there, holding his duffel bag.

He was only a few inches taller than Julia, but solidly built. He stood very erect, with a broad, high chest, slightly puffed, like a pouter pigeon. There was something pouter pigeonesque about his stance, too, which was slightly martial, adversarial. A strong line ran from his nose to the corners of his mouth. His lips were small, precisely defined, and elegant. Like a Greek statue's, Julia had always thought. He wore small round-rimmed glasses, silver-colored. His coarse curly hair was tangled, and now quite gray.

Closer to him, in the small room, than she had been in years, Julia caught his scent: a surprise. It was deeply familiar, that musky, golden maleness, Wendell's drifting aura. She knew it in a private, intimate way—but it was now no longer hers to inhale, she no longer owned it. Her body recognized it, but without response. It felt odd, like the discovery that you could no longer see the color blue. This scent had been part of her life. She'd awakened to it each morning, the sheets had been full of it. The room had been rich with Wendell's presence. But it was now meaningless to her, even faintly distasteful.

Wendell looked slowly around, as though he'd never seen the room before. His glasses glinted, opaque.

"Sorry to have to put you in here," Julia said. "But we're full up. My parents are in the guest room."

She really was sorry. It was humiliating for him to stay back here, crammed behind the kitchen like a hired hand, surrounded by useless stuff, forced to bear witness to the dysfunctional aspects of their life, the abandoned detritus of the marriage.

But she wasn't entirely sorry: it had been Wendell's decision to abdicate. He'd had the rights to the master bedroom, he'd chosen to give it up.

"No, no," Wendell said now, looking around at the shelves. "This is fine."

Through the wall, in the kitchen, they could hear the boys moving, opening the refrigerator, talking. They heard Steven laugh.

Julia lowered her voice. "How did it go, this morning?"

Through the wall, Steven said, "No *way*." A glass was set down on the counter.

"What happened?" Julia went on. "Did you give the money to the guy with the amps?"

"Not exactly," Wendell said.

Steven laughed. The sound was right next to them.

"We can't talk here," Julia whispered. "Tell me later. But Jack seems okay, doesn't he?"

Wendell's glasses glinted and he shook his head, but Julia gave him an encouraging smile, then left the room. He was still holding his duffel bag. There was nowhere for him to unpack it, there was barely room for him to lean over and unzip it.

Julia went into the kitchen, but only Steven was still there.

Upstairs, Jack shut the bathroom door behind him and hooked its flimsy latch. The room smelled familiar, a faint odor of mildew and something spicy, cedary. The walls had been painted white, but were being slowly stained darker by age. Jack set his duffel bag down on the toilet seat, where it hung over on either side. He had trouble with the zipper because his hands were shaking. He rooted inside the duffel, rummaging among the clothes. On the bottom was a brown paper bag, his works. He pulled it out. Now he needed the stash. He began rummaging harder, pulling everything out. Jeans, sweater, shirts. He could feel his heart pounding. He shook them in the air before he dropped them on the floor. The room was small, and there was little room to move. As he shook the sweater, a small glassine bag fell onto the faded bathmat: the stash.

He stepped on his clothes as he moved to the sink. Over this hung an old wood-framed mirror, flecked with toothpaste. Jack stripped off his sweater and dropped it on the floor. He leaned over the sink, avoiding himself in the mirror.

Taking out his works from the paper bag, he set them along the narrow back ledge: the lighter, the blackened spoon, the little bag of cigarette filters. The syringe, the supple yellow-brown snake of rubber tubing. He took down the cloudy plastic glass from its wall bracket and ran some tapwater into it. The pipes groaned going on, shrieked going off. Tapwater had rust in it, it could stop your heart, but everything could stop your heart. Things were getting close now, and there was a muted roaring in his ears.

His hands were shaking harder, and he could feel his pulse as he approached the fix. Leaning over the sink, he opened the glassine packet, trying to control the tremble in his clammy hands. He gently tapped the dirty-white powder into the shallow bowl of the spoon, making a small dry peak. With the syringe he drew a little water from the glass, then squirted it carefully into the spoon, flooding the powdery peak. Then he flicked on the lighter, sliding the flame back and forth beneath the spoon. The little peak of powder vanished, dissolving into the liquid like a magic trick.

He took a deep breath, trying again to steady his hands. He dropped the cigarette filter into the magic liquid, letting it soak up the solution. He set the needle into the filter and carefully drew the liquid up through it, sucking the last drop. He was salivating now. He swallowed, and clenched his muscles to stop the trembling.

He sat down on the edge of the bathtub and rolled his shirtsleeve high on his arm. He looped the yellow-brown snake of rubber tubing around his bicep. He held one end with his teeth, tugging the other end with his other hand. He flexed his muscle against the constricting cord, the needle poised over his skin. He was looking for a fresh unbroken site. He was hardly breathing.

With the back of his hand he wiped the sweat from his inner arm. There were three lines of tracks, the biggest clusters along the best vein, a series of red, moist peaks. Some had little darkened scabs at the tops. He pumped his left arm, opening and closing his fist, to make the veins rise. He set the spike against an untouched patch of skin, along the deep blue line beneath it. He hammered softly, feeling the point grab at the flesh, then set it in and pushed. The needle slid through his skin like a prayer. He drew the plunger back slightly, sucking up; a coil of brilliant scarlet flowered suddenly in the barrel, a tiny dark unfurling of blood. It was the festive signal announcing the arrival in the vein. He pressed down hard, hard, hard on the plunger and sent it home, driving the clear miracle deep into his veins, pulsing, into his private heaven, and he felt the sweet darkness close around him, caressing and comforting him in every way, like water flooding through and finding every surface. He was wrapped by bliss. Everything around him receded. He swayed slightly and closed his eyes. There was nothing more than this, nothing else.

At dinner, Julia put Wendell at the head of the table.

"You there, please," Julia said, pointing.

She wanted Wendell in his old chair, to make up for the punishing bedroom and to show him her gratitude for his coming all the way up here, on what might be an unnecessary mission. Now that it might be unnecessary, she felt especially grateful, and generous.

But as soon as Wendell drew out the chair and sat down, Julia felt a sandy grain of irritation: at the casual, proprietary way he handled the fragile old spindle-back chair, leaning carelessly against it, making it strain and creak. As though he didn't know how delicate and brittle these chairs were, as though it didn't matter if he broke one. As though it still belonged to Wendell, or, worse, as though it didn't matter who owned it.

Wendell, who'd sat in that chair for years, now seemed wrong there. His limbs had taken on some strange Bridgehamptonish configuration. He had become a Long Island species, alien to the Maine habitat.

Katharine, beside him, beamed at her ex-son-in-law. "It's so nice to see you again, Wendell. I've missed you!"

"No, no," protested Wendell, "I've missed *you*! It's *more* than nice to *you*, Katharine. It's *delightful*."

"Oh my," Katharine said happily. "You've outdone me."

Edward looked at his plate: fillet of salmon. Transverse pectoral muscle. An easy cut at an acute angle, dorsal—ventral. He had little to say to Wendell. He was not pleased to see his ex-son-in-law, and he resented Wendell's placement. Wendell was no longer the head of the household and shouldn't be treated as an honored guest. Why should Wendell leave the marriage and his wife (alone now, probably, for the rest of her life) and then arrive to sit at the head of the table as though nothing had happened?

Wendell took things for granted, Edward thought testily. *Someone should let him know that his acts had consequences.* Hadn't he, years ago, fumblingly asked Edward for permission to marry Julia? Hadn't they stood in the living room at Villanova, by the unlit fireplace, before dinner, both of them mortally embarrassed, transfixed by the spotlight of significance glaring down on them? Hadn't Wendell made some sort of promise about his intentions? Certainly a promise had been *implied.* Certainly Wendell hadn't asked Edward permission to marry his daughter *just for a while, just until he found someone more appealing.*

Why was all this treated so casually? Wendell might start off by apologizing to Edward for divorcing his daughter. This was only a fantasy: no one apologized for anything nowadays. No one admitted they'd been wrong. People said nonsensically that they'd "misspoken," as though some impersonal agency had taken over their tongue and forced them to form rogue syllables, or that "an error had occurred," as though someone from outer space had made it occur. *People should take responsibility for what they did.*

Though no one did this now, no one, starting with their president, who was a big disappointment. (Edward wouldn't mention this to Julia, who became too heated over politics. Whichever side she took, she'd be unable to consider the other.)

Look at Wendell, sailing blithely in for a holiday visit to his abandoned family, in this shabby, poorly run home, full of leaks and missing objects. Wendell, free as a bird, everyone friendly and respectful, as though he'd lived up to all his promises all his life.

Katharine, of course, was nice to everyone. You couldn't depend on her for moral indignation. She'd feel it for a moment, out of loyalty, and then it would evaporate. She gave everyone the benefit of the doubt. You couldn't depend on her for being anything but generous. A waste, really.

He looked over at Jack.

"So, Jack," Edward said, "how are things with you?" He focused on his grandson, though he actually had little interest in talking to Jack. His real intention wasn't in talking to Jack but in snubbing Wendell.

"Pretty good, Grandpa," Jack said, nodding vaguely.

"You working?" Edward asked.

"Not at the moment, no." Jack ran his hand through his hair.

"Have a plan?"

Jack nodded. "Yeah. A plan." He drank from his glass. He and Steven both had beer bottles beside their glasses.

Edward kept his eyes on Jack. "What kind of plan?"

"Now, don't grill him, Daddy," Julia said, her voice light but firm. "He's here for a visit, not an interrogation."

Edward frowned. "I'd hardly call this an interrogation," he said. "I'm just asking what's going on."

Katharine touched his wrist. "You did sound a little stern."

"'A little stern,'" Edward repeated, as though it were an unfamiliar phrase. He looked down at his plate, frowning, and cut another bite.

"What about you?" Katharine asked Wendell brightly. "What's going on with you?"

Wendell pulled apart a piece of French bread, and crusty shards exploded across the table. "Things are going well," he said energetically. "Really well."

"Well, good!" said Katharine. "Any particular news?"

"The big news," Wendell said buoyantly, "is that my book is coming out next spring. So they can't throw me out yet."

"Was that a risk?" Katharine asked, teasing. "Being thrown out?"

"Constantly," Wendell said. He shook his head and looked owlish. "Publish or perish. You think you're safe when you get tenure, but you're never safe."

"Do you have tenure?" Edward asked Julia.

"No," she said. "All those years while the boys were growing up I didn't want to teach full-time. For a long time I was an adjunct professor, so I'm just up for tenure now, this year."

"You'll get it," Wendell said with assurance. He smeared butter on his bread.

"Easy for you to say," Julia answered.

"No, no, you will," he said, his mouth full.

"How does it work, getting tenure?" Edward asked.

"A committee's made up of people from your department," Julia explained. "You teach a class in front of them. Then they meet without you and discuss your teaching, your professional accomplishments, all that. They decide if you deserve it." Her stomach tightened at the thought.

"Of course you'll get it," said Katharine. "You're a wonderful teacher. And a wonderful artist. Have they seen your work?"

"They have," Julia said, "but you're slightly biased, Mum. The rest of the world doesn't hold my work in quite the same esteem, unfortunately."

"Oh, they'll give it to you," Katharine told her reassuringly. "You've been teaching there for years. Haven't you?"

"That's no assurance. The committee can decide what it likes."

"Jules, come on," Wendell said, ebullient, aloft on a cloud of his own self-esteem. "Don't be such a pessimist. Of course you'll get it. You don't have to win the Nobel Prize to get tenure."

"Depends on the committee," Julia said. "They've turned people down for reasons no one could figure out. My department"—Julia shook her head—"I seriously don't want to talk about it. It's bad luck to speculate." Not getting tenure would be a disaster.

Steven rescued her. "So, my news," he announced, "is I'm applying to law school."

Everyone turned to him, Julia with gratitude. She recognized that this was diversionary and sacrificial: Wendell would be displeased to learn this in public, along with everyone else. Steven would know this, but had done it, anyway.

Wendell's eyes narrowed. "Law school? When did you decide this?"

"I've actually been thinking about it all summer," Steven said.

Wendell nodded. "What about tuition? What have you been thinking about that?" His face was expressionless.

"I'll get student loans," Steven said. "If you two can help me at all, fine. If not, I'll do it myself."

"Good for you," Edward said approvingly. "I put myself through medical school. I had no help."

"I thought your father put you through medical school," Julia said, frowning.

Edward paused, suddenly uncertain. Maybe she was right. He'd done something self-reliant, independent, though. What was it?

"It was during the Depression," he said forbiddingly. "Times were very hard."

"I know," Julia said, "but I always thought you said your father was proud he'd been able to send you all the way through. That he never fell behind on the tuition, even though it was during the Depression."

Edward frowned. "Maybe you're right," he said. "Maybe it was after medical school. After that I never took a penny more from my father." *How had he gotten this wrong? How could this fact of his own life no longer be available to him? He felt a tiny ripple of alarm.*

"That's right," Katharine said loyally, shaking her head. "You never did."

"Well," said Steven, "I promise that if you send me to law school, I won't ask you for a cent afterward."

"Good for you," Edward said again.

"Only sixty thousand dollars more, and that's it," Wendell said, chopping the air with his hand. Steven laughed, nodding. Wendell lifted his wineglass, watching his son. Julia could feel him considering.

"What does your mother say?" Wendell asked. "Julia?"

Julia hesitated: it would be worse for Steven if Wendell discovered that she'd already known.

"She's only just heard, too," Steven said. "She hasn't really had time to think about it."

Wendell nodded, watchful.

Julia looked at Jack. He seemed to be ignoring all this, the family politics, his grandfather's questions, his brother's plans. He seemed focused intently on his meal, although now she realized that he wasn't actually eating much. He was moving his food around, head lowered. Maybe there was something strange about his eyes. Were they heavy-lidded? And was there something odd about the way he moved? Clumsiness? Or was she imagining it? Jack felt her gaze and looked up. She smiled, worried. Now that she looked straight at him, now that he met her eyes, she felt a sudden clench of fear: there was something missing, something wrong.

"Jackie, tell everyone about your gig," she said. "Your grandparents would love to hear."

She wanted Jack to be himself again, grinning at his grandmother, leaning easily back, teasing her, making them all laugh. She wanted Jack back in his own skin.

"And a 'gig' is?" Katharine asked, ready to be teased.

"It's a musical performance, Grandma," Steven explained. "In case you think it's a horse-drawn vehicle."

Katharine lifted her chin with dignity. "It was my mother who drove around in a gig, not me. Your great-grandmother," she said. "You've got the wrong generation. We said 'buggy.' That was the word, not 'gig.' We would *never* have said 'gig.' It wasn't a word we used."

"Sorry, Grandma," Steven said, laughing. "Pardon me."

"I don't even know what a gig *is*," Katharine said, with mock hauteur.

"Sorry," Steven said again, grinning.

Jack watched them without expression.

"Tell us about your performance, Jack," Katharine said, leaning forward. "Where was it?"

Jack brushed his hair back from his forehead.

Like an adolescent, Julia thought, *he's so uncomfortable.* What was the matter with him? He kept his head down. His hair kept falling forward over his eyes, and he kept awkwardly brushing it back.

"It was at a place in New York, Grandma," Jack said. "Way downtown."

"What was the name of it?" she asked.

"The place?"

She nodded.

"It's called Arlene's Grocery."

"'Arlene's Grocery?'" Katharine repeated. "Really?" She looked around at the others. "Is that the name of a nightclub?"

"Yeah." Jack gave her an odd smile. "It's a pretty funny name." He shifted in his chair.

"Well, it's very different from our day," Katharine said. "In our day those places were called El Morocco. The St. Regis Roof. Things like that. What else were they called, Edward?"

Edward shook his head. "I don't know what they were called."

"We didn't go to them much," Katharine said. "We didn't live in New York. But you read about them: 21—that was the name of one. So now it's Aileen's Grocery. And what instrument do you play?"

"Arlene's," Jack said, brushing at his hair. "Bass guitar. You've heard me play, Grandma."

"I'm sure I have. I've always loved the guitar," Katharine said.

"It's kind of loud, Mother, the one Jack plays," Julia said.

"Guitars?" Katharine said. "Guitars aren't so loud."

"They're all amplified now," Steven said. "Electronically, with speakers. It's not like a regular guitar. It's very loud."

"But I can play a regular guitar," Jack said. "Acoustic."

"I'd love to hear it," Katharine told him.

"So this was a job?" Edward asked, looking up at Jack.

"Yeah. One night." Jack brushed at his hair.

"But you were paid for it?"

Jack nodded.

"Well, that's very good, Jack," Edward said judicially. "Congratulations."

"Thanks," Jack said. He wiped his mouth with his napkin.

"I didn't think you were working," Edward said.

"He works at Aileen's Groceries," Katharine told him. "He just told us. Don't you think that's a wonderful name?"

"Arlene's," Julia said, and stood to get the salad from the sideboard. She offered it to Edward. "Have some salad, Daddy."

Edward did not take it. "Does it have garlic?"

"Don't you think I know by now you don't like garlic?"

Edward took the bowl suspiciously.

"Can't be too careful," Katharine said, looking at the others, smiling.

Jack had mashed his potatoes with the back of his fork, splitting the thin red-brown skin. He lifted a small forkful to his mouth. He chewed slowly, as though the food contained grit.

But there was something wrong. Julia felt the beginnings of dread. There was something holding Jack in its grip. Some black hole was sucking at him, absorbing his thoughts, his attention, his energy. The people around this table were irrelevant, hardly present for him. Something else had become his center. What was left for all of them, for the rest of the world, was this dry husk of consciousness, this simulacrum of Jack. He did not look up at her. *When would they talk?*

When everyone had finished, Julia looked at her watch. "It's late," she said to Katharine. "Why don't you two go on to bed. We'll do the dishes."

"No, no, of course we'll help," Katharine said, rising and groping for her cane. She set off after Julia, the pitcher in one hand, the water sloshing perilously with each step.

Everyone came in to the kitchen to help with the dishes, even Edward stood in the doorway. Julia stood at the sink, clouds of heated steam around her, rinsing the dishes. Wendell stood at the dishwasher, loading: it was the first big expenditure they'd made on the house, decades ago, this rumbling, pounding monster. Jack leaned silently against the refrigerator; Steven cruised around the room with a sponge, swiping at countertops. Katharine, leaning on her cane, watched for tasks she could do one-handed. Julia listened to the others talk, saying nothing, feeling Jack's silent presence. When the dishes were done, she suggested again that her parents go to bed, but again they rallied.

"Oh, we don't want to go to bed *now*. Do we, Edward? It's not often we get to see the whole family," Katharine said brightly. "We want to get as much of it as we can."

This will go on forever, Julia thought in despair. Her parents would never go to bed. They would spend the entire night making small talk, while Jack stood among them all, mute and distant, his eyes opaque.

In the living room, Jack sat at the far end of the room. As the others talked, he yawned again and again, shifting in his chair. He seemed unaware of the conversation.

"Wasn't it, Jackie?" Julia asked, turning to him.

"Sorry?" he answered.

"Wasn't your favorite thing, when you two were growing up, going out in the Whaler?"

"I guess," Jack said. "Yeah. Probably." He nodded. There was a silence.

Steven wanted to move over and simply stand in front of his brother, to shield him: he was so visibly on something. He must have taken it before dinner.

"You taught us, Dad," Steven said, "except you didn't really know how to use the Whaler yourself."

Wendell grinned. "It was a learning process for all of us."

"You'd sit there trying to start the engine and swearing under your breath," Steven said. "I'd try to hear what you were saying without looking as though I were listening. You got quite creative."

"I prided myself on imaginative language," Wendell said. "I was rather good at it. And it was good for you to learn about adversity. Learn that engines don't always start."

"We knew engines didn't always start," Steven said. "Ours hardly ever started." He looked at Jack. "Remember? It would *never* start. Or sometimes it started up and then when we were out somewhere it would cut out. Just quit. I used to think we were going to die."

Jack nodded, smiling oddly. His mouth seemed to rise higher on one side than the other.

"What would you do then?" Katharine asked Steven. "When it stopped?"

"Try to start it," Steven said. "We'd be drifting out to sea, or onto the rocks. There was always some dire peril. We'd yank again and again on the starter cord, I thought my arm would come loose. We were supposed to have oars, but it was too much trouble to bring them down from the house, so we never did. Anyway, we were pretty small; we'd have had a hard time rowing that boat anywhere, against the tide."

"Once you were towed home," Julia said.

"That old guy," Steven said. "Ted Somebody. He told us he'd tow us in *once*, in this disapproving way, like it was our fault the engine had stopped. The implication was that next time he'd leave us out there to die."

"What a miserable creature," Julia said. "I didn't remember that. Do you, Jackie?"

"That old guy," Jack said enigmatically. He set his ankle on his knee. His foot twitched.

"I don't know about you," Edward said abruptly to Katharine, "but I'm ready for bed."

Julia looked at her mother, but Katharine smiled docilely. "I guess that means I am, too."

Julia stood to say good night. She kissed her mother's cheek, soft and warm; her father's, lean and unresponsive. She could hardly wait for them to leave; she felt Jack's strange dark presence flooding the room.

When they had gone at last, she said, "Let's go out on the porch. Come sit with us, Jackie. We've been seeing shooting stars."

For a moment Jack hesitated, and when he stood, it seemed provisional. It seemed as though some unspoken condition hung in the air. He was coming with them *for now*.

They sat in a row, Jack between his parents, Julia between her sons. At first they did not speak, settling into the chairs and gazing sightlessly into the darkened meadow. There was no wind.

"So," Wendell and Julia began, together.

"Sorry," Julia said, "go ahead."

"So, Jack," Wendell said. "We wanted to talk to you about what's going on." He paused, but Jack said nothing. "We're a little concerned about you."

Jack did not answer. He was not going to help.

"We're concerned about what you're doing," Julia said gently. The thing was to make Jack feel loved, not attacked. That he was among friends, that he could let them know he needed help.

"About drugs." Wendell's voice was uncertain: it wasn't clear whether he was disapproving or supportive.

Jack said nothing.

"Is there anything you'd like to tell us?" Wendell asked.

"About drugs?" Jack repeated.

"Please, Jackie," Julia said. "Don't be obstructive."

"Look," Jack said, "I don't know what you're saying. What do you mean?"

"All right," Wendell said. "We'll start at the beginning. Are you taking drugs?"

Too soon, too hard, thought Julia.

There was a silence.

"Are you?" Wendell's voice was quiet and intent.

"Not in an important way," Jack said. He scratched suddenly and urgently at his neck.

"What does that mean?" Wendell asked.

"I mean, I don't do anything significant," Jack said.

"What does that mean, not significant?" Wendell asked.

"Okay, I don't do any kind of drugs, to speak of."

"But what does that mean? What drugs do you do?" asked Wendell. He turned to look at Jack, but Jack stared straight ahead.

"Look, everyone I know takes drugs," said Jack, his voice impatient. "It's different now. It's not like when you were growing up. Drugs are everywhere."

There was a pause. Wendell stared at him.

"Still," Julia said gently, "they can take over your life. You can take too many drugs." She wanted an admission, any kind. "You can start in on drugs that you can't stop taking."

Jack looked down. He shook his head slightly.

Julia turned to Steven.

Steven shifted in his chair. "Uh," he said. "So, look, when I went out to see you in Brooklyn, things looked pretty rough."

Jack lifted his head. "And?" he asked, truculent.

"Things looked pretty bad. I'm worried about you."

"For Christ's sake," Jack said, his voice rising. "What is this, an interrogation? I'm *fine*. I'm living in a friend's apartment. I'm trying to get more gigs for the band. What do you want? You think I should go to law school, too? Be a different person? Is that what you want me to do?"

"It's not that we—" Julia stopped, stalled by his anger. His voice was so harsh, so hostile, she didn't know how to continue. It was as though he had no connection to any of them. As though he hated them, as though this hatred was there, just below the surface, simmering and dark, and the slightest word or gesture would reveal it, bottomless, toxic.

"I'm not going to law school, and I'm not going to work for a bank," Jack said loudly. "And I'm not working for a fucking video store, either! What is this, a family conference? You know what?" He paused insultingly. "It's none of your business what I do. Any of you."

There was a silence. Jack's anger filled the air and made it unbreathable. They were unprepared for this; none of them knew a way to rise up and combat it, or make a way through it.

"Okay," Wendell said, trying another tack. "No one's telling you to work for a bank. But how are you paying the rent?"

"I don't have any fucking rent!" Jack said. "I told you, I'm living in a friend's apartment. Christ!"

It was like a cloud of steam, scalding, blinding, impenetrable.

"Bro," said Steven finally, "cut it out. You've got to have a place to live. You've got to have some way to pay your way."

"I've *got* a place to live. I'm going to pay my way, all right? Is it okay with you if I choose a different life from yours? If I don't tie myself to a tree and wait for someone to cut me in half with a chain saw? You all act like everyone in the fucking world has to do exactly the same thing. Where I live, everyone is doing what I'm doing. Artists, musicians, writers—everyone I know is scraping by. We have different objectives. It's a different approach."

"Jackie," Julia put her hand on his wrist, but he jerked away as though he'd been scalded. "We're worried about you."

"Well, *don't be,* all right? I'm fine. I'm *fine.*" Jack smoothed the hair back from his face with both hands. He cupped his face and leaned forward, elbows on his knees, staring out into the night.

We should have planned this, Julia thought, *the whole thing.*

What were they supposed to do now? They each should have had a goal, some point to make. This was like grasping at mist. Jackie was filled with something. She could feel him vibrating beside her, like a huge smokestack, full of heat and choking black air.

It was less and less likely that he was fine. He was not fine. Julia arrived at this understanding abruptly, as though she had reached a ledge on a mountain. Beyond was the drop: Jack was not fine. This was serious. Steven was right. Something was wrong, something had taken him over. His resistance made it clear, if nothing else. He was furious. He was against them, he was on the side of something else. They had become the enemy. What was he on the side of?

"Are you taking heroin?" Julia asked bravely.

There was a long pause.

"What?" Jack said. His voice cracked high with outrage. "Am I *what*?"

"Heroin. Are you taking it?" she repeated.

"What do you think I am, a junkie?"

Now Wendell spoke. "Are you taking heroin?"

Jack said nothing for a moment. He shook his head.

"No, I'm not. Okay?" His tone was weary and inauthentic. "That what you wanted to hear? I'm not a junkie. Christ." He leaned back.

"Well," Steven said, "I'm sorry, but I'm not sure I believe you."

"Well, fuck you, bro'!" Jack said, voice rising. "Who asked you? And what the fuck do you know about it? What are you all, the narc squad?" He put his hands on the arms of the chair, ready to stand.

But there was nowhere, Julia could see, for him to go. The car keys were in her pocket. He was trapped here, listening to their hostile probing questions. What Jack wanted was to get away, back into some irresistible current. She could feel his urge, his desperation. His realization that he was trapped. It was palpable. How had Wendell managed to get him onto the plane?

"Okay," Wendell said, changing his tone. "Jack, I want a serious answer, not outrage. No shouting." He sounded courteous now, and earnest, as though he were running a meeting. "We're all worried about you. We don't want to get you in trouble, but if you're taking heroin, you need help. That's what we're offering. Help."

Jack jerked his head restlessly back and forth.

"I don't need help," he said. "I'm not taking drugs."

"Show us your arms," said Steven.

"Fuck!" Jack said. "I'm not showing you my fucking *arms*. What *is* this?" He threw himself back in his chair and scratched furiously at his wrist.

Julia held her breath. Some kind of violence was now in the air. Were they going to hold him down and pull up his sleeves? Wendell stood up.

"Don't make this a circus," he said. "If you're not taking heroin, why would you mind showing your arms?"

"Maybe there's a chance I'm *offended* that you don't believe me," Jack said. "By the fact that I've given you my *word* and you obviously don't trust me."

There was a pause. Jack's breathing was now loose and heavy.

"You're obviously all against me," he said angrily. "You've obviously all discussed this, you won't believe anything I say. Why don't you put me in a straitjacket? Why don't you fucking tie me up and call the police? Nothing I say will make any difference to you."

"It's not that we don't believe you," Julia began.

"Then tell Dad to lay off!" Jack said. *"This is a fucking inquisition."*

Julia wondered if her parents' window were open.

"Jackie, please," she said.

Jack jerked himself up to his feet, staggering slightly. "You're all against me," he said. "I don't need any help. Okay? You got that? I don't need any help, and I don't want to be questioned. I'm not in school. I'm an adult. You have no right to ask me anything."

Jack stood facing them, the light from the kitchen windows illuminating his angry face. Julia didn't dare put out her hand to him.

After a moment Jack turned and stepped down into the black meadow. He began walking away, down the path. Steven stood at once and followed him, jogging down the steps. The two figures turned shadowy, vanishing quickly into the long grass, the darkness.

THIRTEEN

"You shouldn't have done that," Julia said.

"What?" Wendell asked, incensed. "What shouldn't I have done?"

"Pushed him to show his arms."

"It was Steven who asked to see his arms."

"But you kept on about it. You shouldn't have."

"Because things were going so well until then, you mean?"

"No, but that—set him off."

"He was already *off*, Julia," Wendell said. "In case you didn't notice. He was not being cooperative."

"But that's what did it. That drove him away."

"What *did it* was us asking him questions. Don't blame this on me. Our son doesn't want to talk about drugs. That's the problem. As long as we don't ask him about drugs, he won't yell at us and storm off into the night. That's the deal."

"But there's a better way to do this," she said. "You don't confront someone who's so touchy. You don't take them on head-on."

"You asked him head-on if he took heroin," said Wendell.

After a moment Julia said, "You're right, I did." There was another pause. This suddenly was overwhelming to her, too large and frightening to deal with, like a landslide. "I don't know what we should have done. I don't know what to do." She shook her head. "Tell me what happened this morning."

"I told you I found a guy called Ralph Carpenter, who runs a rehab center in Florida. We had a couple of long conversations. He was amazingly helpful."

"How'd you find him?"

"The Internet."

"The *Internet*?"

"What's wrong with that?"

"Wendell, he could be anyone."

Wendell looked at her. "Okay," he said. "How are we going to do this? Are you going to challenge everything I say? Because if so, I'll leave now. Okay? I'll head back to Bridgehampton and put on my tennis whites, which you find so amusing, and you can deal with all this yourself."

There was a silence.

"Give me some credit, Julia. I'm not a total idiot. Or give yourself some credit: you wouldn't have *married* a total idiot."

"Okay, sorry," Julia said reluctantly. He was right, she would have to stop. But everything was so alarming now, there were so many things that could go wrong. "What did this guy say?"

"I know you can't go on the Internet here, you can barely make a phone call. So I looked at different places online, and Sandra gave me advice. I liked the look of this place, it's small, and they could take him right away. So I called and talked to him, and I liked him."

"What did he say?" Julia repeated.

"He was very practical. I told him I was going to see Jack, and he said to go first thing in the morning, without telling him, so he wouldn't have a chance to take anything before I arrived. 'Use,' they call it. So Jack wouldn't use before I got there."

Julia said nothing. She hated the idea of offering up their family to a stranger on the Internet. A man taking the call on his cell phone, wearing a loud Hawaiian shirt and standing by a swimming pool. Traffic noise behind him, trashy tropical leaves littering the ground. Shouting advice about Jack, whom he'd never met.

"He thought we should have an intervention," Wendell said. "He wanted to come up and do it with us, but I said we wanted to talk to Jack alone first. He told me it wouldn't work. I said we wanted to try it." Wendell laughed shortly. "Which was such a good idea."

"We haven't completely failed," Julia offered.

Wendell turned to her in the darkness. "Julia. This is really bad."

On the last words Wendell's voice went uneven, and Julia felt fear flooding her own throat.

"This is really bad," he said again. "It's serious. It's how people die."

There it was again, the word she did not want to hear, the word she would not allow into her mind. It was terrible to hear it from Wendell. The word began swelling and shrinking in her consciousness, rising and falling through her mind, as though she'd been hit by something and these were shock waves. Her scalp felt tight.

"Yes, but—not—" She was struggling. "Not—if you know—I mean, can't they fix it? Doesn't rehab work?"

"Jules, this is serious," Wendell said. "Jack's a heroin addict, he uses needles. He's in trouble. Even with rehab, the chances are only fifty-fifty. The numbers are really bad." Wendell's voice was quiet. "Seventy-five percent relapse during the first year after rehab. Even with rehab, only one person in thirty makes it to five years. Most people—" He stopped.

There was a pause.

Julia willed the word out of her mind.

"Yes," she said. "Tell me what happened this morning."

"Well," Wendell said, "what happened first was that I couldn't find his apartment. I took the jitney in from Long Island to the city, and then took a cab. I got some Russian driver who swore he knew his way around

Brooklyn, but of course he didn't, and he didn't have a map, so we got lost. We kept driving around, with him arguing in Russian on his cell phone. He couldn't find it, so finally I had to call Jack on my cell phone, for directions. So by the time I arrived, Jack had done whatever he needed to do."

"Do you think he really did?" Did she have to believe it?

"Carpenter said to look at his eyes. The pupils contract when you're on heroin. When Jack came to the door I could hardly see his pupils. It was frightening, he was like an alien. His eyelids were half-closed, and there was no pupil."

"The pupils," said Julia, remembering. *His strange eyes.* Each of these things was a shock. Hearing them from Wendell, here in front of her, hearing their source from the stranger in Florida, made them real. Each one fell into her consciousness like a weight. It was as though she'd always known them. She hated knowing them.

"Tell about Carpenter," Julia asked. "What's he like?"

"He seems good. He was once an addict himself. He sounds tough, very effective, very capable."

"How do we know he's good?"

"He was recommended by two other places," Wendell said. "And Sandra checked him out. Okay? Are you going to keep doing this? I don't actually like being grilled. Don't be like this, Julia."

"Don't you be like this," Julia said. "Just because you've found things out, it doesn't mean I have. You have to let me ask questions, Wendell. I'm in this, too."

"Fine," Wendell said.

Julia put her head in her hands. "I don't want this to be happening."

"I don't, either."

After a moment Julia raised her head. "Go on about this morning."

"First of all, Steven's right, Jack's place is really awful," Wendell said. "Jack seemed kind of unsteady, but glad to see me. I told him I had the money, and that we'd give it to the guy with the amps, and then go to the airport, as we'd agreed. The whole time I was talking, Jack's eyes kept closing, and he kept scratching himself. He kept lifting up his shirt and scratching his back, as though he had the plague. Carpenter says that's another symptom."

Julia shuddered. "So then what happened? Did you find the amps guy?"

"Well, no. Jack started changing the story. First he said that, actually, the guy who owned the amps thought he did have insurance, after all. So I said, Okay, fine, then let's head for the airport. Then Jack said, No, he had some things to take care of first. I said, Fine, I'd help him. He said okay, and went back to his bedroom. I followed him, as though I were being friendly, and he got kind of angry and asked me what I wanted. I think he wanted to make a phone call. He said he didn't need a bodyguard.

"I was being the good cop, acting as though everything were all right. I mean, obviously, I'd gotten there too late, I'd seen his eyes, but still—" Wendell paused; there was the treacherous break again in his voice. "I mean, he's still *Jack*—"

"I know," Julia said. None of this seemed possible. It kept being new, not credible. It was Jack they were talking about.

"I sat down on his bed. I told him we loved him, we wanted to help him. He calmed down, sort of. He kept nodding, but the whole time he kept scratching. I actually started to cry." Wendell shook his head, his voice rough again. "I asked if he wanted help."

"What did he say?"

"He said no. He said nothing was wrong, he didn't need help. He pretended I was talking about his not having a job or any money. And I'd agreed with you not to talk about drugs until we were all together, so I dropped it.

"I took out the money. I had it in my pocket, this big wad, like a gangster. I said we'd hand it over together to whomever he owed it to, and then we'd go to the airport.

"He kept looking at the money. He'd look away, and then back. He couldn't help it. Finally he said that he did owe the money, to a friend.

I said fine, we'd go and pay the debt, whatever it was. I said I didn't care what it was for. He said he had to call first. I said fine, and didn't move. I just sat there, on his filthy bed, waiting.

"He tried to call, but the line was busy. So we sat there next to each other while he dialed, over and over. Finally he got through. He talked very quietly, as though he were trying to keep from being overheard, even though I was six inches away. I could hear him breathing. He asked someone if he could come over. He said he'd be there in fifteen minutes. So we went over together."

"Where was it?"

"Some woman's apartment. A rundown building, three flights up," Wendell said. "Two girls, there, or women, whatever. God! The way they looked at us. One of them never said anything, never spoke. She was lying on the sofa, playing an electric guitar that wasn't plugged in. She had short spiky blond hair, black roots, pink at the tips. She had on a T-shirt and striped tights. She watched us and played the guitar, without making a sound. She had pale blue eyes, completely empty. Once Carpenter'd told me, I could see it: eyes half-closed, no pupils. She was high. Nodding off.

"The other one was the dealer, I guess—or maybe they were both dealers. Anyway, this one was all business, tall and thin, all angles. Short black hair and a square jaw and eyes like fucking steel screwdrivers. There were cats everywhere. The place stank.

"'I've got the money,' Jack said. He looked at me and I took out the wad and handed it to her. I felt like a criminal. I probably was a criminal.

"'It's what I owe you,' Jack said to her.

"She looked at him and then at me; then she counted the bills, very fast, on the table. Then she looked up again. She was polite, but very cool. She was watching us. And Jack was watching her like a hawk. I could feel something was going on, but I couldn't tell what. Jack didn't introduce me. I stood there, watching both of them. Magenta Hair was watching all of us, too, but as though we weren't real, as though we'd just turned up in her dream. Her head was kind of bobbing, as though it were loose on her neck.

"I felt as though I'd walked into a whole other universe that I'd only just realized existed. There was something going on that I didn't understand, some secret undercurrent, like electronic signals, too high to hear. I didn't know how to pick them up, but I knew they were there. I could feel them."

Wendell's voice was distressed. Julia reached across the empty chair to pat his arm.

"I'm sorry. What a scene," she said. "Then what?"

"I had the feeling something was about to happen, or that it would happen if I blinked, if I stopped paying attention for a moment. So I was determined not to blink. It seemed as though everything were in code, every word, every gesture. I was trying to break it, but I was a kid, a beginner, and they were experts. I didn't have a chance.

"Jack asked if he could use the bathroom, and I thought, That's it. Steel Eyes would take him, it would be somewhere behind her, and they'd leave the room together. I couldn't say I had to follow him to the bathroom. I'd be left there in the living room with Magenta Hair, who was riding high. And then whatever it was Jack wanted to happen would happen. I'd lost.

"But it didn't happen like that. The bathroom was right behind us, down a little hall. Steel Eyes just pointed at it, and Jack turned around and went off alone. Steel Eyes and I stood there waiting. We didn't speak.

"I had the feeling she wasn't human, as though she'd chosen not to be human, to be something else. It was like meeting a vampire, someone with no soul. She'd joined the bloodsuckers. She was ready to ruin Jack's life, maybe get him started sucking other people's blood. Or anyway, she was sucking his.

"I couldn't stand being in the same room with her, I didn't want to breathe the same air. I wanted to get out of there—the secret signals, the stoned girl friend playing her disconnected guitar, the smell of catshit.

"Jack came out of the bathroom, and they kept exchanging these zinging glances, like laser beams. I could feel them passing, and I didn't blink. I stood there, watching them both. I watched their hands, I was like a kid at a magic show. Every move they made, I saw.

"So nothing happened. We left. Jack and I went back downstairs—
he went first—and we got back in the cab with the Russian (who'd made
himself a fortune by not knowing his way around Brooklyn), and we
went straight to LaGuardia. We haven't mentioned it since. On the plane
Jack slept, or pretended to. His leg kept twitching."

Julia sighed. "It's so *sordid*."

"Among other things," Wendell said. "Also illegal. And very, very
dangerous."

"And sad."

The night around them was quiet. There was no sound from Steven
and Jack, no sound but the soft breath of the wind across the meadow.
The silence was broken by a distant mechanical cough, then a loud
rumble, falling immediately to a low drone.

"Is that the Whaler?" Julia asked. "Ours? They can't be going out in
it now."

"Without a light," Wendell said.

The sound of the engine rose slightly, fell, rose again, then steadied.

"They are. It's them, they're going out," Julia said. "I can't believe it."

They listened to the muffled drone.

"They won't go far," Julia said. "They'll come right back. Right?"

"They're idiots," Wendell said.

The sound of the engine was steady.

"They'll come right back," Julia said. "Steven won't let Jack do anything crazy." She listened for a moment, willing the sound to change.
"What do we do now about Jack?" Julia asked. "What does Carpenter
say is next, after you try the family conference and fail?"

"I don't think we've exactly failed. It feels as though we haven't even
started. Or as if we started out and were ambushed." Wendell went on;
"Carpenter wanted us to fly him up here, do the intervention with us.
He charges two thousand dollars, so of course he'd think that would be
best."

"How does it work, an intervention?"

"He says the whole thing is very calm, very supportive and noncon-
frontational. You get the family, his best friends, anyone close to Jack.

Everyone speaks for themselves. You confront him with the situation. You make it clear he can't change on his own, but you tell him you're all behind him. You tell him you'll help him if he agrees to get help. Once he agrees to it all, Carpenter takes him to the airport and they fly down to his place."

"Which is what?"

"It's called New Life. On the west coast of Florida. It's small. I looked it up online. There's a swimming pool, and a bunch of guys sitting around laughing. A gym, everyone doing workouts. It looks like summer camp. Their big claim is they focus on the individual."

"Don't all those places say that?" asked Julia.

"I don't know, Julia," Wendell said, exasperated. "I have no idea what these places are like, this one or any others. *We're in over our heads here.*"

There was a silence.

"I can't believe this is happening," Julia said. "I know that's a cliché, but I can't. My mind keeps going in circles."

"Clichés are signifiers of communal reality," Wendell said. "Everyone feels them, that's why they're clichés."

"We're certain about this, right? That he takes heroin? It's all still circumstantial."

"Pupils like pinheads? Scratching like a madman? Paying the social call to the lovely home of Magenta Hair and Steel Eyes? What do you think was going on there?" Wendell asked. "Julia. You're manufacturing your own lens of reality."

"I know," Julia said weakly, "but he sat with us at dinner. He seems normal."

"*He does not seem normal,*" said Wendell. "He was in a trance at dinner. As though he was on drugs. Stop pretending this isn't happening, Julia. It's happening."

"Okay," Julia said. "You're right. He's probably taking it. But couldn't he be taking it *without* being addicted? Couldn't we talk to him about it, couldn't we help him stop?"

"Julia. Heroin is one of the most addictive substances there is. It's diabolical."

"But couldn't he be taking it without having a habit?" She put her head in her hands. "I don't know what I'm talking about."

If he were addicted, she'd know. She'd surely know, she'd have a feeling about her own child. The thing was, this didn't seem possible. She kept returning to that: it wasn't possible. Couldn't something else be happening, and couldn't they talk to him in some better way?

"Why won't he show us his arms if he doesn't have needle tracks? And if he has tracks, he's addicted," said Wendell. "Either way, why do you think we could talk him out of taking heroin? We couldn't even talk him out of smoking pot, for Christ's sake."

"All right," she said again, not agreeing.

She didn't agree with Wendell, but she couldn't argue with him. What he was saying made sense, it just didn't seem to be part of reality. There were two parts to this: the part Wendell was talking about, and her son.

The Whaler chugged steadily through the dark.

It had been Jack's idea, going out.

The boys had been standing on the dock, looking out across the black water, when Jack had suddenly climbed down into the Whaler. He felt his way unsteadily through the darkness to the stern, groping for the toggle on the starter cord.

"What are you doing?" Steven said, but Jack, without answering, had yanked at the cord, ripping the engine into noisy life. Steven climbed in then, and Jack uncleated the bowline and threw it into the boat, pushing off as the engine snorted, coughed, stuttered, and then found its rhythm.

Jack sat down at the helm, the engine loud. He set out toward the mouth of the cove, heading straight for open water, or where it would be if they could see it.

"This is kind of stupid," Steven said, over the noise of the engine.

Jack did not answer.

There was no chop. The water was flat and inky, a smooth sheet below them in the dark. The small wind of their own movement blew across Steven's face. He could see nothing ahead. They moved out across the invisible sea. It seemed they were going fast, very fast for a boat without lights, but there was no way to know. He had no idea where they were by now—halfway across the cove? nearing the mouth of the cove, setting out onto open water? Would he know when they hit open water?

Jack felt the night wind on his hair. He was squinting into the darkness. He was starting to come down, he could feel himself beginning the descent. He could feel a lowering of the sky, an ominous dropping of atmosphere. The air was beginning to collapse around him. The deep blue-black dome of the night was closing down over him, it was taking on dangerous weight. His legs were starting to ache, and his calves seemed to be on fire. The notion of vomiting came to him. His body might decide to do this. He didn't want to do it, but once it was in his mind, the idea had a certain presence, a significance. The gluey mess of potatoes at dinner had made him start thinking of it, and now it was firmly in his mind. There was the possibility, the awareness of the vile, boiling heave.

Jack licked his lips. They were dry and gritty, and felt like someone else's, someone's lips that his tongue happened to have access to. He was shivering now. His body felt clenched. He felt like a giant fist, leaden and heavy. He was turning to stone. He wanted to stretch out and go to sleep. He imagined lying down, a long limitless reach, the luxurious flex of his muscles, the longitudinal thrust of his limbs. He licked his lips again—someone's lips—and felt his stomach tensing. He rubbed his hands over his eyes and thought of vomiting. He could see nothing, it didn't matter if he kept his hand over his eyes or not. He could steer like this, his eyes covered. It didn't matter.

He had very little tolerance right now, he could feel himself teetering, right on the edge of something. If Steven said anything to him he didn't want to hear, he would throw Steven overboard. He was ready, his whole body was ready to make the move. If Steven said anything to him, he would jump overboard. He never wanted to see his parents again, the thought of seeing them was intolerable. With their questions. He hadn't meant to come here. He was in touch with something else, something slower, deeper, more important than his parents, though hard to keep track of, something beautiful and smooth. Something for which he felt a helpless nostalgic yearning.

His calves were on fire and his head ached. He would have to kick, of course. He would have to kick. This was excruciating, intolerable. He would kick as soon as he could. He would go clean. He would go away, he would go out West and go clean. The thought of vomiting was more pressing. The heat, the flames were running through his body now, his arms and legs. His head felt swollen and strange. Something was ticking inside his brain.

If only he could kick he'd be fine, though he'd also be fine if he could score some dope. If he could only get some dope and get straight. Then he could make a plan to kick. He had nothing left. Fucking Dana hadn't given him any more, she'd stood there in front of his father like she didn't know what he'd come for. She could have gotten him something, could have slipped him a bag. He'd hoped there'd be something in the bathroom for him, but there wasn't. He only owed her six hundred, she could have slipped him something for the other two. Why did she think he'd gone there? She could have thought of something.

Fucking Lisa lying on the sofa, on the nod, her big striped legs splayed out like a doll's. His father looking back and forth, at Dana and then at him, his eyes sliding back and forth like he was in a shooting gallery. *A shooting gallery.*

Jack leaned over, his arms locked across his belly, his stomach clenched. He began to rock back and forth, holding himself from throwing up. He was trying to hold on to something, something that would keep him still, stable.

"Jack?" Steven said.

Jack could not see his brother. He did not answer, rocking back and forth. He let go of the tiller. Steven climbed back toward the stern and took the stick. Jack folded himself tightly over his stomach.

Steven sat beside him and pushed the tiller over, starting a wide turn. He turned his head toward the dock, staring into the night, though he could see nothing. He was calculating the location of the invisible dock. There were no lights.

"Take us back," Jack said, rocking. His eyes were clenched shut.

"We're *going* back," Steven said.

"Now," Jack said. "I need to go back."

"We're going back," Steven said again. He was straining to see through the dark, trying to see the lights of the house. They should be there, there was no fog. He thought for a moment he saw them, though they seemed to disappear. He couldn't be certain he saw them. It was like watching a shooting star, your eye followed it, but did you see it? A question you could never answer. He held the tiller over, steady, looking toward shore. Beside him was the silhouette of his brother doubled over on the seat, rocking back and forth in the darkness.

.

FOURTEEN

"What do you think they're doing?" Julia asked.

"They'll be back," Wendell said. "They're just fooling around."

"I can't believe they're doing this," Julia said. She looked at the corner of the porch, where the oars leaned against the wall. "Going out at night, no light, no oars. Breaking all the rules."

"Yeah." Wendell laughed shortly. "I guess that's the point. They don't have to obey our rules anymore."

They listened. The engine held its steady drone.

"Is it getting fainter?" asked Julia. "Where are they going?"

Wendell did not answer.

They listened, looking hard into the darkness, as if by looking they could hear better.

"What are they doing?" she asked again.

"Just fooling around," Wendell said. "They'll be back."

The engine sound was becoming fainter, more distant against the dense blackness that held them.

"They're not crazy," Wendell said. "Steven's not crazy. They'll be back."

"We think Jack's crazy, then?"

"We don't know what Jack is. If he's an addict, he's crazy. Anyway, he's not sane."

Julia gave a short laugh. "We've done a great job here, with our family discussion. What a success."

"Could have been worse," Wendell said.

"How? We've gotten exactly nowhere."

"That's not true," Wendell said forcefully. "Actually, we know more now. We know it's worse than we thought. We know Jack won't discuss it. We know we have to take steps."

"Didn't we know all those things before?" asked Julia.

"Not for certain. And we didn't know how Jack would act," Wendell went on. "Storming around and yelling, he's showing us how serious it is." Wendell sighed lengthily. "Christ."

"What if he doesn't want to get help?" Julia asked. "We can't force him. We have to talk to him again."

"Carpenter says these interventions work," Wendell said. "Hazelden recommends them, if the person doesn't want to go into rehab."

"So why don't we send him to Hazelden?"

"Two-week waiting list. Carpenter could come up tomorrow."

They sat again in silence. The sound of the engine was much fainter.

"How much gas is there?" Wendell asked.

"No idea," Julia said. "Steven took it out a few days ago. I don't know how far he went, if he filled up afterward, or anything."

Wendell stood up. "It will be all right." He set his hands on his hips.

They listened. The air was taking on the deep chill of midnight.

"Who do you know who has a boat?" Wendell asked.

"Dan Ellsworth," Julia said. "Remember? That contractor. He's next door now, he built a house just up the cove."

Wendell put his hands in his pockets and rose onto his toes. "They'll be fine," he said decisively.

The engine was a soft muted sound, a small tear in the fabric of silence around them. The night felt huge.

There had been accidents along this coast, of course. People had been lost. Things went wrong: the wind came up, the engine quit. The boat shipped water, wallowed, capsized, foundered. The tall green seas rose and sank around it. People hung on to the boat, fingers clamped to the side of it as it drifted through the loose shifting waters. Hypothermia, that was the risk. People clung until their stiffened fingers no longer held, and then their helpless bodies were simply lifted away, taken by the cold green swell.

"Those idiots," Julia said.

"It's Jack," Wendell said. "Steven wouldn't do this."

"It's not just Jack," Julia said. "Do you think Jack's holding him hostage? Why is Steven letting this happen?"

"We don't know what Steven will do, actually," Wendell said. "This is going to be hard on him."

"He doesn't have to wreck the boat just because he's upset," Julia said.

But now it seemed stable, steadier, the sound. Didn't it? They listened, focusing, trying to measure it. Was it louder? Softer?

"He's not going to wreck the boat," Wendell said. His voice was quiet, abstracted.

"All right," Julia said. "You're right. They're grown-ups. They've been going out in the Whaler since they were eight. They'll be all right."

Wendell sat down again, the chair creaked heavily. "Right."

"So what do we do about Jack?" Julia asked. She was still listening.

"Carpenter says you need some kind of proof. He said we have to talk to his friends, his girlfriend, his boss, his landlord. Get something that's hard fact. Otherwise Jack'll just lie."

"Is it coming closer?" asked Julia.

They said nothing. The sound hovered on the edge of definition, faint, remote.

"Maybe," Wendell said at last.

After a moment Julia said, "We don't know any of those people. The other band members, maybe, but he doesn't *have* a job or a landlord or a girlfriend. Who's the guy whose apartment he's staying in?"

Wendell didn't answer.

"And if Jack's doing it, the other band members probably are," Julia said. "Don't you think?"

"I guess."

"And why would they tell us? I don't know," Julia said. "What kind of proof can we get?"

"His arms," Wendell said. "We have to look at his arms."

"Then what? We call your friend?"

"I guess then we call him. We've kind of screwed it up," Wendell said. "I don't know, really. I thought we'd be in a different situation by now. I thought we'd have gotten somewhere with our discussion."

"Will Carpenter come up here? Even if we've already made a mess of it?"

"I guess. If we pay him."

"How much does he charge? What does the whole thing cost?"

"Twenty-five thousand a month."

"Jesus. How long does it last?"

"As long as it needs to. A month, anyway. He said count on three months."

"Will insurance cover it?"

"Don't know yet."

"Well, we can't afford it. How could we pay that?"

"I don't know. I suppose if we have to, we do."

The sound of the engine had been drifting through the night, a faint thrumming line connecting them to their sons. It faded, rose, faded. Julia was no longer sure she could hear it.

"Has it stopped?"

Wendell did not answer.

"Has it stopped?"

"I'm not sure."

"I think it's stopped."

"I can't tell if it's stopped or if I just can't hear it," he said.

They sat without speaking. The night seemed emptier now. The sea had come nearer. They could feel its presence in the darkness, the damp salt air moving up onto the land, across the meadow, against the skin.

"I think it's stopped," Julia said again. Had it?

"Maybe they're back at the dock," Wendell said, but they both knew that the sound, before it had vanished, had been distant.

"They'll start it up again," Julia said. They listened, waiting. "I'm getting cold. It's cold out here."

"Can you call that guy? With the boat?"

"Dan?" Julia said. "Do you think I should?"

They listened, listened, listened for the engine.

"Let's get flashlights and go down to the dock," Wendell said. "Let's try to hail them. They may be fine. They may have turned off the engine and are just talking."

Why, thought Julia, standing up, *would they do that?* Turn off the engine and drift in the dark? If the engine had merely quit, they might be able to get it started again. But if they'd run out of gas, then they were drifting with the tide, out into open water, in a small boat. *The cold green swell*. She felt it in her chest, she would not let herself think about the cold green swell.

She and Wendell would walk down to the dock with flashlights. They would call out, and the boys would answer, explain. They would make this into nothing. Instead of calling Dan, the Coast Guard. *They were idiots, her sons. Jack was an idiot, an idiot.*

The grass was drenched with dew. Julia felt the damp soaking through her jeans. They each held flashlights. Julia went first, but out of courtesy she'd given Wendell the new one, the one she'd bought after her father's complaint. His was the stronger light, so they moved slowly, Julia squinting at her own faint colorless beam that barely lit the trampled path.

Down at the dock the water lapped quietly against the wooden pilings. Their footsteps were hollow; beneath the planks were waves. They could hear the night now, the soft sound of quiet sea, the faint movement of the breeze. It was silent. There was no sound of an engine.

They stood on the edge of the dock and swept their flashlight beams into the darkness. There was no moon, and the shafts moved back and forth in the dimness, lighting the flat colorless sea before them. There was nothing there. Blackness pressed in on them.

They took turns calling, they called in unison. They cupped their hands around their mouths. Their voices went out into the darkness. They called, and then they paused to listen. Julia closed her eyes, to hear better. Below them, the water mouthed the dock, lapping against the posts. The sea was quiet. There was the rope, the discarded bowline, tossed in a careless scribble onto the damp planks.

"Those idiots," Julia said.

"They know better than this," Wendell said.

"That stupid Whaler," Julia said. "It needs a new ignition." How could she not have gotten a new ignition? The shifting cold green swell, rising, sinking away, translucent. Drifting bits of pale spume dissolving into the wave. Her breath shortened.

They listened, they listened. They stood facing the night, focused and intent. They listened. The dark sea stretched out beyond them.

"What's the tide?" Wendell asked.

"High around eight. It's going out. What time is it now?"

"Nearly eleven. They've been gone almost forty minutes. Those jackasses," Wendell said angrily. "Steven! Jack!" he bellowed.

They were silent.

"Listen!" Julia said, though they were already listening. "Isn't that something?"

There was something faint, a wisp of sound. A response. Was there? Had they heard it? Did it come again?

"Jack!" she shouted. Her voice was becoming hoarse.

Nothing. No sound.

"We have to do something," she said. "They can't have meant to turn off the engine, way out there. We can't go on thinking they're fine. The engine's quit, or they're out of gas. They're in trouble."

Wendell did not answer. He stood peering out, the strong beam of his flashlight sweeping back and forth.

"Wendell," Julia said.

"All right," he said, and at the words fear swept through Julia, cold and swift.

Back inside, they stood by the phone. Julia's jeans were soaked from the grass, and she was shivering. Her legs were trembling, tremors rippling up her body.

She dialed Dan's number.

"Dan? It's Julia Lambert," she said. "From next door."

"Julia," said Dan.

"We've got a problem," she said. "Jack and Steven went out in the Whaler forty minutes ago, without a light. We can't hear the engine anymore, we think it's stopped."

"I'll pick you up at your dock," Dan said.

"Wendell's here, too," Julia said. "We'll bring flashlights. Should we call anyone else? Should we call the Coast Guard?"

There was a pause.

"How long did you say?" Dan asked.

"Nearly an hour, now."

"I'd think so," said Dan.

It was bad, then. Julia thought of the big Coast Guard vessels, their high imperious hulls, their gigantic engines and churning wakes, their stony-faced crews.

"We'll call and come down to the dock."

"Bring blankets," said Dan, and hung up.

"You call the Coast Guard." Julia handed the phone to Wendell. "I'll get blankets and coffee."

The phone was answered on the first ring.

"U.S. Coast Guard," a man said. "Is this an emergency?"

"Yes," said Wendell.

"Can you identify the situation for me, sir?" The voice was clear and crisp.

"My two sons are out in a Boston Whaler," said Wendell. "We think they're in trouble."

"How long have they been gone?"

"Nearly an hour."

"Can you give me your location?"

"We're just south of Symington. Peterman's Cove, near Halsey Point. They left from our dock, on the west side of the cove."

"Size of vessel?"

"Twelve feet long."

"Occupants?"

"Two young men."

"Ages?"

"Twenty-two and twenty-four."

"Clothing?"

"Jeans and sweaters," Wendell said.

"Emergency equipment? All vessels are required to carry flares."

"I don't know," Wendell said. "It's not my boat."

"In your understanding, what is the problem?"

"I'm not sure," Wendell said. "I'm afraid the engine has quit, or that they've run out of gas. We thought we heard the engine stop. I'm afraid they're drifting out to sea."

"What other local capability is there? Is there a marina nearby? Any local official boats? Police? Fire?"

"We've called a neighbor, Dan Ellsworth. He's taking us out in his Whaler to search."

"Can I ask you to stand by for a second, sir?"

"Of course," Wendell said.

The line went mute, silenced, though not dead. Behind the curtain of silence, procedures were being carried out. Wendell waited. The seconds ticked away.

"Hello?"

"I'm here," said Wendell.

"Okay, sir, we're going to issue a Safety Marine Information Broadcast. This will inform all local vessels about the situation and ask them to identify themselves, give their locations, and tell us if they can help. We'll deploy the available local assistance and see if they can locate the vessel. We will be monitoring the situation. If the vessel has not been found before 1:00 a.m., call us then."

"Right," Wendell said, "okay."

"If you do find the vessel, call us immediately."

"Right," Wendell said again, nodding. "Right."

Julia and Wendell, wearing slickers, waited for Dan on the dock. They carried blankets, flashlights, a thermos. They heard Dan's boat approaching, a steady liquid chug. A narrow beam of light cut through the dimness. The Whaler neared and the engine gulped, swallowed, then idled loudly.

Dan stood at the helm in the stern. His slicker glistened in the beams of their flashlights. He brought the Whaler alongside the dock and nodded greetings. "Climb aboard."

Dan was solid, not tall, with a square face and blue eyes. His thick eyebrows glinted with sea mist. His skin was ruddy and weathered, his cheeks faintly pocked. He moved with authority.

Wendell steadied the boat for Julia, then climbed in after her. Dan shifted the tiller and the boat moved off, the mounted spotlight sending a shaft of light out across the dark water.

"Call the Coast Guard?" Dan glanced at Julia.

"I did," Wendell sat balanced on the gunwale.

"What'd they say?" asked Dan.

"They didn't seem to think it was an emergency. They asked about local assistance and I told them about you. They're putting out some kind of broadcast, telling all the boats in the area."

"They're not sending someone out now," Dan said.

"No."

"It's their policy. They don't go out for people out of gas."

"And what happens to them?" Wendell asked.

"The Coast Guard is fed up with tourists who don't check the gas tanks before they go out," Julia explained.

"So you die of exposure?" asked Wendell. "Or how are you meant to get back?"

"The community is meant to look after its own," Julia said. "That takes the burden off the Coast Guard. And it means you have to deal with your neighbors if you keep running out of gas." She felt protective of the Coast Guard. It was like God—someday you would need it, and then it would save your life. You didn't mock it. And she didn't want Wendell to alienate Dan.

Wendell turned, looking ahead into the gloom. Julia sat across from him. The boat moved steadily across the water. The wind was freshening, and they were heading into the chop. Each small wave slapped against the bow.

"How are we going to go?" Julia asked Dan. "Just in circles?"

"Head to the mouth of the cove first," Dan said. "Make a few loops there. We don't find them, we'll head out to open water and start making squares, east to west."

The idiots, thought Julia. *Idiots.*

The chop was getting heavier, the waves smacked against the bow.

FIFTEEN

Steven sat in the bottom of the boat, leaning on the stern seat, his spine grating against its narrow edge. A thin film of cold sloshing water was seeping into his jeans. They were outside the cove now, beyond the protection of the point. Out in open water, and the wind coming up. The waves were bigger, the chop stronger, and the boat was beginning to toss. It was safer to stay down: a big wave, coming up unseen, could take you overboard in seconds.

The tide was still pulling them out, toward the sea and into the dense tangle of local coastal currents. One of these, strong and fast and unpredictable, could take them anywhere: far out to sea, or slamming onto a rocky headland, or, miraculously, drifting quietly into the shore in a quiet bay.

The Whaler was a light craft, twelve feet long, made for short trips in calm waters. The gas tank was empty, and without the engine there was no way to steer. For some reason there was only one life jacket, on which Steven was sitting. They had not brought the oars.

Jack sat on the middle seat, leaning forward, his legs apart. His elbows were on his knees, his head in his hands. His body seemed loose and unstable, swaying and shifting with the Whaler's movement. The boat slopped roughly in the chop.

"You okay?" Steven asked. In the darkness he could see only his brother's silhouette.

Jack did not answer.

Steven raised his voice. "You okay?"

"No," Jack said, without lifting his head. "I feel like shit."

"What's the matter?"

"You wouldn't understand."

"Try me," Steven said.

"I'm coming down," Jack said, without moving. "Jonesing."

There was a pause. The boat rose sideways, rocked down.

"What's it feel like?" Steven asked.

"Like fucking hell. My skin is on fire, I want to scratch my whole skin off. My head feels like someone set off a bomb in it, and I want to throw up. I wanted to throw up all evening."

"So it was a really good idea to take the boat out."

Jack did not answer.

The damp sea air wrapped closely around them, black and endless. The boat rocked, slapped by the waves. Above them was a sudden smooth flapping sound, rhythmic and steady. Muffled wings: a seabird was passing overhead. The shifting pinions sounded a faint unearthly chord with each beat, like the shadow of music. In seconds it was gone, unseen.

"Okay, so maybe it wasn't such a good idea to take the boat out," Jack said, his head still down. "So what?"

"So here we are being carried out to sea in the dark," Steven said, angry. "I'd actually just as soon be back at the house."

Jack shook his head without raising it. He spoke slowly and with effort. "I don't give a fuck where you'd actually just as soon be. I'd just as soon be dead."

"What were you planning?" Steven allowed his voice to become insulting. "You thought you'd come out here in the boat to get off heroin?"

There was the word. He had said it without thinking. It hung in the air now, electric.

"I wasn't planning anything," Jack said, his voice muffled. "How do I know what I thought? I thought maybe we could head for a marina."

"A marina? There isn't a marina for fifteen miles. What are you talking about?"

Jack lifted his head. "I don't know what I was doing. I was going to get away from Julia and Wendell being assholes. I couldn't use the car, Julia had the keys."

There was another pause, then a wet smack against the bow. Rudderless, the boat rocked in every direction, without rhythm.

"Here, put on the life jacket." Steven pulled it from beneath himself and held it out to his brother. "You're up higher than I am."

Jack shook his head.

"Take it," Steven said, his voice rising.

Jack did not move.

Steven felt a sudden rush of fury rise up in his chest, fury at Jack for getting them into this: the small open boat, the open water, night. Drifting on the outgoing tide, lost at sea. They could capsize easily, in an instant, they could die. All of it Jack's fault. Selfish, reckless, crazed: he was putting their lives at risk, for no reason, for nothing. An addict. Fury suffused him.

And beneath the fury Steven was choked by pity and fear for his brother, sitting like a deadweight, his body swaying alarmingly with the rocking waves, his head in his hands, his body racked by mutinous turmoil. His brother had become altered. His life had been somehow taken over. Some aspect of him had been lost to Steven.

Steven rose to a crouch. Carrying the life jacket, he moved over to Jack, staying low.

"Here," Steven said. "Put it on." It was a bright orange vest made of flat linked panels. Straps and buckles dangled off the front. He pushed it against Jack's shoulder. "Here."

Jack said nothing, his face still buried in his hands.

Steven pushed harder. *"Here."* He was angry again: it wasn't enough that Jack was putting them both at risk, he wouldn't even accept the small measure of protection they did have. *"Here."*

Without raising his head, Jack swung his arm out in a loose, hard, back-handed blow that knocked the jacket from Steven's hands. Steven grabbed for it, his hand clutching; he clutched air, grabbed again, he felt the damp fabric against his fingertips, felt it slip away. The jacket hit the water with a soft, dead splash. Steven lunged against the edge of the boat, grabbing for it again, the water cold on his hand. The jacket bobbed just out of reach. Phosphorescent, pale and glimmering against the dark water, it drifted lightly just beyond his fingers, half-submerged, the straps trailing.

"You asshole," Steven said, pushing himself up against the edge of the boat. "You fucking asshole."

Jack said nothing, his face still hidden.

"Why'd you do this?" Steven said. "Look at us," he said. "We're in an open boat headed for the middle of the fucking *ocean,* because you have to get hooked on heroin. You *ass.* We may both die because of this."

"You have no idea," Jack said thickly, "how good that would be."

"Shut up!" Steven said. "You may want to die, but I don't! I don't care if you want to die! You complete asshole!" He was shouting now, shouting at Jack's lowered head, inches away.

Jack turned his head slowly, laying it sideways on his knees, so that he faced away from Steven.

"Don't just turn your head away," Steven shouted. *"Listen to me."*

"I won't listen to you," Jack said, his voice gravelly. "I can barely hear you. I don't give a shit what you say."

"You have to listen to me," Steven said. "I'm going to make you listen to me. You've screwed everything up. You got us both out here in this boat in the dark, *Christ.*" Steven shook his head, furious. The boat was rocking now, sliding up and down each wave, bullied by the oncoming wind.

"Yeah, well, you're the one who ran us out of gas," Jack said. He was speaking into the wind, his voice faint. "You took the boat out last."

"Well, you're supposed to check the gas before you take it out," said Steven. "If you'd done that, we wouldn't be in this mess."

"Well," Jack said slowly, his voice hollow, "if you'd filled the tank after you used it, we wouldn't be in this mess either."

"*You asshole*," Steven said. "Don't blame this on me. We're out here because you don't have any sense. We're out here because you're a heroin addict. *You're a fucking junkie.*"

Steven felt as though the words had blown him apart from his brother. He felt swollen and gigantic, enraged.

Jack said nothing.

"*What's the matter with you!*" Steven was now shouting. "*Why do you do this! Why do you always screw up? You've been screwing up your whole life. All you do is piss people off! Why do you do it? You asshole! You complete asshole! You flunk out of school, you lose the job, you smash the car—what's the matter with you?*"

He waited, furious, crouching low, close by his brother. Jack's body was tense, frozen.

"That's the question, isn't it," Jack said, his voice muffled. "Same old, same old."

"You complete fool! You fool! *What are you doing?* You're going to kill yourself like this." Steven's throat was thick.

Jack said nothing.

"You know what? You're going to die."

With difficulty, Jack answered. "You, too."

"Don't be a fucking smartass!" Steven told him. "You're acting like a lunatic. Christ! We're out in an open boat and you just threw the only life jacket overboard."

"I did?" Jack lifted his head, confused.

"You did!" Steven said. "It's gone! It's gone! Why do you think I'm so fucking mad? You're an asshole, a complete fuckup."

"Sorry," Jack said, squinting. "Why didn't you put it on?"

"Because you're the one sitting high up here on the seat, asshole,"

Steven said. "And because you're the one who's sick. You should have put it on. At least one of us could have worn it." He made his way, crouching, back to the stern. "Christ." He sat down again, settling into the thin film of sloshing water. The bilgewater was now deepening with the slapping waves, cold each time it washed against him.

"Sorry," Jack said. "I didn't know I'd done it. I didn't mean to."

He did not sound contrite but preoccupied, as though something were taking him over. He lowered his head again into his hands and made a slow, horrible retching noise. It sounded deep and inhuman.

"Throw up into the boat," Steven said unkindly. "If you lean overboard in these seas you'll fall out."

Jack did not answer. He retched again, deeply and lengthily. His body heaved as though something inside him were trying to get out.

Steven looked away, then, unwillingly, back at his brother.

Jack put his head lower, between his knees. He began to vomit, his body convulsing with each heave. Each contortion seemed terminal, as though it were dragging the last of something out from the interior. He made guttural sounds. The smell was vile.

Steven watched his brother's body as it shuddered and clenched. Between heaves, Jack went limp, his limbs drooping, head hanging between his knees. He breathed loudly. The boat tossed without rhythm, slapped randomly by the waves. Jack swayed unsteadily. He made a moaning noise.

Steven wondered if Jack were in any danger. The vomiting seemed extreme, violent. Did that mean something? How did you know if it were projectile? What did you do if it were? Steven had nothing to offer him, no water, no heat, no blanket. Could you die from heroin withdrawal? What would happen? Fever, nausea, aches, dizziness—the body in protest. Was it serious?

The vomit lay in loose drifts on the bottom of the boat, dissolving into the briny water. Jack retched again and again, his body contorting horribly with each surge, though after a time nothing more came out. Then it seemed worse, the body in useless spasm, heaving emptily.

Steven's jeans were now completely soaked. Sitting in cold seawater was tolerable; sitting in seawater mixed with vomit might not be. It might now be worth the risk of moving up onto the seat. Though it would be stupid to go overboard because he didn't want to get vomit on his jeans.

He wondered what his parents were doing, how long they'd wait before making the call. Making the call meant things were really bad; they'd postpone it. They'd keep hoping to hear the sound of the Whaler coming back in to the dock. He wondered who they'd call. Probably that guy down the cove first. Maybe the Coast Guard. Something would be done, people would set out in boats to find them. There would be lights sweeping back and forth through the darkness, there would be the loud blast of foghorn signals. There would be voices, shouts carrying across the waves. He thought of how they would sound.

He imagined them shouting names—*Steven! Jack!* Or maybe it would be more impersonal, generic. *Hello!* If it were not his parents, probably the voice would be calling "Hello-o-o," long and slow. He imagined the way it would sound. He heard the calls in his mind. *Hello-o-o-o.* All he actually heard was the noise of the waves sloshing against the boat— uneven, repetitive—and the wind.

The ocean, the night, had spread out around them. It seemed they were nowhere, now, and nothing: a drifting spar. He felt lost, unloosed from the world. Wherever you were was at the center of things; you were at the heart of your own universe. Other people came into view, but you, your consciousness, was the center. Now, in this endless featureless drift, Steven was not at the center of anything. It felt alarming, vertiginous, as though he were sliding over the edge. He imagined the boat seen from above, seen from the air, tiny, rocking aimlessly, lost, nothing. They were lost in the world. They were no longer within the comforting curve of their own cove, they were probably not even near the familiar jagged line of local coast. Now they were anywhere, nowhere, out of sight of land, the boat shifting unevenly, tossing in the tide and the crisscrossing currents.

The wind seemed to be rising, and the sound of it was a kind of whistling across the water. Steven's legs began to tremble with cold.

Jack was motionless, leaning over, his arms wrapped tightly around himself, his head on his knees.

Dan stood with one hand on the tiller, legs apart, braced against the rocking of the Whaler. The spotlight tossed with the motion of the boat, its beam rocking skyward with each wave. Wendell and Julia sat on the gunwales, across from each other. They faced the bow, pointing their flashlights forward, scanning the water ahead. Their slickers were wet from sea mist. A pile of life jackets lay in the bottom of the boat.

"How far have we gone?" Wendell asked.

Dan spoke without looking at him. "We've left the cove. We're in open water, heading west. We're parallel to the shore. We'll go west for two minutes, then south, then east, then north. Making squares, like a grid."

The compass was mounted beside the spotlight, and Dan glanced at it every few moments. The boat slapped steadily against the waves. The wind was against the tide, raising rough little peaks.

Julia leaned forward. Her flashlight was barely functional, the beam gray and indistinct against the shifting seas. She stared hard into the darkness, visualizing the boys, preparing her eyes to see them, as though the imagined sight might conjure up the real one.

She imagined the boat appearing in the weak beam of her light, rising up suddenly on the crest of a wave, broadside to them. She imagined seeing it from behind; she imagined both boys turning, waving, shouting, their voices distant, fragmented by the wind. She imagined the pale glimmering life jackets over their dark sweaters.

With each shift of the water, with each tilt and change in the liquid kaleidoscope of the ocean landscape, she could see the boys, the boat, for a moment in the new picture. Then, reading it more carefully, she lost them. The waves shifted, peaked, lifted, fell, empty. There was no glimpse of orange, no color at all. The sea was gray, the sky black and impenetrable.

The engine changed. Dan was throttling back, the boat slowed. Julia looked at him hopefully. He'd turned his head to the left, but there was no urgency in his gaze. She saw he was merely making the turn, starting the square. Nothing else.

Dan leaned down and picked up a life jacket. He tossed it to Julia.

"Getting rough," he said. "Better put it on." He tossed another to Wendell and strapped one on himself.

Julia caught it, fingers stiff with cold. She put her arms clumsily through the armholes, pulled the straps taut, and struggled with the narrow buckles. She turned back to the waves, staring out along the weak beam of her flashlight. What was that? There was something—wasn't there?—on top of a wave, vanishing, then appearing again? The water shifted constantly, she lost it, then thought she found it—though was it anything? Or was it just a pallid line of foam along the crest of a wave? She strained to see it in the dim light. It was something.

"What's that?" she said, pointing.

Wendell turned his beam on it. They all saw it now, small and pale, riding the edge of a wave.

"A life jacket," Wendell said.

No one else spoke. Dan turned the boat, and they headed over. Julia leaned over the side, ready to grab it; it drifted, rocking, alongside. As it neared she saw a name in big block letters across the back: LAMBERT. Magic Marker, her own hand. She felt sickened. She grabbed it, the water bitingly cold. She pulled it into the boat and shook her hand hard, flinging off the icy drops.

"Well," she said. "I wonder what . . ." She stopped.

She could think of nothing good that it might mean. She felt her chest tighten and took a shallow breath. *It could be something simple,* she told herself, *it could mean nothing.* Fear rose in her. *How could it mean nothing?* She thought of the boat overturned among the waves, the life jacket drifting out of reach, chilled hands reaching for it. The cold green swell. *She would not think this.* She would not allow these images in her mind. Thinking them would make them possible. She would keep them from her mind. She would not allow panic to enter into her.

She took a long breath, filling her lungs, to calm herself. She looked at Dan. He was frowning, staring straight ahead. He'd corrected the course, veering back to the invisible square.

This was the way it would go, Julia told herself. Dan would do it. They'd chug steadily along in these slow methodical squares. They'd cover the territory. They'd find the boys. The life jacket meant the boys were somewhere near. Didn't it? Or would the life jacket drift through the waves at a different rate of speed, in a different direction for some reason? It was like a math problem: *If two boys in an open boat . . .*

The description, the words "two boys in an open boat" frightened her again. Panic rose up in her throat, she fought to keep it down. Why wasn't one of her sons wearing the life jacket? Which one did not?

She would not let herself think that.

She would hold the thought of them in her mind: safe, sitting in the boat. That was the image. They were sitting in the boat, rocking silently, waiting to be found. Her two sons were warm and alive. They were carrying within them the sum of their lives, their bright potentials, the long hopeful reach of their futures. They were safe, their hearts were beating, they were alive. They were cold, wet, angry, maybe frightened, but they were alive. Julia held tightly to that image. She pictured them: Steven, sitting for some reason on the bottom of the boat, in the stern, Jack on the middle seat, head in his hands. They sat rocking in the boat, in the dark. Waiting to be found. Alive.

Dan had turned the boat back again, watching the compass, making the last side of the square.

SIXTEEN

"What's that?" said Wendell. He straightened, squinting intently.

Julia stared where he pointed; she saw nothing but shifting water. "Where?" she asked.

Dan said nothing. He looked ahead, down to the compass, back up again. The flashlight beams swept back and forth across the waves.

Finally Wendell spoke again. "It's nothing," he announced. "I'm seeing things." He frowned and shook his head. "Can't we go any faster?" He looked at Dan.

Dan's gaze shifted to him, then back to the water ahead. The sea mist was thickening, and he had pulled up the hood of his slicker. The spotlight below gave off a dim aura of ambient light, but his face, in the shadow, was nearly hidden.

Julia heard Wendell draw in his breath to speak again.

Don't, don't. This was not the moment for Dan to turn taciturn, Wendell offended. She turned, looking out into the dark waves. Everything was going wrong, getting worse. Her stomach was knotted and tight. *And where were they, her sons? Where were those beautiful smooth-skinned boys, her darlings, somewhere out on this tossing sea?*

The boat was pitching now, forward and back. The wind was rising, she could no longer pretend it was not rising. Dan held course, glancing down at the compass, back up at the waves ahead. Julia set her hand on the gunwale, to hold on. She could see nothing.

Wendell spoke again. "Sorry. I don't mean to make suggestions. I can see we're not going any faster, but could you explain why?"

"Two reasons," Dan said. "One, it's dangerous. These waves are too big to move through fast. Two, we're making a grid. The size of these squares lets us look at the whole area at this speed. If we go faster, we might miss your boat."

Wendell nodded. "Thanks."

He frowned. The muscles jumped at the corner of his jaw. *He has nothing to offer here, there's no contribution he can make,* thought Julia, *he could only stare into the waves while another man took charge.* She felt, unexpectedly, a wave of sympathy. Wendell was out of his depth. They both were. There was nothing they could do. They were in Dan's hands, or God's, or whoever was in charge.

Dear God, Julia thought suddenly, surprising herself: it was what her mother used to say. *Was it cheating, to call on God if you weren't sure you believed in one?* Might you somehow be punished for it, your wishes deliberately unfulfilled? But if there were a God, surely it would be a merciful one, not petty and punitive. Surely it couldn't hurt to call on God in distress. *Dear God,* she thought again.

Again Julia pictured her sons silhouetted against the night, the two of them still and mute in the rocking boat, taken over by the silent watchfulness that comes with fear. She saw their figures dark, now, without life jackets. She saw their boat rising rapidly upward, then plunging vertiginously down, into the trough, as a big wave passed beneath them. *It's all right,* she told herself. *They're in the boat, they're safe.* She held to this thought, the image of the boat, steadily rising and falling.

"What's that?" Wendell said again, his voice urgent, pointing with the long beam of his flashlight. All of them stared into the darkness. A long minute passed. Julia squinted hard out at the water.

"Nothing, I guess," Wendell said, reluctantly. "Sorry."

Again Julia felt sympathy: Wendell was desperate. They both were. *How was this happening? How could their sons be out there in the night, lost, floating in darkness?* An hour ago they had all been together, all of them safe, their lives not at risk. They'd been sitting on the porch, doing something that had then seemed violent and dangerous, explosive—arguing with Jack about drugs—something which now seemed unthinkably simple, so innocent, so safe. If only they were still sitting on the porch now, arguing violently, angrily, about drugs. How had this change taken place? Now death was hovering over them in the darkness. They still seemed so close, those earlier hours, it seemed as though it would still be possible somehow to correct their course, now that they knew that this was not the way they'd wished to go. As if they could will things to spool backward, for the night to reverse itself, just briefly, so they could find themselves sitting again on the porch, arguing, and then not let Jack stride off into the darkness.

Anger was nothing, it was the littlest thing. They could all be still sitting together, angry over something tiny and insignificant. Heroin addiction, something like that, anything at all. If only they were on the porch again, if only heroin addiction were the problem now, something they could solve.

Julia shifted on the hard seat. Her right arm was tired, and she put the flashlight in her left hand, scanning the waves awkwardly. Something in the gloom caught her eye. Something glimmered just beyond her range, there was some flicker of reflection from a hard surface—wasn't there?—something solid, something besides the restless liquid surge. She shone her light back and forth where she thought she'd seen it, scribbling with the dim shaft of light. She saw it again—didn't she? She didn't want to say *What's that*, like Wendell, when twice it had been nothing. But there was something there. Again she saw something hard and solid, reflective; then it was gone, obscured by a wave.

"There," she said, pointing.

Wendell turned his beam, and Dan looked. Nothing now.

"I'm sure I saw something," Julia said.

They all peered. There was nothing but plunging waves. Wendell's strong beam swept back and forth across them.

"Boys!" Julia shouted. "Jack! Steven! Hello!" Her voice was lifted by the wind, taken into the dark salt air.

"Hello!" shouted Wendell.

They listened.

"Would we hear them, with the engine on?" Julia asked no one. No one answered. She raised her voice again. "Hello!" It was a strange word to use, but it seemed the call ought to be public, impersonal. "Hello!" she shouted again, stretching it out.

She listened. The boat was tossing now, the waves were heaving it up and down in long rolling plunges. She had heard something, she thought she had heard something. She looked at Wendell. "Did you hear that?"

Wendell stared at her intently.

There was something, some faint noise, over the engine. Wasn't there? She looked at Dan. He had heard it. He was turning the boat. The rising waves had lifted the horizon, so they could not see far ahead. White foam frothed against their bow. A wave broke on it, and water raced in a smooth cold surge down the bottom of the boat. Julia held the gunwale with both hands.

"Boys!" she shouted. "Hello!"

Now they all heard it: something human, some kind of response, high and distant. Brief. Then it came again. Wendell stood up. Dan held the tiller steady. The waves broke over and over against the bow.

"Hello!" Julia called again.

When they saw the boat, it was surprisingly close, sliding down the side of a wave. The Whaler's white sides shone luminous in the beams of light. The two boys were seated and motionless. It was the image she'd been holding in her mind—the white boat, pitching and plunging in the waves, the two figures. They were both facing Dan's boat, and now they were waving. Everyone was shouting, both of the boys, and Wendell was shouting, too, as though this thread of contact must be maintained as they made their way through the water.

. As they drew closer, she could see the boys' faces, lit by the thin beams of light. They looked drained and ghastly, their eyes huge and black. Jack sat on the middle seat, holding on to the thwart with both hands, his face white and pinched. Steven was in the stern. The night was black around them. They looked like figures in a dream, caught suddenly by the eerie beams of light, surrounded by the immensity of the night.

"Hello!" called Steven, as they drew close.

"We're here!" Julia called back inanely. Their boat rocked and dropped.

Dan steered alongside, the engine now loud, nearly idling. The water was too rough for the boys to board their boat. Dan threw a coiled line toward the Whaler, its loops unraveling in the air. Steven caught it. The heaving waves threw the two boats together and away, together and away. Steven cleated the line quickly, held up his hands to show he was done. Jack watched without moving. He was hunched over miserably, his arms wrapped around himself. *He must be cold*, Julia thought, *he must be freezing.*

"Here," called Julia. She threw over two life jackets, wheeling them across the water to Steven.

"Thanks," Steven said. He put one on and handed one to Jack. Jack looked at it.

"Put it on," Steven said to him. Jack did not move.

Steven turned back to the other boat. Dan steered in a slow half-circle, his eyes on the compass. As his boat took on the weight of the boys' Whaler, the drone of the engine changed, and they felt the drag.

They got under way, heading back through the jostling waves. Julia watched the boys. There it was, the sight she'd made up in her head. They were sitting in the boat, drenched with spray and mist, cold, silent, alive. *They were alive.* She could not take her eyes from them. Each time a wave rose between them she lost them from sight, they were taken again by the night and the water. She held her gaze where they had last been, and miraculously now they reappeared. The rope between the two boats cut steadily through the shifting water, rising, dripping, from a wave; going suddenly slack as a wave slid the two boats closer, then tightening again as another wave flung them apart.

Once they were inside the cove, the water quieted, the waves flattened to a mild shifting moil. The engine pitch changed again, rising slightly, and they moved faster. Now they could see lights on shore, lights from their own house.

Alongside their dock the water was flat. Dan slowed the boat to a guttural idle. Julia climbed out first, stiff from the cold. Steven jumped onto the dock to fend off, holding the two boats apart with his foot. He uncleated Dan's line and threw it to him. He made their own line fast to the dock, then leaned down, into Dan's boat.

"Thanks," Steven said, holding out his hand.

Dan shook it, his face breaking into a small smile. "You're welcome. Glad you're back."

"I was glad to see you out there," Steven said.

Dan blinked kindly, nodding. "Know what it's like." The others called thanks and he lifted his hand, giving them all a small courteous salute, already shifting gears. The engine sound changed, and the boat began to move slowly away from the dock, out into the water. The spotlight cut into the translucent sheen of the night, heading deeper into the cove. Within moments they could not see the boat, only the cone of light moving off into the darkness.

SEVENTEEN

Jack was still sitting in the Whaler, hunched over, his arms wrapped around himself. Julia leaned down toward him. "What's the matter, Jackie?"

Jack was silent.

"Jack?" Wendell said.

After a moment Steven said, "He's feeling sick."

"Sick?" Wendell said.

"He was throwing up," Steven said, his voice neutral. "The boat is full of vomit."

Julia wondered what this meant. *Was it to do with drugs? Did everything now have to do with drugs? Or had Jack simply been seasick, tossing on the nighttime seas?*

She leaned in. The boat reeked, the smell of salt and vomit were mixed horridly together. She shone her flashlight on the hunched figure. Jack did not look up.

Julia crouched down. "Jacko, you're home. Time to come in." It was what she'd used to say when the boys were little, when they'd gone to sleep in the car on the way home from the movies. "You're home."

Jack shook his head quickly and oddly. His shoulder jerked.

"Come on," she said again. "Time to come in."

Now Jack looked up, into the circle of light. He was shivering, his whole body twitching. His face was pale and glistening from the damp. His skin looked stretched and taut. There was a smeared residue around his mouth, his cheeks, his chin. The smell was very bad.

Jack stared at her for a moment, then stood unsteadily. Julia put her hand out and he seized her forearm, stepping awkwardly onto the dock.

"There," she said. "Let's go up."

She held on to his arm. Jack walked slowly and with difficulty. Behind them were Wendell and Steven with the blankets and thermoses. No one spoke. The grass was dense with dew. The flashlight beams drifted along the path.

Julia opened the back door: the kitchen was miraculously light and warm, another world. Here it was dry, stable, safe. Steven and Jack came in behind her, damp and shivering.

"You need hot showers," Julia said.

"Yeah," Steven said.

Jack said nothing, and Julia patted his sleeve. "Jackie?"

He jerked his arm from her.

"Come on," she said. "You're like ice."

"*Don't paw me,*" he said, moving away.

"Jack," Julia said.

In the light he looked much worse. His face was pale and drawn, shining with moisture. His eyes were like black holes, deep circles beneath them. His cheek twitched suddenly, he raised his hand to cover it.

"What is it? What's the matter?"

"I feel really shitty," Jack said.

"You're chilled." Julia came closer. She put her hands on his chest, on the sodden sweater, and felt him shiver. "You need a hot shower. Maybe a bath."

Jack shook his head quickly. "Get off."

Julia pulled his arm. "Come on. I want you both upstairs. You're like ice."

"*Christ!*" Jack said. He ripped his arm away from her. "Don't touch me! *Leave me alone.* I don't want a shower."

He stared at her, his eyes black and furious. Now the pupils seemed enormous, limitless.

Julia stood motionless. Her hand, shaken off, hung in midair. She felt a tightening in her scalp.

"What's the matter?" Wendell asked. "What's going on?"

Jack shook his head. "Leave me alone," he said, frowning, his face twitching. He scratched violently at his neck.

"No one's touching you," Wendell said reasonably. "But you're cold and wet. You need to dry off and warm up."

Jack stared at him. "What do you mean I'm cold and wet?"

There was a pause.

"Jackie, you're drenched. You've been out in the boat for hours," Julia said coaxingly.

"What the fuck are you talking about?" Jack asked, furious.

There was a pause.

It was possible that they were right. He did now remember the boat, the waves, the endless slosh and chop out on the black water. He actually was cold, if he thought about it, but there were other things that had his attention: his leg, the twitch that caught him in his calf, the clenching grip that seized his leg as though a giant took it in his hand and squeezed it unbearably.

He kicked his leg violently, as though he could shake the giant's hand loose; he kicked again, kicked. His face kept twitching, he felt his cheek leap under the skin.

"What is it, Jackie?" asked Julia. "What's the matter?"

Jack shook his head. His stomach was roiling, at any moment he might retch again, though there was nothing left to heave; he was empty, raw.

"Wendell, there's something wrong with him," Julia said. "Jackie, tell us what's wrong."

"I feel shitty," Jack said, croaking. "I'm in pain. All over."

"What is it?" Julia put her hand on his brow. "You're clammy and sweating. Do you think you have a fever?"

"I need something for the pain," Jack said.

"What pain? Where do you have the pain, Jackie?" Julia asked. "You're trembling."

Jack grimaced and rubbed at his stomach. "Here." He doubled over. "My legs. All over. I hurt everywhere."

"I don't think we have anything for your stomach," Julia said.

"I hurt everywhere! Christ! I just need something for the pain!"

Julia looked at Wendell.

"Okay, Jack," Wendell said. "We'll get you something. You go get cleaned up. I'll call."

"Something strong," Jack said, his face twisted. "Vicodin, or Percoset." He expelled a long painful breath.

Wendell nodded. "I hear you. Now go up and get dry."

Steven put his hand on Jack's arm. "Come on, bro. We're both soaked."

Jack yanked away. "Get off." He stood, swaying.

Steven raised his hands. "Fine," he said, "I won't touch you." He left. After a moment, Jack followed. He walked slowly and painfully, bent over.

Julia and Wendell looked at each other.

"What should we do?" Julia asked.

"I'm calling 911," Wendell said. "Something's really wrong. He's in withdrawal or something. I don't know what that means. If it's dangerous."

"It might just be flu," Julia argued. "Chills and shaking, aches and pains. And he's been seasick."

Wendell stared at her. "Julia, the reason I'm here is that *we think Jack is a heroin addict.* What's happening is part of that. He's acting irrational."

"But calling 911 is overreacting," Julia said. "He may just be overwrought."

"Overwrought from what?"

"Look what he's just been through!"

"What? Steven's just been through exactly the same thing, and he's not tearing anyone's arm from the socket."

"Jack isn't tearing anyone's arm from the socket, Wendell," said Julia angrily. "Don't exaggerate! Jack doesn't want to take a shower—big deal. We don't have to call the police."

"Don't minimize this, Julia," Wendell said. "Jack is acting crazy, and he's sick. He's having some sort of chemical reaction. We don't know how to deal with it. I'm calling 911."

He left the room.

After this there'd be no turning back. *Each moment drew them further into it. Here was the public declaration, the admission of shame.* She felt fear surround her, dark and breathing. She wanted to resist all of this, keep it away from her. *Damn Wendell,* she thought, *damn him.*

She began cleaning up, rinsing out the thermoses. On the windowsill stood the little spray of spotted feathers, still jaunty against the black pane. *The unbearable pathos of objects.* It was so strange that they all looked just as they had yesterday, though everything around them had been caught up in violent change. It was like a neutron bomb: a huge detonation, shattering all the humans but leaving the objects intact. *And how could it possibly still only be night? By now, after all this, it should at least be day. By now it should be tomorrow, or the day after.*

Overhead she heard the steady low drum of the shower: *Good,* she thought, *Steven's got him in.* She wanted Jack warm, dry, *normal,* not wet and miserable, his hair damped down, mouth smeared with vomit. Hostile and strange.

Checking on her parents, she stood outside their door, head bowed, listening: only the faint sound of deep, slow breaths. They'd slept through it all so far—the runaways, the rescue, the return. She hoped they would sleep through the next ghastly passage. Would there be a siren?

She felt her parents' presence like a steady wheel rolling quietly along beside this large uneven one that was Wendell and Jack and Steven and herself. Their own was taking on velocity, spinning faster and faster. She could hardly keep her parents' rolling steadily beside them, she could hardly pay attention to her parents at all. She had wanted, this week, to offer them some kind of respite—from everything, from their own aging, from the world outside, from all the vicissitudes of life—but she was not managing any of this. Instead, they were being drawn into this violent commotion that seemed increasingly powerful, about to engulf them all.

EIGHTEEN

There was no siren, only a firm knocking on the front door. Two police-men stood outside, their faces sober, their blue uniforms glittering with badges and insignia.

"Mr. Lambert?" The policeman was solid, with a smooth red face. "Officer Wood and Officer Powers, Hatchard Police Department. You're having a problem with your son?"

"That's right," Wendell said.

They came inside, filling the front hall.

"Tell us what the problem is," said Wood.

Wendell explained: the trip, the rescue, the agitation. "We think he's in withdrawal from heroin."

The word again. How could he use it in public?

Wood nodded. "Could you tell me your reasons for thinking this?"

"His lifestyle and general demeanor," Wendell said.

Julia admired the word "demeanor."

"Earlier this evening we asked him directly if he took heroin," said Wendell. "He got very angry. That's why he went out in the boat."

Wood nodded. "Did he admit to drug use?"

"No," Julia said. "This is speculation."

Both policemen looked at her.

"When we got home, he got more and more agitated," Wendell said again. "He didn't seem to remember he'd been out on the boat. He was angry and nearly violent and delusional."

"Well," Julia said, minimizing.

"He shouted at his mother and told her to keep her hands to herself," Wendell went on.

"He didn't hurt anyone," Julia said to Powers, "but he's violently ill. He has cramps and nausea. He's been vomiting."

"Where's your son now?" asked Wood.

"Upstairs, taking a shower."

"Does he know you've called Emergency Services?"

"He thinks we called a doctor. He wants something for pain."

"There's an ambulance outside," said Wood. "If your son needs medical attention, they'll take care of it."

There were footsteps upstairs. The shower had stopped.

"Let's give him a minute to get dressed," Julia said.

They stood in silence. Steven came downstairs, jogging easily until he saw the policemen. He stopped, then came down to stand in front of his father.

"I thought you were calling a doctor," he said.

"I called 911. This is who came. Where's Jack?" Wendell asked.

"Getting dressed," Steven said.

"Is he alone in his room?" Wood said. "Does he have any drugs up there?"

Wendell hesitated. "We don't know."

"We'll go up," Wood said.

"Let's give him another minute," Julia said, but the policemen were already moving past her.

Steven said to Wendell, "Why did you do this?"

"Because your brother's sick and acting crazy," Wendell said. "He's in withdrawal, and I don't know if he's in danger." He started after the policemen.

"But why did you lie about the doctor?" Steven asked, following his father. "Why did you lie to him?"

But Wendell, behind the policemen, had reached the second floor and didn't answer. Jack's door was open. He was now dressed, but still looked ill, hunched over, holding his belly. He straightened when he saw them.

"What the fuck is going on?" he said.

"Officer Wood, Hatchard Police," Wood said. "Your parents notified us of some disturbance."

"Get out of here!" Jack lunged for the door, slamming it shut.

Wood stepped next to the door. "Jack," he said, raising his voice, "your parents called us because you seemed disturbed and in pain. You want to talk about what's going on?"

"Get out of here," Jack called. "I don't know what the fuck my parents were talking about, but I want you to get out. And tell my parents to get away from me. They're trying to have me locked up."

Wendell moved forward. "We don't want you locked up, Jack," he said. "We're worried about you."

"Tell these cops to get out of here! I haven't done anything! I'm not going to jail!"

"You're not going to jail, Jack. All I'm asking you to do is calm down and come out," Wood said. "We can talk things over out here."

"I'm not talking. I'm not going to jail," Jack said again.

Wood spoke against the door. "You're not going to jail, Jack," he repeated. "We want to get you some help. There are some medical folks here who'll get you to a doctor if you'll come out."

There was silence.

"Jack," he said, "we'd like to get you to a hospital. Get you something for the pain."

Silence.

"Come on, Jack. I'm going to open the door now. We're going to get you some help."

Julia felt sick.

Wood opened the door quietly: it was unlocked.

Jack was crouching beneath the eaves, rifling through his duffel bag. Clothes littered the floor.

"Get out of here," he said weakly.

"Calm down, Jack," Wood said. "We're going to get you some help."

"Christ," Jack said. He dropped his head and stopped moving.

"Come on now, Jack," Powers said.

Jack looked up. He was sweating now, his face glistened. A wave of trembling passed through him. His teeth chattered, and he clenched his jaw to stop.

"I need something for the pain."

"I know that," Wood said. "We'll take you to a doctor."

"I don't want to see a doctor."

Wood shook his head. "Then you'll have to put up with the pain."

There was a long silence. Jack closed his eyes again. His whole body shook.

"Come on," Power said. "You need some help."

There was another silence. Jack stood slowly, meeting no one's eyes. Hunched and stiff, he walked over to the policemen.

"Good boy," Wood said. "We'll take you out to the ambulance."

"Get me out of here," Jack said. He didn't look at his parents. "I need something for this pain."

"Show us your arms," Steven said suddenly. He looked at the policemen. "Show us his arms. He wouldn't let us see them."

Wood glanced at Jack. "Jack? Okay if we show your arms?"

There was a pause, then Jack put out his arms, palms up. The policemen slid back his sleeves.

"Jesus," said Steven.

The inner forearms were like a battlefield, the skin red and inflamed. Bloody oozing scabs lay along the veins.

This was the silky, elastic skin of her child, that miraculous inner skin, so nacreous and fragile, which Julia had stroked and smoothed so many times. Here was the beloved body she had thought of as hers.

It had been pierced and invaded, over and over. Julia felt sickened. The air darkened, closing around her head. She put her hand against the wall, which seemed treacherously unstable. She lowered her head. Her knees buckled. The darkness rose up. She felt Wendell's grip on her arm, around her shoulders. She swayed, the blackness abated, she straightened.

"Jackie," she said.

"Get me out of here," Jack said, not looking at her.

It's all new then, she thought, dazed. *All new from here on. We haven't been here before.*

They stood at the front door as Jack went out with the policemen. Outside the front door were the medics, sunburnt men in yellow neon vests. They moved forward, around Jackie. Beyond the meadow, in the driveway, were the scarlet lights of the ambulance glowing in the darkness.

"Where will they take him?" Wendell asked Wood.

"Gaud County Hospital."

"Then what?" Julia asked.

"Medical evaluation," said Wood. "Ask for Crisis Response."

"We'll follow you," Wendell said.

Wood nodded, setting off down the path.

"Thank you for coming," Julia called politely after them. *Was that what she meant? Thank you for taking away our son? But they'd done them a service, you had to say something.* She was crying, she realized.

Julia turned to Wendell. "Now what?"

"Now we go after them," Wendell said.

"But do we call your man in Florida? Or someone local? Do we need a lawyer? Heroin's illegal." Julia's voice sounded high. "And what about my parents?"

"Leave a note for your parents," said Wendell. "Steven, are you coming?"

It was not really a waiting room, merely a jog in an open hallway. In the angle, one wall was lined with orange molded plastic chairs, and a battered turquoise sofa stood against the other. On both walls hung framed posters of blurry landscapes in pastel colors. A scuffed wooden table held an untidy scattering of obscure dog-eared magazines. Around the corner was the nurses' station; their low intermittent conversation could be heard but not understood, like voices in a dream.

Wendell and Julia sat on opposite ends of the sofa, their legs stretched out, their feet on the table. Steven sat on a plastic chair. He was leaning forward, flipping through a magazine. He had changed his clothes, and his hair was slicked and combed. His face was solemn. They had been here two hours.

Julia reached out with her foot and touched his knee.

"You okay?"

Steven nodded without looking up. He ripped through the pages at speed.

Julia turned to Wendell. "I think you should call your guy. In Florida."

"The one you were so keen on," said Wendell.

"Don't," said Julia.

"Let's talk to the doctor first," said Wendell.

Julia looked at the doorway. They seemed to be the only people here, the hallways beyond the nurses' station were silent. It was nearly three o'clock in the morning, and she could feel exhaustion settling into her brain. *Maybe they should take turns dozing. Would that help?* Something about this seemed logical; something, not. Each thought seemed difficult. How would they manage to make a decision? The idea of a decision seemed immense, impossible to achieve.

"What do you think we should do?" she asked. "Steven, what do you think?"

Steven frowned, his mouth pursing with distaste. "Why ask me?" He kept flipping through the pages.

"What do you mean?" Julia asked.

"I'm not a drug addict. Why do you think I know more about this than you do?" He looked up at her, the magazine open on his lap.

"Of course you're not a drug addict," Wendell said. "But you know more about drugs than we do."

"What makes you think that?" Steven asked. He leaned back in his chair, looking hostilely at his father.

"Steven, it's not an indictment," Julia said. "We're asking for your help. It's just generational."

"What does that mean?"

"*Stop it,*" said Julia. "Don't do this, Steven. What is it?"

"Look, I'll do whatever I can," Steven said, "but I'm not an expert on this. I'm not Jack's spokesman here." He put on a public announcer's voice. "'Welcome to heroin! Let me tell you what drug abuse really means!'" His voice turned normal again. "I'm in the dark here, too. Don't act like I'm in charge of this, I'm not." He stared angrily at his parents, his arms folded on his chest. "I've never taken heroin, and very few of my friends have. I've never taken stuff like this."

"Steven," Wendell said.

"Okay," Julia broke in. "Okay, Steven. No one wants to assume anything. We only want you to be a part of our team. We want your advice because you're part of the family."

How could they be going so wrong already? Now they were alienating Steven, too.

"Fine," Steven said, still staring at them angrily. "I'm not the fuckup."

"What do you mean?" Wendell asked.

"*I'm not the fuckup,*" Steven repeated. "I'm not the one you have to call the doctor about. I'm not the one you go to the emergency room for."

"We know that," Julia said. "Steven, what is it?"

"I'm sick of this," Steven said. His voice shook suddenly. "Sick of the whole family racing around *in crisis* because Jack's screwed up again." He stared at them, his mouth tight. No one answered.

"He does it all the time," Steven went on, "he's always done it. Every time there's a lull in the conversation, Jack screws up! Now he's going to have to go to rehab—"

"We don't know that," Julia said.

"Oh, he's going to snap his fingers and quit?"

"I mean—" Julia stopped.

"We don't know what your brother is going to do," Wendell said loudly. "We don't know if your brother's still alive."

Still alive, thought Julia, *what does that mean?* The words circled dizzily in her mind. *Still alive.* Things were beginning to fly apart.

Steven made a noise of exasperation and jerked his head to one side. He shook his head and looked down again at his magazine. Wendell stared belligerently at him, leaning forward over the battered table.

The poster on the wall showed an afternoon party on the lawn, a flag fluttering in the sea wind, bright water beyond. People sat at a table, teacups and plates scattered on the cloth before them. It was strange to see a world like that; it had nothing to do with her. She could not imagine it.

Julia looked at her watch: ten of three. The information was useless; she could not remember when they'd arrived. She felt as though waves were washing up over her, higher and higher. She was dazed by exhaustion and fear, and this new complication with Steven was bewildering. How could he now feel like an enemy? How could he not want to help them? How had they made him feel whatever this was—resentful, jealous, antagonistic? How would they be able to keep on going if everything in their path rose up against them? It was more than she could absorb. She felt stunned by all this, as though she were water-logged and beginning to sink, bobbing lower and lower.

Wendell sat back against the sofa and crossed his leg over his knee, watching Steven.

"I'm not the fuckup," Julia thought. Of course he wasn't. What was he thinking? Why was he so angry?

There were purposeful footsteps in the hall, and they all looked up.

"Mr. and Mrs. Lambert?" The doctor was a short man with thinning hair. He wore rimless glasses, a white lab coat, and khaki pants. He carried a clipboard.

"And Steven," Wendell said.

The doctor nodded at Steven, then looked back at Wendell. "I'm Dr. Hughes." He pulled over one of the plastic chairs and sat down facing them. "I'd like to ask you some questions about Jack."

Julia sat up straight. "Of course."

She was ready to answer, ready to comply. Jack had always been healthy, and shouldn't that count for something? Shouldn't he get credit for that? She wanted to speak on his behalf. She was ready to offer Jack's medical past to the doctor; she'd offer him anything. She'd prostrate herself on the floor.

Dr. Hughes asked about Jack's drug history, making notes as she talked. They told him about the marijuana, the problems at school, the whole of it. Steven's warning, Wendell's visit. It was a relief, finally, to tell everything, to be candid with someone who was knowledgeable and authoritative, someone who would not expel Jack from school or put him in jail.

When they had finished, the doctor looked up.

"Can you tell me exactly what happened last night? What were the first symptoms that occurred, and what preceded them?"

"Jack was fine all evening," Julia began.

"He was actually sick all evening," Steven interrupted.

She looked at him. "He was?"

Steven nodded, looking at the doctor. "He told me in the boat. He started vomiting then. He said he'd felt sick all night. He was in withdrawal from heroin."

The word.

"Did he say that word to you?" Julia asked Steven.

He nodded.

"He used that word?"

He nodded again.

Julia turned to the doctor. "Do you think he's a heroin addict?"

The doctor looked at her. "Have you seen his arms?"

"I wondered if there was a test," Julia said meekly, "a blood test."

"Most conditions present with a variety of symptoms. Judging from everything I know, I think your son injects himself frequently with heroin, which suggests addiction. When do you think was the last time that he had any interaction with the drug?"

"Yesterday morning," Wendell said. "It was my fault. The driver got lost. We drove around and around Brooklyn. He didn't have a clue where we were going."

The doctor looked at him for a moment. "Brooklyn?"

"I picked him up there to take him to the airport," Wendell explained. "We came up this afternoon. I was trying—"

"We were trying to have a sort of intervention," Julia said. "Just the family. To talk about the problem."

The doctor nodded again. "What about later on? Was he under your observation from then on?"

Wendell and Julia looked at each other.

"Every second? I don't think so," Julia said. "But he was with us, in the house. I mean, I think we'd know."

"We wouldn't know," Wendell said, shaking his head.

"He probably took it again," Steven said.

"You think so?" The doctor turned to Steven.

"He was high at dinner," Steven said. "I think he took it when he first got to the house."

These were the things you never told your parents, never told the adult world. Steven felt like a traitor. His brother's life was at risk, he told himself, Steven was part of the team trying to save him. It was his responsibility now to tell his brother's secrets to this blank-faced stranger. This was part of the rescue effort, it was essential knowledge. They had to have knowledge in order to save him. *He was trying to save his brother's life. He was a traitor, he was betraying his brother in his darkest moments. This was the true crime, the great crime. Invading someone's secret life, offering it up stripped and bare, without protection, to strangers who will destroy it.*

How did you decide when you should take over someone's life? You were always wrong. It was always their life. Betraying your brother was the great crime.

"So he probably used drugs again before he went out on the boat," the doctor said.

"It's possible," Wendell said. "What does that mean?"

"Just that there would be more in his system. We're waiting for lab results now. Your son has tested positive for opiates. Right now I think he's in acute withdrawal from heroin. The worst phase will last four or five days or more. It can be severe: nausea, chills, violent cramping, pain in the joints, pain everywhere. It's extremely unpleasant but not life-threatening, so we don't usually keep heroin patients in the detox unit. Often we give them medication to relieve the symptoms, then release them."

"Release them?" asked Julia. "Just like that? Wouldn't he just start taking it again?"

"This is not a rehab facility. If your son wants to quit, we'll offer recommendations for treatment."

"What if he doesn't?" Wendell asked.

"Jack is twenty-two," Dr. Hughes said. "This is going to be his decision."

He looked back at Julia.

"He has an infection in his bloodstream, which is fairly common among intravenous drug users. So we're going to keep him here for now, monitor him and give him intravenous antibiotics."

"This infection," said Julia, "is it from needles?"

The doctor nodded. "Very possibly."

"Is it serious?"

"It can be," he said. "It can go straight to the heart. It can be fatal." Julia nodded.

No matter what you were prepared for, it was not enough. There was always more. Straight to the heart.

"What happens next depends on you," said Dr. Hughes. "When the infection's cleared up, we'll release him. He'll still be in distress, though the medications will relieve his symptoms. When the acute phase is over and the physical pain subsides, then psychological pain begins to predominate. He may experience deep depression."

The infection, thought Julia, did it mean AIDS? But she could not say the word.

"What about rehab?" asked Wendell.

"We give recommendations for both outpatient and inpatient programs," said the doctor. "If he wants to quit."

"How long would it take to get him into a local program?" Wendell asked.

"There are wait-lists. Usually about four to six weeks."

"Until then he'd be living at home," Wendell said.

The doctor nodded.

"Can we see him?" Julia asked.

Dr. Hughes hesitated. "When parents are responsible for the addict being brought here, their presence may cause agitation, so we often keep them apart. But I think Jack's stable now. You can see him, but briefly. Keep things calm."

"We just wanted him to get help," Julia said, stunned. *Agitation? How could they have become Jack's enemy?*

"An addict may see any interference as personally threatening."

"But we want him to stop," Julia said stupidly.

"Yes," said the doctor.

There was a silence.

"Is there anything else we should know?" asked Julia. "This is all new."

Dr. Hughes looked at her. "This is the first experience you've had with Jack's addiction?"

"Really, yes," Wendell said.

"Well." Dr. Hughes looked down, as though he were waiting for something to settle, then looked up at Wendell. His voice turned quieter. "You need to prepare yourselves for a real struggle. Heroin addiction kills most people. Very few survive it, no matter what they do."

Good, thought Julia, *good.* What she felt was relief. Now it was out in the open, now they knew the worst. Knowing it was the first step.

This was a challenge, and they would meet it. Knowing the danger made it possible to avert it. They would rise up to this and conquer it. Hearing about the problem made Julia feel powerful and determined. She listened carefully, focusing on every word.

Afterward they went to see Jack. The door to his room was ajar.

"Knock knock," Julia said, peering in.

The room was small. Jack's bed filled most of his space; a white curtain hanging beside it suggested another bed beyond. A metal stand stood beside Jack's bed, with an IV bag suspended from it, half full of a clear liquid. Narrow plastic tubing looped down to Jack's arm, where it vanished beneath a bandage.

Jack was in bed. He looked awful, his face pale and glistening with sweat. There were huge shadows beneath his eyes, and his eyelids drooped heavily. Julia bent over to kiss him, but he flinched and she drew back without touching him. There was nowhere to sit, and the three of them stood awkwardly along the wall.

"How are you feeling?" Julia was nearly whispering, as though not to wake him.

"Better," Jack said, his voice normally loud. "They're giving me Klonopin."

"Is that a painkiller?" asked Julia.

"Antianxiety." Jack swallowed, making a horrible phlegmy sound.

There was a silence.

"Is it helping?" Julia asked.

Jack shrugged. His eyes looked not quite focused.

"We're going to get you help," Wendell said.

"Yeah," said Steven. "We're with you."

Jack nodded, his gaze on the wall ahead of him.

"We're going to get you out of here," Julia said.

Jack closed his eyes, opened them.

Julia remembered once when he'd been sick, as a child. Six or seven years old, and in bed with a fever. She'd come into his room to take his temperature. Jack had opened his mouth like a tiny bird, folding his lips around the glass shaft. His eyes were dark, dulled with fever. She sat on the bed and smoothed his forehead, waiting while the mercury rose: he was like a small soft radiator. She could feel the heat from him. He watched her, his mouth closed over the thermometer, his gaze mournful and trusting. He had been so small and brave; she had been so certain of curing him, so effortlessly powerful.

Now there was a long pause.

"Jackie?" Julia said.

Jack roused himself. "Yeah," he said. He was still staring at the wall. "Okay."

Suddenly it was very late.

"We're going," Julia said. She gently patted his knee, barely touching it through the sheets, but he grimaced.

"We'll come back later," Steven said. "When you feel better."

"We'll see you," Wendell said, nodding.

The halls of the hospital were silent, and they walked through them without speaking. The sound of their footsteps seemed very loud. Julia could hear the discrete squeaks of her sneakers, every step. At the elevators Steven pushed the button with the heel of his hand, holding it down hard. The elevator took a punishingly long time to arrive. Down in the lobby, they each pushed through the revolving door into the fresh damp air of the summer night. It was a release: they were freed from the stale air, the steady, maddening lights, the claustrophobic labyrinth of hallways. Still no one spoke, and they crossed the parking lot and climbed into the car in silence.

Driving home, the empty roads glimmered black in the headlights. Julia finally spoke. "He looked awful."

"He *was* awful," Steven said.

"I'm calling Carpenter in the morning," said Wendell.

In the backseat, Steven leaned back and folded his arms across his chest. *It would be all of them against Jack.*

PART III

PART ONE

NINETEEN

Coming into the kitchen, Edward found it empty again. Exasperated, he turned on the kettle, then began noisily opening and closing the cupboard doors, looking for cereal. He found it, fixed himself a bowl, and sat down, listening. There were footsteps upstairs, brisk creakings, and once he thought he heard someone on the phone. He ate slowly, waiting for someone to appear.

Edward had slept badly. His night had been full of vivid dreams, and he'd found himself awake over and over. Even when he opened his eyes the dream-images had persisted, and he'd lain awake in the dark, his mind filled with urgency. The troubling scenes had entered into him somehow. He could not rid himself of their weight, their potency. Usually anxieties vanished at daybreak, but today a sense of disturbance lingered. Deep anxiety, like a dark mist, drifted over him, soft and suffocating.

Sometimes he dreamed about surgeries, nightmare scenes that went wrong. The premature rupture of an aneurysm, arterial spasm, intracranial bleeding. The sudden plummeting of blood pressure, alarm blazing through the operating theater, the eyes of the assisting nurses and doctors glancing over their masks. The hurrying urgency of speed, speed, speed, the circular trail of blood moving incessantly through the system, unable to pause for a second. The burden of responsibility, the feeling of looming dread. The loud rhythmic thud of the magnified heartbeat, monitory and punishing. Edward resented these disturbances. He'd worked hard his whole career, he should now be able to get through the night without interruption.

But this was not what he'd dreamed about last night, was it? It was something quieter, larger. When he'd finally awakened for the day, he was tired and unfocused. Katharine, beside him, was still asleep, as she had been all night, easy and tranquil.

Katharine slept well, she'd always done so, and he'd always envied it. Sleep for him was elusive, fugitive. During all those years he'd practiced, he'd resented the fact that Katharine could reach sleep so easily and he could not. He'd *needed* sleep, he'd *deserved* it. Katharine had not needed it, at least not as he did, yet she'd been the one to have it, effortlessly, in abundance, at will. She could take a ten-minute nap, at once falling away from consciousness, as though she were dropping into the sea.

Edward felt deprived by this, as though his wife were deliberately keeping something from him. Those endless long nights, listening to her steady breathing—the long slow inhalation, the pause, the nearly noiseless exhalation—as he stared at the dim ceiling, trying to avoid the infernal message of the clock. Finally, in exasperation he'd get up and go into his study and find a book, though he disliked reading. The wasted hours would make him heavy-handed and slow the next day.

The night before a surgery he'd always been scrupulous, never drinking, never staying up late, but actually reaching sleep was beyond his control. His insomnia had infuriated him. He'd not discussed it at the hospital, it was better not to reveal your failings.

In surgery, slow hands were a risk. There was always the fear of clumsiness, a fatal slip. He'd made them, everyone did. Human error.

He'd once severed a vestibulocochlear nerve, and still remembered the moment perfectly, the fine white filament suddenly snapping back, unloosed, coiling in on itself, glistening. Sickening, irrevocable. There was no going back, no fixing it. Nerve tissue was not like bone, you couldn't clamp the severed ends together and let them knit. It couldn't be undone.

The patient was a woman in her forties; she'd had a tumor settled deep in the anterior temporal lobe. He'd diagnosed it, it was operable and discrete, and he'd removed it. The surgery was a success, and she'd survived, though she'd be deaf in that ear for the rest of her life. But it was only because he'd removed the tumor that she'd *have* the rest of her life.

Patients had come to him in fear and desperation, losing their eyesight, their balance, their hearing, their sanity. They came from all over the world; he'd become famous. Neurosurgery, during the course of his career, became increasingly effective. And he'd been a pioneer, he'd designed instruments and techniques that were still in use. He did what he could for his patients; many he healed, most of them he helped.

He'd saved probably the mind, certainly the eyesight, of a Hollywood producer's daughter. Afterward, someone had called Katharine and asked for her favorite color. "Blue," she said, and a week later a blue Mercedes appeared in the driveway. They'd kept that car for years. Katharine used it like a wheelbarrow, driving it to the nursery, loading it full of plants until the trunk wouldn't close. The producer had founded a research chair at UCLA in Edward's name. He'd been a star. He'd helped hundreds of people, and loved what he did. There was nothing so exhilarating.

The nervous system was his own private universe, vast and beautiful, wheeling through its own space. The elegance of the brain, with its dizzying whorls and layers, its branching deltas of blood vessels, the rounded, scalloped, ruffled lobes. Its symmetry, its geometry, its unimaginable complexity. People had no idea what it was like, how it worked. The mysterious web of connection between thought and tissue, tangible and intangible, reason and emotion. Physical movement, perception of pain, thought, and feeling: everything that defined the human experience had its origin in the brain.

The nervous system had its own language: *amygdala, hippocampus, the circle of Willis.* Those were things that had never been described or even imagined before. They'd been identified and named like new continents, the features of a newly discovered landscape. *The tenia of stria terminalis.* All of them were places he'd been, places most people had never heard of. No one understood it completely, even now. It was still being discovered. He had a profound, unutterable respect for it, all of it.

The kettle began hissing, but he ignored it. He was still working his way through his cereal. He felt, not tired exactly, but heavy. Weighted down by something—his lack of sleep, or those dreams.

For most of his career, the hospitals held periodic panels to review medical errors. They assessed and investigated them and assigned blame. That had stopped because of lawsuits: now the hospitals couldn't risk admitting errors, so the errors went unacknowledged and unaddressed. A *mistake,* Edward thought, *an abnegation of responsibility.*

That panel had been powerful. Edward had been called before it more than once, everyone had. The first time was over that severed nerve. A row of sober faces, your peers, impending judgment. It was serious, appearing before it. They hadn't called him in over those surgeries. They hadn't been his errors; they hadn't been considered errors at all. Leucotomies. *Jesus.* At the time, those operations were common. Nothing to do with him.

The hospitals chose the patients, the violents and intractables. Without surgery they'd have spent the rest of their lives in straitjackets, that was the belief. After the war there were thousands of them. Conditions were appalling then; the hospitals were desperately overcrowded. It was a serious public health crisis. He and a partner had gone twice a month to the VA. The surgeries were brief and simple.

It didn't do to think about it now. *Those hospitals. The smells in the dim corridors. The look of the patients. You could feel it, what went on in the wards. Violence, abuse. You could sense it.* It didn't do to think about it now.

The kettle changed its trill to a low wheezing sound. Edward spooned the last milk from his cereal bowl. He felt physically weighted down. *What was the point of remembering all that?* Fifty, sixty years ago.

When Julia appeared in the doorway, he saw she was preoccupied, her mind elsewhere.

"I didn't sleep well," he announced, pushing his empty bowl away.

"I'm sorry," Julia said. She turned the kettle off, its voice now a high silvery whisper. "Is Mother up?"

"She was asleep when I left," Edward said. "Your mother can sleep through a tycoon."

"Typhoon," she said.

Edward frowned, vexed.

Julia made them mugs of coffee and sat down with him.

"I'm sorry you didn't sleep well," she said again.

"I think I'll live," Edward said.

Then why tell me about it? Julia thought, with a surge of exasperation. *Why bother to complain if you don't want your complaint taken seriously? Why contradict everything everyone else says? Why is yours the only correct version of the world?*

"I have to tell you what's going on," Julia said.

"'What's going on?'" Edward repeated. He remembered the dim commotions of the night.

"Jack's in the hospital." Julia took a breath: this felt like jumping off a cliff. "He's in withdrawal from heroin."

"Heroin?" Edward whistled. "That's pretty serious."

"I know," Julia said. Did he think she didn't?

"Exogenous opioids," he said. "Very hard to shake."

"Wendell's found someone who's coming up from Florida. He's going to help us stage an intervention."

Edward nodded. "Intervention," he said. "I don't know how well these things work." *She might as well know the truth.* "Counseling, meetings. All that talk."

"We don't know what will work, Daddy," Julia said. "We don't have a lot of choice."

Edward sipped his coffee. *Heroin addiction was chemical, not psychological. Opiates destroyed the dopamine receptors. The structure of the brain was altered. Trying to cure it by talking was like trying to set a broken leg with meditation.*

"This man who's coming, he wants the whole family to be a part of this," Julia said.

"What do you mean, the whole family?"

"As many members as possible."

"Do you mean your mother and myself?" demanded Edward.

"Yes," said Julia.

Edward was silent for a moment. He was filled with distaste. "Ted and Harriet?"

"I called them," Julia said. "Ted can't come, but Harriet's flying up. She'll get in late tonight. She's staying at the B&B in town, there's no room here. We'll meet with this man first, without Jack, and then when Jack gets out of the hospital, we'll all meet together."

Edward nodded. *He could not imagine Harriet being helpful with this. Nor himself: it was all nonsense. Palliative.* "Who is this person?" he asked.

"His name's Ralph Carpenter," Julia said.

"What does he do?"

"Runs a rehab program."

"What are his qualifications?" Edward asked, testy.

Instead of answering, Julia dropped her head. Edward waited, but she said nothing. She shook her head without looking at him.

He could see she was frightened. There was no point in pursuing this. There was no single successful protocol. The statistics were very bad, there was no point in frightening her more.

"What's Harriet supposed to do?" he asked finally.

"We're all meant to do the same thing," Julia said. She raised her head but did not look at him. "We're supposed to be very positive, very supportive."

Edward nodded.

"We're not meant to judge him," Julia said.

"In what way?"

"For taking drugs."

Edward nodded again. "And how is this meant to work? Telling him how great he's been."

"We're not telling him he's great to take heroin, Daddy," said Julia. "We're telling him he's a great person, and that we love him."

There was a silence.

Of all the useless strategies, thought Edward.

"And how his behavior hurts us," said Julia.

"And why is this meant to work?" Edward asked again.

"I don't know," Julia admitted. "I've never done it."

"When does this fellow arrive?"

"Tonight. He's staying at the B&B, too."

"How long has he been running his operation?"

"I don't know."

"What's his success rate?"

"I don't know, Daddy," Julia said. "High." Then she added, her voice changing, "Actually, I don't know. Nobody's rates are very high. Don't be like this."

"Like what?"

"You know. An interrogator, trying to find the flaws. We don't—there isn't a perfect way to do this. Do you think there's some better way?"

"It's a difficult situation," Edward said, "medically speaking."

"Thank you," said Julia. "My point. If everyone agreed on one method, that's what we'd use, but they don't. This one seems—" she stopped. Her throat seemed to be closing.

It still seemed, at moments, as though an alternate reality was possible.

Mightn't someone announce a mistake, a misdiagnosis; mightn't there be some way in which this had not happened? Might she not be meant to be in some other body, some other life?

"It's an extremely difficult problem," Edward said.

"That's what I'm saying. I'd appreciate your help, not having you sit around disapproving of everything we do."

"'Sit around?'" Edward said. "I hardly disapprove of everything you do, nor do I sit around. As a matter of fact, every time I try to make a contribution, you reject it. That sink is still leaking, you know."

"It was never leaking," said Julia. "And you know exactly what I mean. Just stop it." She felt sickened by herself. Would she never stop this inane, roiling, adolescent struggle with her father?

Edward did not answer. *Maybe she was right, maybe he was somehow being antagonistic. And it was better to say nothing. He wished Katharine were here, to put an end to this disagreeable conversation. He didn't know why Julia was so angry at him. And in fact he had nothing to say. Usually he knew exactly what to do, but now he did not. And there was still something drifting near him, dark, insubstantial, troubling.*

TWENTY

Harriet's room was small and airless, and it smelled faintly of mold. She had arrived in Portland on Saturday night, too late to make the drive to Julia's. She spent the night in a motel near the airport.

Her room was long and narrow. Against one wall was a synthetic-looking bureau missing a handle and a massive armoire containing a TV set. Against the other were two queen-sized beds covered in gold synthetic quilting. She wondered why hotel rooms always had two large beds in them. Was it for group sex? This small cheerless room would be the last place on earth for an orgy. The pillows beneath the scratchy gold spread were nearly flat; the windows overlooked the parking lot, and did not open. The room was utterly inert, it seemed to oppose motion.

Harriet kicked off her shoes and lay down on the bed to call Allan. When he answered she felt relief.

"Hi," she said.

"Hi there," he said. "You've arrived."

"Just at the motel," she said. "I'll drive up to Julia's tomorrow." She could hear crowd noises in his background.

"How is it?" he asked.

"Like a motel," she said. "What are you watching?"

"The Sox," he said.

She was comforted by this, too, by the idea that her life, her real life, was still going on at home. Allan, in his stocking feet, was sitting in the big gray chair in the living room watching the ball game.

"Who's winning?"

"St. Louis," he said, and his voice changed. "Oh no. *Oh no.* I can't *believe* that play. Oh my God."

"What's the inning?"

"Top of the fourth. Why do they keep that guy on the team? They want us to lie down on the floor and weep. They want us to tear our hearts out and let them bleed. They want to watch that happen."

Harriet said nothing. She listened to the tiny swelling noises of the crowd, the announcer's voice, rapid, urgent, unintelligible.

After a moment Allan asked, "How are you doing?"

"As well as can be expected," Harriet said.

"It'll be better than you think," Allan said.

"You always say that," Harriet said. "I don't know why you think it's true."

"I don't know why you don't," Allan said.

She laughed.

When she hung up, she sat without moving. Someone nearby was watching TV, she could hear it through the thin walls. She wondered if it was the Sox game. She thought of turning on her own TV and entering into a triangulated companionship with Allan, long distance.

She undressed to take a shower. The carpet was gritty and unpleasant against her bare feet, and she wore her sandals into the bathroom. The room was small, and it filled quickly with steam. When she brushed her teeth, the mirror was clouded and she could not see her reflection. When she went back into the bedroom, the smell of mold was stronger.

She slept poorly, waking up several times in the night. Her own used breath seemed to fill the room, and in the morning she had a headache.

Downstairs she checked out and walked through the lobby, her small suitcase trundling obediently behind her. She pushed through the smudged glass doors. The sky was overcast but full of glare, and she squinted, looking for her rental car. The lot was full of cars, almost all of them similar, blunt amorphous shapes in dull metallic colors. She tried to remember what her car was like: she thought it was not large and not white. She headed for where she thought she'd parked it, beneath a tall lamppost in the corner. What if you really couldn't find your car? It would be a nightmare. She'd always hated those huge parking garages with ramps and floors and elevators. Low-ceilinged, dimly lit, dirty and labyrinthine, they seemed perfectly designed as crime sites.

Was this it? She stopped and aimed the key at a small dull red car, a meaningless name written in silvery script on the trunk. She pressed the Unlock button, and to her relief the car beeped obligingly, recognizing her. She heard the metallic sound of interior locks clicking open. She put her suitcase in the back and got in. As she backed out of her slot, she tried to remember the name written in script—*Karillin? Maxira?*—but it was already gone.

The street wound toward the highway past gas stations and fast-food restaurants, with their bright signs and dispiriting products. She'd read once that Julia Child was a great supporter of fast-food places, because you knew exactly what you were getting. Was that it? She couldn't remember exactly—why would it be reassuring to know that the tasteless bits of chicken, the thin patties of beef would always be the same? But it was Julia Child, she must have had some good reason.

At the second light there were signs to I-95 and she headed up the ramp, sliding the little red car into the northbound traffic.

All the cars on the road seemed to look alike. She wondered again about the name of her own car. What was the point of made-up names? Words that existed nowhere but in the mind of a Japanese marketing executive? What was the point of words without any meaning? Wasn't

the whole point of words that they had meaning? These names were chosen because they had no meaning in any language: Starion, Altima.
They were devoid of content, like artificial food. They were the opposite
of names.

She was now drifting along in a pod of cars, caught in the stream of
traffic like a fish in a school.

Though maybe names acquire content only through association,
she thought. "Chartres" would mean nothing if we didn't know about the
tall, elegant, unequal spires, the glowing windows. We've invested it
with the presence of its cathedral. Maybe the Japanese marketer, whispering the syllables to himself at his desk, hoped that "Altima" would
create a place for itself in the world—a smooth, bullet-shaped place,
unique and irresistible.

But didn't the Altima look like every other small car on the road?
She thought them all indistinguishable, but maybe that was her age.
She'd stopped looking at cars the way she'd stopped listening to new
music. The marketer's nemesis: the aging population, wanting consis-
tency and familiarity, indifferent to novelty. But we're big, she silently
reminded the marketers, don't ignore us. We're a huge bulge in the
demographics. You should pay attention to us.

She had settled into the stream of traffic. The speed was moderate
and steady, the weather was mild, and there were no decisions to make
for another hour or so. There was nothing for her to think about except
what lay ahead.

On the phone Julia had been abrupt.

"I have to tell you something," she said. "Jack's a heroin addict."

Harriet was shocked at the fact and that Julia had told her.

"We're having an intervention," Julia said, "we need the family.
Mother and Daddy are already here, and Ted can't come. You're it. Can
you come?"

No surprise about Ted, who lived in Oregon. His wife was from
Seattle, and they rarely came East. In any case, theirs was a family that
didn't get together. They lacked the gathering gene.

'We need the family'; 'You're it.' So peremptory, as though this event had given Julia the right to be in charge of the world. Harriet's partner had just gone to Sicily for two weeks; it would be a nightmare for her to leave the office right now.

But the event was a nightmare. It was a calamity. *Heroin.*

"I'm so sorry," Harriet said.

"Thank you," Julia said. "Can you come?"

"Do you need me?"

"It would be great," Julia said, and to Harriet's horror her voice broke on the last word.

It was bad, then, thought Harriet. It was very bad.

Before she left she'd done some research; the numbers were frightening. Most people died from this. Heroin was an opioid, an opium derivative, like codeine and morphine. It had an insidious chemical grip that coiled around the brain like a python.

Heroin was diacetylmorphine, a synthesized form of morphine with extra chemical boosters that delivered it quickly to the brain. Opioid addiction destroyed the natural patterns of behavior, including those of survival. The craving subsumed everything else. In one study, rats were offered morphine or food. They chose morphine, over and over, until they died of starvation. It was a scientific anomaly, a brain stimulation pattern without biological value. Most brain stimulation patterns benefited the organism—fear, food, sex. But chemical addiction had no benefit; in fact, the reverse. It was quite interesting, actually, a mystery.

It wasn't interesting, it was terrifying. Heroin was a war zone. Julia must be frozen with fear—Wendell, Steven, all of them. It was terrifying.

Harriet wondered what her father had to say about this, her mother. She was glad she was staying at the B&B and not at Julia's house, in the midst of it all. She dreaded entering into this, whatever it was going to be. It felt like a tornado, a violent twister, dark and ominous on the horizon, swirling closer, picking up houses, cars, trash. Whatever was going to happen—what did you actually do in an intervention?—was going to be messy and chaotic, giant whirlpools of emotion and drama. Harriet dreaded it.

The thought of them all taken over by the storm, all of them caught up in emotion, unburdening themselves, accusing and apologizing and weeping, was unbearable to Harriet. She wanted to keep herself clear of it, draw herself taut and hold her breath until it was over. She dreaded entering the hot dark vortex of the family: Julia, with her emotional sagas; Edward, self-absorbed and tyrannical; Katharine, unbearably cheery and self-sacrificing. All of it was excruciating.

One reason Harriet worked with animals was that they didn't talk. You didn't have to hear from anyone who had, suddenly and sickeningly, become in touch with their feelings. Animals were always perfectly in touch with their feelings, and never felt the need to discuss them.

And animals were innocent. None of them was responsible for their troubles. The dogs looked at her hopefully and moved their tails when they saw her, even the very sick ones, with the gentle, unbearable eyes. The dogs met her gaze with their own, full of trust. That gaze was the reason Harriet had chosen her profession.

Animals had no choice; people decided their lives. She could hardly bear to think about her animals, the ones she couldn't help. She wouldn't let herself think about them now, she would not let herself near the thought.

She pressed the accelerator, surging past a high-axled SUV driven by a grizzled man wearing sunglasses. What she wanted was to get on with things, get on. She was afraid of the wringing of hands, accusations and justifications. Edward's endless triumphs and vindications: her father was always right. It was not possible for him to admit he'd made a single error in his entire life. Or if he had, he'd taken possession of it, somehow; he'd forgiven himself. There was nothing he felt sorry for doing, nothing.

After the scene over the Cape house, and her father's furious diatribe, Harriet had decided she would never again argue with her father. She wouldn't ask for his approval or disagree with his opinions. She simply would not engage. Nor would she engage with Julia, who felt such undying condescension at the fact that Harriet was not a New Yorker, an artist, a wife, a mother.

Julia's condescension was irrelevant now. It had been years since she and Julia were close, since Julia left for boarding school. When Julia came home on vacations from school, she'd been too sophisticated to be friends with her little sister, and in college it had been worse. Julia had been unbearable: bohemian, insufferably pretentious. Harriet and her friends mocked Julia behind her back, with her stupid hair and artsy clothes. Then there had been the awful time when Harriet had announced her plans for veterinary school, and Edward had been so horrible. Julia had sat there without speaking, as though she didn't even know Harriet, as though they'd never been friends.

After that Harriet had deliberately withdrawn from her family. She had her own life: her practice, her research. She and Allan had their own friends, their own vacation places, their own habits and routines. She'd agreed to come up here for Julia and would do whatever was necessary to help her out—*though what would this be like?*—but she would draw a careful line around herself. She would not talk to her family about anything but Jack. Not about their emotional lives, and certainly not about her own. Nor would she talk about her practice, about which her father was caustic and derisive.

Thinking about her father's insufferable views was actually calming. In a way Edward's elitism had been responsible for her own views of animals. She'd become interested in animal consciousness partly because Edward believed it didn't exist. His view had been strictly behaviorist; he saw animals as being more or less like plants: no capacity for emotion, self-perception, reason, or "higher" intelligence. A huge chasm was meant to yawn between man and the "lower" animals. This was useful in maintaining man's amour propre; the belief that animals lacked consciousness—and the ability to feel pain—conveniently eliminated ethical issues about using them in lab experiments.

Anyone who actually worked closely with animals—shepherds or hunters or dog sledders or the blind—knew from experience that animals had emotions, consciousness, and intelligence. But those people didn't much intersect with animal behaviorists, and didn't much care what scientists thought.

Harriet spent her professional life treating animals and observing their responses. She'd also been observing a slow, fierce ideological struggle, in the scientific world, over the perception of these responses. She'd stopped thinking of her father in this context, except as someone whose unmediated wrongness wholly vindicated her own position.

She was interested by the ideological struggle, by the scrutiny of "tool" and "consciousness"—animals used lots of tools, it turned out, and their consciousness was surprisingly complex. She found animals themselves deeply interesting: their use of the world, their trust in their emotions, their adeptness at being wholly present. Harriet was fascinated by their alternate universe, the way they inhabited their senses, their instincts, their own landscapes.

Harriet loved her animal patients. She loved Allan, her insanely hardworking boyfriend (or partner, after eight years of cohabitation, or whatever the term was now), with his sharpened pencils and precisely rolled-up sleeves and perfectly level bow ties. It was only her family she had trouble with. It wasn't exactly that she didn't love them, either, just that she didn't like being around them.

Harriet bore down on the accelerator, urging her little car past a van with tinted windows.

She'd do this, whatever she was asked to do, but she doubted that she could help much. She hardly knew Jack, she hadn't seen much of him for years. She wasn't close to her family, and why should she feel guilty about that? Why was it a cardinal virtue, being close to your family? What if your family happened to be made up of people with whom you had little in common, whose company you didn't enjoy? Why wasn't your family equally to blame, for not being close to you?

Though apparently it was some sort of cardinal virtue. Everyone, even the religious right, *especially* the religious right (despite their high divorce rate), thought family should come first (though the religious right thought that Jesus Christ and dinosaurs were cohabitants of the planet, which always made her feel as though everything—all ideas, theories, logic, the earth—had been stuffed into a paper bag and shaken hard).

But where would they be as a society if family came first? Nowhere. There'd be no inventions, no thinkers, no planners, no science. (No wars, either, of course.) To move ahead as a society, ideas had to come first, and work. Work was what engaged you. All the rest was emotional blackmail.

Heroin, though. Jesus.

The word stopped her. Each time she met the word itself, it stopped her again. Poor Jack, poor Julia, poor all of them. It was a misery.

She turned on the radio for the news, to get away from this. It was no better: more deaths in Iraq, more suicide bombers, more kidnappings. This loathsome president, who lied and lied and lied. His monstrous arrogance, his appalling ignorance, his suicidal insularism. Harriet loathed him, his piggish little eyes, his moronic stuck-out ears. This was physical. It was also bigotry, she thought. This is how bigotry is born, the transfer of the intellectual to the visceral. I'm a bigot.

She turned off the radio.

It would be strange to see Wendell there. She'd never been crazy about him. She'd always thought he was a lightweight, a pseudo-intellectual who liked talking better than thinking. When Julia told her about the divorce (though not the reason, of course, Julia hadn't told her anything about her private life in years), Harriet hadn't seen it as such a tragedy. She'd always suspected Wendell of having a wandering eye, and hadn't seen his irresistible attraction in the first place. Besides, why did everyone feel they had to be married?

Julia had offered to give her directions over the phone, but Harriet had declined. She hadn't wanted to take directions from her older sister, and was sure she'd remember, once she got there. Wasn't this the exit?

Turning off the highway, she found it less familiar than she'd expected. It looked like any town, anywhere, like the one she'd left an hour earlier: gas stations, chain stores, and fast-food restaurants. Harriet groped along, making guesses at a traffic circle, a bridge, and the traffic lights. She finally turned off onto Route 3, setting off cross country. She hadn't been here for years.

The landscape became visible again, low rolling swells and rises, thickly wooded, then open and swampy. The soil was poor, the vegetation low and scrubby. Those early farmers, struggling with thin soil and long winters: that had been a real hardscrabble life.

When she saw the sign for Goose Cove Road, the turn seemed familiar, and the name. It looked right: open fields slanting away from the road. A few gnarled and lichen-covered trees, their branches twisted from the wind. Old white clapboard farms, the house and barn built into each other in a sort of accordion stretch. What was it called? Something charming and folksy.

The light was strong and raking, slanting across the fields. She'd forgotten how bracing it was, how harsh and bold. Different from the Cape. The Cape: the little saltbox house on its grassy knoll. The cluster of scrubby pines behind the back porch, the jungly mass of honeysuckle with its sweet yellow trumpets, tumbling down the hill. The pond below, shining in the morning sun. The high dimness of the silent barn, dark and hot, with its sour bat smell. Hard to believe that none of it was there anymore, or anyway not for them. Now it existed only in their minds. The new owners would have torn out the honeysuckle, evicted the bats. She'd lost it for the family.

Though she'd had to sell, for a million reasons. It was too far from Philadelphia, she could rarely get up there, the house was falling to bits, and she needed the money to start her practice. And the house had been hers, after all.

Edward had been enraged. He walked up and down in the front hall, his face furious, shaking his finger in the air like a striking serpent. Her father thought all the decisions in the world should be made by him. It was a wonder he'd stayed head of his department so long, that he hadn't been assassinated years ago by an outraged colleague.

At the next intersection she slowed, wondering whether to stay on Goose Cove or take the unmarked road that wandered across the salt marshes. She couldn't tell where the sea was from here. She'd have thought she'd be able to sense it. Suddenly she could feel everything drawing closer—her family, this whole thing, looming. She felt herself bracing for it, drawing taut. The house was coming nearer, her parents, this event. Julia's demands. All this commotion. She felt it rising inside her. She hated it.

She wished she were back in her office, wearing her comfortable clogs and scrubs, standing at the high steel examining table, surrounded by the thick stench of disinfectant and dog hair. Ushering in a young mother with a cat carrier, a three-year-old daughter clutching at her thigh. The big gray diabetic cat inside sitting quietly, eyes black with alarm. A difficult animal, ready to sink his teeth into her wrist or swipe her arm with long red stripes: she wore long padded gloves when she worked with him. She felt only affection for him, though: his world was distorted by pain. When the medications were working, he showed the sweetness of his real nature, the clumsy, head-bumping caresses, the boiler-room roar of his purr.

"What's going on with Twombly?" Harriet would ask, closing the door.

She longed for this familiar territory, knowing what to do.

She took the unmarked road, then pulled over to the side and stopped the car. She put her hands over her face. She might not be able to do this. She could feel the approach of something—panic, or fear—flickering around her mind. Her chest felt hard and full. She opened her eyes: the gnarled, wind-twisted trees along the road, beyond them the wide weedy fields, stretching on and on. It was unbearable, this landscape.

TWENTY-ONE

Jack rolled his head slowly back and forth on the pillow. He wondered who was behind the curtain, the other patient. The nurse went there to do something noiseless. Maybe whoever was there was mute. Maybe asleep. Maybe comatose. *That'd be good.*

He felt nauseated again, his stomach cramping. He'd vomited all day, there was nothing left inside him but a foul-smelling gruel. He could feel it coming on again, though, his gut starting to heave. He considered calling the nurse to ask for the basin.

The nurse was vast and disapproving, with limp blond hair and a small mean mouth. *Well, why wouldn't she hate drug addicts? It's our own fault. We could quit any time and we just don't. Instead, we take up space in the hospitals, and the doctors' time, and the fat nurse's. Feeding off the system, taking advantage.*

He rolled his head again. It was in his calves now, his knees, the muscles jerking and cramping hard; it was like being squeezed by a demon. It came and went in waves.

He'd hated it when his parents came in, and Steven. His mother tried to kiss him and he'd flinched. He couldn't stand being touched, it was like something electric crawling on his skin. *Don't worry, Jackie. We're going to get you out of here,* she said, *we're going to get you well.* They'd come again today, talking about rehab. Everyone crying, he'd cried, too. *All right, I'll quit.* Of course he would, if he could. He was always ready to quit. He hated remembering it, crying and stumbling around in that fog of shame and nausea.

It was night now. They didn't really care about the pain. Things were getting bad again, he could feel it starting up. He wanted the nurse, but he didn't want her to see him like this, kicking. He closed his eyes tightly. *This was so fucked up.* The nurse was supposed to be giving him something, and why wasn't she? He opened his eyes, which were watering, and lifted his head.

He felt for the cord laced through the bed railings. He found the button and pressed it. Where was she, his monstrous angel? She was hiding somewhere on the ward. She had shut herself into some closet, or she was ducking down beneath some counter, eating, wolfing down cake, stuffing food into her giant belly. She must eat all the time, to maintain that mass. He imagined her intestines, snaking back and forth, dense, compacted, a hideous mass of jellied eels, stuffing her skin to bursting. *Where was she?* He pressed the button. His calves were on fire, his legs.

What was the point of these things if they didn't work? He lay back on the pillow. His legs were on fire, he could feel them kicking and jerking. His arms had no power in them. Deliberately he tensed the muscles in his arms, then relaxed them.

He kept his eyes closed. He could see them, his inner arms, the bruised, flaming skin, the secretive blue lines of the veins below. *Sweet,* he thought, and at once all of this fell away and he was longing for the endless black velvet, the sweet dark place. Panic rose in his chest. *Christ,* he thought, *Christ.* He rolled his head from side to side again. He would have to get out of here. The muscles in his calves clenched horribly. He began to shake, a wave of chills and panic swept through him, and it became hard to breathe. *He was alone in here. He was alone and in danger. Anything could happen to him now.* His hands, he realized, were fists.

The nurse appeared in the doorway.

"We can hear you, you know," she said. "When you ring. The first time."

Jack looked at her. *Wasn't that the point?* "Sorry," he said. "Did I hold it down too long?"

"What is it?" she asked.

"My legs," Jack said. "I've got cramps. And nausea. Plus the chills."

The nurse waited, her mouth pursed. Her dress hung smoothly from her enormous waist. *How could a dress be that big?*

"Can you give me something?" asked Jack.

"You're having withdrawal symptoms," the nurse said.

She was slouching, her weight leaning against the door. She didn't hold herself well: *No pride,* he thought. *No pride in being a fat nurse.*

"Right," he said. "I am. I wondered if you could give me something to take the edge off." *Take the edge off:* a junkie's phrase. He shouldn't have used that. He shouldn't sound like a junkie, he should sound like a straight person, upstanding, responsible, normal. He should say something like "I wonder if you could do something to alleviate my symptoms, which are becoming severe." *What the fuck.*

Jack smiled stiffly at her, raising his eyebrows in appeal. "I feel like shit." Now it was his spine, an injection of fire. His leg suddenly jerked, hard and uncontrollable.

The nurse did not smile back. She had one hand on the doorknob, ready to leave. "You're having withdrawal symptoms," she said again.

"Please," Jack said. He closed his eyes as the wave of chills and shivering hit him, then opened them again. "Look, the doctor said he'd give me something. He told me."

The nurse lifted her chin and stared at him. On her great bosom— which was not actually so big, given her size, but anyway wide and deep—was a card with a name on it. He couldn't read it from this far away. He wondered what her name was: *Meredith? Angelica? Tony Soprano?*

"You've been given clonidine," she said accusingly.

"That was then," Jack said. "It's worn off." His body felt light and useless, as though it were about to be discarded. Nausea rose up again, it seemed to have taken up residence in his body, spreading through him at intervals like a tide.

The nurse raised her eyebrows without altering her expression.

"Could I have some more?" he asked. He closed his eyes again for the chills, opened them.

"You had your medication at eleven-twenty," Ms. Soprano said. "I can't give you any more until one-twenty."

"*Jesus,*" Jack said distinctly. "Can I talk to the doctor?"

"He's gone home," said the nurse, sounding pleased. She set a hand on her great hip with satisfaction. Her hands were tiny but fat. "He left instructions. Is there anything else? Because I have other duties."

"Yes," Jack said, arching his back. He closed his eyes against the pain. "I'd like a great big wet kiss."

The nurse closed the door behind her. Jack opened his eyes in the silence. He was sweating, and his nose was running. He looked at the ceiling, then at the curtain that hung between his bed and the next. He listened. A distant radio somewhere, no voices. He could hear no footsteps, no traffic in the halls. He drew in a long breath, expelled it slowly. *Fuck.* He felt like shit. It would get worse. The dope was roiling around inside him, declaring war. *It was the absence of dope, really. Hell hath no fury like that of a habit scorned.*

His calves clenched again, and his leg kicked. He felt the wave of contraction move through his whole body, a paroxysm. He would stop this. He had to end it. When his muscles unclenched he sat up, squinting as the shivering started, and slid his legs out of bed. He was naked except for a faded green hospital gown, open at the back. He put his bare feet on the floor and tested his weight, then stood, shakily. He ripped the bandages off his arm and peered at the IV needle. Such a waste, that beautiful clean little entry. He slid it out. A bright bead of blood grew on his skin.

There was a locker in the wall. He tottered to it and opened the metal door. He dressed quickly, pulling on his clothes. *Fuck:* no shoes. The fucking policemen had brought him here in his bare feet. The shivering went through his body again.

He moved silently to the curtain and peered around it.

A man lay in the next bed. He was tall and heavy, with graying hair. His head was thrown back on the pillow, exposing a reddened throat, rough and scraped, like chicken skin. Taped over one side of his head, covering one eye, was a huge white hump of bandage. The visible eye was closed.

"Yo," whispered Jack, watching him.

The man was motionless beneath the sheets.

"Dude," Jack said quietly. The man did not stir. His chest was barely moving. He was silent. Jack moved past the bed, to the locker. He raised the metal fastener carefully, sliding it upward, trying to muffle its sound. His head rang with pain. On the locker floor was a pair of work boots; Jack set them quietly on the floor. He slid his bare feet into the heavy boots. He felt the cold fixed shapes of the silent man's feet, his own feet like small impostors. He slid his hospital gown under the sheets on his bed to hide it—let them think at first he was in the bathroom—and opened the door to the hall.

It was empty. The scuffed linoleum floors gleamed dully in the fluorescent light, the view both bland and melancholy. Jack turned left, and started walking fast. He was nearly tiptoeing, holding his full weight from the heels.

Halfway down the hall, Jack saw the edge of a countertop projecting out from the wall. A nurses' station: he turned abruptly and started back, boots squeaking on the polished floor. He looked at a closed door: *Room 412.* What was his own room number? He didn't know. What if he needed to duck back into it? Too late, he'd burned that bridge.

He was nearly running now, stepping awkwardly on his toes. One of the rooms he was squeaking past was his, behind one of these doors was the one-eyed man lying motionless in his bed. His boots stolen, though he didn't know that yet.

Jack reached the end of the hall and paused, peering cautiously around the corner to another vacant hall. At a distance, too far to read, was a sign: maybe to the elevators.

There was a tide rising around him, lifting him up, he could feel its surge. He was on his way out of here; the tide would carry him. He felt himself beginning to swell and harden with power, with capability. In his head was a high chanting, kind of a headache, kind of something else. He was on his way out of here.

He was half sprinting now, taking long strides on his toes. This corner was the point of no return. From now on he could no longer duck back, undetected, into his room, the number of which he did not even know. He had no plan. If a nurse stopped him, the tide would carry him on. What he was doing felt illegal, though it couldn't be. He could leave the fucking hospital if he wanted. He wasn't under arrest. *Though if he got caught they'd come after him, take him back. The fucking police would come after him again.* He knew that. He wouldn't get caught, he could feel it. There was a pounding in his head, the chant. What he was looking for was a back stairway, though he'd take an elevator if it came first, he'd take an open window, he'd take anything to get off this floor, out of this building. The wave of chills swept up him again, and he felt his left eye twitching. The twitch felt huge, spasmodic, as though his whole face were contorting, though he knew it never looked like that. Though it might, the nurse would know. The fucking nurse would know if she saw him jumping down the hall on his toes, in some redneck's boots.

He heard voices and footsteps. He stopped his leaping and slowed deliberately to a normal walk. *What was a normal walk?* How did he look? Should he smile? He couldn't remember the normal way to walk.

Two figures rounded the corner, a young doctorish-looking woman with a stethoscope around her neck, wearing a white lab jacket and khaki pants, the man beside her in green scrubs and a shower cap. They were talking; they looked up at him as he approached. How were they looking at him? Were they suspicious? Should he smile? How would he act if he were normal? His eye twitched horribly. He met their eyes, their sober gazes. He felt transfixed by their sober gazes. He didn't have to speak, did he? Did he look guilty? His face felt paralyzed. Except for the twitch.

They came closer, no longer talking. They were both watching him. The man in scrubs wore light green paper slippers over his shoes, round rimless glasses. Jack looked at them, he could not look away. His eye jumped grotesquely. He could feel his throat contracting; he swallowed. His feet in the strange boots were carrying him past them, he had not stopped walking. His head felt oddly high, his chin oddly tilted. He was walking slowly, he had devised a plan of walking slowly, right past the doctors, who were staring at him closely—were they? Or were they simply walking by someone in the hallway? In an agony, trying to look normal, Jack came abreast of them. He nodded—was this the way you nodded? His calf muscles suddenly clenched, and he sniffed audibly. He was frowning, though, letting them know he was focused on something else, not on them. The way you let a policeman know you were worried was by looking at him. So instead you looked past him, you never looked at him. That was the trick. He'd nodded to the doctors, and now he looked past them, frowning toward the elevator, the back stairs.

The two doctors were quiet—quiet because they were waiting to talk about him? He felt his breath in his chest. He wanted to turn around and look, he would not turn around and look. It wasn't against the law to leave your room. They would come after him, they would take his arms and legs and put him back in that bed beside the silent man beyond the curtain, with the terrible white hump over his eye; he would roll his head back and forth on the pillow, vomit gruel onto the floor. He could hear his breathing now.

He would not run, would not rise onto his toes. Normal people walked heel first, he concentrated on the heel. His skin, in the strange boots, felt raw and tender. *The boots were hostile, they were enemy boots. No, they were not enemies, they were helping him escape.* He would not turn and look at the doctors.

The sign at the end of the hall said: LABORATORY. AUTHORIZED PERSONNEL ONLY. The arrow pointed left. Jack turned right, heading down another hall, praying for stairs. Where was the fire exit? He'd be dead by now from smoke inhalation. He was on his tiptoes again, the boots squeaking. *The fucking squeak.* He felt the rush of the tide again, carrying him forward.

A door opened and he slowed at once, like a child in a game. A nurse came out into the hall and glanced at him, her gaze staying on him for an extra moment—did it? He felt his breath in short puffs, as though he were about to break into tears. No, she had turned and was walking ahead of him. It wasn't the giant nurse, not his avenging angel, who wanted him to writhe in agony as punishment for being a drug addict. She was hunched in a broom closet somewhere, head low, wolfing down doughnuts. He could hear her gulping, her solitary chewing. Get down as many as possible: that huge body needed constant stoking. She must smuggle the stuff in, hide it under her giant skirt. Like drugs: this amused him. *Hey,* he thought.

He followed the nurse down the hall, slowing his steps to match hers. She was older, gray and parched, wearing a white shirt and pants, squeaky white shoes. She passed an open doorway and paused in it. *Go in, go in,* thought Jack, coming up behind her, but she only paused, and went on. He walked behind her like a marionette, his joints now loose, barely connecting his limbs.

There at last were the elevators. *Christ.* If she got in, he'd wait for the next one, he wouldn't get in alone with her. She walked to the doors and pushed the button, then turned to him. Her glasses magnified her eyes, making them large and bleary. Her short gray hair was slicked back like Elvis's. She looked at him. He stared up at the red light over the elevator doors. She looked away. He could feel her next to him, hear the papery rustle of her pants. At any moment she could turn on him, she could have him taken back to the darkened room, the silent roommate.

The elevator doors slid open.

"Going down?" she asked.

He shook his head.

"You're going up?" She was frowning: a poor choice, then.

"I mean no," Jack said, shaking his head. "Going *down*."

He waved her on. They both faced the door, which slid closed. Jack watched the floor numbers change: they'd already been on the next to highest, that's why she'd frowned. The top floor was probably off limits, labs or something. He felt himself begin to sweat. It was breaking out on his forehead and his neck. Could someone else see it? Could you see sweat? The nurse was looking at him. Closely, it seemed.

"Are you all right?"

Apparently you could see sweat.

"Yeah!" Jack said. "I'm fine." He grinned, meeting her eyes; then he looked back up at the illuminated numbers.

The nurse was still watching.

What did he have to do to be fine? How did you look normal?

"You seem distressed," she said levelly.

"I've been visiting my son," Jack said.

He couldn't believe he'd said that. Big mistake. Big mistake.

"Your son," the nurse said, with a little frown.

Christ. What time was it? The middle of the night. And where was the pediatric ward? Jack looked up at the numbers over the door again; the elevator slid abruptly to a stop. The doors opened onto the high-ceilinged lobby. A looping line of rope cut the space in two; a guard on a raised chair sat at a gap in it. Beyond him were revolving doors. Jack glanced around: he had no recollection of this space. Where was he? How had he gotten here?

"Thanks," he said idiotically, nodding. Was the tic showing? His eye felt huge, as though the tic were enlarging, like her glasses. He smiled in a preoccupied way and started toward the door. He would not look around. He kept his strides slow, heel first. A blister was starting on his chafed skin. The guard, in a dark sweater and khakis, sat slumped in his chair, gazing out. He wouldn't check anyone leaving, it was people coming in they were careful about. Though why did they care who came in—what were they afraid of? Terrorists? Drugs. It was drugs. Everything was drugs. He could feel the pounding in his head, the chant. He could feel the nurse behind him, watching. His legs were on fire and his feet burned in the heavy boots. He pushed through the revolving door, which went on turning slowly behind him; he had the uneasy feeling that it might never stop.

TWENTY-TWO

Outside was an empty circle of pavement. Arc lights shone down on him, infernally bright, like a prison. He walked fast, squinting, following the curve of the sidewalk—the nurse still watching, he could feel her gaze on his back—as though he had a destination. Beyond the curve was the parking lot, and rows of dark vehicles. He needed a road, people, cars. A drugstore, you could find something at a drugstore. As soon as he reached people, he'd be all right. He kept walking toward the parking lot. He needed shade, his eyes hurt in these arc lights. It was night, he'd have plenty of shade.

In the parking lot things were better. The night felt cooler there, and his eyes watered, relieved. The nurse could no longer see him. So what if she had seen him, so what if he'd said that thing about his son, he was free, he was gone. They couldn't arrest him for leaving his hospital room. He thought of the silent man, the hideous hump of bandage. Around him, behind him, the lights sizzled, or something did. He felt light-headed now, dizzy, and his legs were on fire. Still the rising tide was carrying him.

There were reflections on the row of cars, light outlining the sleek curves of fenders and roofs. He was limping now. The boots were killing his feet—should he take them off? *Bad idea.* Barefoot you looked crazy. He might *be* crazy. How would he know? His feet were impostors in these boots.

He paused and set his hand on the curve of a car. That nurse would say something to someone, she was definitely suspicious. He should never have said that about visiting his son. He looked too young to have a kid. Didn't he? Though he felt old. He felt the same age as his ghastly roommate in the hospital. He felt suddenly that he *was* his ghastly roommate, in the damp molded boots, as though he was in the man's body, stuck in his life. How would you know whose life was yours? *Fuck.* His head was pounding with pain, it was lifting off, drifting away. He opened the door of the car. The interior lit up in welcome and he got in.

Shutting the door, he slid his hands along the visors. He leaned down—his stomach gave a huge lurch at the movement—and swept the floor with his fingers. The light went out, and he was left in darkness. He leaned back against the seat and closed his eyes. It was the first time he'd stopped moving since he'd stood up beside his hospital bed. That was long ago. The silent room, awash with the contempt of the fat nurse. That fat nurse: he'd like to see her now, out here in the dark, on a level playing field. His stomach clenched and his cheeks suddenly puffed out with the urge to vomit, then relaxed; the moment passed.

He wondered what time it was. It felt late. It felt like the deep middle of the night, just starting to tilt toward dawn. The air was cold and damp. He opened his eyes: he was alone in a stranger's car. It felt safe but temporary. He scanned the dashboard for a clock, but everything was dark. His fingers groped across the dashboard for the ashtray. Something gave way and slid open. He dipped his fingers into it: bingo. The keys. At once the headache worsened, a muscular hammering pulse inside his brain.

There you are, he thought, *but where was that? About fucking time.* He did not know what he was saying. He slid the keys into the ignition.

He felt an overwhelming relief, as though he were offering up his body to God. Tension was sliding away, it was leaving him, except for the pounding pulse. He turned on the engine. The car had a rich, faintly unpleasant, organic smell. Something moldy or rotten maybe, food scraps under the seat, crumbs in the cushions. *Christ, it was the fat nurse's car, Dunkin' Donuts boxes under the seats. It had to be.* He fiddled with the instruments, and the windshield wipers rose up suddenly and began their sweeping arcs. He switched them off and groped for the lights. Before him was a sudden illumination, a low glowing oval of light. The pavement glistened slightly.

He drove slowly, looking for the exit. In his head was the pounding, the high near-chant, in some not-quite-distinguishable language. His legs were cramping, his calf muscles seized up suddenly, jerking as though bitten. Once he kicked out involuntarily; his foot left the accelerator, and the car slowed. He straightened his knee and set his foot, in the heavy boot, back on the accelerator. His skin was goose-bumped.

What he needed now was money. He still had his wallet and knew what was in it: four bucks. He needed more, just enough for a bag or two. Just enough to get straight. He wondered what he could sell: his boots. As if anyone would buy them. He should look in the trunk, maybe the fat nurse had left her vacuum cleaner in it, on the way back from being fixed. Maybe her CD player. Or maybe her brand-new laptop computer, still in the box. A gold Rolex. He remembered his father counting out the money into Dana's hand, all those bills. Fucking Dana (not her real fucking name), staring at him with those cold dead eyes. And all that H in the back room, with the scales, the razor blades. The little glassine bags of powder, stamped with Dana's clever mark. All of it just a few steps away, in the back room, his father watching them every second.

Jack's eyes watered; he was swept with chills. His teeth began to chatter and he punched knobs on the dashboard for heat. He turned the radio on, then off. He was freezing. He stopped the car and closed his eyes. The pounding in his head grew louder, and he opened them again.

What he needed was to quit altogether. *He needed to get clean.* The thought washed suddenly through him. This was awful, it was sickening. *He had no life.* He would quit, he would rid himself of this, it was torture. Though first he would have to get straight, just to get through it all: the pounding, the aches, the chills. He needed help. He was sick, right now he needed something to stop the sickness. Then he would end it, he would quit. He would get clean.

The exit was a short curving drive to a main road. No traffic light, no sign, a few unlit buildings. He turned right. The clock on the dashboard, now illuminated, said 3:48. He was in Maine: nothing would be open at this hour, even if he found a town. *Fuck.* The wave of chills passed through him again and the pounding in his head increased. All the Valium had worn off now. If he had those empty bags with him he could have sniffed them, licked them, gotten something from the dust. Rubbed his nose in them. He thought of opening a bag and tilting it, tapping the powder carefully into the blackened spoon. The way it moved from the bag into the shallow bowl of the spoon, in a controlled slide, the tiny granules tumbling over one another, nearly unbearably seductive. Pressing the shaft of the syringe home, sending the solution into his veins, the magic spell. The deep luxury of its arrival in his consciousness. Sinking into its presence. He sniffed deeply; his nose was running. He could feel his eye twitch.

Rounding a curve and descending a small slope, he came into the town. He crossed a little bridge to the intersection of two main streets lined with brick and granite buildings. On the corner was a stone building with the name of a bank etched over the entrance door: now it held a chiropractor and a family therapist. Nothing here, all the real stuff was over at the mall.

Somewhere outside the old town was a wide-open place, paved, dotted with familiar presences: Pizza Hut, AAMCO, the bank, McDonald's. He needed the mall, with its cheesy, neon brilliance, its sleazy corporate presence. Something would be going on there, something might even be open all night, a drugstore. He stopped at the intersection for the light, though it took too long to change and he couldn't wait. The streets were empty. His legs were on fire, and he stepped on the accelerator, heading up the hill, past an old movie theater, shops, all of them closed and dark.

He was sweating again, and his neck hurt. He turned his head from side to side, his eyes on the road.

At the next intersection he turned right, onto a row of houses. They were hung with professional signs, now lawyers' and dentists' offices, and all dark. Ahead were big lit-up signs.

The mall parking lot ran along the road, huge and indeterminate, an ocean of blacktop. He turned in at McDonald's (closed) and began to cruise. He headed farther in toward the long low row of lit-up buildings: dry cleaners, Pet World, Radio Shack. Everything closed and silent. Why wasn't there an all-night Rite Aid? He could have gone into it and lifted something, Christ, baby aspirin, Lavoris, shampoo. Anything to make this stop. Heat was rising through his body again, sweat starting up on his forehead. Nausea bloomed inside him, his stomach seized in a testing, preparatory way. He stopped the car, jerked open the door and leaned out, retching onto the pavement.

As he raised his head, he saw the car pull up in front of him. First he saw just the tires, bright and colorless in his headlights, then, raising his eyes, the word POLICE on the side in big letters. Jack closed the door, though the overhead light stayed on, illuminating him. The cop sat in his darkened car without moving. He was parked broadside in front of Jack. *Fuck. Fuck Fuck Fuck.*

The policeman got out and came over to the car, carrying a flashlight. Jack rolled down the window.

"License and registration please," the policeman said. He shone the flashlight in on Jack's face.

"Hi, Officer," Jack said, blinking, trying for cheer. "Is there a problem?"

"Hope not," said the policeman. "Can I see your license and registration?" He pointed the flashlight down at Jack's lap.

"Hold on," Jack said. His heart was thundering in his chest. He slid his hand into his pants and pulled out his wallet. He opened it up and handed it through the window to the policeman. The policeman said nothing. He was red-faced, with a wide nose.

"Hold on," Jack said again, and leaned over and opened the glove compartment. *Wouldn't you leave the registration in your glove compartment? Always in the car, so you'd never find yourself in this precise situation, a policeman holding a flashlight over you as he waits for you to hand it out to him? Wouldn't you leave it in the glove compartment, in a little plastic folder with the insurance folder?*

He rooted hard. Maps slid onto the floor. A thick owner's manual. The folder: he grabbed it.

"Here you are," he said, handing out the registration.

The policeman said nothing, turning to go back to the cruiser. He climbed into the front seat and started talking on the radio. He was checking to see if the car was stolen. That nurse wouldn't be leaving yet, would she? Weren't the shifts from eight to midnight, midnight to four? Or was it eleven to three, three to seven? Maybe she'd stay and have coffee with a friend. Maybe it wasn't the fat nurse's car after all. It had only been missing for twenty minutes. How would anyone know?

Jack smiled in the dark, practicing. *Thank you, Officer.* You thanked them for everything. He leaned his head back against the seat and closed his eyes. This was agony. His joints were now on fire, his knees, his wrists, his elbows. His hips felt as though the insides had been carved out with a spoon, carved bare. The nurse's shift wouldn't be over until six. She wouldn't know yet.

After a while he heard the car door open again and close. The policeman walked back with his cards. He handed them to Jack and leaned down inside the window. He pointed the flashlight into the interior, irradiating the inside of the car. Jack held his hands up in mock arrest.

"Everything all right?" the policeman asked. "You're a long way from home."

"Fine," Jack said. "Just waiting for a friend." *Shut up! Shut up! Don't get tricky!*

"What's the name of your friend?" asked the policeman.

"Ricky Wigmore," said Jack, a name from grade school.

"And where does Ricky live?" asked the policeman.

You asshole. Why did you start this?

"He lives in New York. He's staying with friends up here. I don't know exactly where. With his mom and stepfather, I think. We just said we'd get together."

"And where are you staying?"

"With my mom. She's rented a house with a friend, down on the coast." *Why! Why! Why lie?*

"You're meeting Ricky pretty late," said the policeman.

Jack smiled at him. "Yeah. I guess."

The question was, had the cop seen him run the light? He had run the light, hadn't he? He thought he had. But that was the key. If not, then there was nothing to bring him in for. At least for once there was nothing on him, not a crumb, not a flake, not a grain, not a whisper of heroin. Unless the fat nurse was an addict and there was some in her car. That would be ironic, wouldn't it?

The thought of irony made Jack want to retch again. He felt the wave ripple through his stomach. He held it from coming up his throat.

"All right," said the policeman, shining the flashlight into the interior again. The beam withdrew suddenly. The policeman became a dark presence, a voice outside the car. "All right, Jack. Be careful."

"Thank you, Officer," Jack said, raising his eyes to the policeman's. "Thanks for stopping. Good night." *Why? Why? Why say anything? Shut up!*

Jack saw his bulk move away in the darkness. He heard the hard shoes on the pavement, and then the engine start up.

TWENTY-THREE

Something was interrupting, again and again. In between were great reaches of time and silence. Around Julia was darkness. The sounds came from miles away, another planet. Julia lay without moving, pulled unwillingly from the grasp of sleep by each insistent noise, hoping each would be the last, until suddenly her mind flashed on—*telephone*—and she leaped from bed.

She pulled on her robe and hurried down the steep stairs, sideways on the narrow steps, her bathrobe flapping against her legs. She crossed the dining room in the dark, not pausing at the light switch.

"Hello?"

"Mrs. Lambert?" A woman's voice, a flat downeast accent.

"Yes?"

"This is Monica Savage, at Gaud County Hospital. I'm calling to tell you that your son Jack is missing."

"Missing?" Julia repeated. Jack was *at* the hospital.

"He is not in his room. As far as we can tell, he's no longer on the premises."

"What does that mean?" Julia asked. *How could he be missing?*

"I don't know, Mrs. Lambert. He left the hospital without going through discharge."

"But he was sick. He was on an IV." She could not bring herself to name his condition.

"Apparently he disconnected himself. We are not a restrictive facility," Monica reminded her. "We're a hospital."

"I understand that," Julia said. "But still, I'd have thought—" she stopped.

She'd have thought a child would be safe in a hospital. When they'd seen him, Jack had been helpless and twitching, racked with aches and chills. No condition to sneak off. And why would he? He needed help.

"Do you have any suggestions?" Julia asked meekly.

"I'm sorry, Mrs. Lambert. You might try the police. We'll call if we have any further information. He may contact you."

"He had no shoes," Julia said, remembering.

"He seems to have taken his roommate's," Monica said.

"What do you mean?"

"The other patient in his room had boots in his locker. Now they're gone."

"Oh," said Julia. Each new piece of information was worse. "Well, thank you for calling." She hung up before she heard any more.

Julia moved through the nighttime rooms without turning on lights. Wendell's door was closed. Julia knocked gently, whispering his name. She heard nothing; she whispered again.

"What is it?" Wendell asked suddenly. He sounded completely awake, alert.

She opened the door onto pitch blackness.

"The hospital called." Julia spoke into the dark. "Jack's gone. He's disappeared."

"Shit," Wendell said quietly. She heard him grope for the light. Its sudden glare revealed him sitting up in bed, blinking, bare-chested. The hair on his chest was graying. "What do we do now?"

"Call the police, I guess," said Julia. "Or do we? If we call them, they're on the lookout for him. Do we want him arrested?"

"We can't ask them to find him. He's not a runaway child, he's an adult. And he hasn't done anything."

"Not yet," Julia said gloomily. "But he hasn't gone off at four o'clock in the morning to find a good job."

"*Shit,*" Wendell said again. He rubbed his hand over his scalp.

"Isn't there a drugs hot line?"

"What would we say, our son has gone into the night looking for drugs? Then what?"

Julia folded her arms. "What makes me furious is that we have to sit here waiting for the next awful thing he does. *Why does he act like this? Damn him.*" She paused. "He still has that infection, he's still on intravenous antibiotics. Is he crazy?"

"Yes," Wendell said. "While he's an addict, he's crazy."

"God." Julia put her face in her hands.

Wendell sighed. "Yeah."

Julia raised her head. "I thought we were getting somewhere. I thought we were, you know, on our way."

"I guess it's not going to be that simple."

"I didn't think it would be *simple*," Julia said, "but I thought we'd be working together, all of us. Now it feels as though Jack's working against us. I didn't expect that. Right now he may be hitchhiking back to New York, back to his dealer."

"So what am I doing here?" Wendell said, looking at the crammed shelves looming over his bed. "How long do I stay in this fucking storage closet, waiting for him to show up? Why was this such a good idea?"

"What should we have done instead?" said Julia. "What do you do if your son is a heroin addict?"

"We should call Carpenter," he said.

Carpenter had arrived the night before, too late to meet with them. He'd called from the airport, then rented a car and driven himself to the B&B.

"We can't call," said Julia. "He doesn't have his own phone there."

"We'll go over."

"Right now? At four in the morning?"

"Right now is when we need him. It can't be the first time something like this has happened."

"What about Steven?"

Wendell paused. "What do you think?"

"I hate to wake him up," Julia said. "And I think he's getting sick of Jack's emergencies."

"We'll go alone." Wendell got out of bed. His legs were bare. He was wearing only boxer shorts, and his pale muscular thighs were blue-white. Suddenly Julia could smell his body; she turned away.

"I'll get dressed. Meet you at the front door," she said.

When she opened the front door Julia was met by a wave of night air, as fresh and cool and tranquil as though Jack were lying quietly in bed upstairs. The lilacs were dark masses against the paler meadow, the sky was lightening along the eastern edge. Dawn was not distant; she could feel its approach, everything gathering smoothly toward its miraculous transformation.

She could not reconcile the extreme beauty of the landscape, the rustling grass, the sweet air, the mysterious sense of anticipation in the lightening sky, with her sad and frightening errand. How could they both exist in the same time, the same place?

Wendell appeared, and they set off in silence. Julia brushed through the long grass, cold and wet. The car windshield was silvered with moisture, and the wipers swept dark fan-shaped streaks on the glass. The headlights made a long bright tunnel in the darkness.

At the end of the driveway, turning onto the paved road, Julia spoke.

"I can't believe he's done this."

Wendell said nothing.

The village was still dark. The main street was quiet and empty, the trees along it deep shadowy shapes. The B&B was a tall Victorian house near the center, set back from the road. It was prim and well-tended, the clapboards pale yellow, with white eaves and gables. Edging the neat front lawn was a line of magenta petunias, shadowy in the darkness.

The house showed no lights. Julia and Wendell went up the stone pathway and stood at the front door. Wendell knocked on the screen. Every noise seemed loud.

"Maybe we should have called first," Julia whispered.

"Well, we didn't," Wendell said. He knocked louder. *"Hello!"*

A light went on upstairs and he knocked again.

"Who is it?" A man's voice.

"The Lamberts," Wendell called quietly. "It's an emergency. We need to see Ralph Carpenter."

"Just a minute."

Another light. The stone front step was cold and damp. Julia, in sandals, felt the chill on her feet.

Inside there were footsteps on the stairs, a light in the front hall. The front door was hung with white curtains. They heard the metallic shiftings of the lock, then the door opened onto a man in pajamas and faded brown bathrobe. Below wild thatched eyebrows his eyes were stupid with sleep, his cheeks thick with stubble..

"We're so sorry to bother you," Julia began.

"It's a family emergency," Wendell interrupted. "We need to see Mr. Carpenter."

"He's coming," the man said. They stood in silence, the man in the bathrobe blinking slowly, nearly asleep again. Carpenter's legs appeared, in close-fitting jeans. Barefoot, bowlegged, he came springily down the steps. He wore a blue V-neck sweater and no shirt. He was stocky and muscular, with a round face and a tanned, balding head. His gold-rimmed glasses glinted in the overhead light.

He was already talking. "Come in, come in," he said expansively, as though he'd invited them there. He was fully awake, brimming with energy. He moved like a boxer, light, agile, powerful. He turned to the man in the bathrobe. "Where can we talk?"

The sleepwalker motioned them into the living room, turned on a light, and left, shuffling back upstairs. The living room held a suite of stiff green furniture and a glossy maple reproduction table. On the wall were faded bird prints.

Carpenter turned to them.

"Ralph Carpenter," he said unnecessarily, holding out his hand first to Julia, then Wendell. His grip was strong, lasting a moment longer than she'd expected.

Wendell and Julia sat down on the sofa and Carpenter flung himself into a high-backed wing chair. He set his ankle on his knee, his leg angled flat. He laced his hands over his midriff. His black eyes were intent. "What's going on?"

"Jack's left the hospital," Julia said. "They called us."

"Walked out," Wendell said, "without telling anyone."

"Okay," Carpenter said, nodding. He seemed unsurprised. "He's looking for drugs."

"What will he do?" asked Julia.

Carpenter shook his head. "We have to prepare for the worst," he said. "Right now, Jack is not the person you knew. You understand that?"

They both nodded soberly.

"Yes," Julia said, then added rebelliously, "No, not really."

"You have to start learning it," Carpenter said firmly. "You have to start realizing that, on heroin, Jack is no one you know."

He waited, watchful.

Julia said nothing.

"So we have to treat him like someone else." Now he sounded milder. "Right now, you need to learn that everything you know about your son is no longer relevant. All your memories, everything you've built up to deal with him, are useless."

He paused. Carpenter gave off a kind of heat, an energy-based authority. He seemed not to blink; his eyes were like a snake's, round and black.

"The way we deal with people is through memory," he said. "Each time we see someone, we're using our knowledge of past behavior to predict future behavior. We create a body of knowledge about the person."

He waited.

"But none of that applies to a drug addict," Carpenter said. "While he's under that chemical spell, his personality is altered. Everything you know about Jack is no longer valid. It may be valid again, sometime in the future, but it's not useful now. Don't say to yourself, 'This is just temporary, like a fever. Jack is still there, he's still available.' He's not. Right now, he's gone. Right now, you no longer know your son."

Carpenter paused again, his eyes moving from one to the other. There was something oppressive and reproving about his manner.

"Jack's not available to you right now. Everything you know about him is not true. All your memories of him are false."

Julia thought of Jack standing in her apartment that day, looking so strange. His gaze speculative, purposeful, frightening.

"He's been taken over by something stronger than he is," Carpenter said. "He can't help himself, and right now he doesn't *want* to."

"So what do we do?" Julia asked. She hated all this, hated hearing it, hated Carpenter's bossy authoritative manner.

"Right now, we wait," Carpenter said. "It's unlikely he'll come home on his own. He'll probably be picked up by the police. He might be hitchhiking, he might have stolen a car. He has no money?"

Julia shook her head. "He didn't even have any shoes. He stole his roommate's."

"He's going to do something to get some drugs. He's in severe withdrawal right now. It could go on for days. He's in agony, by the way." Carpenter's voice turned gentler, though it was still commanding. "You should know how painful this is for him. Heroin addicts have very low pain threshholds, and withdrawal is excruciating for them."

"Great," Julia said. "He's in agony, he's no one we know, and he's going to commit a crime." She heard herself crying, her voice awkward and raw. She should have brought Kleenex.

"This is hard," Carpenter said, nodding.

Julia found a wadded-up tissue and blew her nose.

"When we find him, our job will be to convince him to stop." Carpenter looked from one to the other.

There was something about this he enjoyed, Julia thought. Power: he likes the fact that we know nothing and he knows everything. He was like a magician, revealing one dreadful fact after another, forcing his knowledge on his audience. There seemed no possibility of challenging him: there was the top hat, there was the white dove, fluttering nervously on his arm.

"You can't force an addict to stop," Carpenter went on, "he has to want to do it. He may say he does, because he knows you want him to, but he doesn't. Or he may want to quit, but he can't. He'll say anything you want to hear, to keep you quiet. He'll say anything: addicts are manipulators. They're players. I was an addict myself."

He looked at them each again, his eyes penetrating. *What did he want?*

"I went into rehab three times," he said. "Each time I swore to my parents I was quitting, that it was all over. I asked them for help and for money. Finally, my parents had enough. They said, 'Ralph, we're through. We're moving to Europe. We won't give you our phone number or address. We won't even tell you what country we're in. You'll have no way of reaching us. We wish you luck with your addiction, but you have to solve it yourself.'"

He spoke slowly.

He liked telling this story, Julia realized. He relished being the bad boy, the shameless reprobate, and then being transformed, becoming the star, the hero. There was something horrible and exhibitionistic about his performance, but also mesmerizing. She had no choice but to listen to him, take his advice. There was no recourse, it seemed.

"Each time, I'd told my parents I'd changed. I lied to them. I stole from them. I told them I was weak, that I'd had a breakthrough, that I needed their support—whatever I had to say to get heroin." He paused, looking at them.

"I know it's hard to understand what's happening right now with Jack. It's hard to believe it. Sometimes parents hold a kind of private reserve for their son. I can see them thinking, Well, that's not what's happening to my son. Things aren't so bad for us." Carpenter paused again. "Everyone thinks that things aren't so bad for them. But you need to know something: heroin has the same effect on everyone. And most people on heroin die from it."

Julia shook her head and began to cry again. "I don't want to hear this."

Carpenter waited a moment. "The only way to get through this is to talk our way through."

"Fine." Julia tried to stop crying. "What shall we say?"

"Let's talk about Jack," said Carpenter. He leaned back against the chair. "Tell me about him. How did all this start?"

Wendell shook his head. "He's been on drugs for years. It's always been a problem."

"We could never stop him," said Julia, "even from smoking pot. He was always on the outer edge. But our older son, Steven, never had a problem. It's so strange."

"It often happens," Carpenter said. Now he seemed genuinely gentle. "It seems unfair."

"It could have been the divorce," said Julia, "that sort of drove him to it, but Steven went through it, too."

"Your sons are different people," said Carpenter.

"Things were different for them, though, when they were growing up," Julia said. "We were stricter with Steven. With Jack, we sort of thought we'd already done it." She shook her head, pained. "I don't think we were paying attention."

"I think we were paying attention," Wendell said.

Julia looked at him. Was he going to disagree with her? *He's not even your son.*

"We were more permissive with Jack," she said to Wendell. "Now it seems crazy," she said to Carpenter. "Now everything we did seems crazy. How could we have let this happen?"

She felt like a supplicant, as though, if she offered exactly the right combination—confession, obedience, trust—to this black-eyed, muscular man, he would cure their son. What could she offer him?

"Blaming yourselves isn't useful," Carpenter said. "It gets us nowhere. I was a drug addict, and you know what? It wasn't my parents' fault. It wasn't my friends'." He tapped his chest. "It was my fault. I took drugs, I liked them, I hung out with people who took them. I got hooked. Chemicals do that to you. My parents were not to blame."

"I think I was hard on Jack," Wendell said slowly.

"There'll be a time to say that," Carpenter said. "Right now, don't blame yourselves too much. We're going to look ahead, not back."

"I know I was," Wendell said, as though Carpenter hadn't spoken. He was looking down at the rug, as though he were looking back through the years and could see himself, critical, exigent.

"Don't," Julia murmured.

It seemed, too, as though there was something risky about this, about offering too much of themselves to this stranger.

"Really," Carpenter said, shaking his head. "It's not useful. We can talk about family patterns, but right now, blame isn't useful. This isn't Freudian therapy, we're not going back to the womb."

A *good thing,* thought Julia.

"This is a long process. Right now, what I'm saying seems impossible and unreal. We'll go over and over the same ground until it feels different. Until it feels true."

She did not want any of this to be true.

"Also, this may be a legal matter now. If Jack is found by the police, there may be charges against him. If so, there'll be an arraignment. We may want to ask the judge to remand him into rehab. There may be the possibility of jail."

"What do you advise?" Wendell asked.

"Depends on what Jack does." Carpenter steepled his hands. "And what his habit is. It sounds pretty serious."

"Jail," said Julia miserably. She put her hand over her eyes.

"Remember that Jack isn't the son you know right now," Carpenter said. "Heroin has taken him over. It's the only thing in his life. Nothing else has any significance for him. Nothing. Not even you. As a human being, he's pretty much hit rock bottom."

There was something hypnotic and dreadful about Carpenter, his intensity, his ferociousness, his penetrating stare. It felt perilous, putting themselves so completely in his power. She disliked his self-importance, his jargon, and she detested everything he was saying. But he was the professional: what choice did they have but to trust him? Julia could not think of a way, or a reason, to resist him.

TWENTY-FOUR

Jack watched the police cruiser as it slid off across the parking lot, watched its headlights until it turned slowly out onto the road.

Leaning against the door, he was swept again with a wave of trembling. He closed his eyes, his teeth began to chatter. He slid down and curled up on the seat, hugging himself for warmth, waiting for the wave to pass.

He thought of the drugstore he hoped to find nearby, its dry, faintly noxious chemical smell, its narrow aisles and loaded shelves. The good stuff would be behind the high counter, maybe locked in a safe, or in a narcotics drawer. In New York it was harder. On the Lower East Side, metal bars scissored across the drugstore windows at night. In Harlem, articulated metal shades unrolled heavily to the sidewalk, ending with a padlock. They took no chances: *those fucking junkies.*

He'd take any kind of downers—painkillers, sleeping pills, hair tonic. Over the counter, off the shelf, whatever he found. Tylenol PM Extra Strength had codeine in it, he'd heard. Vicodin, Percodan, he might get lucky. Lortab, diazepam. Some drugstores even sold methadone, though that was too good to be true. But he'd find something: maybe Oxy, though it was getting scarce. The thought of drugs excited him. The thought of their nearness, their presence, was starting to crowd out the rest of the world. Certainly he would not think of his parents asleep at the house, the thought of them like static on the radio. Below the static—below everything—was the thought of heroin, beautiful and dark, a slow wide stream like honey. Heroin lay beneath everything.

As though he were having a vision, he thought of the moment when the needle first went in, unbearably beautiful, that moment of delicate piercing. Drawing up the tiny flower of blood. *The orchid.* The bright scarlet unfurling into the clear liquid. *The inside touch.* The way the needle felt in your vein. *It was the beloved. It was the arrival of the beloved.*

Jack felt suddenly exhausted, resentful about his abstinence, as though not using had been his choice. He felt aggrieved, as though he were owed something, as though he deserved a reward for having refrained for such a long time. It had been hours, *days*, since he'd used; it was time for all this misery to be over.

Chills swept through his body again. All this—abstinence and solitude and silence—was like being in the desert, trudging through the empty dunes. An image came to him: a landscape, pale and bleak, unnaturally lit like an early Renaissance painting, the light coming from everywhere. Himself struggling through it like a pilgrim, a saint. Who was it, out in the desert? For forty days and forty nights? The ravens brought him food. The silent flap of ragged wings against an empty sky. *Where would he find it, how would he find his way back to his dark honeyed beauty?* His whole body was lit up with the sense of it. There was no way not to draw near. His teeth clattered in the silence as he shivered, the sound loud and unnatural. It was strange to have your body doing something without your direction.

The drugstore would have a back door. He'd go around there. What he needed was a tool. Still lying on the seat, on his side, Jack reached for the glove compartment. The tiny light inside flared on the tiny crowded cubby, stuffed with papers, maps, CDs, a battered packet of Kleenex. He rifled through it. *Nothing.* Why didn't the fat nurse keep a nail file in her car, some scissors? Even a pen. Or a heavy rock. *Why didn't she keep a heavy rock in her glove compartment? Why would you not?*

All he needed was a few minutes before the alarm went off. It would be ten, fifteen, maybe twenty minutes before anyone arrived, out here in the boonies. Or maybe in the boonies there'd be less time, since there was nothing else to do. He had to do it soon or it would be light. And that policeman might come back. He had a bad feeling about the policeman. It seemed suspicious that he had driven away, because surely he himself had aroused some suspicions? The made-up name, the made-up place at the shore. Sitting there in the middle of the night, waiting for someone without knowing where he was. He could hardly believe the words as he heard them coming out of his mouth, but the policeman had nodded and let him go. Who knew what goes through the minds of policemen? Maybe he had snuck back around without headlights and was waiting nearby, behind him. But probably this was paranoia, junkie thinking. The police had other things to do besides pick up a guy jonesing in a parking lot.

Jack eased upright and waited for his stomach to unclench. Still bent over, he started the engine. Without turning on the lights, he drove very slowly toward the line of shops, squinting ahead into the darkness. He could see the white lines of the parking lot, the darker mass of the buildings as he approached them, dim neon glows in the windows. He drove carefully, inching along.

Now it was thirst. Now he could hardly swallow, and his eyes itched. Once you thought about swallowing you had to do it. His throat was parched, it was like canvas. His hands itched, the backs of his hands. He scratched at one with the other. Nearing the buildings, he slowed down further, squinting at the dark outlines against the dark sky. He jerked his chin in the air and scratched suddenly at his neck; at the same time the car thudded to a heavy stop and his head snapped back against the seat. He peered through the windshield into the darkness: *Fuck.* He'd driven right into the building. Though only at five miles an hour, maybe two.

Maybe he'd been lucky. Maybe he'd hit the drugstore, maybe he'd broken the lock on the door. That was a thought. *The car was a tool.* He backed up a bit and got out, scratching at his hands. He wished he had a fork to scratch his skin with, a knife, a saw. *Christ, Christ, it itched.* Who was it, who had it been, out in the desert? Alone and starving, under the empty sky. Saint Jerome? Robes black against the red cliffs, the great reach of sand behind him. Too much space, too much empty sky. The image was unsettling, he tried to dismiss it.

The low buildings of the mall stretched out in both directions. He peered in at each dim window, looking for the drugstore. Dry cleaners, a toy store, a men's clothing shop. He clopped along, his feet swimming painfully in the heavy boots. His knees hurt. Was there a way to scratch the backs of both hands at once? Some trick of coordination? He could not manage it. His neck itched again. His throat was horribly dry, he could barely swallow. Swallowing made him realize how dry he was. He tried not to, he could not help it. *Swallowing was like heroin. Once it entered your mind it was all over. Though heroin had always already entered his mind, it was always there, lying dark and silky at the bottom of his mind.*

Through the dimness he saw a glowing pink sign advertising sunscreen, and his heart lifted. In gratitude he scratched hard at the back of his hand. Growing and blooming inside his mind was the thought of smack, and the long black drop into pleasure. It was nearly unbearable. *Christ.*

There might be methadone. There'd be painkillers, something. Maybe morphine. If it wasn't all locked up. Whatever he got now he'd trade later for H. He'd find something, even over the counter, to damp this down, what he was feeling, to get straight. All he needed was to get straight. His head was swollen, it felt bursting. His calves were on fire. *The itch, the itch, the itch.* He rubbed furiously at his eyes.

The door was made of heavy glass, with a horizontal bar across the center. He tried it: locked tight. The back door would be solid metal, probably. Better to get a rock and go for this one. Where would a rock be?

The idea of going back to the car and driving somewhere else to look for a rock was unbearable. He could hardly walk. Every part of him hurt. The idea of shifting his body, changing things around, was unbearable. He was here, standing in front of the glass door. He swayed slightly. Where would a rock be? In a shopping mall?

He turned and looked into the darkness of the parking lot. The sky was beginning to lighten faintly along the lower edge, the air turning dimly translucent instead of opaque. It would be dawn soon, and he'd be visible. He needed something, anything. A rock, a length of wood. A two-by-four, *was that too much to ask?* Innocuous, hardly dangerous, why not leave it out on the sidewalk in front of the drugstore? *For someone like him, who actually needed it. Was that too much to ask?* The sidewalk seemed, in the darkness, heartbreakingly empty, devoid of rocks and two-by-fours.

He worked his way along. He'd have to move fast, before the nurse discovered her car was gone. When would her shift be over? Four? Six? Dawn was coming, an excruciating thought. He could hardly consider its arrival, the horror of it, the violent and punishing illumination that would flood the landscape. He shook his head in protest. A mistake: pain. He breathed out loudly, closing his eyes. He kept moving, always kept moving.

And there it was, against his foot. Someone had, in fact, left something heavy on the sidewalk. He groped for it with his hand: a rock. He could have wept at the graciousness of fortune. He picked it up, feeling its heft: heavy Maine granite. He felt a flash of pride for his state, for its treasure, its remarkable mineral properties. He started back to the drugstore, hurrying, in the too-big boots, hobbling toward the faint glow of the suntan lotion.

At the door he stopped, feeling for the lock. He'd smash the glass, then reach in and open it from inside. If the whole window shattered, he'd just climb through it, not even open the door. Opening the door would set off the alarm. He raised his arm and brought the rock down hard against the glass. He felt a violent shock, like the kick of a shotgun. A thud, but no sound of shattering. He raised his arm again, staggering slightly. Closing his eyes, he swung it harder, as hard as he could.

There was a high shivering sound, and he felt the light lethal rain of splinters. He opened his eyes and leaned down: in the dim glow he couldn't see what was glass and what was opening. *Why didn't the nurse have a flashlight in her car? Who would drive around without a flashlight?* He ran his fingertips delicately along the broken edges of the glass. It felt jagged, dangerous.

He closed his eyes and used the rock again and again. Shards flew into the air and peppered his hair, his face.

The crossbar on the door was higher than his waist, the door was too narrow for him to jump onto the bar. He'd have to climb through it, resting his ass on the broken glass as he shifted from one foot to the other.

He picked at the pieces left in the crossbar, trying to hurry. The door might be alarmed, though. If it had gone off, he had about ten minutes. Maybe fifteen. He ran his fingertip along it: smooth enough. He wished he had something to throw over it—*what kind of person drove around without a blanket in her car?* He lifted his right foot as high as he could, over the bar, and threw himself over, trying to hold his crotch away from the crossbar, feeling the broken glass rake against his thigh. His foot crumpled as it hit the floor, and he went down on his side, lunging into the darkness, hitting his head against something as he fell.

He struggled to his feet. His hands were hot and wet, and his right thigh burned. He hobbled along the aisle, peering at the shelves. The farther he got from the neon glow at the window, the less he could see. He'd have to risk turning on a light. The alarm had already gone off, he could feel it.

He felt his way into the back and slid his hands carefully along the walls for the light switch. The sudden illumination was like a blast of sound. The silence turned brazen. He glanced around the store—three narrow aisles, display shelves packed with shampoo, toothpaste, soap— and stepped behind the high counter. Below it were the shelves of dispensing bottles. The really serious stuff would be double-locked, then there was the single-locked drawer, and even the good unlocked stuff would be dispersed among the stock, so it wouldn't be so easy to make a grab for it. But he could sense the presence of what he wanted, his nerves were pulsing. He touched the bottles, the big dispensing jars full of pills and capsules. He looked along the shelves for hydrocodone, codeine. Vicodin, Percoset. Just in case they'd been left out on the shelf last night.

There, below the counter, was the locked drawer: that's where the good stuff was. He could feel it. The controlled substances. His pulse was rising, his body could feel the approach of it, it was like salivation at the approach of food. It was better than food. The ravens circled around him, laden, their big black wings flapping. This was what he wanted.

He tested it: the drawer was locked tight. Where was a weapon? Where was something that would pick a lock, or break it? What was wrong with that nurse?

He looked again along the shelves. He took down a big jar and opened it: the capsules were small and yellow, a bright synthetic color, like yellowjackets. He took some and stuffed them in his pocket. Never pass up drugs. The color looked dangerous, subversive. He could always sell them. He could sell them as anything. Junkies would buy any kind of drugs. He opened another jar: two-colored capsules, deep electric blue and tan. He shook out a handful and stuffed them in his other pocket. He should get some painkillers off the shelf, he should get them right now, just in case. He should clear out, get to the car and get going, before the police came. The locked drawer was full of what he wanted. The keys wouldn't be here—would they? He opened the smaller drawers, looking for the keys, yanking them open, slamming them shut. There were empty pill envelopes, unused labels. Supplies. Nothing.

He looked along the shelves. There were other bottles he should take, only he didn't know which ones. He should leave right now. The alarm would have gone off, people were on their way, cars were speeding along these silent roads, he had to get out, had to throw himself back through the shattered door, but he couldn't bring himself to move. He was fixed and frozen by the proximity of the pills, the drugs, with their faintly sour chemical smell; the fact that what he needed, what he longed for, was right here with him, inches away. His heart pounded in his chest and he felt a kind of ecstasy rising through him; he wanted to finger each of these bottles, the big capacious manufacturers' bottles, so carelessly, luxuriantly full, the tops so casually closed, opened with just the twist of the hand, of the wrist: all his. He stood in the blissful current of triumphant arrival, feeling its balm upon his soul. He stood bathed in the overhead light, bathed by its radiance, in this ecstatic moment of possession.

The light around him began strangely to change, turning more brilliant and ruddy, and somehow pulsing. It was part of this strange blissful moment, this stilled ecstasy, and he waited expectantly for it to expand and unfurl. There was the sound of an engine, and his chest closed and tightened, and he swore. He heard the slam of a car door and dropped down, below the counter. Was there a back door? Could he reach it? It was too late to turn off the light.

"POLICE OFFICER." The voice was unnaturally loud, electronically amplified, and blurred, impersonal. There were footsteps coming closer, the voice grew louder. "COME TO THE FRONT OF THE STORE WITH YOUR HANDS UP."

Jack crouched on the floor. He would not move. He would never move. They couldn't make him move. His wrists ached to be scratched, and his knees were on fire again, his body returned to him with a vengeance. The inside of his thigh burned where the glass had cut it.

He thought of the pills in his pockets. He would take some pills right now, they would do something. This was the moment. He straightened enough to reach into his pocket, felt his fingers close on some yellows. He pulled out three: he wouldn't be selling these now. He gulped them down, stiff and dry in his throat. Outside, the policeman was still booming. COME TO THE FRONT OF THE STORE WITH YOUR HANDS UP. On the wall above him, flickering against the banked bottles and jars, was the reflection of the circling red light.

What was he thinking? He couldn't bring the pills with him. Was he crazy? That was possession. He straightened again, stooping, and pulled the rest out of his pockets, scattering them on the floor. He would be in possession of nothing. *He was just trying to find a place to take a piss, that was all, Officer.* He'd taken nothing. The voice outside was relentless. He hated the way it sounded, loud and demanding. COME OUT WITH YOUR HANDS UP. YOU ARE UNDER ARREST. In a minute he would feel the codeine starting to seep beautifully into his bloodstream, he held that in his mind, but now, now, YOU ARE UNDER ARREST, that fucking cop would not stop, and he could feel his heart pounding, maybe he should come out, he did not know exactly what to do, the voice was so loud: COME OUT WITH YOUR HANDS UP, and there was no back door, nowhere for him except right here, crouched under the counter, COME OUT NOW the policeman said, and hearing that, he suddenly understood that the policeman held a gun.

And at that, at the notion of guns, of a bullet crashing through the small shop hard and fast, blasting through the plywood counter and finding him there crouching dismally behind the shelves like a terrified animal, the metal blasting into his own body, through his rib cage, living bones, tendons, white glistening tissue, pulsing blood vessels, at the thought of that, something in him gave way, he felt fear wash over him like the tide and something in his bladder released and he felt a hot wet rush along his thigh.

He thought, *Christ. I'm being arrested.* And he thought, *I've pissed my pants. It will stink up his car.* And he thought, *This isn't how it is, this can't be real, I'm not here in this strange place I've never seen before, I'm in the desert. Elijah, that's who it was, ravens circling around him, food in their yellow beaks. Manna. Like heroin.* And he thought, *It's me, though, and I'm here,* because he could smell the rich stench of his own urine, pooling dismally beneath him on the floor. And he thought, sickeningly, as he heard the slow crunch of the policeman's footsteps on the shattered glass on the sidewalk, and heard him start to work on the lock, *It's me, I'm here, there is no desert, I'm about to be arrested.*

And he thought of his parents, and the look he would see on their faces. He could hear the heavy movements of the policeman at the door and he could feel the anger flooding through his body, his rage at the absence of smack, but he could also see his parents' faces, wounded, shocked, and none of this was what he had intended, and *Fuck,* he thought, *Fuck.*

TWENTY-FIVE

Edward stood by the bedroom window, getting dressed. Long bars of sun slanted across the rush-bottomed chair, the drop-leaf table, the painted floor. Edward buttoned his shirt with difficulty; his fingers were not working well.

Edward's night had been bad again. He'd slept little and had disturbing dreams. The night had been full of commotion. Now, in the stillness and early light, Edward felt oddly unsure of himself. He felt something hovering on the edge of his consciousness. It was as though he'd just lost a train of thought, but it wasn't that, it was his own mental placement, his mind, himself. Uncertainty had invaded him. Today it seemed strange for him to be here in this room, standing by the worn rush-bottomed chair in his daughter's house. His daughter Julia.

Sometimes, now, it took a conscious effort to remember something he knew intimately: the name of his own daughter. It was a shock. The neurons fired more slowly and less frequently as you grew older, the brain shrank. He knew this happened, but it outraged him in himself.

Katharine, in her faded lavender wrapper, leaning on her cane, came in from the bathroom. "All yours."

"Thanks," said Edward. He sat down to put on his socks. *Where else had he been? What was that train of thought?* He felt he was somewhere else. *A reel was running somewhere in his consciousness, playing scenes from the past.*

The surgeries. Not the recent, familiar ones, the trephine craniotomies, the intracranial aneurysms. The reel was running on the early surgeries.

He stopped, a blue sock in his hand.

The images in his mind were stronger than the ones in front of him, the patterned tablecloth, the sun slanting onto the floor. *The shadowy hallways, the stench. The frightened faces, the greasy feel of the straitjackets.* The last thing he wanted was these unwilled memories swirling through his mind.

Those surgeries were done with local anesthetic. The patients heard the sound of the drill going through bone. They were strapped down. They lunged, moaning.

He didn't want the memory in his mind. During surgery they'd stop screaming. The surgery stopped the anxiety, that was the purpose. Leucotomies, not lobotomies; that was a misnomer. The lobe was not removed, this was only a severing of the neural connections to the frontal lobe. It was a simple operation. *He didn't want those faces in his mind.*

Edward leaned over. He was still here in this yellow room, the walls lighting up in glowing panels as the sun moved across them. It seemed decades that he'd been sitting here, those reels playing in his mind, but Katharine was still standing at the bureau, the same radiant oblongs of sun lay on the floor.

He was in two places at once. Those V.A. hospitals, and here in the yellow room. The patients had been fully conscious, twisting and crying.

The operations had been performed in good faith. They'd been to cure schizophrenics, or at least to save them from a life in the wards. That was the intent.

Edward slid his foot heavily into his shoe. He felt weakened by this flooding tide. *What was the point of it? Why was this happening?*

"I hate thinking of the past," he said to Katharine, surprising himself. Usually he liked thinking of the past, reviewing his successes, thinking up retorts.

"Well then," said Katharine reasonably, "think of the future." She was still at the bureau, he could see her reflected in the tilting mirror.

"What sort of future should I think about?" Edward asked irascibly. "I'm eighty-eight."

"Any sort at all," Katharine said. "You choose." She leaned her cane against the bureau. Balancing unsteadily, she took off her wrapper, then her nightgown.

"I don't have much of a future," Edward informed her. "I don't expect to live much longer. There's not much future to think about."

"There's today." Katharine eased open the top drawer and took out a bra and sweater. "You can plan for today."

Her own plan for today was to wear her favorite sweater. It was short-sleeved and flat knit, a deep raspberry color, a present from Julia. She liked being encased by a gift from her favorite child. She'd never told anyone Julia was her favorite; for years she'd felt guilty that she had a favorite. But she'd stopped feeling guilty: it was how she felt.

She drew her bra around her waist, hooked it in front, and slid it around to the back. She couldn't reach around in back anymore. She dropped her breasts into the cups with her hands. Her breasts were still heavy, her skin white and soft, but none of this mattered now. Her skin was worn and papery, its sensation dulled. Ecstasy no longer lay just beneath its surface, as it had once. When she was younger, she'd lived in her skin, a touch would set her alight. Just seeing Edward come into the room sometimes would do it, head slightly lowered, looking at her from under his brows. Now nothing could, but she didn't miss it.

When you were young you thought sex was the most important thing there was. You pitied the old, so impoverished by its lack. You couldn't imagine that once it was gone you wouldn't miss it, but that's what happened. Once it was no longer present in your body, it was absent, part of your past.

She and Edward had had decades of wonderful sex. All that was still hers, it still lived in her memory, what she had left of it. It had been their secret. She suspected that Edward had had his own secrets, apart from her. Still, he'd stayed with her, never left. She'd trusted him, and she'd been right. He was bossy and demanding, but he was also brilliant and charming. She found him endearing, and he loved her. She knew that, though he had trouble saying so. It didn't matter. They loved each other, they had grown around each other like a pair of trees. They were interlocked. He was hers, and this was her life.

She reached ponderously for the sweater. Getting dressed now took half the morning, all this tugging and struggle. The cane slid sideways, off the bureau, clattering to the floor.

"Anything for attention," she said, of the cane.

"Shall I pick it up for you?" Edward was now dressed, waiting for her.

"Don't bother," said Katharine. "It'll just fall over again." She pulled the sweater over her head with difficulty.

"I'm going out to have breakfast," Edward said abruptly. He turned and headed for the door.

Katharine's head emerged, and she pulled the sweater down over her shoulders. "I'm losing my memory," she said.

Edward turned and looked at her. He could not remember hearing Katharine complain before. "We all are," he said finally.

"No," Katharine said. "I can't remember anything. I can't remember what you said to me yesterday."

"About what?" Edward asked.

"I don't know," Katharine said. "I can't remember."

She pulled the sweater down to her waist, lapping herself in Julia's rosy love. She watched him steadily, with a small rueful smile. The smile frightened him.

"Now, Kattie," he said. He came over to her.

"I mean it," she said, "my mind is going."

What he felt, a sudden jolt, was loneliness and fear. *Might she leave him?* "Kattie." He put his hand on her shoulder.

"I suppose there's nothing to be done," she said. "I suppose it's that awful thing."

"What?"

"That disease. I can't remember its name." She laughed, her eyes troubled.

"What disease?" He would not say its name.

"You know it. When you lose your mind." The words caught in her throat. She was frightened.

But Edward rallied. "You're overreacting," he said. "We all lose cognitive functions as we get older. Memory loss is a normal part of aging." *Though he was not losing his memory; the reverse, it seemed.* It was flooding in on him like an excoriating tide.

Katharine said nothing, watching him, distress in her eyes. *Was she going to cry?* This was frightening to him. She never cried.

He patted her shoulder gently. "Don't be frightened. What you have is what everyone has. It's old age. Come out and let's have something to eat."

They stood for a moment, searching each other's eyes.

If this were the worst, Alzheimer's, she was right. There was nothing they could do. Edward felt stripped of something necessary. It was a curse, right now, knowing the nervous system, the brain. He'd have stricken the knowledge from himself if he could have.

He knew exactly what was happening, how it looked. The hippocampus lay deep in the temporal lobe, a twinned pair of elegant structures, curved and coiled. This was where memory was made, where the sights and sounds and feelings that make up the bright continual cinema of daily life were mysteriously transformed into neural impulse, then stored in neural tissue.

During the hideous reign of Alzheimer's, the neurons in the hippocampus were gradually invaded by granular clumps of plaque that formed fibrillar tangles. The plaque displaced the glia—the support system for the neurons. The clumps and tangles strangled the neurons from within, choking off the blood supply, dissolving the synapses that allow the transfer of information. The cells were starved and suffocated, which meant that new memories could not be formed. The patient became a captive in a locked chamber: nothing new could be learned. First short-term memory would go, then, as the plaques and tangles spread, the stored long-term memory was destroyed. The private realm, that secret treasure, the accumulation of the self, began to seep away.

Where would she go if she left him? It was his life, too, that she remembered. They had shared it.

Edward was silent. He raised his hand and stroked her hair. It was thin and soft. She watched his eyes. *My poor Kattie,* he thought. Her face, with its high rounded cheekbones, the fine net of lines around her mouth, her large, deepset eyes, was very beautiful to him.

"I'm still here now, though," Katharine said, making an effort to smile.

"I am, too," Edward said gently.

"I don't want to leave you."

He shook his head mutely.

He had not thought of losing her.

He'd always assumed that he'd go first. Now he could see what lay ahead for them: it was the ebbing of her mind. From now on, at each moment like this, when the two of them looked at each other, they would share less and less, she would become more and more absent. It would mean she would be slowly, continually leaving him, moving out like the tide. He would be helpless to help her, increasingly bereft.

Right now, after what had been filling his mind—*the faces of those young men, their cries, the grimy straitjackets*—he could not bear to learn this. He could not bear to think of the damaged brain.

TWENTY-SIX

In the kitchen, Edward fixed breakfast for them. As they ate, Edward found himself covertly watching Katharine, her eyes, the muscles along her jaw, as though they might reveal her condition. Though if it were Alzheimer's, the mental symptoms would long precede physical ones.

Katharine, feeling his scrutiny, looked up. "What?"

"Nothing." He shook his head.

He was frightened. A dark wing swept back and forth behind his eyes. He wanted to go back into the bedroom and lie down again, re-make the pattern of the night. He wanted to sleep soundly, then wake refreshed, not like this, tired, troubled by dark memories that hung about him like mist, by Katharine's awful news.

They ate in silence, Katharine absorbed by her own thoughts. He had never wondered what they were. He had always considered her his property. Now he saw that she had her own domain, where he could not enter; he could only ask her what lay inside, as a supplicant. This made him feel ashamed. The fact that he'd never thought of it made him ashamed.

He'd often kept his thoughts to himself, but he'd never wondered if Katharine could understand them. Now he would have to: this would be a terrible new landscape. He'd be alone in it. *Would his daughters help him? What could your daughters do?*

"Coffee?"

"I thought you'd never ask," Katharine said. What she'd wondered was if he'd asked already, and what she'd answered.

Edward stood to find the coffeemaker, though he was doubtful of his ability to make it work. These things changed designs every year, you needed directions now to find out merely how to turn things on. *What was wrong with a button marked On/Off? What was so terrible about that?*

"Good morning, Daddy." It was Harriet, standing in the doorway. He'd forgotten she was coming.

She held herself upright, her chin lifted, aloof. She was cool, Harriet, ready for flight. Julia was hot, ready to fight.

"Harriet," he said.

She hadn't expected to find him there; she was ready for Julia, not her father. But there he was; she would have to kiss him. She crossed the room, nearing the dangerous presence. The lined skin, the pale blazing eyes, the faint old man's breath, the flyaway hair. The bones so close now to the surface. She felt irritation, and something else: *he was so old.* How had this happened? Why did it make her angry? She reached out to brush her face against his dry cheek, then drew back.

"Harriet! Good morning," Katharine said, pleased, smiling. "How lovely to see you."

Harriet kissed her mother, the soft worn skin.

"Have some coffee with us," Katharine said.

"No thanks," Harriet said. "I just had some at Santa's Little Workshop. With the elves."

"Santa's Little Workshop?" repeated Katharine.

"I went straight to the B&B. Everything's ruffles and flounces. All the curtains have bobbles. It's Elfland."

"Maybe you could fix us some coffee," Edward said. He had no idea what she was talking about. "All I can find is instant."

Harriet stepped forward.

It was a relief to have her take charge of the coffeemaker. This was also new to Edward, that things might be beyond his capabilities. He watched Harriet, trim in her green sweater and khaki pants, move briskly around the kitchen. She took apart the machine, emptied the grounds, ran water hard and fast. Her gestures were smooth and unhurried. She was at ease with the physical world.

She was a surgeon, too, of course. He wondered if she had troubling memories, errors that haunted her. All surgeons had them. They taught you about it now in medical school, how to deal with them. When he'd trained, you learned for yourself. You never talked about this.

Was it worse to make a mistake on an animal, who didn't understand that you were trying to help? Who struggled under your touch? At least human patients knew the doctor was trying to heal them. *Though not those struggling men.*

This was new: he'd never aligned his work with Harriet's before.

"Harriet," he asked, "how much surgery do you do?"

"Twice a week," she said, "Tuesdays and Fridays."

"You have an assistant, or do it all yourself?"

"An assistant," she said, "an intern."

Harriet stood with her back to him. The coffeemaker pulsed beneath her hand, little bubbling eruptions. She held herself clenched, ready for his next remark. It would be belittling, a reminder of the lowly nature of her profession. She waited, but he said nothing, and she turned to face him.

"No microscopic cameras," Harriet said, "no video screens. Just my primitive techniques and my worthless, lower-order patients. A waste of resources, I know."

Edward looked up at her, silent.

She was so strange, Harriet. So abrasive and hostile. Something had set her off, and there was no point now in asking her what he'd been thinking about. Why were his children like this? So adversarial. It felt wounding to him. He'd have liked comfort.

They heard footsteps outside, and Wendell came in from the porch.

"Harriet," he said in a welcoming voice, "good to see you."

"Wendell." Harriet wondered if they should kiss, as they'd always done. Perhaps divorce had changed their relationship; perhaps they were no longer kissing kin. A hug was less charged, but didn't seem to be happening. Should they shake hands? Polite, but so formal. They smiled, moving slightly, though not toward each other.

"So," Wendell said. "We have some bad news. We got a call from the hospital late last night. Jack's vanished."

"Vanished?" Harriet said.

Watching Katharine, Edward could see now that she was struggling for clues, trying to keep abreast of the life around her, trying to keep her secret safe. He wondered if this was how it was for her now. *His wife was tender, fragile, dying. Things were falling away, layer after layer of the world was collapsing inward.*

Julia appeared in the doorway. She had made a run to the market, and her arms were loaded with bags of food. She saw Harriet standing in her kitchen and for a moment her heart lifted. *Oh good, Hattie's here,* she thought, and she felt deep relief. But at once she saw that Harriet's expression—closed, impatient—did not alter, and her heart sank back down.

"Hi there," Julia said lightly. "You're here." She set the bags on the counter and turned to face her sister, in case Harriet made a move.

"Yep," Harriet said, motionless.

"How was your trip?" asked Julia.

It was useless, she thought. Nothing would break down the barrier between them. Why had she asked Harriet to come? Rigid, judgmental, adversarial, Harriet was just like their father. She'd make things worse. Why had Julia thought her family would help? She began unloading food.

"The trip was fine," Harriet said. She brought mugs of coffee over to Edward and Katharine.

"You all set at the B&B?"

"I've just come from there. It's fine. Apart from a terminal case of the ruffles."

"I think they all have that," Julia said. Of course Harriet would be disparaging. "Sorry there's no room for you here."

"You can have my room," Wendell said gallantly.

"No, thanks," Harriet said. "I think it may get too hot for me here."

"It may get too hot for all of us here," said Wendell.

Putting jars and cans away, opening and closing cupboards, Julia waited for her to say something consolatory about Jack, voice distress, offer sympathy, anything, but Harriet was silent.

Harriet sipped from her mug, waiting for her sister to raise the charged subject of Jack, the addiction, the crisis, the reason they were all here.

"You've heard Jack's gone," Julia said. She'd thought she could keep her voice level while she said this, but found she was wrong.

"Wendell said," Harriet answered, disturbed by the unevenness in Julia's voice. "Is there a plan?"

"No plan. We wait," said Julia. "We don't know what he's done or where he is. Anything."

Harriet watched her, moving swiftly, putting things into their places: the cleanser beneath the sink, the paper towels high in the larder closet. Julia's response to the worsening catastrophe around her seemed so practical, so conscientious, so *good*. Harriet felt something shift inside herself, like the opening of a small sluice.

"I'm sorry about all this," she said inadequately.

"Thanks," Julia said, not looking up.

Harriet glanced around the bright, shabby, cluttered kitchen: the battered wooden counters, the faded diamond pattern painted on the floor. The open shelves of china, the colorful plates, the bright hanging mugs. It was all nicer than she'd remembered. Warmth, order, and cleanliness. The tiny spray of spotted feathers in the cobalt blue bottle on the windowsill. The row of smooth stones, a small painted teapot, the neat jars of herbs, all of it woven into a bright changing pattern. It struck Harriet suddenly that this—here—was the life of an artist. This kitchen was a modest manifesto, part of Julia's declaration for beauty.

It was not small, she thought. To choose beauty, to insist on it—this was a large gesture. Harriet felt abashed, never to have noticed something so central, so large, in her sister's life. How could she have missed something so important? It was a small revelation.

But Wendell was talking to her, she was being briefed.

"So, Harr, the guy who's doing the intervention is coming over," he said. "Ralph Carpenter. He's staying at your B&B. We're going to start things today and then meet with Jack. Assuming he turns up."

"You should have had him put in a restricted area in the hospital," Edward informed Julia. "Patients in detox are often put in a psych ward. Those are locked."

"We weren't given a choice," Julia said. "Hospitals don't ask you where you'd like to put your son the heroin addict."

"There might have been options you didn't know about," Edward said. *They might have included him in all this, asked his advice, used his name. Doctors gave each other professional courtesy.*

"There might be a lot of things we could have done differently, Daddy," Julia said. "But I don't want to hear about them now."

"Jules," Wendell said. "Your father's trying to help."

Julia turned to them. "How could he do this?" She was nearly crying. "He still had that thing in his arm. He stole his roommate's boots. How could he act like this? *What is the matter with him?*"

Edward looked at Katharine. She shook her head, mystified. *Boots?*

Harriet shifted uncomfortably. This was like seeing her sister naked by accident.

"He's an addict," Wendell said. "Remember what Carpenter said: he's not the person we know."

"I don't want to hear what Carpenter said," Julia said. She took the cutlery basket from the dishwasher and began rattling silverware into the drawer.

"Opiates alter the chemistry," Edward informed everyone. "They change the personality. They produce a physical change in the makeup of the brain."

"I don't want to hear any of this," Julia said. She set down the cutlery basket and put her hands over her ears. "I want him back."

TWENTY-SEVEN

Carpenter arrived just before lunch, and Julia brought him into the kitchen to meet everyone. He was wearing jeans again, and big sneakers. A long-sleeved collarless jersey, gray, shapeless, and looking vaguely like prison issue.

They stood together in the doorway.

"I want you all to meet Ralph Carpenter," Julia said, "who's going to be helping us with Jack." She looked around the room; everyone nodded politely.

"Edward Treadwell," Edward said sternly, standing up. He did not move toward Carpenter.

"Edward." Carpenter nodded, looking at him intently. "Ralph Carpenter."

Edward nodded, irritated by the use of his first name.

Harriet disliked Carpenter at once: he was too intent, too aggressive, those challenging black eyes. Too small and muscular and bouncy. Her father must loathe him; he'd called him "Edward." Those awful gigantic shoes, the sloppy collarless shirt.

When she introduced herself, Carpenter said, "Glad to meet you, Harriet," and looked at her too hard. "Thanks for coming."

Harriet nodded curtly. She was irritated by the first name, too. And he had no business thanking her; she was here for Julia, not him.

During lunch they sat in the dining room. While he ate Carpenter asked questions.

"Where do you live?" he asked Harriet. "How long have you been there?"

Harriet felt interrogated, and gave him short answers.

He went on around the table, fixing each of them with his black gaze. He asked what Steven was "up to," and where Edward and Katharine lived. How many children did they have? Where did Ted live?

Everyone answered politely: they had given him the right to come here and ask them these questions, despite the discomfort they felt.

It was like seeing a strange doctor, thought Harriet, *having to take off your clothes, expose your most private and dysfunctional aspects to an unknown gaze.*

When his plate was empty, Carpenter leaned back in his chair and looked around.

"So," he said, "I'd like to get started. We'll have three sessions: the first now, the second this evening, and the third with Jack, when he turns up, which I hope will be soon."

He tore off a ragged piece of bread, the crust splintering jaggedly, and set it on the table.

No manners, thought Harriet, pleased.

"I'd like to say first," he went on, "that I admire you all for coming here. Jack's at serious risk right now. You may be saving his life." He looked at each of them soberly. "This is hard for a family. You're going to have to pull together to make this work, but I believe you can do it."

So earnest, Harriet thought. *Like a high-school basketball coach. And why on earth did he believe in them? This family had never pulled together in its life. Her parents hadn't made any effort at all, they'd happened to be here. Her father had never helped any of them. She'd never dream of asking him for help: helping wasn't what this family did. Nor did they ask for it. She'd rather beg in the streets.*

"Let me explain how this will work," Carpenter said. "The intervention. We're here to help Jack, not punish or blame him. We're not going to force him to do anything. We're going to tell him how we feel about him, and what effect his behavior has on us. We're going to tell him the consequences of his addiction, and ask him to change."

The room had turned quiet. Carpenter looked around the table.

"Let me tell you something about drug addiction. It's frightening and shameful. It's a family's dark secret," Carpenter went on. "No one wants to admit to it. Including Jack. Who is, by the way, right now, not in his right mind. He's not the Jack you know anymore: he's been taken over by his addiction. He's been colonized. He's been invaded by heroin. You can't imagine how powerful this is. It's a physiological state, a kind of illness."

Wrong, thought Edward triumphantly. *Addiction is not an illness. A fundamental mistake in terminology before we've even started.*

"Jack's ashamed of his condition," Carpenter said, "but he can't help himself. He's ashamed of what he's doing and ashamed he can't stop. He's caught in a vicious cycle. We're not here to judge him for this." Carpenter looked searchingly around the table. "What we're here to do is offer support." He paused. "And love."

The word: it sizzled in the silence like a live wire, electric, dangerous. Love was not a word their family used. It was not a word they would tolerate from a stranger.

"Together, you can save Jack's life," Carpenter said. "I have confidence." He looked around and smiled.

You don't know us, thought Harriet. *You have no idea.*

"So," Carpenter said, leaning forward. "Let me tell you what Jack's going through. What it's like to be an addict.

"Someone who tries heroin is usually already a drug user, so the idea isn't really foreign to him. He's been using all sorts of things—pot, hash, probably some hard stuff—but heroin's a giant step up from everything else, into the big time. Heroin gives you status. Heroin is the king of cool." He paused. "And heroin gives an unbelievable high, a pleasure you can hardly imagine. It's rapture. There is nothing, *nothing*, so great as the first heroin high. Nothing." Carpenter sounded severe, as though he were daring them to disagree.

Is he boasting? wondered Harriet.

"So. At first it seems pretty harmless. It only costs ten or fifteen dollars a bag. But your body will always compensate for a foreign substance, bring things back to normal, and so, as the user's body starts to adjust to it, he needs more and more heroin to get high. And once he's addicted—which can take several weeks or several months—his habit starts to interfere with everything in his life.

"Getting heroin and using it take up a huge amount of time. And it's expensive: he needs more and more money, and is less and less able to hold a job. So he turns criminal. This isn't such a big deal, though, because he's used illegal drugs for a long time. In a way, he's been living outside the law for years. He's used to breaking it. So now he starts breaking promises, lying to get money, maybe stealing it. It feels normal, though, because everyone around him is doing this, too—lying and stealing, selling, buying, and using an illegal drug. His whole community functions outside the law.

"When he starts committing crimes, sometimes his first victims are family members, because they're the easiest targets. He slips a twenty out of Mom's wallet, he picks up Dad's digital camera from the seat of the car. It's a terrible irony, if you will: the people who most trust him, who most want to help him, are the ones he first betrays."

Julia drifted in and out of attentiveness. She hated the way Carpenter talked—"*a terrible irony, if you will*"—that pretentious psychospeak. She hated the way he talked about Jack as though he were a member of some ghastly defective tribe. He'd never even met Jack.

When Carpenter described taking money from her wallet, she stopped listening. She actually felt she couldn't bear this, it was like being hammered on the head, the relentless deluge of bad news, these devastating assertions and assumptions. The fact that they were true.

Julia looked at Steven. His arms were folded on his chest, his eyes cast down. She wondered if all this was news to him, if it was as dreadful for him to hear as it was for her. She wondered how much of it she could safely not listen to. What if she listened to none of it? None of it was what she wanted to hear. Carpenter was a sort of beast, there was something predatory and gloating about him.

She saw that he'd balled his napkin and left it on the table, beside his plate. It sat there like something mauled and abandoned. *Put your napkin in your lap,* she thought reprovingly, *and don't lean back in that chair.*

He was wrong about Jack. What about the person Jackie was, besides the heroin addict? Jackie had such intelligence and vitality, such talent and potential. Carpenter made him sound like some hopeless loser, without brains or resources: he was wrong, wrong, wrong.

"On some level he's ashamed of this, which is another reason to take heroin—as a protection from shame and depression. Heroin becomes a shield. By this time it's no longer such a big source of pleasure. His body's adjusted to it, and it's increasingly hard to get high.

"Once he's addicted, he has no choice. He has to take heroin constantly, all the time, or he'll go into withdrawal. This is called jonesing. It's a craving, and it's excruciating. He'll feel as though all his joints are on fire. And it will do strange things to his mind: he may want to vomit at the sight of red, something like that. It's weird stuff.

"So now he's using for both physical and psychological reasons. If he tries to quit, he gets an unbearable craving and he's horribly sick. So usually he ends up by using again, and because he's failed to quit, and is ashamed of that, he uses more.

"For someone young—Jack's age—it's especially hard. He doesn't have a long successful period in his life to look back at for reassurance. If he had trouble in school, for example, he may be secretly afraid that he's never done anything right and he never will be able to. That he's a failure as a person. And that's frightening. So he has another reason to take heroin."

Carpenter paused.

He made it sound like a documentary, Harriet thought. *The Addict's Story.* As though there were only one way for this to happen. As though only Carpenter knew what it was. At the same time, she had the uneasy feeling that he was right.

"Now he's trapped," Carpenter said. "He can't get out of this by himself. It's not just a question of using willpower. Heroin is big-time, it's one of the most powerful addictions we know. Jack needs help. This is where all of you come in." Carpenter looked around the table, holding them each in his gaze. "You, each one of you, are at the center of this. I can offer you direction, maybe clarity, but it's you who will make this work. You can save Jack's life. It's your love that can make this happen."

No one spoke. The word seemed less painful now. It sounded like an option.

"So," Carpenter said, "here we go." He smiled around the circle. "We're going to start off first just by talking. I want you to talk about Jack before he took drugs. Him at his best. Your favorite memories. We're going to remind ourselves of what a great kid Jack is. Why he's worth saving."

Carpenter nodded at Katharine. "Katharine? Would you like to begin?"

Katharine smiled. She'd been listening carefully, but it was only intermittently clear. *They were going to talk about something important, but was it about the family? What was all this about an addict, and why did he keep mentioning Jack? Where was Jack? Wasn't he here, or had that been another time?*

Katharine cocked her head demurely. "I think I'd rather not go first. Let someone else have that honor."

Carpenter turned at once. "Edward? How about you?"

Edward frowned again at the name. "I've been thinking about this a good deal," he said, as though this set him apart from the others.

"Have you?" asked Carpenter encouragingly.

"Opioids are some of the most addictive substances we know. This is pretty serious," Edward said challengingly.

"Do you think we aren't taking it seriously?" asked Carpenter. "What would you suggest we do?"

"Well, it's not my field," Edward said snobbishly. "I'm not an expert. But I'd suggest you get a neurologist, someone who specializes in opiate addiction. It alters the chemistry of the brain. Destroys the dopamine receptors."

"That's one theory," Carpenter said courteously. "Another is that it creates new ones."

That's one theory. Harriet felt a thrill, a shock: here was a direct challenge to Edward.

Edward leaned forward. "May I ask what your training is?"

"Daddy," Julia said, *"stop it."*

"I've given my credentials to Wendell and Julia," Carpenter said politely, reminding Edward that he was not in charge, "but I'd be happy to give them to you. MSW from the School of Social Work at the University of Pennsylvania, with certification in intervention and treatment of addiction disorders."

Edward said nothing, betrayed. *His own institution.*

"Addiction causes changes in the brain," Carpenter went on, "you're right about that."

Edward snorted. *He didn't need Carpenter to tell him he was right about the human brain.*

"They now think it creates a kind of supermemory that never fades," Carpenter said.

"What are you talking about?" Edward asked.

"It's a new theory from MIT. Certain drugs release surges of dopamine, which create memory. Normally, these memories relate to survival—we get dopamine surges about food, sex, and shelter. But addictive drugs create something they call 'extreme memory.' It reinforces drug-taking, reminding the addict how great it is. They think it may never fade, which is why addicts can be clean for years and then have terrible relapses."

"I've never heard of anything like that," Edward said dismissively.

"It's new," Carpenter said. "They're doing tests with D-cycloserine, trying to destroy old memories so that new patterns can replace them."

"D-cycloserine is used for tuberculosis," Edward informed him.

"At higher doses," Carpenter said. "These studies were done with rats—maybe you know about them, Harriet?"

But Harriet was not ready to transfer allegiance from her antagonistic father—who was, after all, her father—to this stranger.

"There are lots of studies done with animals," she said. "I'm afraid I'm not familiar with them all."

Carpenter nodded, not as though he'd been rebuffed but as though this proved his point.

He was more artful, more powerful, than Harriet had thought. He could not be dismissed.

"Let's get back to Jack," he said. "Edward, we're starting with you. Could you tell us what Jack used to be like?"

"Well," Edward said, "I'm not sure what you want me to say." Giving praise made him uncomfortable. "Jack's always been lively. Always had a lot of musical ability."

The fact was that Jack had always been difficult. Always a problem. Edward frowned and rubbed his knees under the table.

"What are your feelings for Jack?" asked Carpenter.

Edward smiled angrily. *There was no end to these invasive questions.* "He's my grandson," he said. "I suppose I'd have to say I loved him."

"Daddy," said Julia, "do you think you could just say straight out that you love him?"

Edward looked at her. "I think that's just what I said."

"No," said Julia, "it's not. You sound as though you were being forced at gunpoint."

Edward started to answer, but Carpenter raised his hand.

"Let's stay on track here," Carpenter said to Edward. "You love Jack, let's start with that. Do you have any early memories of him?"

"Early memories," said Edward. "Well. One year I gave both boys chess sets at Christmas. Steven liked the whole idea, and I started teaching him to play. But Jack—" He shook his head. "First he lost his bishop. Not to another piece—he dropped it out the window, or something like that. So he'd ruined the game. Then he sat down on his board, which was cardboard, and ruined that. He'd destroyed everything in about fifteen minutes."

Edward snorted and shook his head again. He was smiling, and looked around, but no one smiled back. The story was meant to be funny: he felt uncomfortable. *He didn't like this. Carpenter leading them. Bullying them into saying things they didn't mean, didn't feel.* He felt manipulated.

"So," Carpenter said, "Jack was a lively, challenging boy. What other memories do you have? Good times? Times that made you proud?"

"I heard him sing in a Christmas program once," Edward said. "When would that have been?" He looked at Julia.

"Sixth grade," she said, smiling faintly.

"A very beautiful piece of music," said Edward. "He sang a solo."

"He had a very beautiful voice." Julia put a faint emphasis on "voice."

Edward said nothing. *He'd be damned if he'd pay compliments on demand.*

"So, Edward, you remember Jack singing a beautiful solo at school. What about after that? More recent times?"

"I don't see Jack very often," Edward said. "I live in Philadelphia and he lives in New York. He doesn't come down much."

"No," Julia said. "You're critical of him."

"What do you mean?" Edward asked.

"You make him feel bad. You bring up whatever he's done wrong," Julia said.

"I tell the truth," Edward said. *The fact was that Julia had been very lax toward Jack. Both of them had, both Julia and Wendell. The boy had been given no limits.*

"You make him feel bad," Julia said. "You do it to Steven, too. You do it to Ted. Why do you think he lives three thousand miles away?"

Carpenter raised his hands as though quelling the tides. "Okay, let's keep the focus. Edward, thanks for your thoughts. We're going to move on."

"What in the world are you talking about?" Edward asked Julia. "Ted lives in Oregon because of his job."

Julia did not answer.

This was excruciating. Steven wondered what would happen if he simply stood and walked out of the room. He imagined the chair scraping across the floor, himself in the doorway, turning to speak. "I can't do this. I'm sorry."

He remembered that Christmas, the awful chess game. Jack's face as he sat down on the board, crushing it beneath him. He was calm, alert, ready for what would follow. He knew how Jack felt, trapped and claustrophobic in their grandfather's rigid presence.

Carpenter turned to her. "Harriet?"

It was like a ghastly game, she thought, waiting for your name to be called.

"I'm really here for Julia," Harriet said, adding silently, *though I hardly know her.* "I don't really know Jack very well. I haven't seen much of him as he's gotten older. I'm afraid I'm not going to be able to be very useful." She gave Carpenter a candid, fellow-professional look.

"It's generous of you to come all the way up here from Philadelphia," said Carpenter. "You're a very good sister."

"Hardly," Harriet corrected him, then stopped. She felt stung by his characterization and confused by her abrupt response. Why did she resist being called a good sister? *She was not a good sister. Hearing herself called one was like wearing someone else's medal.*

"I think you are," Carpenter insisted. "I know it means a lot to Julia to have you here."

Harriet felt her face flush. *What had Julia said about her? It couldn't have been complimentary. What kind of sister was she?*

Carpenter was watching, smiling encouragingly.

"I'm sorry," she said. "I'll have to think some more. I'm not ready for this."

Carpenter nodded. "Think about it." He looked at Julia. "Julia?"

"There are a thousand things I could tell you about Jack." Julia shook her head. "One time when he was little, four or five, I was in the kitchen with both boys. Steven had done something to make me cross, I don't remember what. I was leaning over, scolding him, and he was very downcast. Jackie was right there, watching, and finally he moved in between us, facing me. He looked up and said, 'Don't get mad at 'Teven. I did it. Get mad at Dack.' He was so tiny and brave. So generous."

Thinking of these moments was like flipping through a catalogue, the pages flickering past, offering glimpses of him, year after year. The small boy with his pearly skin and machine-gun laugh. That time in the kitchen when he'd picked up a wooden spoon and begun to play the row of hanging pots like drums, a rattling, clanking, hilarious staccato beat. The time he'd walked into the air beyond the dock. The time he'd sent her flowers. How many of these was she allowed? She began, unwillingly, to cry. *This was her son's life, all those bright memories, and where was her son? And who was this intruder, forcing them all to say these things?*

Carpenter waited.

"Sorry," she said.

He shook his head. "It's all right." He waited, then asked gently, "And what about after he began taking drugs?"

Julia sighed, wiping her cheeks. "There are a million of those, too. One afternoon I was on a bus, going through Central Park. We stopped in traffic, and I saw a bunch of kids under the trees. They were looking kind of goofy—loose-jointed, shambling—and I realized they were smoking pot. The way they were holding the cigarettes, the way they were moving—they were high.

"It was starting to rain, and one of them threw his head back and spread out his arms. His mouth was open to catch the drops. He was just wearing a T-shirt, no coat, and I thought he's going to get soaked out here, too high to come in from the rain. The others were staggering around, laughing. The bus started up again and we got closer, and I saw it was Jack, with his arms out and his mouth open.

"My first thought was to get off the bus and go get him. He was sixteen. He'd already been caught at school; we'd already had all the conversations, the scoldings, the curfews, the warnings. I was furious. I wanted to go and grab him by the scruff of the neck and take him home.

"But they don't let you get off in Central Park, and I had to sit there and wait, and by the time I'd gotten to the other side, I'd changed my mind. There wasn't much I could actually do. I couldn't keep him from going to Central Park, he was sixteen years old. I couldn't actually keep him from doing anything—going to school, seeing his friends, getting drugs, stretching his arms out and opening his mouth like a fool, high as a kite in broad daylight." She shook her head. "We went right past them all. I watched him as we drove by, staggering around, his arms out, as though everything was so great. All his friends stoned out of their minds. All those promises he'd made, all the rules, all the systems we'd thought up, all the threats—" She paused. "Nothing."

The room was quiet.

"Wendell?" Carpenter said. "Would you like to go next?"

Wendell drew himself closer to the table, his chair legs scraping the floor. He took a deep sighing breath. Something in the room shifted, the air was darkening. They were entering a different place.

"Okay." He set his elbows on the table, looking down. "This is hard for me. I really didn't want to believe it."

"Believe what?" Carpenter asked.

Wendell looked at the table, up again. "That Jack takes." He stopped. "That my son is a heroin addict."

The words were terrible.

Carpenter nodded. "Hard to believe."

"I *didn't* believe it," Wendell said. "Even though he asked for money all the time, even after I saw his apartment and heard him on the phone. When I saw that woman, his dealer—even now, it's hard for me to believe it." He looked down; he rubbed his hand on the table as though erasing a spot.

"It's like trying to realize that someone has died. You know it, but you don't. Your body doesn't believe it, or something. Part of you believes, but part of you hasn't learned it yet." Wendell looked up again. "I guess on some level I still don't believe it."

Carpenter nodded. "All right. Why is that?"

"Because," Wendell said, even more slowly, "it can't be true. It's not the Jack I know. I know Jack as my son. I know his whole life. I know him now as a young man, and I knew him before, as a little boy, and as a baby. I taught him to ride a bike, I taught him to do crossword puzzles. I've known him all his life, and that's not what he's been. It's never what he's been. It's like hearing now that he's Chinese, or that he's not my son. How can I believe this?" He looked around the table, his face troubled.

Carpenter nodded again, gently. "It's very painful to learn that Jack is not the person you know. It will take a while to become real. It doesn't happen like that. What else?"

Wendell said slowly, "It's as though there are two tracks going simultaneously in my head. One of them saying, 'This can't be true,' and the other one saying, 'Here's the evidence.' And the evidence track is delivering a lot of information." He paused painfully. "Jack's asked me for money, over and over, in the last few years. There was always a good reason. I thought we were supporting his creative life. He was a musician, he was struggling, I was glad we could help him get started.

"A few months ago he called and asked me for eight hundred dollars. He said he really, really needed it. His band had been offered a gig, and they needed the money for travel expenses. Tennessee, somewhere. Memphis."

"Memphis?" said Julia, startled.

Wendell nodded. "They needed to rent a van, and pay for gas and motels, rent equipment, a lot of stuff. He had all the details." He looked at Carpenter. "I'm an impecunious college professor, not a hedge-fund manager, I don't have an extra eight hundred dollars lying around. But it seemed like a good way to support his music. The only way the band could succeed was by playing, and this seemed like an important gig. I thought I was being a good dad." Wendell folded his hands on the table.

"So a few weeks later, I called. I said, 'So, Jacko, how was Memphis?' There was a little pause, and he said, 'Memphis?' Then he remembered, and said, 'Oh, it was great, really great.'" Wendell shook his head.

"The whole thing literally made me sick. My stomach hurt every time I thought about it. I didn't tell anyone, not even Sandra. I was ashamed to. How could I tell anyone I'd been tricked by my own son? That he'd lied to me to get money?" He shook his head again. "I didn't let myself think about it at all. I didn't let myself think of what he wanted the money for, though I guess somewhere I knew. But what could I do? He's an adult."

"He told me exactly the same thing," Julia said. "I gave him the money, too. But I didn't have the nerve to ask him about it afterward."

"One night this spring we had dinner together," Wendell went on, "Jack and Sandra and I. He was kind of strange, twitchy and nervous. He didn't seem to be concentrating on anything we said. I kept talking, myself, to keep him from having to say anything. I was embarrassed to have Sandra see him like that. Afterward, on the sidewalk, he seemed a little off-balance. I asked him if he was okay, and he said yes. But when we said good night he asked if he could have cab money back to Brooklyn. There was something about the way he asked that made me uncomfortable. I gave him a twenty, and he was so grateful. Effusive. Then I felt guilty and gave him another twenty.

"He thanked me over and over. I felt kind of disgusted, it was like being thanked by a beggar. And then suddenly I got it. That was the whole point of the evening, the only reason he'd come in to have dinner with us was these two twenties I was handing him. Of course he'd take the subway home, not a cab." He looked at Carpenter. "It made me really angry."

Carpenter nodded again. "Go on."

"I'm angry at him." Wendell's voice rose. "He's lied to us over and over. He's asked us for money again and again and again, lying and lying and lying. *I hate being lied to.*"

"I don't blame you," Carpenter said.

"It's unacceptable," Wendell said. He brought his palm down on the table. "But Jack's behavior has *always* been unacceptable. He's *never* done what we asked him. He's always been a screwup. He's always screwed up in school, he'd barely pass or he'd flunk out. If he manages to get a job he gets fired—what has Jack ever done that we could be proud of?"

"How can you talk that way?" Julia asked, furious. *"He's your son! You can't talk about your child that way."*

"How should I talk about him?" asked Wendell. "He's deceived and betrayed me. He's done it to you, too."

Julia shook her head. "But you've always been like this to him! You've always looked down on him, and he's always known it. How can he not? Why *wouldn't* he screw up?"

"He's lied to you, too, Julia," Carpenter said quietly.

"You stay out of this," Julia said. "This is between me and my husband."

There was a silence.

"I know this is hard on you," Carpenter said.

"Don't patronize me!" Julia said.

Carpenter said nothing. He leaned back in his chair and folded his hands, lacing his fingers across his stomach. He waited.

Julia put her hand over her eyes. "Of course I know he's lied to me," she said. "Of course I know that. But he's still my son. I still love him."

"He's Wendell's son, too," Carpenter said. "But you both have a right to be angry. Jack has betrayed your trust. Why wouldn't you be angry?"

Julia shook her head and said nothing, her hand still covering her eyes.

After a pause Carpenter said, "Jack's disrupting the family. He's betraying you all. This is the reality. You'd like to defend him from this reality, but he's created it. This is what addicts do," he said. "This is what happens. Addiction robs you of the person you love. Addicts betray our trust."

"I hate this," Julia said. "I hate it."

This was like watching someone being flayed, thought Harriet. This awful little patronizing man, with his professional empathy, who seemed—horribly—to know everything. The awful story of Jack.

"Steven?" asked Carpenter. "Anything you'd like to say? This will be hard, I know."

Steven drew a breath.

He didn't want to say anything. He didn't want to be here, to "share his feelings," to parse the activities of his brother. All of it sickened him. This stupid know-it-all ass, holding forth about someone he'd never even seen, like he was the supreme authority on Jack, as though he could tell all of them what Jack was like. His parents telling stories on Jack, on themselves. It was like everyone was under some horrible spell. Himself, he was under this spell, too.

Everyone was waiting, their eyes on him. He would have to say something, he would have to enter into this somehow. He would be forced to.

"I've been worried about Jack for a while," Steven said reluctantly. "I guess I'm glad something's finally being done."

Carpenter nodded.

But Steven balked. He refused to dredge up touching moments and offer them to Carpenter on demand. His whole life had been spent with Jack; his whole childhood was Jack's. It was his, and theirs; it was private. Each of these shared memories flooded him with a dark tide of sadness. It was no one else's business.

He remembered the time riding bikes with Jack in Riverside Park. They were kids, he was twelve or so. It had been late afternoon, Jack wobbling behind him on the paved walkway. He rose manfully up to thrust down on the pedals, wrestling with the handlebars as though he were riding a steer. It was autumn, with the moist smell of fallen leaves. The leaves crackled pleasingly as they rode over them. Below them, on the hillside sloping down toward the river, he saw a group of boys moving uphill. They crossed Riverside Drive casually, apparently ignoring the cars, and headed up the hill. They moved in a drifting crowd, spread out across the grass. They wore long loose T-shirts, baggy pants. At the moment he saw them approaching, Steven realized it was turning dark. They had stayed out too late.

The other boys moved closer to them, and he felt fear knock in his chest. He saw their gazes light on Jack and himself. Their eyes were bold. *Stay close behind me*, Steven said quietly to Jack, without turning around. *Keep going, and don't look at them.* He gripped his handlebars hard, as though that would help. The boys arrived, drifting around them. There were four or five; Steven and Jack were more or less surrounded. The boys stared at them. Steven looked straight ahead, pedaling. He felt as though he'd painted a sign on his brother's bike: TAKE ME.

One of the boys, short and stocky, in a faded yellow T-shirt, stepped forward and grabbed Jack's handlebars, jerking him to a sudden stop. Jack's wheel wavered and he cried out. The boy laughed, his teeth white in his face. He thrust the bike away from him scornfully, letting go and stepping back. Jack went down sideways with a crash. The boys laughed, hooting. They did not move, and for a moment there hung in the air the clear prospect of something more, something worse, unthinkable. It seemed that the boys might move in closer, surrounding them both.

Steven stepped down from his pedals, straddling his bike. He was frozen: should he step forward and help Jack up, and yell at them for pushing over his brother? He was afraid if he did that, if he did anything, the boys would move closer and attack them both. Silence and immobility seemed the wiser choice. Jack lay struggling beneath the fallen bike, arms and legs thrashing. Steven, unharmed, did not move.

The moment swelled, then ended. The boys suddenly lost interest. The tallest one turned restlessly away and said something incomprehensible, the others looked at him and turned. They were supple and lithe, their movements smooth. They still housed some dreadful possibility; Steven felt sick, watching them. They went on, heading uphill with long strides, moving across the ground in shifting patterns, like a pack of wolves. When they were gone, Steven helped Jack back onto his bike.

"We shouldn't have stayed out so late," he said.

It was his fault, he'd been in charge of them both. Of his little brother. At home, Steven went into his room and shut the door. He sat on the bed, his heart pounding, still in that moment. They'd been helpless, surrounded, and the light was going, beneath the trees dusk was invading the landscape. He felt sick. For months afterward that moment came to him at night, when he was trying to sleep. Closing his eyes he saw the circle of hostile faces, the gathering darkness. They might have done anything.

He wouldn't tell that story now, though, how he'd been irresponsible. Everyone here was sitting around the table waiting for him to break their hearts. He wouldn't do it, deliver himself on command, reveal dire moments in the life of Jack's brother. And he wouldn't tell stories about Jack the fuckup. It was true that Jack was a fuckup, but why tell those stories?

He didn't want to say anything at all, though he was here, he knew he would have to say something.

Reluctantly he began. "I went to see him last week," he said. He told about waiting outside the door, Jack's sluggish voice, his heavy-lidded eyes.

"It smelled so bad I could hardly breathe," Steven said, "but Jack didn't seem to notice. He hardly knew I was there. We went out for coffee. I gave him some money."

The worst thing, the hard black thing inside him, was that this was his fault. He should have prevented it all, all of this, too. The stinking apartment, the stupid lies about Memphis, this aggressive jerk telling them what they should think about their lives, passing judgment on everyone. It was his fault that it had come to this. He, Steven, should have done something long ago, should have stopped it. He'd always known it was happening, he'd always known Jack was taking drugs, too many, and too hard. He was the one who'd always known, and he'd said nothing until now, when it might be too late.

"Go on," Carpenter said. "And how long have you been worried like this about Jack?"

There was the time he'd visited Jack at college and Jack had been high all weekend. Steven slept on the floor in a sleeping bag, and on Saturday morning he waked up to Jack, still in bed, scrabbling in a dirty plastic bag. Leaning on his pillow Jack rolled a joint, took a long toke, and offered it to Steven.

"Want some breakfast?" His voice was high and choked with captured smoke.

Lots of times. That beach party out on Long Island, when Jack was falling-down drunk. He couldn't stand up, and Steven had to drag him across the sand to his car, and he'd thrown up all over Steven's jeans and feet. Steven stood in the sandy parking lot with his brother's dead weight in his arms, the hot wet mass of vomit soaking through to his skin, his feet coated with the warm disgusting mass, feeling rage and revulsion and despair.

The time in New York, at some restaurant, when Jack came out of the men's room glassy-eyed and groggy. He collapsed in the booth, head leaning back, eyes shut, that blissed-out grin. There was some girl with him, she'd done it too, come out and collapsed against the seat. She wasn't really a girlfriend, Jack never really had girlfriends. There were always girls around him, they were drawn to him, that glitter, but he wasn't drawn to them. He had something better than girlfriends, better than sex: he had that wild, gorgeous, golden secret, waiting for him all the time, every minute.

There was the time just last week, waiting outside in the hall while Jack shot up. There was the time Jack set fire to the scrapbasket. It was always too dangerous, Steven could never stop him, never fix it.

"All his life," Steven said, and to his horror he began to cry. *It was his fault. How had he let it happen?* He raised his hand to cover his crumpling face.

"It's not your fault," Julia said; Wendell put his arm around his shoulder.

There was a long silence in the room, broken by Steven's uneven breaths. Julia was crying, too. The air in the room was denser.

"I'm sorry," Carpenter said. "I know this is hard."

Stop it, thought Harriet, *stop patronizing us.*

"Darling," Katharine said to Julia, "what is it? What's the matter?"

Julia looked at her. "It's Jack."

"But what about him? He's here, isn't he?"

"We don't know where he is," Julia said. "He's a heroin addict."

Katharine looked around the table. "Heroin," she said. *Then it was bad, it was very bad.* She put out her hand to cover Julia's. "I'm so sorry."

It was terrible watching this, thought Harriet. She felt the hard place in her chest start to loosen in a frightening way. She looked down at her hands, afraid she, too, would start to cry.

Carpenter was talking again, telling them more about heroin, more about what they should do next, but Harriet couldn't concentrate on anything he was saying. She could hear Julia crying, for Jack, and for her family, and for herself, and she could hear Steven crying, harsh awkward sounds. She thought of Jack staggering on the sidewalk, thanking his father for the two twenties. She felt as though her sister's life were being laid bare. Things were breaking down.

Carpenter was still talking when the telephone rang. Julia stood to answer it. The others sat silent, listening.

The conversation was brief. She hung up and turned to them.

"Thank God," she said. "Jack's in jail for burglary."

TWENTY-EIGHT

Suddenly, instead of being provisional, everything was urgent. Jack's arraignment was the next day, Monday morning. Miraculously, through some professional network, Carpenter had found a lawyer, in a strange state, on a Sunday night. Now they were to hope that the judge would remand Jack into Carpenter's charge, on condition that he go immediately into a rehab program. Then they'd bring him home from court and have the intervention. Afterward, he and Carpenter were meant to leave in time to catch the last flight to Boston.

Apparently the intervention was still important, even though Jack would have no choice but to participate. Carpenter told them that his chances of success with rehab would be much better if Jack went through the process. And now that they were halfway through it themselves, it all seemed more serious, more effective. The words, Carpenter's earnestness, the whole enterprise no longer seemed so alien.

Carpenter had asked them all to write letters to Jack.

Be specific, Carpenter said. *Tell him what this has been like for you. Tell him what will change if he keeps on.* They'd all met before dinner and read their letters out loud. *Very good*, Carpenter said, looking around, when the last letter had been read. *Now I want you all to rewrite them. This time, no blame, no accusations.*

Now, after dinner, Julia sat in her bedroom at the rickety white writing table. The yellow pad lay before her, the paragraphs full of crossed-out words, second thoughts laboring sideways along the edges. What *had* it been like for her? What would happen if things went on like this, unchanged? What was it she should say to her son?

Don't blame yourselves, Carpenter had said. *Don't blame Jack, that's not what we're doing here. Just talk about what it's like for you.*

Horrible was what it was like for her. Nearly unbearable.

On the table was a chipped vase of rugosa roses and Queen Anne's lace. A few satiny pink petals and a dusting of creamy pollen had fallen on the white cloth. Julia brushed at them with the edge of her hand. She thought of her mother's timid gratitude for the flowers in the guest room, and her own dismissive response. Julia, her face frozen, had pretended that the flowers meant nothing, though in fact she'd put them there for her mother, knowing her mother loved rugosas. She felt a familiar stab of pain, shame, rage at herself. *Why was she like this? So cold, withholding.*

She stared at the inky page. She felt the confusions of the family pressing down on her. Her anger at her father, her distance from her mother. Her disgust at herself for not being more forthcoming, more open, more loving. Her intent, as a parent, had been to interrupt that pattern, to be open, loving, available to her children, but she had made as many mistakes as her own parents had. What if Jack—or Steven, for that matter—felt the same rage toward her that she felt for her father? How terrible to be judged by your child, to be found wanting. Of course you would be found wanting. What if Steven withheld himself from her, as she did from her mother?

The task, the task, the inky page. She began to write. At least she wouldn't have to move to Europe without a phone, like Carpenter's parents. Thank God, they had caught all this early, when it was curable. Thank God, they were dealing with it now. She filled three pages.

When she was finished, she pushed her chair back from the table and went out.

At the core of the house was a massive stone chimney, opening downstairs into fireplaces in the living room, dining room, and guest rooms. Upstairs, the chimney was covered with stucco, and its presence dominated the tiny hall. It rose up almost directly in front of the steep staircase; at the top there was space for only a single floorboard. Leaving her room, Julia sidled along the narrow board past the rough chimney, then went down the hall to the boys' rooms.

Steven's room was small, the ceiling sloping sharply down to the eaves. A rickety bureau stood beneath the window, with narrow iron beds on either side of it. One bed was covered with Steven's clothes, surging from his duffel. On the other bed lay Steven, leaning on a pillow smashed against the wall. He was reading a paperback, and looked up as she came in.

"Can I sit down?" Julia asked.

He slid his legs sideways to make room for her. She patted his knee.

"How're you doing?" she asked. "With the writing. Hard, isn't it?"

"I'm not doing it," Steven said.

"What do you mean?" Julia asked.

"I'm not doing any of this. I quit," Steven said. "I don't want to be involved." He looked back at his book.

"Don't read, Stevo," Julia said. "Please talk to me. What do you mean?"

"What I said," Steven said. "I'm not doing it."

"But we need you," Julia said. "We all have to do this together or it won't work."

"I don't care," Steven said.

"Look," Julia said, "you started all this. It was you who said we had to do something."

"This is crap," Steven said.

"You can't stop now," Julia said. "What's the matter?"

"It's completely different from what I thought it would be. I don't like this guy, and I don't want any part of this."

"Why don't you like him?"

"He's an asshole."

Julia sighed.

"All this bullshit about emotions and love and pulling together," Steven went on. "How do we know it'll work? Even if Jack does go to rehab, half the people who go there stay addicted. As soon as they get out, they're back on drugs again. Just going into a program doesn't mean you're safe."

"Sandra says this is a good program," Julia said. "And we have to trust someone."

"Fine. But count me out."

"You can't quit, Steven. This won't work without you."

Steven shook his head. "It's like hunting an animal. We're all going after him, trying to break him down. It's sickening."

"So what do you think we should do instead?" Julia asked.

Steven kept his eyes on his book. "Okay," he said. "I know you're trying to help him. But he's my brother. I can't take your side against him."

"No one's against him. It's not us against him."

"That's how it feels," Steven said.

"Which is worse? All of us doing something to save him, or all of us just watching as he crashes?" Julia asked. There was a pause. "Please help us, Stevo," she said. "He might die."

Steven looked at her stubbornly. "I can't go on with this. It's sickening. We're all going to sit around him in a circle like jackals. It's brutal, and I'm not doing it."

"It's not brutal," Julia said. "You have to help us, Steven."

Steven said nothing, and Julia began to cry.

"Don't you understand how dangerous this is? People die from heroin. It's lethal," she said, "it's lethal."

Steven lay motionless. He could feel his mother's body against the side of his leg, and for some reason he thought of the tree trunk against his back, the rough bark. He remembered the huge trees crashing through the air, the silence of the fall, the enormous sound when they hit the ground.

It seemed futile, all of this. Terrible and futile. Jack had always been like this, the wild center of the storm. Because of him, plans were changed, vacations canceled; they'd had family meetings, school conferences, fights and scenes. Their parents had fought horribly over Jack. Everything had always revolved around Jack. His parents had nearly missed his college graduation because they'd had to stay in the city and talk to the principal of Jack's school: he was about to be thrown out again. There was always an emergency.

Now here they all were in Maine, everyone rallied for this new crisis, everyone dropping the threads of their own lives for Jack's emergency. Of course they should do this. Of course Jack's life should be saved. Of course the money for law school should be diverted to pay for Jack's rehab. Of course this was the correct thing to do. He remembered the sound of the trees as they hit, it was huge.

"I can't hold this all together," Julia said. "I don't like it either, but I think we have no choice if we want to save Jack. If you drop out, my parents will, and probably Harriet. My father's already muttering. It won't work." She put her hand out, stroking the hair from his eyes. "You're killing me, Steven. You're killing the family if you do this."

"You're the one who killed the family," Steven said. *He hadn't meant to say that.*

"What do you mean?"

"You got the divorce. It was your idea."

"Are you serious? You think *I* killed our family?"

Steven shrugged, then nodded.

"Steven," Julia said, and then stopped. She looked down at her hands. "I wanted nothing more than to save the family. Nothing. Do you not know what your father did?"

Steven moved away and stood up. "I don't want to know what my father did," he said. "I don't want to know what you and he did in your marriage. But you're the one who wanted the divorce. That's what happened."

"Because your father left me," said Julia, *"for a woman in his department."* She stared at him. "Did you not know that? How can you accuse me of destroying our marriage?"

"He said *you* had an affair."

There was a long pause. They watched each other.

"So don't try claiming the moral high ground," Steven said. "Don't ask me to join in your campaign against Jack, okay? You have no moral grounds to say anything." He folded his arms. "You and Dad have fucked things up between you."

Julia stood, ducking her head from the eaves. "I can't believe you've raised this now," she said. "I can't believe your father has."

She left the room.

What she wanted was Wendell, the holy jerk, the criminal weasel, the royal fuckup, whom she needed, right now, as a partner and ally.

Downstairs, she tiptoed down the hall past her parents' room, praying no one would come out, then past the kitchen to the little back hall to Wendell's door.

"Come in," he called.

Wendell was sitting on the unmade bed, his cell phone pressed against his ear. He looked up and spoke into the phone. "Hold on."

He was calling Sandra, of course. He had an ally already.

"I need to talk to you," Julia said.

"Call you back later," Wendell said loudly. "Yeah." He nodded, looking at Julia as though she could hear what was being said. "Bye." He clicked off. "Sandra sends her best. Says to tell you you're doing a great job."

Julia nodded stiffly. "Thanks. Give her my best."

"The cell reception's terrible here, it kept cutting out. I could hardly hear," he said cheerfully. "So, what's up?"

Wendell's friendly face, the message from Sandra, and, for some reason, the sight of him sitting placidly in his untidy nest—*why did men not make their beds?*—made Julia hesitate, her rage abate.

"I was telling Sandra what's going on," he said, "the arrest." He shook his head.

"There's more," Julia said. "Breaking news. Steven's decided not to participate."

"What do you mean?"

"He's not going to be in the intervention."

"And why is that?"

"He doesn't want to take our side against Jack."

"'Our side against Jack'?"

"That's just what I said. He feels it's us against him. The ends don't justify the means. How did he get so priggish?"

Criticizing her son to his father: the pleasures of complicity. The luxury of complaining about her son to the one person in the world who loved him as she did.

"He said we'd destroyed the family already," she went on, "by getting a divorce. Actually, he blames me for destroying the family. He thinks the divorce is my fault." She felt the rage returning.

"Why your fault?"

"Steven says you told him I had an affair." She was now furious again.

"Well, you did," said Wendell.

"*Goddamnit*, Wendell, how many affairs did you have?"

"But you're the one who wanted a divorce."

"Well, *yes!* After you took up with that lowlife T.A., and practically moved out!"

Wendell shrugged his shoulders. "It was you, actually, who asked for the divorce," he said. "I wouldn't have."

"*It was you, actually, who destroyed the marriage,*" said Julia. "*I wouldn't have.*"

Wendell looked down at his hands. "Look," he said pacifically, "we have different views on this."

"No, we don't, Wendell. Don't suddenly pretend now that you didn't want a divorce. *You left me.* Don't pretend now that something else happened."

Wendell spread his hands out, the fingers wide. "Julia," he said quietly.

Julia covered her face with her hands. "Oh my God," she said. "How can you talk like this? How can you start all this up now? What were you thinking?"

"I didn't start anything up now."

Julia raised her head. "Why did you just tell Steven I had an affair?"

"I didn't just tell him. I told him years ago, I don't remember when. Why is he raising it now?"

Julia stared at him. "Well, he is. Why did you tell him in the first place?"

Wendell shrugged. "I must have been angry at you. I don't remember."

"Angry at me! You're the one who left! Why were you angry?"

He shrugged again. "I told you. I wouldn't have gotten a divorce."

"If you didn't want a divorce, why did you do what you did?"

Wendell looked away. There was silence.

"Why did I." He sighed. "From this perspective, now, impossible to say. Stupidity? Arrogance? Restlessness? I have no defense. I think I thought what I was doing was sort of minor. Acceptable, somehow. I didn't think I was doing too much damage. I didn't take it seriously. I thought you wouldn't. It was partly the times, it seemed as though everyone was fooling around. By the time I realized I was wrong it was too late."

"'Sort of minor.'"

"I know."

"Well, you did it, and you're stuck with it. If you didn't want a divorce, why did you get remarried so fast?"

"To get on with things. You didn't want me. I wanted a life."

So that was how marriage can happen, she thought, *just like that. Decide you wanted it, choose a partner for life. It was only men who could do this, though, just decide it would happen. Willing women lined the streets, waiting for a man who'd decided this, that he wanted a life.*

"Do you cheat on Sandra?" she asked.

"No. I learned my lesson." He looked rueful. "I'm kind of disappointed in myself: I don't even want to. Do you think it's age? Or fidelity?"

Why did Wendell sound so reasonable, so steady, so nice? She needed someone to be angry at, to blame.

"I want you to tell Steven what you did, Wendell. It is not okay for him to think it was all my fault."

Wendell folded his arms uncomfortably. "Right," he said. "I don't think this is the moment, though."

"This is the moment he's raised it, Wendell! This is the issue he's brought up! What are we going to do?" Julia stopped. "This whole thing will fall apart if he quits."

"Okay," said Wendell. "Let's think about this."

"We have to get Steven to cooperate. *He has to do it.*"

"Okay," Wendell said.

"He thinks I ruined our marriage," Julia said. "I want you to go and talk to him. Tell him whatever else you want, but tell him I didn't ruin it. Take some responsibility. Tell him we were both at fault then, and we both want this now. And we have to do this together. All three of us."

"Right," Wendell said.

"I'll come with you," Julia said, "we'll tell him together." She paused. "Or is that a good idea?" She shook her head. "Maybe not. I don't know," she said helplessly. "I don't know what to do."

She was flying apart: this was too much for her. Trying to repair the damage done to their son by the divorce, trying to give Steven what he needed, trying to hold Jack safe in her mind, trying to comfort her poor befuddled mother, trying to break down the barrier between them, protecting herself from her cold, hostile father and sister. The intervention teetering on the brink, and now Wendell announcing that he'd never even meant to end the marriage. All that pain, all that howling misery, that vast wilderness of unhappiness, had been for nothing.

"Jules," said Wendell.

"What is it?"

"I think we can't impose this on Steven."

"*Impose it*! You sound like him!" Outrage bloomed again. "This is not an imposition, Wendell, it's not a favor we're asking. He's a member of our family. He has to be an ally. It won't work without him. He has to cooperate."

There was a pause.

"You're right." Wendell's voice was meditative. "But I don't think we can do it that way. I think we have to listen to Steven. Ask him how he'd like to help Jack and hope he comes around to it. I think we can't coerce him. He'll just say no."

"Then what do we tell Carpenter? If Steven refuses, everyone else will drop out."

"We'll tell him the truth. It can't be the first time this has happened. We can't force Steven."

Julia hesitated. Part of her knew Wendell was right, but part of her wanted to rise up and impose her will on Steven. She could feel her own ferocity. She could feel something dark and tyrannical, overbearing, dictatorial, *her father's will*, breathing inside her. She wanted to command Steven to do as she wished. *She was like her father*, she thought, appalled.

Wendell waited, his expression gentle, and she was reminded that there were times when he'd been a good husband, a good father. Times when she'd trusted him to make a kind of order, find a sensible path.

"Okay," she said. "You talk to him."

She left the room, closing the door behind her.

This, too, was out of her control. It was beyond her scope. Wendell would manage to get Steven to help them or he would not; the judge would release Jack or he would not. It was out of her hands. But she wanted, through sheer force of will, to bring Jack home, to make him responsive and humble and loving, to make him safe. She wanted to lift him to the sunny turquoise pool in the photographs. She wanted to *will* him cured. She wanted to smother his will with hers, to make him clean, safe, free, as she wanted, not addicted, imperiled, bound, as he wanted.

But what was she to do with this shameful, unwanted thought: *she was like her father?*

TWENTY-NINE

The courthouse at Buxton was a large, majestic building, four stories high and faced with the local blue-gray granite. Below the elaborate cornice, in a carved frame, were the words "Gaud County 1894." The building was set into the side of a long hill, just off the main street, beyond its own big parking lot.

The courthouse lot was full, and Julia parked out on the main street. This sloped down, between neat Victorian buildings, to the narrow turbulent river. During the nineteenth century the river had made Buxton a thriving mill town. The mill had closed during the 1940s, and several decades later the center of town had declined, its traffic and vitality leached away to the new malls on its outskirts. But now, in the new century, gentrification was setting in, and the handsome buildings were being painted and restored. Now the shabby discount store on the main street was flanked by a Mediterranean restaurant and a health-food shop. Across from these was an art gallery; up the street, a neatly painted house with bow windows and a round slate-shingled turret held a small law firm.

Just before nine o'clock on Monday morning, Buxton was already busy. Pickup trucks and small cars moved slowly down the street to the light at the bridge; the shops were opening up. As Julia, Wendell, and Carpenter walked toward the courthouse, a woman approached them, plump and graying, with a round, pleasant face. She wore khaki pants and low scuffed heels and carried a small brown bag, stained lightly with coffee. On her way to the office, thought Julia. She'd hang her jacket on the back of the door, sit down, and open her coffee. The woman smiled cheerfully as she passed, a small-town reflex.

Julia smiled back gratefully.

Would she smile if she knew where Julia was going? Not to an office and a blameless life, but to put up bail for her son, in jail for burglary?

A wave of shame hit Julia. She had been moved into a different part of humanity. She was now behind a high wall, in the shadow. Other people, other parents, walked about on the other side in the sunlight, talking and laughing. How could this be her life now? *What would happen to Jack?*

The granite façade of the courthouse glittered in the glaring sun. They mounted the broad front steps and pushed through heavy swinging doors into sudden semidarkness: high oak wainscoting, dim polished floors. They took the wide wooden staircase winding stiffly upward.

In the upstairs hall a white-haired man in a dark suit stood waiting. He carried a flat briefcase under his arm, and when he saw them he came toward them. He wore thick-soled shoes that creaked with each step.

"Mr. and Mrs. Lambert? I'm Charles Olson." He put out his hand.

Olson had pale, dry skin and light blue eyes. His forehead was deeply creased, his cheeks seamed. His eyelashes were very pale, like a lamb's. He talked to them about what would happen at the arraignment. Carpenter had found him by phone. Listening, Julia watched his long pale face: was this the man who would get her son out of jail?

"This judge doesn't like drug abusers. He sets very high bails," he said. "As I told you, I expect it to be around $100,000 cash, or $50,000 surety." He looked at Wendell and Julia. "Have you decided what you want to put up?"

Julia pulled the envelope from her pocketbook. "The deed to my house."

Olson held up his palm, forestalling. "I want to be sure you understand this," he said. "If Jack doesn't show up for trial, you know you'll lose the house."

"He'll be there," Julia said steadily.

They'd had no choice. They couldn't raise $100,000 in cash (or not without going to her father), and there was no other surety they could offer. Julia's apartment belonged to Columbia, and Wendell's belonged to Sandra. But offering the deed—only a piece of paper—didn't seem such a risk. The trial wouldn't be for another six months, and in two days Jack would be safe with Carpenter, safe in Florida. Six months from now he'd be long past the hard part. It was a lifetime away.

And the offer felt proper to Julia, appropriate: it was an exchange. She'd gladly trade her house for Jack's freedom, not just from jail, but from this affliction. She was making a pledge, taking a vow of honor. In fact, the house was the only thing that could reflect the gravity of all this. Money wouldn't do it.

"But it's only to guarantee Jack's appearance, right?" asked Wendell. "As long as Jack turns up, Julia keeps the house, even if he's found guilty?"

"Correct. As long as Jack appears for his trial, the house stays yours," Olson said. Julia handed him the envelope and he put it neatly into his folder. "Okay. We all set? It'll probably be about twenty minutes, half an hour, before our case comes up. Here we go."

He pushed through the swinging door into a long high-ceilinged room, mostly filled by rows of benches. At the far end was the raised desk, the judge in his black robes seated behind it. He was a brisk elderly man, balding, gaunt-necked. Below him, to one side, sat a fat woman in glasses and short curly hair. She stared around the room as her fingers pecked steadily at a narrow machine on a stand before her.

They sat near the front. The activity was steady and confusing: people came in through a swinging door, lawyers stood and made requests; the judge nodded or questioned them, made cryptic pronouncements, banged his gavel. Papers were gathered, briefcases zipped, people sat down, stood and left the room. New ones came in.

Olson turned to Julia and whispered, "Now."

The swinging door on the right was pushed open, and a deputy in a gray uniform came through. Behind him was a thin man in a stiff neon orange jumpsuit, hands behind his back. His head was lowered, his hair unkempt: a homeless person. Julia looked beyond him for Jack. The prisoner jerked his head to one side, scratching with his chin at his shoulder, and Julia realized suddenly that he was handcuffed, and that he was Jack. The room came terribly into focus.

"Jack Lambert," the deputy announced.

The judge nodded. "Please read the charges."

Olson rose and approached the bench. The prosecutor stepped forward, a tall man in a tan suit with metal-rimmed glasses.

"Your Honor," said the prosecutor, "Jack Lambert is brought before you today on a charge of car theft, grand larceny, and burglary, Class B. Breaking into a commercial property after hours, possession and intent to possess scheduled drugs."

The words, in the enemy's mouth, sounded fearful.

"Does Mr. Lambert have legal representation?" asked the judge.

"I represent him, Your Honor," said Olson. "Charles Olson. The family has asked me to represent Mr. Lambert."

"Mr. Lambert," said the judge, looking down at Jack. "Do you understand why you are here?"

Jack nodded.

"Please answer the question," said the judge testily.

"Yes, Your Honor," Jack said.

The black-robed judge looked down on Jack from his raised desk. Behind him was the deputy, with his trim gray uniform, his bright badge, his epaulettes and holstered gun. Jack's neon-orange jumpsuit was both meager and conspicuous. His arms, emerging from the stiff, short sleeves, were bare. It looked like a medieval morality play, thought Julia. The uniforms of power, the livery of humiliation.

"Mr. Olson," said the judge, "how do you plead?"

"Not guilty, Your Honor," said Olson. "My client was under the influence of drugs. I hold that he was not responsible for his actions at that time."

"Tell me, Mr. Richards, what do you propose for bail for Mr. Lambert?"

The prosecutor folded his arms. "Your Honor, this is a serious offense. Mr. Lambert did not simply pick something off a counter. He stole a car and then deliberately destroyed private property to gain illegal access to the premises, in order to take illegal possession of controlled substances. This was a series of intentional criminal acts, and I suggest that bail be set at not less than $200,000, in cash or surety.

"The Lamberts are not a local Maine family, but summer residents from New York City. Jack Lambert has come here as a representative of a drug abuser's community, not of ours. He's broken out of a hospital, stolen a local woman's car, damaged a local merchant's property, and taken illegal possession of scheduled drugs. He's shown himself to be a calculating criminal, and I think bail should be set accordingly high."

"Mr. Olson?"

"Your Honor." Olson gave a courteous nod. "I would like respectfully to remind you that this is the first offense for Mr. Lambert, and that his acts were neither violent nor aggressive. He did not break out of the hospital but merely walked from his unlocked room. His parents are both professors in good standing at a highly respected university in New York City. They have also owned property here for eighteen years. They are solid and contributing members of this community, and this is a tragic moment for them and for their son. Mr. and Mrs. Lambert are willing to put their best efforts into helping their son deal with the terrible curse of addiction."

"What are the plans on release?"

"Mr. Lambert has been accepted at a rehabilitation program where he will go this afternoon, if released. The head of this institution, Mr. Ralph Carpenter, is here today to vouch for him. I would request that Mr. Lambert be released into his custody."

The judge looked at Carpenter.

"Please approach the bar."

Carpenter stepped forward, a sheaf of papers in his hand. They spoke quietly. Carpenter handed him his file and the judge leafed through it, asking questions. Carpenter stood easily below him, courteous and composed.

Julia, watching him, thought, *Thank God.* *Thank God we have Carpenter.*

The judge pushed the folder back to Carpenter and raised his voice.

"Mr. Carpenter, are you prepared to take on the burden of responsibility for Mr. Lambert?"

"Yes, Your Honor," said Carpenter, and at that moment Julia felt an upwelling of pure love for him.

The judge looked at Wendell and Julia, fixing them with his gaze. "Mr. and Mrs. Lambert, do you understand the nature of your son's situation?"

"Yes, Your Honor." They spoke together, as though they were married.

The judge read the conditions of Jack's release. He must remain at the facility at all times for thirty days. He must refrain from the use of scheduled drugs, he must avoid all contact with any individuals that contributed to his drug-taking activities. There was a list of curfews, reminders, restrictions.

"You agree to these conditions on behalf of your client?"

"Yes, Your Honor." Olson stood with his hands folded in front of him.

"You agree to take personal responsibility for carrying them out?" The judge looked sternly at Carpenter.

"Yes, Your Honor," he said.

"Mr. Lambert," said the judge to Jack, "these good people, Mr. Carpenter and your parents, are vouching for you. They are prepared to take responsibility for your behavior. Are you prepared to commit yourself to this program?"

"Yes, Your Honor," said Jack. His voice was thick, and a bright glaze of mucus ran from his nose to mouth. *Didn't the officer have a Kleenex?*

The judge rapped his gavel on his desk.

"Request granted," he said. "Bail is $200,000 cash, or $50,000 surety. Next."

The house, then.

For the first time Jack looked at them. He raised his hand in a sort of salute, then the blank-faced officer herded him back out through the door.

The jail was in another part of the courthouse complex. There was a tunnel through the hillside for the prisoners, but everyone else had to go outside.

They went back downstairs, emerging into the sunlight on the granite steps.

Julia turned to Olson. "We can't thank you enough."

Olson nodded. "Glad I could help. But you know, this is just the beginning." His voice was cautionary.

Julia shook her head. "We have him back. That's all I care about."

"You did a great job," said Wendell. At his voice, Julia looked at him: she could see he was angry, but he said nothing more.

The jail was newer than the courthouse. It was squat, made of pale brick. Inside the front door was a narrow hall with a high counter at one end. Folding chairs were scattered near it. On one wall was a closed elevator doorway. Behind the high counter sat two policemen, their eyes lowered, working at computers.

"Good morning," Olson said. "We're here for Jack Lambert."

One of the policemen looked up. He was pudding-faced, with wide full cheeks and a gap between his front teeth. His expression was empty. He looked down again, searching. They were silent. He looked up at Olson.

"Right," he said, "we have him."

Julia watched his face. She was ready to smile, but he ignored her.

She was waiting for a sign, a lightening, some softening of the expression, some hint that Jack was no longer in disgrace. A sign that they were all members of the same community and Jack was a child of it. She'd been in this situation many times—a supplicant to authority, pleading on behalf of her son. She'd watched the face of someone in charge, scanning it for humanity. In the past she'd always found it, on the face of the principal, the dean, the director. They'd been, at heart, on Jack's side, they'd always wished him well.

But now she found no such response to her timid smile. The policeman's face was blank, as though she were not there. He offered nothing. She saw that they had reached a great divide: Jack had passed into adulthood. No one was wishing him well. He was no longer someone's child, but a criminal.

Though he was not a criminal, he was her son.

She stood silent and humble. Right now, below these heavy, powerful men in their complicated uniforms covered with arcane paraphernalia, their creaking holsters and jingling devices, she felt guilty of everything.

The pudding-faced policeman slid papers across the counter.

"Sign this, sir," he said to Wendell. He made "sir" not respectful but severe, monitory. They all signed. The policeman stapled forms, then looked back at his computer, tapping at it. "All right," he said. "When this comes through, you can take him home." He looked up. "You'll have to bring him back for trial."

"We know that," said Wendell.

"You're his parents?" The policeman glanced from one to the other.

"Yes," said Julia.

"All right, then," he said. "Wait here."

They sat down on the folding chairs. The policemen ignored them, talking inaudibly on the phone, looking down at their screens. One stood and left through a door behind the counter. Wendell stared ahead, his face dark. Julia watched the door, wondering if he would reappear with Jack. She wondered how long this would take.

There was a mechanical creak beside them. The elevator doors slid open to reveal Jack, familiar, in his own clothes. Beside him stood the deputy from the courtroom.

Jack stepped off, his hands behind him. The policeman asked, "Ralph Carpenter?"

"That's me," Carpenter stepped forward.

"I'm releasing Mr. Lambert into your custody," he said ponderously. He leaned down and did something behind Jack's back, then stepped away, like a magician loosing a dove. Jack brought his hands in front of him and rubbed his wrists together, grimacing. Everyone drew around him, Julia hugged him. Carpenter was introduced, and he and Olson stood on either side of Jack.

"Mr. Lambert," Olson said.

Jack looked at him, then away.

Olson began talking to him in a low tone, explaining everything, his voice urgent and serious, like a coach before a game. Carpenter listened, his head lowered, his face intent. Wendell stood watching Jack. Jack was frowning, as though he were trying to concentrate on something else.

Olson raised his finger. "One single infraction," he said warningly. "One single one, and you're back inside. You understand?"

Jack nodded without expression. He said nothing.

"Would you answer Mr. Olson, Jack?" Wendell said.

"Okay," Jack said to nobody.

Olson turned to Julia and Wendell. He put his briefcase under his arm and stuck out his hand. "Okay. We'll be in touch. Good luck."

Wendell looked at Jack. "Jack?"

"Thanks," Jack said.

"We can't thank you enough," Julia said, before Wendell could say anything more.

"Okay." Carpenter put his hands together with a gesture that was almost a clap. "*Vamonos.*"

The policeman behind the counter looked up. Julia caught his eye and smiled. He nodded curtly, and looked down again. They pushed through the heavy doors.

They walked in silence to the car. When they reached it, Carpenter opened the rear door. "Jack and I are going to sit in back."

Jack looked at Carpenter for the first time. "Think I'm going to jump out?"

"I don't know what you're going to do, Jack," Carpenter said pleasantly. "I don't know you. But I gave my word that I'd stay with you, and I'm going to keep it."

Jack said nothing. He climbed into the backseat and turned his face to the window.

It was midmorning now, and the sun was high. The light was bright and diffuse, glaring. They drove through Buxton's small downtown, then a dreary residential neighborhood. The houses and yards were small and bleak. Clipped scrawny shrubs hugged the concrete foundations. The August-brown lawns, seared by the heat, were shaved and listless.

Julia had asked Wendell to drive so she could talk to Jack. She turned now to face him over the backseat.

"So, how are you feeling? What was it like in there?"

"Okay." Jack looked out the window. "It was okay."

"Not scary," Julia said, half a question.

"I didn't get raped, if that's what you mean," Jack said. "There were two other guys. They were drunks. No one got raped. We all had other things on our minds."

Wendell looked up at him in the rearview mirror. "I hope you know how serious this is."

Jack stared out the window.

"Mr. Carpenter is here—" Wendell said.

"Ralph," Carpenter said.

"Ralph is here to help us with all this. We're going home to talk about it."

"Not just us," Julia told him.

Jack looked at her, frowning. "Who else?"

"Your whole family. Your grandparents. Your aunt. Your brother."

"Your behavior affects more than just you," Wendell said.   ·

Jack was silent.

"This is serious, Jack," Wendell said, looking at him in the mirror.

"He knows it's serious," Julia said.

"I'd like to hear that from him, if it's all right with you," Wendell said.

Jack said nothing.

"This isn't the moment, Wendell," Julia said.

"Maybe I could be the judge of that," asked Wendell. "I'd like to hear a response from my son. He has criminal charges against him and I have yet to hear him say a single word about it."

"He was in *jail*," said Julia, now angry herself. "He was in *handcuffs. He knows how serious it is.*"

"*I'd like to hear that from Jack, Julia,*" Wendell said. "How about 'Thanks for getting me out of jail'? How about 'I'm really sorry for all this'? How about that?"

"What's the point of all this?" Julia asked. "Why are you harassing him?"

"I'm not 'harassing him.' I'm asking for a civilized response," said Wendell.

"I'm sorry, Dad, okay?" Jack said loudly. "Okay? *Thank you. Thank you for getting me out of jail.* Okay?"

There was a silence.

Wendell looked up at Jack in the mirror. He looked down at the road, then back again at Jack.

"What about what the judge said?" he asked the mirror.

"I heard what the judge said," Jack said, his voice flat and impatient. "I'll do it."

"You'll do what? *You'll do what?*" Wendell cried. He swerved abruptly, pulling the car off the road and onto the gravel shoulder. They jolted violently to a stop. "What will you do? Sneak out in the middle of the night, looking for drugs?"

"*Stop it, Wendell,*" Julia said. "*What are you doing?* Jack was crazed. He was in withdrawal. He's not going to do it again."

"Wendell," Carpenter said.

"*He was crazed, right. He's always crazed. He's a heroin addict.*" Wendell twisted around to look directly at Jack. "Your mother put up the deed to her house to get you out. Do you know what that means? You have a felony charge. If they find you guilty, and I don't know why they won't, it will be on your record forever. *Do you understand what you're doing to your life?*"

Jack said nothing.

Wendell brought his fist down on the seat back. *"Goddamn you!"* he said. *"How could you act like that? Stealing a car! Breaking into a drugstore! You're a common criminal!"*

"Leave him alone," Julia cried.

"Wendell," said Carpenter.

"Leave him alone? Then what will he do? We left him alone in the hospital for twenty-four hours and he committed two felonies. *Jesus Christ!"*

"What do you want me to say, Dad?" asked Jack angrily. "I don't know what you want."

"Wendell," Carpenter said firmly, leaning forward, "this is counter-productive."

"I'll tell you what I want," Wendell said to Jack. "I want your assurance that this will not happen again."

"Fine," Jack said. "Fine. *All right, Dad."*

"All right *what?"* asked Wendell.

"It won't happen again."

Wendell waited for a moment. *"It's not enough!"* he shouted. *"Damn you! Make me believe you."*

"What do you want me to say, Dad?"

"Wendell, stop it," Julia said.

"All right, Wendell." Carpenter put his hand on Wendell's shoulder. "Really. Come on. This is going nowhere."

There was a silence.

Wendell stared at Jack, then he turned back to the steering wheel and pulled the car out onto the road. For the rest of the trip no one spoke.

THIRTY

The house was quiet when they arrived. Coming into the silent hall, it felt as though the house was empty. The others went into the living room. Julia went to the kitchen to fix coffee, then brought in a tray.

Jack and Carpenter were sitting awkwardly side by side on the sofa. Julia found herself assessing Carpenter physically. He was shorter than Jack, but seemed more powerful, more in control of himself. She wondered if he could overpower Jack if it were necessary. If Jack were to—*what? Run out the door? Beat someone up?* It was absurd.

Julia set the tray down on the table and looked at Jack. Up close, she could see he was exhausted. There were deep blue circles under his eyes. His hair was matted, and reddish stubble covered his cheeks.

As Carpenter reached for his coffee, Jack stood.

"I'm going to go wash up," he said.

"Okay," Carpenter said. He stood, holding the mug. "Where're we going?"

Jack's eyelids fluttered with irritation. "I'm going to the bathroom."

"From now on, just think of us as joined at the hip. I'm coming with you."

Jack stood motionless, staring at him. Then he threw himself, hard, back on the sofa. He folded his arms.

"The bathroom here is pretty small," he said. "I don't think there's room for both of us."

"I think we can squeeze in," said Carpenter. "We'll have to." There was a silence. "I'm not your enemy, Jack."

"You're not my friend," Jack said. He stretched his head up and scratched at his neck. The skin rasped beneath his fingers.

"Actually, I am."

There was a silence.

Jack shook his head slightly, exasperated. "I'll wait."

"I'm not going anywhere," Carpenter said mildly.

Jack turned to him. "What is this? You're going to follow me around like a cop?"

"If it wasn't for me, you'd still be in jail," Carpenter said. "Still in handcuffs. Real cops would be following you around."

"Look." Jack sat down again and crossed his legs, his ankle on his knee. "I don't know you, Mr. Carpenter—"

"Ralph," said Carpenter.

"—but it was my parents who got me out of jail. Okay? I owe them a lot. I don't even know you."

"Okay. Let me tell you who I am, Jack," Carpenter said. He put his mug on the table. "I run a drug abuse program in Florida. As you heard the judge say, you've been remanded into my care. You're going to get to know me very well," Carpenter said. "Your parents asked me for help because they think you're in trouble."

"I'm not in trouble," said Jack.

"I think you are," Carpenter said. "You were taken to the hospital because of uncontrollable agitation. You ran away from the hospital, stole a car, broke into a drugstore and stole scheduled drugs. You were arrested and charged with burglary. Those are felonies. That's trouble."

Jack closed his eyes and shook his head. "This is all bullshit."

"What's bullshit?" asked Wendell. "What are you talking about?"

"Why is that?" asked Carpenter.

Jack shrugged. "I left the hospital because they wouldn't give me anything for pain. I didn't steal the car. I just had to get away, it was the middle of the night. I borrowed it. The nurse told me where the keys were."

Could that be true? Julia wondered.

"She said you stole it," said Carpenter.

Jack shrugged. "Lying."

"What about the drugstore?" asked Carpenter. "Why did you break into the drugstore?"

"I didn't break into it. I told you," Jack said. "I wanted some Vicodin." He shook his head suddenly from side to side, wildly, like an animal. "I'm still in pain, for Christsake. I'm out of my mind with pain."

"Jack," said Julia, "if you're in pain, you go to a doctor. You don't break into a drugstore."

"*I didn't break into a drugstore,*" Jack said.

There was a long silence.

"Why don't you go and get cleaned up," Julia said.

"That's what I was trying to do," said Jack.

"So let's go," said Carpenter.

Jack didn't look at him. He shook his head.

"Do you not understand this?" Wendell asked. "Did you not understand what the judge said? Do you not understand the conditions of your release?"

"*Christ!*" Jack slammed his fist onto the chair, his face dark. "Don't you trust me? My own parents? What the fuck do you think I'm going to do?" He looked at them accusingly.

"Of course we trust you," Julia said.

"Actually, we don't trust you right now," Wendell said.

"*What's the matter with you? You're all paranoid,*" Jack said, furious. "*What the hell do you think is going on? Christ! I have the flu, a stomach flu, I feel like shit! I ache all over, and you won't even get me a painkiller.*"

He started to stand, and Carpenter stood at once. Jack sank down again, but Carpenter stayed upright, standing over him, hands on his hips.

"We don't trust you right now, Jack," he said, "because you're not telling the truth. That's the problem."

Jack stared at them. His leg jumped. He shook his head. "You have no idea what I'm going through."

"Actually, I do," said Carpenter. "I was a junkie for eight years."

"We're trying to help you," said Julia.

Jack made a sound in his nose. "By putting this asshole on my case?"

"You got it," Wendell said.

Upstairs, Jack stood in front of the small sink, a towel around his waist. His face was covered in thick drifts of soapy lather. He stared at himself in the mirror. His limbs were leaden and his head felt heavy, as though the lather carried weight. He leaned hard on the sink; his knees were in flames. He drew the blade of Steven's razor through the white foam. Each stroke opened a swath of moist skin, the lather piling weightlessly up against the plastic shaft. His face was revealed incrementally, streak after pale streak exposed to the world.

The contours appeared, dismally familiar. The line of the lip, with its slight, sickening upward curl, the low flat troglodyte brows pressing heavily over the eyes. The narrow slanting nostrils, dark and humid within. The vile nose hairs—the sight of his face filled Jack with dread. Here was something deadly and immutable, some kind of bond to the tangible world that could not be broken. *Here he was again.* He'd hoped for something better, he'd hoped for a different face, one that showed a different relationship to life. He'd rather have stayed masked, rather have kept the shaving cream on forever, his face hidden behind high festive drifts, only his eyes visible. He avoided his eyes in the mirror. He did not want to meet his own gaze, to admit to what the eyes knew. He watched the blade as he drew it along his cheek.

In the reflection he could see Carpenter behind him. He was sitting on the closed toilet seat, leaning back, his arms folded across his chest. He was watching Jack like a python. While Jack showered he'd stood on the other side of the curtain, and when Jack turned off the water he could hear Carpenter breathing.

Carpenter was an asshole, but strong. He'd gripped Jack's arm for a moment, Jack felt the fingers close on him. Carpenter was all over the place, jumping up from the sofa, leaning over him, those black eyes.

Jack rinsed off the flimsy plastic razor, the suds collapsing into the sink, swirling into the blue-stained drain. He raised the razor to his face again. He tried to imagine using the razor as a weapon, brandishing its narrow slanted surface at Carpenter. He could not. He could not imagine challenging Carpenter in any way. That dense wrestler's body, the springy step, the watchful stare. Something about Carpenter suggested that he would move swiftly into street-fighting combat without hesitation. With joy, in fact.

Jack himself wasn't up to it. He wasn't up to any physical struggle now, actually. He had become weak. It was a surprise to him: he'd been used to being strong, his body capable. Now he was aware that there were things that were beyond his strength. Almost everything, in fact. He could barely stand up.

Jack let go of the sink and cupped both hands beneath the faucet. He leaned over and splashed water onto his face, closing his eyes. Shutting his eyes gave him vertigo; he might tip over. He opened them. His head ached, and his stomach was in a continuing boil. He rinsed his shaven neck, then scratched it. He scratched deeply, into the skin. His calves were pulsing and twitching as though something were inside trying to get out. His whole body hummed, as though he'd been wired for electricity and someone had turned on the switch and walked off, leaving him there, sizzling and twitching forever.

The air around him was filled with dread and panic, like a smell. He didn't want to meet his eyes in the mirror. He was afraid he might be gone, he might be dead, the eyes empty, there might be nothing left but his body. A wave of claustrophobia spread through him: he had to get out of here. He needed to get out of his skin, his mind, his whole fucking life. He wanted to exist in a different way. He wanted smack. His body yearned for it.

Smack was the answer. There it was, the beautiful thought. He longed for it. The answer to everything, the different way of existing. It felt so unfair, that everything prevented him from it. The whole world was in league against him, while his needs were so simple. He wanted one thing. Everything urged him toward it, it was a tide moving through him. The only question was how to reach it. *The journey of a thousand miles starts with but a single step.* What was the first step? He would reach it, he would get there.

The shock of the cold water on his skin was bracing, and for a nanosecond he felt better. Then his face caught fire, and desperation returned. He was living nanosecond by nanosecond, it was intolerable.

At least he was back home, better than being in fucking jail. Though jail had not actually been so bad. Mattresses on the floor, but clean. Nicer than his apartment, actually. Clean, and no one had hurt him. At least that asshole Carpenter had not been in there with him, staring at him every second. Jack squeezed out a line of toothpaste on Steven's toothbrush.

"I want to make sure you understand what's going on, Jack," Carpenter said from behind him. "What I said in court, about your going into treatment, is true. You don't have a choice. It's that or jail. So you and I are going to spend a lot of time together."

Jack raised the loaded toothbrush to his mouth. He now met his own eyes in the mirror as though they were those of a friend. He locked onto his own gaze and began brushing his teeth, pretending he was alone. *Nothing was true until it happened.*

"We're going to work on this together," Carpenter said. "I want you to think about quitting."

Jack leaned over and spat loudly into the sink. Of course he was ready to quit. Only not right now, not exactly at this moment, feeling the way he did, *in agony, for Christsake.* What he needed right now was a fix, just to get himself straight, just to stop the unbearable tension of vibration and pain running through him. Then he'd talk about quitting, he'd talk about anything. Just a bag, one bag.

Carpenter waited.

"Jack?"

Jack wiped his mouth with his hand. The toothpaste had a synthetic peppermint tang, disgusting.

"It's time to quit," Carpenter said. "Your options have run out." His eyes bored into Jack.

Jack lifted his chin to scratch his neck. He met Carpenter's gaze in the mirror.

"How do you figure that?" he asked. All this was talk, it would go on forever. He felt swept by a desperate boredom. Despair and boredom at once, he was stretched unendurably between them.

"You've been arrested, Jack. You were in the slammer. You were booked on felony charges. That's big-time. You know that, right? Major. You're out on bail on one condition—you go into treatment. That's what's going to happen. It's your only option, so let's talk about it."

Jack shrugged his shoulders. He leaned over again and cupped his hands, buried his face in the cold water. Again, the shock on his skin felt good, and for an instant he felt better. Then his face went hot again and the desperation returned. What he was doing was living nanosecond by nanosecond. He was getting through them, one at a time. They stretched before him forever, the endless dry landscape. It was intolerable.

"I'm guessing you're not feeling very well right now," Carpenter said. "What's your habit? How many bags you on?"

Jack dried his face on the grimy hand towel and stuffed it back onto the rack. He looked at his reflection. His pupils were dilated now, enormous and black. He had to get out of here.

"I don't know what you mean," Jack said. He leaned close to the mirror, his face looming. He drew down his lower eyelid, examining the glossy liquid curve of his eyeball. Suddenly close and huge, it was deep yellow and bloodshot, the color of pus, laced with tiny serpentine blood vessels. The sight gave him a voluptuous satisfaction.

"What is it?" Carpenter asked. "I want to know how bad it is."

Jack looked at him in the mirror. "Five a day."

Carpenter watched his reflection. "I think you're lying," he said.

Jack said nothing. *It was none of Carpenter's business. Why should he tell him anything? Carpenter wanted a major habit, the big time. He wasn't going to perform on command.*

"I also think you feel like shit," Carpenter said.

Jack said nothing. *This, too, was none of Carpenter's business.*

"Let's be candid here," Carpenter said.

Jack released his eyelid and looked at Carpenter in the mirror. Bargaining time: he could hear it in the tone of voice. A deal was about to be offered, some kind of drugs. Valium would be fine, anything was fine, anything better than this. He'd take it. Anything was a step on the road to smack. He wanted just enough to take the edge off.

He was not actually being candid here. What he actually wanted was enough smack to suck himself out into deep space, to planet Mars. To Pluto, which was no longer Pluto, for some reason. His legs jerked, nearly simultaneously, but not quite. His joints ached and he was freezing cold. His skin was covered in goose bumps. He was shivering. He was desperate to get out of this.

No one ever died from heroin withdrawal, they only wished they could. That was the joke, though not much of one. Why was it meant to be funny? Death looked very good from here. It would be so easy. Where was he going, if not there? It was just a question of how much you sucked into the barrel. It was easily within reach. In fact—he let the idea bloom in his mind, erupting upward like a mushroom cloud—it was unbearably appealing. Sliding blissfully off into the darkness, peace. No more of this pain and vileness, the sores on his face, the look in his father's eyes, no more hating his own despicable self.

The idea of dying was smooth and alluring, the ultimate high. Junkies who OD'ed and were brought back said it was the best high of their lives. Heading into deep space, looking for Pluto, sinking into darkness at a million miles an hour. Beautiful.

His body was now infested by some kind of living itch that dwelt in his bloodstream. He was surrounded by endless low bare hills of dread. Everything he saw was fatal. The space around him had become infused with fear, he could smell it. Everything he saw had some sinister hidden counterpart that lay just beneath the surface of itself. Like an iceberg, most of what surrounded him was concealed and dreadful. It was dangerous to move. *Fear and Trembling*: who wrote that? Wittgenstein? No, someone farther north, another double letter. The Scandinavian. Had he been a junkie? Because he was right, it was the perfect description of life in the world. The color red was now a horror. *He himself was a horror, let's not leave that out.* He closed his eyes and opened them again. Carpenter was still waiting.

"What do you mean?" Jack asked. He put both hands on the sink and leaned heavily on them, taking the weight off his unreliable legs, putting it onto his unreliable arms. He dropped his head.

"Okay, don't tell me," Carpenter said. "I suspect you take eight or ten bags a day, and you feel like shit. If you hadn't left the hospital, you'd still be on IV painkillers. You chose to give them up. It was your decision. Now you feel like shit, and you're on your way to rehab. You're giving everything up. You promised that in court."

"You promised, not me," Jack said.

Carpenter raised his forefinger. "I promised it on your behalf. If I hadn't, you'd still be in prison. You have a criminal record now. It's time to quit." He leaned forward, resting his elbows on his knees. He lowered his voice. "I want to help you, Jack. I know what you're going through, and I'm going to help you get through it if I can. I promise you I'll help you. But I want you to know something. You can't fuck with me. Don't try. Do you understand?"

Jack heard the voice ringing in his head. It went on and on. *Trial, a criminal record.* Right now he was upstairs in the bathroom, holding on to the sink with both hands. The room surrounded him with itself.

A wave of shivering passed through him, and he looked down. There was the terrible blue stain around the drain, the slow nauseating whirl of dirty water.

Standing in the kitchen, Julia called to Wendell as he passed by on his way to his room.

"What is it?" Wendell paused, his voice unfriendly.

"I want to talk to you," she said.

He came warily into the kitchen.

Julia was at the sink. "You have to stop acting like this."

"Why? Why should I stop it?" Wendell folded his arms on his chest.

"Because it doesn't get you anywhere." She turned off the water and turned to face him, wiping her hands on the dishcloth. "I'm serious, Wendell. You have to stop being angry at him."

"He's a fuckup," Wendell said angrily. "This is huge. He's acting like a maniac. Should we pretend he isn't?"

"We have to go on," Julia said. "It is huge. We have to go on."

"We have to acknowledge it," Wendell said. "*He* has to acknowledge it. I'm not going to ignore what's just happened."

"No one's ignoring it, Wendell. We've just spent the morning in court. Jack spent the night in jail. That's hard to ignore." She leaned against the sink. "But we've agreed to do this thing with Carpenter. It means we can't just yell at Jack for what he's done. We're trying to give him support for quitting, not to attack him for using."

"So Carpenter says." Wendell shook his head, his mouth tight.

"You have to stop being angry," Julia said.

"What's the point of doing this whole thing?" Wendell said, keeping his voice down. "What's the fucking point? When we started out with it, we didn't know where Jack was, and we were going to have an intervention to persuade him to go into rehab. Now he's been ordered to go by the court, he has no choice. So what are we all doing? This is absurd."

Julia tilted her head. "It's not. This isn't like shipping a dog to a kennel. He's a participant. It all depends on his attitude. Carpenter says he has a much better chance of recovery if he goes through this. All the programs say that. Starting with an intervention is much better than going in cold, if the addict doesn't want to go. It means he's willing, he's committed."

Wendell shook his head.

"Don't be like this," Julia said angrily. "Why did you come all the way up here? Why did you talk Steven into doing this? We're meant to be supporting Jack, not blaming him. If you go on acting like this, Carpenter will ask you to leave. What good are you doing, yelling at Jack?"

"How should I feel?" Wendell said. He folded his arms. "How the fuck should I feel? Happy about this? Not angry?"

"I'm not going to tell you how to feel," Julia said. "Think of how Jack feels. Think of what will be best for him. *He's our son, Wendell.* His life is at risk. Fifty percent of heroin addicts die from it. Think about that, instead of your amour propre."

Wendell glared at her.

"Or do what you want!" Julia flung the cloth onto the counter. "Do whatever you want, Wendell." She threw her hands in the air. "It will be fine. My father will tell Jack every single mistake he's ever made, my mother won't remember who he is, Harriet has hardly ever seen him, Steven will refuse to show up, and great, why *don't* you tell him how really angry you are at him. Tell him how badly he's fucked up, which I'm sure he hasn't noticed. It'll be a huge success. You'll be really helpful." She folded her arms on her chest.

There was a long silence.

Wendell's mouth began to change. He raised his eyebrows, the corners of his mouth shifted.

"Don't smile at me!" Julia said. "Don't change the subject! Don't turn coy and come-onny, don't get charming! You have to decide if you can be a grown-up.

"Remember what you said the other day, how you thought what you did wouldn't matter to our marriage? How you just did what you wanted? And how badly you screwed everything up? Okay, now, this is your chance to make something work. Try *not* to do what you want. Try that, Wendell."

She was leaning back against the sink, her arms folded on her chest, her head high, her feet set close together.

They watched each other.

Wendell looked away, looked back at her.

"It's not my *amour propre*," he said. "Or maybe that's part of it, but it's something else, too. The way he acts, not looking at us, not talking to us, not admitting what he's done, as though he's too cool to deal— he acts *contemptuous* of us. It feels to me as though he devalues everything I've ever done for him. He devalues the fact that I love him. He devalues himself, the whole enterprise of having him and raising him—he acts as though it was all worthless. He doesn't care about any of it.

"Having a son, bringing him up, is one of the great experiences *of my life*." Wendell stared at her. "He's ready to throw it all away. Like that. He acts as though it means *nothing*. He's contemptuous of everything we've ever done as parents." Wendell paused. "That's what really pisses me off. Who is he to decide that what we've put so much into is worthless, trash? How *dare* he? How dare he take this so casually, his part in our lives? We were a team, he and us. We all agreed that he was valuable, his life was valuable." Wendell shook his head. "Who does he think he is, to say now that it's not? I want to grab him, I want to shake his fucking head off."

Julia watched him. "I know," she said, and sighed. "It's awful. You're right. But we can't act like that now. We can't be angry. We're doing something else. We're trying to reach him another way. Carpenter—"

"Carpenter's a jerk," Wendell said.

Julia narrowed her eyes. "Okay, Wendell. You take charge. You figure it all out. Let's fire Carpenter, and you do it all."

"Okay," Wendell said. "He's done a lot, I grant you."

"Just gotten Jack out of jail, is all," said Julia.

"—but he's a power freak. He makes me want to throw up."

Julia lifted her shoulders. "He's in charge, Wendell. He's running this. We have to trust him. Either we do it his way or we have to come up with a whole other plan. And if we do it his way, we have to believe in it. We have to do it right. *You can't act like this.* You have to stop feeling this way."

"What do you mean, *stop*. How should I stop feeling this way?" Wendell said angrily. "You can't just stop feeling something."

"Try thinking of someone else besides yourself, Wendell," Julia said. "Try thinking of our son. Think of what might be best for him. Think of the fact that he might die if we don't do this right."

THIRTY-ONE

Katharine and Edward came slowly into the living room and settled side by side on the sofa. Katharine laid her cane down at her feet. It would be difficult to reach later, but at least it wouldn't suddenly clatter to the floor in the middle of something. She leaned back and looked around. There was Harriet, had she been there before?

"Good morning, dear," she said, smiling.

"Morning, Mother," Harriet said.

Harriet seemed tense, and Katharine wondered if she and her sister were at odds. They often were, which pained Katharine. She herself had been close to her own brothers, and why did this current of antagonism run so strongly between her daughters? Hostility in the family seemed such a waste. But she'd learned years ago that she could do nothing to fix this. If Katharine raised the subject with either daughter she'd turn angry, blaming Katharine for interfering, blaming the sister for something she'd done. There was some continual aggrievement, some perennial wound; she couldn't end it or heal it.

Sometimes she wondered if it had been something she'd done, or Edward, years ago, while the girls were children, that still fueled this. Had they created some awful pattern of blame and anger? Had they not paid the girls enough attention? Given too much of it to one of them? The crimes you paid for, as a parent: excruciating, to be blamed for something you'd never dreamt of doing, of hurting someone you'd give your heart's blood to. But it was the girls who grieved her, not herself. It saddened her that her daughters were not close.

It saddened her, too, that she was not close to Julia. They'd been close once, easy, warm. Julia was her darling. How had they lost this? They'd been close all through her childhood, even through adolescence, while Katharine held her breath, waiting for Julia to turn closed and hard. She and Julia had always shared a sense of humor, and the two of them used to catch each other's eyes and fall into fits, laughing at the same things, speechless, rocking. That was gone. Something had changed, sometime in college, and Julia had become gradually closed to her. Katharine had thought then that it was a late reaction. It seemed all children had to rebel against their parents, you had to expect it. Katharine had held her tongue and waited for her to get through that awful stern phase, impatient, exasperated, disdainful of everything her mother said. But the phase had never ended.

Now Julia was somehow remote and distant, no matter what Katharine said, no matter how she tried to reach her. She wondered if she'd said something, years ago, that had triggered it. Something she'd done? Had it changed when Julia married Wendell? Was it the problem of the mother-in-law, all those jokes?

It was true that the husband resented the mother's presence. The mother was the true threat to the marriage: no one had been more intimate with the bride than the mother, no other boyfriend, no roommate. It was the mother who was the enemy of the husband, if there were an enemy. Not that she'd ever felt like Wendell's enemy, she was very fond of Wendell. But these things were so subtle, so complicated. She might have said something, or done something, without thinking.

Or maybe not. Maybe Julia had gone to a therapist and reconsidered her childhood. Therapists seemed always to be on the side of the child, rightly probably, but why forever? Why not sew up the torn and tattered mess they'd made of the connection to the parents? Why not work around, in the end, to some kind of forgiveness?

Or maybe it hadn't been therapy. Maybe Julia had simply decided that she would no longer be close to her mother. Maybe in New York, among Julia's friends, it was fashionable to dislike your mother, to make cruel jokes about her, to hold her forever at arm's length. That was possible. She would probably never know what had happened.

It seemed such a waste: Katharine had loved her own mother. When she went away to college, when she married, she wrote her mother long letters; in those days phone calls were expensive. She still had all their letters. She had loved having her mother visit. She had called her "darling," they had called each other that. Katharine could not imagine Julia calling her darling.

She'd waited for Julia to return to her former self—children went through phases, all their lives, didn't they? For years she had waited for this to happen, but it had not. Katharine had given up: it seemed that this phase was permanent, or anyway, that it would last for the rest of Katharine's life. Which would not be too much longer, her time was running out.

As you grew older, you became aware of a difference in the way you looked at time. When you were young, it lay before you, endless, inexhaustible. This summer, next, some other time, you would visit Africa or Patagonia, your friends in Wiltshire. Now Katharine knew how few new things she would do, how many things she would never do again. She would never run back upstairs for a sweater. She would never even rise quickly to her feet. Her world had narrowed.

Katharine missed her daughter. She missed her especially when Julia was with her, the masked face, the controlled voice. The withheld self. It seemed so heartbreaking to lose her this way. Nothing Katharine said, nothing, would soften Julia's stern face, nothing would make her laugh outright, the way she used to. Nothing would reawaken that old connection.

Still, Katharine took the pleasure she was allowed in her daughter's company. She hoped things might change, hoped she might have her daughter back before she died. One thing you learned as a parent was humility.

And as her memory failed, it was worse and worse each day, she was losing certain parts of her life. Maybe, as a kindness, she would lose this part. Maybe she would forget that Julia had been cold. Maybe Julia would return to her, and then Katharine would forget they had ever been apart.

Steven appeared, and sat on a low bench in front of the empty fireplace. Julia and Wendell came in, and Julia went to get a chair from the dining room.

"When's this going to start?" Harriet asked Julia. Her voice was cool, Katharine saw they were at odds.

"In a minute," Julia said; then admitted, "I don't know. Whenever Ralph brings him down. He's cleaning up."

Katharine looked from Harriet to Julia. "And just remind me again what it is that's going to start." She spoke in a half-whisper, humorous.

Her daughters looked at her.

"We're going to talk to Jack about his addiction to heroin," said Julia.

"Heroin!" said Katharine. "Oh, dear, that's very bad, isn't it."

Julia nodded. She could hear footsteps overhead. "Very bad."

Katharine turned to Edward. "Did you know about this?" Her voice was lowered.

Edward looked at her, his eyes full of grief. He nodded.

Kattie's announcement that morning had wakened in him a sense of shame. He felt as though a blazing mirror had been held up to him. It was as though his entire life were being reassessed by someone else. He was powerless to control it, forced to observe it.

He found himself wondering what sort of a marriage Katharine had had, a question that had never occurred to him before. The idea itself was a kind of shock, that there might be another, alternate view of their life together. He'd always seen himself as the center of things, moving across the landscape of their life like a roiling storm center on a weather map. His work, his needs, his friends had determined everything—where they lived, who they saw, how they lived. This had always seemed right to him. He had given them all a good life, his family, hadn't he? He was proud of the life they'd had.

But now it seemed different, he could no longer see it from inside himself. He thought things might have been different for Katharine. That she might have been at the center of another system, possibly just as strong, just as roiling, but invisible on his map.

Getting older, it was impossible to see things the way you'd always seen them before. It was some sort of trick of perspective, the landscape shifted. You could no longer see things as they'd always been. This news of Kattie's was changing everything.

He didn't think she'd resented him. What he was afraid of was something else. He imagined a wave of loneliness washing over her as he'd set off in the morning for the hospital. Or worse, a wave of loneliness while he was with her, still absorbed by his world. Had she asked him things, told him things, that he ignored? Had she felt solitude while they sat at dinner, or as he lay in bed, thinking about the surgery the next day, or taking a foreign student into the program, or writing proposals for new equipment? Those were the topics that had drawn him, he'd spent his whole life thinking about them. What had Kattie's life been spent on? He could not say. The whole machinery of his life had excluded her. What had she thought about while he was thinking of these things? The life they'd led had been his.

Katharine was touched by his look, at his being so moved by Jack's trouble. She patted his hand.

"Sad, isn't it?" she whispered, and he nodded.

Had she felt appreciated? Had she understood that he'd needed her? He had. But whatever kind of marriage it had been, it was nearly over. More than fifty years: it was too late for second thoughts, making reparations. All those years had been lived.

He understood that she'd delivered herself to him in a way he had never done for her. Her life had been offered to him. She'd lived his life without complaint. This notion was so powerful, so humbling, that he could hardly think of anything else, could hardly focus on all this, the reason they were here.

There were heavy footsteps on the stairs, then in the dining room. Jack and Carpenter came into the room. Jack moved slowly and self-consciously, his head down, as though he were in church. Carpenter looked around at them all, nodding, but Jack looked at no one.

Jack sat down in the wicker rocking chair, which creaked heavily under his weight. He was clean and shaven, his hair combed. He looked much worse. Everything now stood out against the moist sheen of his skin—the pallor, the sores around his mouth, the dark circles. His eyes looked black, the pupils huge and unfocused. They seemed to fall on things without recognition.

Carpenter sat down in the chair beside him. He looked around.

"Sorry to keep you waiting," he said. "First of all, I want to thank you all for being here. You're doing something remarkable." Carpenter's voice was rich, full of certainty.

Julia wanted to twitch: he was so full of himself, so controlling, so dramatic. It was excruciating. But they had given themselves up to him, they had to trust him. At the meeting the night before, everyone had read their pieces out loud, and everyone had been corrected and asked to rewrite them. Carpenter had been like a teacher, strict, critical, relentless. Julia was afraid that her father would rebel, but Edward had said nothing. Maybe Carpenter had wanted to give them a sense of camaraderie, group pride.

But it didn't matter how they felt, all that mattered was saving Jackie. All that mattered was opening Jackie up to what they said, filling him with their conviction, changing his attitude. *Please let this happen,* Julia thought.

Carpenter leaned forward, fixing each of them with his black gaze as he talked. He kept using the word "love." Julia did not dare look at Harriet, did not want to see the cynical lift of her eyebrows. But everyone seemed serious, intent on Carpenter's words, attentive, responsive. Maybe this was working, maybe Carpenter had done something to their disparate, antagonistic, intransigent family. Julia had no sense, now, of what would happen, how anyone would behave. They were all loose cannons, anything could happen.

Jack heard the start of the familiar litany—*we want to help you help yourself, we love you, Jack*—and he began to rock, very slightly, keeping his eyes on the floor. They were all looking at him. He rocked with small discrete movements, setting up a kinetic screen between himself and everything around him. *One step at a time. Nanosecond by nanosecond.* The goal, his bed of crimson joy, his dark secret life, lay somewhere ahead. It would dispel this lowering anxiety, this gathering doom.

He paid attention to the movement, not listening to the voice, creaking off the seconds. He was holding his breath in his mind. Each creak brought him a moment closer to what he wanted.

They were here to do something to him. They had drawn around him like a noose. They were going to talk to him, say something that would rip his heart from his chest. He could hear it in their voices. He was surrounded. He was the bird in the underbrush, they had nets.

They all had sheets of paper; they were taking them out of pockets, unfolding them, spreading them out.

"All we ask from you, Jack," Carpenter said, speaking slowly, "is that you listen."

Jack leaned his head back. The chair creaked at his slightest movement, and this was somehow comforting, like a secret signal. He was still getting the waves of pain, chills, the aches passing across his body, sheets of fire going through his joints. His heartbeat was quickening, his breathing seemed strange. Whatever they were planning he would resist. He did not look at anyone.

He heard from Carpenter's voice that he was drawing to a close. Next they would all read what they'd written out loud, and it would tear Jack to pieces. That was the plan, he could hear it in Carpenter's voice. Jack was not allowed to speak. They wanted him to be undone. But that would not happen, he would simply endure it. He would endure anything.

Carpenter nodded at Harriet. "Harriet? Would you begin?"

Harriet spread open her sheet of paper.

She'd spent the morning in her claustrophobic room at the B&B, which was filled with the cloying scent of chemical potpourri. Sitting on a stiff plush love seat (bright red, bolt upright), she bent uncomfortably over a low table, rewriting. Everyone had been asked to rewrite. Hers had been too impersonal: could she write from her own experience?

Outside, beyond the deeply ruffled curtains, the tidy lawn, the rows of purple petunias, Harriet could hear the steady stream of cars going slowly by. It was the summer invasion, tourists looking for a parking place, an ice cream parlor.

"I don't want to do this," Jack said suddenly.

"All we're asking, Jack, is that you listen," Carpenter said.

"I don't want to," Jack said, "this is a load of crap."

"We're just asking you to listen to what we have to say," Carpenter said, shaking his head slightly.

He sat very still. Jack knew that if he stood up, Carpenter would be up at once beside him. Like a python.

Jack flung his arms across his chest and pushed himself back in the rocker, tipping back hard. *All right, then. Nanosecond by nanosecond.*

He tried not to hear, but words and phrases came through. Apparently he'd given Harriet a stopwatch one Christmas. He remembered that.

"Now you can have turtle races, Aunt Harriet!" Harriet smiled, saying this, he could hear it in her voice, though he was not looking at her. Each moment was one closer. It had been sweet of him, apparently, to think of her working with animals. She had found that touching, *touching, touching.*

"I don't see much of you now," Harriet said, "but when I see your mother, I know how painful it is for her to talk about you. You've become lost to her because of this. Because of heroin."

Julia, listening, felt invaded. *She'd never talked to Harriet about Jack, about heroin. She'd never talked to her about pain. But how transparent she must have been, how exposed she felt: she had managed to conceal nothing. How humiliating to learn this here, now.*

Harriet went on: "You're my sister's child, my nephew, you're part of the family that will carry us into the next generation. I don't have any children: you and Steven, and Ted's girls, are my representatives. You're our future family. So I care about you; we're connected in a way you might not even think about."

He was keeping himself separate from all this, he was holding himself apart. It was torture, actually, being here. He was in pain. He kept his knee jiggling, a constant movement, the steady creaking of the chair, to keep himself separate. He had a cause. He was a jihadist. He could resist this mindless onslaught of talk. He would keep himself pure.

Harriet looked at him. "What you're doing makes me sad. You look so ill. Your skin is bad, your eyes are dull. Junkies don't last, you know. They have short lives."

Smack was medicine, that's what they didn't know. You never got sick on smack. Everyone knew that.

"And I want you to live. I want you to have a long, challenging, interesting, wonderful life, full of energy and ideas. Not like the one you have now, which is out of your control, and full of misery and desperation, and which can't last. You're part of my family, whether you think so or not, and I love you."

He was becoming breathless. The words kept coming toward him; he was trying to dodge them, trying to keep up the steady stream of creaks, to combat them. He didn't want them in his brain. All this was crap, and what he wanted was not here, but ahead of him.

"Katharine?"

Now his grandmother would say something that made no sense. She smiled at him: she had a story. When he was little, apparently, he'd brought her a cup of tea and it had spilled.

"'Here it is, Grandma, all weak and wobbly,' you said, and you laughed so hard you nearly fell over." Katharine was laughing as she remembered: Jack had been so funny, his laugh so infectious. She looked around to see if anyone else remembered: Julia was laughing, too.

He remembered it, it was stupid, so what? The tea, the laughter. This was like being dragged over stones.

"I remember another time," Katharine said, no longer reading from her paper. "One time you'd done something naughty, I don't remember what. Your father spanked you, and you were being so brave. Each time his hand came down you said, 'That doesn't hurt! That doesn't hurt!' As though you were, you know. Oh, what's the word." She looked at Edward. "Invulnerable! But then finally you burst into tears."

Katharine paused. She wasn't sure why she was telling this story. She remembered Jack's small face, years ago, braced and tense against the tears, desperate, holding out as long as he could. Or had it been Ted? Had it been Edward, spanking?

It was once funny, or it had been told as a funny story, but she could see now that it was not. Not with Jack sitting there, braced in the rocking chair as though ready for flight, his face bleached by pain. The story was not funny, and poor Jack was in agony. She could not remember what came next.

"I love you very much," she said gently. *It was heroin, that was it. Terrible.* "I don't want to see you in such trouble. I know you're having trouble with drugs, and I'm so sorry. I hope you'll be able to stop, you know, get nonaddicted. Edward, what's the word I want?"

"Kick," Steven said.

"What?" Katharine asked.

"Kick the habit," Steven said.

"Well, if that's what I mean," Katharine said, "I hope you do it. And if I can help you, I will. You know I climbed Mount Washington, when I was young."

Edward listened in distress. It was painful to hear her mind wandering. That spanking—it had been him and Ted. It was painful to hear. And Kattie—how had he not realized before what was happening? Poor Kattie, her memory unspooling, the core of her brain under attack.

Why had he not paid her more attention, why had he not appreciated her before? Now it had begun, she would never not be in decline. It was already too late to see her at her best, to memorize it, applaud. Edward glanced down at her hands lying in her lap. They were thickened by arthritis: he felt an impulse, which he suppressed, to pick one up and kiss it.

"Edward?" Carpenter said.

Edward slowly took his paper from his breast pocket. He began to read, but he was still thinking of Kattie and the awful story about spanking Ted. He did not want the family stories of him to be about an ogre. Were there good stories about him? Charming, funny ones? He was telling Jack about a time he'd sung in the *Messiah*. The thing about your children was that they grew up and judged you. Though Ted lived in Oregon because of his job. What if Edward had been someone else to his family, without realizing it?

All those years in the hospital, doing his work, thinking his family was living its way along behind him, like the wake from his boat—what if it had been different for them? He felt a pain in his chest.

He looked up at Jack as he was reading, his bruised arms, his scrambled thoughts and twitching limbs, his vacant eyes, his system in thrall. How dreadful to be his parent, fear that you were being judged somehow by this. What a harvest to reap, what dreadful fruits of your labors.

"Jack," he read, "this is your life. It matters to us. You matter to us. We love you. You mustn't waste your time on this, or your life. You have a great time spread out ahead of you." Edward thought of fall training, the springy dirt road beneath his feet, the soft damp scent of the golden leaves. "I want you to enjoy it."

Jack nodded, rocking. *How long would this take? When was the flight?* He couldn't stand much more of this. He had no choice. He could remember the world, he could remember it in glimpses. He could remember sitting in a restaurant in the morning, having coffee, feeling good. Strange to remember a life without this color in it.

That wasn't where he lived now. Now this ballooning presence was everywhere, that sweet presence around him, but where was it? Listening to this was like having double vision, hallucinating; he was here, listening, *he was here, his whole body was waiting for smack. He was here.*

Now it was Steven standing up to pull his paper from his jeans pocket. He sat down and unfolded the paper, holding it up to read. His hands were shaking. Jack closed his eyes.

"When we were kids," Steven said, "we used to ride bikes together in Riverside Park. There was a group of bigger kids around, tough ones, and we used to watch out for them, but once you told me you always felt safe with me. It made me feel great. For a long time I felt I could protect you. I was your big brother. I tried to protect you."

He didn't want to hear all this, that was the thing. All of this cascading down on him. These stories of the charming rapscallion, the scalawag. These little vignettes of the ne'er-do-well. The piece of shit, actually.

"I used to know what was happening in your life. I used to talk to you all the time. Now I can't reach you. I can't talk to you, you're usually high. Your apartment is filthy, and so are your clothes. I don't even think you're playing music anymore. It makes me really sad."

They were all in a circle around him. There was nothing he could do. His parents were next. There would be weeping.

Wendell opened up his paper. He looked up at Jack. Julia watched him.

"Dear Jack," he began, "I love you." They had been told to write a letter. "You're my son, and I love you very much.

"When you were little, you were so quick and bright, and so funny. We've always depended on you to make us laugh. I remember one time when you were about ten and you broke a clock of mine. It was a red one from Hammacher Schlemmer, your mother gave it to me for Christmas. You broke it into smithereens. When I asked you about it, you said you did it on purpose. The label said it was indestructible, and you were testing it with a hammer." Wendell shook his head. "I got mad at you and said, 'Why do you do these things?' You said, 'Well, I never do the same thing twice, Dad, so I guess sometime I'll run out of bad things to do.'" Wendell looked up at Jack.

Jack was holding himself tilted back, at the highest point of the rocker's arc. The words were coming at him fine and hard like shards of glass.

"It still makes me laugh, you were so plucky." Wendell's face turned somber. "For a long time, when you got in trouble, I'd remember that. I hoped you were just working your way through the possibilities of the world. Sometimes I agreed with your choices, sometimes I didn't, but I thought—I hoped—that eventually you'd run out of mistakes to make." Wendell looked up again.

He remembered the red plastic clock, heavy and durable, the solid feel of the hammer in his hand. He hated this.

"I don't think that's true anymore," Wendell said. "I think you're making the same mistakes over and over. I think drugs are ruining your life, and that makes me very sad."

Well, right, he was a fuckup. Not exactly news. But it was his life, wasn't it.

Rocking the chair back and forth was like jiggling his knee, which he was also doing. They were both ways of keeping his father away from him, of setting up another arena he could gallop around in and not listen. He didn't want to hear all this. *Jack, Jack, how sad we all are. How ashamed we all are of you, how you've let us all down.*

What he wanted was smack, smack, smack, my bed of crimson joy.

Wendell went on. "When you first used to come home from college, you used to talk about what you were studying, and you were so excited about literature. I remember you reading the Romantic poets, and it was as though you were discovering a new country. One night you read them out loud. It was wonderful, you were so passionate. 'Listen to this,' you said, as though no one had ever read that poem before. 'O Rose, thou art sick!'" Wendell shook his head. "What you want in your children is passion. It's the great thing. It was a joy to me."

"When I saw you last week in New York, you looked terrible. You could barely open your eyes, and your speech was slurred. Your apartment was filthy and unkempt. There were empty bottles and trash on the floor, dirty sheets on the bed, no food in the kitchen. It was awful to realize this is the way you live now.

"I called you a couple of months ago. You could hardly speak, you were so high. You could barely get one word out after another. I can't talk to you anymore. You're my son, and you live in Brooklyn, but we might as well be strangers, three thousand miles apart. I can't reach you anymore."

Jack put his head back against the wicker and clasped the arms.

"I feel as though you're doing something now, over and over, that we can't help you with. And there's no stopping you." Wendell's voice broke.

He took off his glasses and put his hand over his eyes. "What you're doing now, Jack, you can't control. And we can't help you with it."

Wendell paused for a moment. He swallowed, then went on reading.

"If I've been a part of this in any way, I apologize. I'm your father, so I guess I must have been. Parents are always a part of their children's paths, part of what they do. I'm sorry for whatever I did to contribute to this. If my attitude toward drugs made this easy, I'm sorry. If it was the divorce, I'm sorry for that. If I was too hard on you, while you were growing up, or when you were a teenager, I'm sorry for that. I love you, and I've always loved you. You have always been one of the great joys in my life." Wendell paused again. "But I also want you to know that I won't let you go on like this. I want you to commit to giving up drugs, and if you don't commit, I won't help you out in any way. I want you to give up this abomination"—he paused again—"which is killing you."

There was silence. Carpenter waited, looking around the circle.

"Julia," he said.

Julia looked down at her paper. She had one chance, they all had exactly one chance. Jack was sitting now before them, maybe listening, maybe not. It was all they could do now, read these letters, hold them up like magic spells against the unthinkable.

"Dear Jack," she began. "I remember you once, when you were six or seven. You were taking a bath, playing with a toy in the tub. I was in the bedroom, and I could hear you." Julia started to smile. "You laughed and laughed, you had that infectious, jelly-belly gurgling laugh. I thought how wonderful it was to think the world was so hilarious. You thought everything was so funny.

"One time you put on a talent show, with the dachshund we had, Noodle. You wore an old skirt of mine over your shoulders, like a cape, and you'd penciled on a mustache. We all sat in the living room while you walked around and told us the tricks Noodle was going to perform. You told us Noodle was going to sit and stay. He was going to shake hands. He was going to bark on command and count to ten. Noodle wagged his tail every time you said his name.

"Then you started giving commands.

"Of course, Noodie didn't do anything, he had never been trained and wouldn't do a single thing we told him to. The more you told him to do, the more excited he got, and he started jumping up in a frenzy and trying to lick you, and barking, and whirling around in a circle. You stuck out your leg and told him to jump over it, and he barked and jumped up and tried to lick your face. You said he was jumping over your leg, and finding the ball, and counting to ten. All he did was bark louder and louder and wag his tail. Then you said that, for the grand finale, he was going to fly through the air, singing the Marseillaise!

"We all started laughing, and Noodie started running back and forth to us, jumping and licking and barking and whirling in circles, and we all laughed—you were completely unfazed by Noodie. 'He will now fly through the air, singing the Marseillaise,' you said again. 'Here he goes!' It still makes me laugh," Julia said.

"But now, Jackie, you break my heart."

Jack leaned back in his chair. *Moment to moment. Nanosecond to nanosecond.*

"Last year I went downtown to hear you play at a bar. I waved to you when I went in, and you smiled. I could see right away there was something wrong. You couldn't really open your eyes, and you lurched. Once you staggered, and I was afraid you were going to fall down." She stopped. "You weren't drunk. It was different. As though you weren't in charge of your body. I went up to talk to you after the set, and your eyes were strange, and your head kept bobbing. You couldn't really concentrate on anything I was saying, and finally I stopped. I couldn't really have a conversation with you. I felt as though I'd come to the wrong place. I'd gone all the way down there and didn't get to see you. My son wasn't there." She drew a breath.

"I want you to stop what you're doing." She wiped quickly at her eyes. "You must stop.

"When you were little, you had such beautiful pearly white skin, much whiter than anyone else's in the family. I used to call you my pearly-baby. Now your skin is yellow. And I've seen your arms."

Everyone looked at Jack.

What the fuck, he thought. *As long as they didn't touch him.*

"Needle marks," Edward said gravely. It was a new way of seeing his family, as though a membrane had been pierced and some interior fluid were seeping among them. He had now become part of it. His daughters no longer seemed hostile and difficult, but troubled and in pain. Even Jack: it was impossible to judge him; he was also troubled, in pain. Who could say how it had happened? He remembered Ted's desperate face. These things were complicated, no one meant to cause pain. Blame was useless: it was a strange thought. Why had he been so full of blame? Who was he to judge?

Julia was crying. "It makes me so sad," she said. "I love you. You're killing yourself. I know who you are, Jackie. I know the person you are. I can't bear to see you doing this. You must stop."

Jack was rocking in tiny movements, the wicker creaked faintly with him. His head and joints ached, he ached everywhere. The creaking was in his ears. He'd had enough of this. He was in a blue spotlight, the horrible radiant pallor flooding around him. He could feel it on his eyelashes, it was caught in them like milk. He was desperate.

"Okay," Jack said, "okay." He squeezed his eyes shut. He wanted this over with, he wanted out of here. He did not want them to touch him. "I'll quit."

"Jack." Wendell stood and put his arms around his son. He squeezed him hard, rocking from side to side as though they were dancing. Wendell was choking, his breath caught deep in his chest. Jack stood within his father's embrace, stooped, trapped. His face, unseen by his father, was contorted. The embrace was excruciating, Jack nearly cried out.

Edward, sitting on the sofa, rubbed his knees and said, "I'm proud of you," but only Katharine heard him.

"What's going on?" she asked Edward.

Julia could not stop crying.

PART IV

THIRTY-TWO

The odd thing was that her life kept on going.

All that fall and winter, when Julia woke in the mornings she was already exhausted, the day lay ahead, insuperable. She felt as though she were trying to move something enormous up a mountain. All day long she struggled to shift its monstrous weight; by the end she had the sense that she'd moved it slightly. She never got it where it should be, and in the morning there it was again, the massive, inert presence, the steep looming mountain.

She was continually tired, and could not sleep. At night her brain seethed endlessly, like water in a tidal strait. She could not stop picturing Jack, out somewhere in the dark night, on the streets, in an alley, in a shooting gallery.

The mordant wit of heroin slang: a shooting gallery was an abandoned building, where addicts went to inject themselves. She knew all this now. She knew the nicknames and street talk, the drug slang, *horse* and *smack* and *downtown*, *China White*. She knew about the treatments, methadone and buprenorphine, she knew the theories. She'd talked to therapists and specialists, psychologists and doctors. Sometimes the weight of the knowledge was unbearable: it was not useful, as it turned out, because there was no way to apply it.

What was so strange was that the mornings kept arriving, long after she was able to receive them. Things kept happening, as though the world were still turning.

On the evening of her opening Julia arrived early at the gallery. Angela, her dealer (she could no longer use that word without thinking of Jack's), was in the front room, standing at the desk, leaning over an open drawer.

"Good, you're here," Angela said.

Angela was tall and commanding, with bold dark eyes and thick iron-gray hair pulled to the nape of her neck. She wore a white dress with a pleated skirt, and very high stiletto heels. She looked statuesque and authoritative, which pleased Julia. Angela's presence was command-ing, and she hoped it would convince people of the merit of Julia's work in a way that Julia's own presence—which often felt tentative and uncertain—did not.

Julia glanced quickly at the walls, a preliminary scouting, then back at Angela. She didn't want to look yet at the work. The shows were al-ways hung by Angela, who never let her come in before the opening.

"I'm looking for a red marking pen," Angela said. "I'll let you look around by yourself." She stalked majestically back into the office, the stilettos making two separate sounds with each step, like a small, very elegant pony. Ca-lop, ca-lop.

The gallery was in Chelsea, and it was a good space, with two big handsome rooms with polished dark floors, glowing light fanning un-obtrusively down from the ceiling. It was a good gallery, a good place to show. *Wasn't it?*

Coming into it each time, Julia felt anxious, wondering first if the gallery were good enough for her to show in. Should she be somewhere

else, in one of the huge impressive, famous places run by a legend?
Gogosian, Matthew Marks? David Zwirner? Should she move?

Her next thought was fear that she was not good enough for the
gallery, and how lucky she was to be anywhere at all, how lucky she
was to have a good dealer who took her work seriously. She had friends
who'd lost their dealers, who'd had their link to the professional world
severed. Friends who'd fallen from the sky, plummeting horribly into
ignominy. Julia was fortunate, fortunate to have Angela, who was definitely serious, if not legendary. Maybe she actually was legendary.
Maybe there was a small seedling legend here, growing. How would
you know?

Julia glanced up at the wall of work again, quickly, then away, her
heart sinking. *It was not what she hoped. It was never what she hoped.*
She could see she hadn't done what she'd intended. Nor was she breaking new ground: she wasn't combining video with cake, or making sculp-
ture out of garbage, or using pigment from moose urine. She was only
trying to work deeper into the presence of landscape, to find something interior that had not been revealed before. She was trying to create a certain set of relationships. She was trying to do something like
what Wolf Kahn did, creating his own glowing, mystical terrain. Why
shouldn't you work deeper into a tradition, instead of breaking out of
it? Everyone worked within some tradition, even if it was the tradition
of subversion, rebellion. What she wanted was her paintings to mean
something, to have their own speaking presence.

Like Albert York's, those small, powerful, enigmatic windows into a
world of deep feeling. *Feeling.* And those big portraits of her children
by Sally Mann, the enormous blown-up close-up faces, gorgeous and
somehow exotic, like nineteenth-century travelers in Egypt. Julia had
walked through those Sally Mann rooms over and over, staring at the
images, made breathless by their magnitude and glory, and wondering
why they had such power. It was feeling, it was passion. The pictures
celebrated those faces, raved over them: those huge portraits were the
Hallelujah chorus. Passion was what she wanted: Giotto's tiny angels in

the Scrovegni chapel, weeping and wringing their hands, quivering with grief like anguished hummingbirds.

Julia had no interest in art that jeered at passion. Irony was the suicide mode of art, so parasitically dependent on the culture around it, so instantly obsolete as the culture evolved. Who read Dean Swift now? Or "The Rape of the Lock"? Who cared about those ancient needle-sharp skewerers, so exquisite, so excruciating, so on the mark, so of the moment, so hopelessly outdated?

Whereas *King Lear* would be read forever. When everyone lived in spaceships, spending their adolescent light-years speeding out toward wherever Pluto used to be, they would still be reliving King Lear's tenderness and anguish, still writing about him for their senior papers. Passion would still drive the universe.

Julia glanced up at the wall obliquely, more slowly, then away again. She wanted to encounter the pictures in stages. She didn't want to catch them unprepared. She looked deliberately up at the nearest, then away.

She came closer, and began to walk, bravely, from canvas to canvas, her heart thudding. They were utterly unfamiliar. This was an artist whose work she'd never seen: these were totally unknown rectangles, filled with incoherent configurations. She stared at them with apprehension.

Although, looking carefully, she recognized some of the colors. She knew those umbers and ochers, that cadmium red. An ultramarine. And a familiar silhouette: the barn blurred into shimmering shadow by high noon. The image sounded a note, like a bell. She felt a pulse of surprised pleasure. The paintings stretched out in an even row along the immaculate white walls, small labels beneath each one: *Cove, Meadow II*. The dates.

She studied the next one: another passage that was good. She felt a surge of private, proprietary happiness. In fact, this transition, this whole section of the canvas was actually quite rich and gorgeous. And this white was bold, startling. She walked slowly along the row of paintings, not stopping. But one of them, she saw, was dead, the whole canvas dead. She felt it in her throat. It was wrong, an insult, mortifying. How had Angela allowed it to hang? She would get it taken down. But the others stood their ground, made their claims, said their pieces.

She stood back. What was it that she had meant to do? Was this it? This row of colored panels, these flat bright things hanging against the plaster walls?

Now, looked at from a distance, it might be a failure again. There had been something else, something quick and liquid, something deeper. That was what she'd been trying for, she'd wanted to make a large bright place, larger, more radiant, more frightening than here, but like it. These were only awkward, shorthand comments, hurried, incomplete versions of the larger thing. She had failed, as always; she'd come nowhere near the mark. She would have to stand here and listen to people offer kind words about the work, a low drone of pity thudding beneath the false congratulations.

On the white wall, in large letters, was her name. There was her name; there was her work; here she was.

Julia stood still in the middle of the room. She was wearing a long full skirt and a scoop-necked sweater. Her low, Bloomsburyish heels, with two neat lace holes, reminded her of Virginia Woolf. Her earrings, delicate, dangling, were a present from Simon.

It had begun. She could not change things. The pictures were done, they were up on the walls, they were presenting themselves to the world.

She had failed, maybe, but maybe not. Maybe what she was trying for could not be achieved. She had come as close, perhaps, as she could, as anyone could, given the limits, right now, of herself. All she could do was make things come close, as close as she could get them, to the real thing.

And actually, now that she let herself look at them more easily, these were close to what she had wanted to say. Even the dead picture seemed revived, it no longer seemed inert. There was the work to be judged, and there she was, accepting authorship. What she hoped was that people would see her intentions, that she was striving for that bright, liquid, melting thing. Now she felt giddy and anxious, full of alarm and anticipation. And also full of pleasure: it was an honor to be a part of this dialogue about art and beauty and value. Everything was near-misses, wasn't it? *Fail. Fail again. Fail better.* Suddenly she felt deliriously happy, inflated and buoyant with pleasure, simply to have the opportunity to participate in the great discourse.

Angela came out of the office and ca-lopped toward her. She smiled in a professional, proprietary way. "How does it look?" She was asking for compliments.

"Beautiful," said Julia. "You did a beautiful job."

Angela nodded. She liked hearing this. "I think it looks very good."

Angela would never say the work itself was good. She never gave compliments. When Angela saw new paintings she looked at them carefully. Sometimes she said, "Interesting," sometimes she said, "I like that one." Sometimes she asked questions about technique. "I hope you go further with that." At the end she nodded and said, "When will you be ready for a show? Can we talk about dates?"

Once, Julia had said, "What do you think of it?" What she was hoping for was something juicy and delicious, something she could take home with her and gnaw on, at night, in bed.

"I think you're moving in the right direction," Angela said coolly, her eyelids shuttering.

After looking at new work Angela took Julia out to lunch and they talked about their lives, and movies, and people they knew, but never about art. Julia understood, from the lunches, and of course from the shows, that Angela continued to believe in her work. She had learned not to expect praise. Sometimes, rarely, Angela said, "It's strong," or, "That's really good." Julia treasured those words, and she did gnaw on them later, in bed.

Actually she didn't want fulsome praise from Angela. There was nothing you could believe about your work from other people, nothing. Praise sounded false; criticism, mean. Everything was biased, of course, there was nothing objective about responses to art. There were a few friends you could trust to tell you the truth, but it was only *their* truths. Nothing made you certain of your place in the world of art. You had to find it yourself and then make it your own. You had to create your own balance, your own certainty. No one else knew what you were trying to do. You had to find your own faith, you had to stand up for it against the assaults of logic and fear and the articulations of the whole critical world. You had to close your eyes to everything else, repeating your personal creed, reminding yourself of what you were doing, why you were doing it.

What she thought about each day was like a symphony carried on in her head, the endless melody of daily life, finding the other shoe beneath the bed, listening in a departmental meeting, setting on enough stamps to match the latest rise in postal rates, all those tiny steps that made up each day. Underneath that, all the time, was the repetitive bass line of Jack. The same thudding note, over and over. He was there in everything; it was a shock each time she re-encountered the thought. How could the rest of the world be trundling heedlessly along like this? There were times on the bus, on the subway, in a class she was teaching, when the bass line seemed to drown everything else out and she was unable to hear the other music, and then she felt as though she had lost some link to the world, some connection to the way it ran for other people. Then she wanted step forward, to her class, or the other people on the bus, and say, *Do you understand what's happening?*

By six o'clock, Angela was standing out in the front room with Julia. Camilla, Angela's assistant, with smooth blond hair and watchful eyes, was back in the office. Julia and Angela made desultory conversation, waiting for the first arrivals.

"Nice shoes," Julia said to Angela. She was sucking up, but also she liked them.

"Thanks." Angela raised one foot behind her, like a racehorse. "Manolo."

"They make your legs look great." This was purely sucking up.

Angela glanced down with satisfaction at her legs, which were too thin and had no shape.

"I like those shoes by what's-his-name," said Julia. "The French designer. With the red soles."

Angela looked at her reprovingly. "Christian Louboutin. They start at six hundred dollars a pair."

What you had with your dealer was not exactly friendship: power was too present in that landscape. With Angela, Julia walked a delicate line. She knew that Angela wanted to be the one who had the expensive shoes, the names to drop. It was understood between them that Angela was meant to be the one who inhabited the great world, full of important people and expensive things. Julia was meant to be the artistic one, bohemian, impecunious, and unworldly. It was better for Julia not to mention her house in Maine, even though all the paintings were done there, even though the house, the barn, and the meadow were endlessly present to Angela, and in fact they were what Angela depended on professionally. But Julia knew that it offended Angela, on some level, that Julia had a place in Maine. It offended her that Julia had gone to boarding school and Angela to public high. Angela resented those things. She thought Julia should be poor and struggling and grateful.

And Julia *was* poor and struggling and grateful, in fact. But she also knew it was not wise to be too poor, because then she would seem pathetic and Angela would drop her. She knew she had to demonstrate some sort of power, some connection to the world that Angela recognized as important.

It would be better, Julia thought, if she were unaware of all this, if she were simply an artist, thinking only about doing her work, but that was impossible, and she was not. The awareness of the balance between them was always there, it was present at every conversation.

"Oh, did I tell you? I got tenure," Julia said.

Angela nodded. "Congratulations," she said neutrally, as though this were merely form. Of course Angela's artists would have tenure. "The *Times* came in," she said casually. "This afternoon."

Thank God, thought Julia. "Good," she said. Of course Angela's shows would be covered by the *Times*.

Angela nodded, watching the door.

Julia stood beside her, mindful of the work on the white walls. She could see it, the long row of quadrangles, without looking at it. She was sure of nothing. It was out of her control. Here it all was, to be judged, waiting to be judged by the *Times*, by the people soon to arrive.

Your task as an artist was to create another body, another you. You produced a metaphysical self, a counterpart to the physical. This was one that grew as you aged, that took on mass and weight and authority as your own body declined. These, now, were the shapes and forms that defined you, they would be what you left behind. It was on the work that you would be judged. No one cared what Picasso was like (ruthless, sexually voracious, diabolically competitive), or that Robert Frost had been brutal to his son, who had finally committed suicide, or that Norman Mailer had stabbed his wife. It was the work: that was how you'd be seen, how you'd be judged.

You'd be judged in any case. You were judged all the time, by the critics, by your colleagues, your peers, your students, your family. Your work and your life. You were judged as a person as well: there was some code, moral, ethical, that underlay everything. Julia felt that. Some large judgmental force. She understood that she was always striving to be good, to be virtuous; she could not have said for whom. Virtue was her true north, she charted her course by it.

She wondered if all this was different for men. Did they feel it, this endless impulsion toward virtue, the sense of obligation? She thought they did not. What a relief not to have this endless beat in your head, the fear of making mistakes, of letting people down, of disappointing them and the world. Did men not have it? Was it only women who were so intent on being *good*, on not stabbing their spouses, on not being diabolically competitive or cruelly disloyal, on not breaking the rules? Was it only women who felt the need to present, to some invisible arbiter, a blameless life? Did men not feel that? Did they not feel guilt? Julia felt guilt all the time. Judgment and blame stalked her, their eyes blazing.

There were different kinds of judgment, there were different parts of your life. She was ready to be judged as an artist on her work, but nothing more. To be judged as a person, as a mother, to be judged on her children, her marriage, made her throat close with anxiety. *God forbid,* she thought. The bass line thudded in her head.

Julia went into the other room for a drink. A tall silver vase filled with calla lilies stood on the desk, and a bar had been set up. The floors were clean and newly polished. The space was brimming with silent expectation. The bartender stood behind a white-draped table, a young man in black-rimmed glasses and a short white jacket. He had a diamond stud in one ear and a narrow little spirit beard. He was so blond that the beard looked as though it had been drawn on his chin, then smudgily erased. He looked at her, attentive.

Julia asked for mineral water. He poured a plastic glass full of chemically enhanced bubbles and handed it to her.

"Congratulations," he said respectfully, nodding at the walls.

"Thanks," Julia said. "Are you an artist?"

They all were, the waiters and waitresses at these things. Someone had made a movie about them. It was their day job, or actually usually the night job. Julia felt a rush of warmth: they were so professional, so careful. They worked so hard. Everyone worked hard, she thought.

The bartender nodded again. He frowned slightly, looking serious, to show that he was in it—art—for the long haul.

"Good luck," she said, smiling. She didn't ask anything more. Right now she couldn't take on the weight of anyone else's needs, their hopes. She didn't want to learn about his M.F.A. from BU, about the mention of his work by a critic, in his first group show, or the theory connecting physics and religion that underlay his approach. Right now she couldn't tolerate the burden of anyone else's aspirations, though she wished him well.

She turned a little away from him and smiled at Camilla, who was sitting behind the desk. Camilla stood politely, and folded her arms over her honey-colored blazer, her white silk shirt.

"Congratulations, Julia," she said. "The work is beautiful."

"Thank you," Julia said. It didn't much matter what Camilla said. Angela had a new assistant every few years. They were always smart and good-looking, always courteous and smooth. They moved on, to an art magazine, to a museum, to graduate school. While they were at Angela's, they were creating a network, getting to know the dealers, the collectors, the artists. They were always pleasant to Julia, respectful. It was part of their job, it meant nothing.

She stood again beside Angela, sipping at the stinging bubbles. She shifted from one witty little Bloomsburyish heel to the other and wondered where Jack was. The question was never not in her mind.

While Jack was in Carpenter's rehab program in Florida, she'd heard from him every day. Not because he was dutiful but because it was one of the judge's stipulations. She'd flown down to see him, she'd met his counselors and his friends. She'd gone to the family sessions, she'd sat beside him on a folding chair in the circle.

Everything was going well, she'd thought. Jack was healthy, he'd gotten over the infection, he'd tested negative, thank God, for AIDS. He'd seemed—well, committed was not quite the right word, but he'd seemed positive and sensible. *Engaged.* Conscientious. Wasn't he? He'd seemed engaged by the process. He took it seriously. Julia had never asked him if he was *committed.* She'd asked how things were going, what the people were like. She'd never said, *Jack, do you swear you will never again take heroin? Are you making this your lifework?* She didn't have to say that, did she? Those things were the whole point of rehab. She had never asked those particular questions, and Jack had never volunteered his response.

She'd met with Carpenter privately, in his small office. The walls were white. He sat behind his smooth-topped desk, his black eyes boring into her. He held a pencil with both hands, rolling it slowly between his fingers as he talked. He talked about the way rehab worked, and the way chemical addiction worked.

By then Julia knew how chemical addiction worked. By then she'd read widely about heroin. She'd scoured the Internet. She'd read books. She knew heroin addiction was nearly a national epidemic. She knew about the addiction of the young, educated middle class. She knew about distribution by gangs, she knew what countries specialized in it, what it was called on the street. She knew about tying off and booting up. She knew where the opium poppy was grown—the Golden Triangle, Southeast Asia—and how it was made into heroin. She knew it was grown, too, in Afghanistan, which received a huge U.S. agricultural subsidy, and where the heroin industry supported the Taliban. She knew heroin had been legal, at its inception, in the late nineteenth century. That it had been created, named, and distributed by Bayer, the same German drug company that made aspirin. That it had been patented and sold briefly as a painkiller.

Julia had been to NA meetings and support groups. She'd heard the terrible stories. She'd talked to recovered addicts, who stood too close to her, looking too deeply and earnestly into her eyes, telling her that Jack could do it, he could definitely do it, stay clean.

That first time she went to see him, Carpenter, rolling the pencil back and forth in his fingers, said Jack was doing fine, he was doing very well. Carpenter held her gaze with his, watchful, intent.

The program had cost thirty thousand dollars and their insurance paid for seven. Julia and Wendell had scraped the rest of the money together, and Steven (bless him) had agreed to apply for student loans for his tuition. (The thought of Steven was a small, painful, constant irritant. He was something she must attend to; she could not do it, she could not, not yet. She had meant to have a celebratory lunch after he'd submitted all his applications, but she had not, not yet.)

Julia still had Jack's rehab schedule in her desk, with its reassuring rota: exercise, group therapy, art therapy, maintenance work, community service. Most of the residents' time seemed to be spent on exercise and therapy. Jack did yoga, and he sat in circles at Group, and he talked about whatever it was he was supposed to talk about. He admitted that he had no control over his addiction, he gave himself up to a higher power. He admitted how bad he felt about everything. How fearful he was about going on with his life. He learned it would get better. He breathed through one nostril, he did child's pose, and downward-facing dog.

When Carpenter called, she heard at once in his voice why he was calling. "I'm sorry to say I have some bad news," he said, but she'd known it when he said her name. "Do you have a moment?"

The bad news was that Jack and another resident had been expelled from the facility for using heroin. Needles.

Julia flew down to Florida. She still felt then that she could get to the bottom of things. She still felt that if she could just get hold of things, she could make them go right, she could force them to go right. She still felt that then.

Carpenter explained the program's fixed rule: no one there could use drugs. There were no second chances; he was sorry. But he did help get Jack into a sort of halfway house, with a part-time work program. The probation officer in Maine permitted this move as long as Jack was still under supervision.

By the time Julia arrived, Jack had already moved out of the rehab facility. He was living in a stucco house that had been painted turquoise, but with gray patches on the wall where the outer, turquoise, layer had fallen off.

Inside, the house felt damp and smelled of mold. The door opened onto a dirty room with a stove and sink in one corner, a brown sofa in another. An arched doorway led to a narrow hallway. Jack was in a small back bedroom. The walls were white, with meandering cracks in them. There was a bed and a bureau. The bureau was painted tan, but one of the drawers was apparently from another bureau, and was red. Jack's duffel bag lay on a limp rug.

When she came into the room, Jack looked up at her. He was sitting on the bed.

"Hi," he said, nodding.

"Hi," she answered. She knew better, now, than to touch him.

She sat down on the single chair. Jack leaned forward, elbows on his knees, staring straight ahead. His face was empty.

"So what happened?" Julia asked.

Jack looked at her, then away.

"*Jack,*" she said.

"*What,*" he said, exasperated.

"Why did that happen?"

He shrugged and looked down.

"*Jack,*" she said.

"I fucked up," he said.

"*Why?*" she asked. "Why did it happen?"

He shrugged again.

"You have to try harder," Julia said. It was like shouting into the wind. "*Jack,*" she said again, loudly.

He said nothing, staring into space.

"*Goddamn it,*" she said. "*Goddamn you. What's the matter with you?*"

Later he'd been thrown out of that place, too. Apparently there were odd gaps in the legal system, which meant that he was not sent back to jail. Technically he should have been, for violating parole, but it seemed that Florida was too far away for anything to actually happen to him, there was some sort of ambiguous gray area here, and then he got into another halfway house. That meant he was still staying in touch, still working his way through rehab programs. Nothing would happen to him now until the trial, Olson said. Each time she spoke to him, Olson reminded her about the trial.

This time Jack found a new place by himself, in North Carolina. This time Julia sent him a ticket for a bus, not a plane. She planned to go down and visit him there, but before she could, he was thrown out. After that, he came back to New York and got into a halfway program in Brooklyn.

Everyone agreed that New York was the worst possible place for him, Carpenter, Olson, everyone. Your new life was meant to be entirely separate from your old. You weren't supposed to see anyone from your addictive life, and how could Jack be avoiding his old friends, his old ways? But Jack said he was. He swore that he saw no one from the bad old days. He swore he was calling Olson every day, though Julia knew he was not.

"I'm telling you," he told her on the phone, "I'm not seeing anyone I used to see."

"What are you doing for a job?" Julia asked.

"Working in a café. Waiting on tables."

"What's the name of the café?" she asked.

"Dar es Salaam," Jack told her, but when she looked it up, it was not in Directory Assistance.

She had no idea where he was. He said he had no phone. She was tempted to buy him a cell, but she had stopped giving him anything that could be converted into money. He was unreachable. Days went by and she had no idea where he was, or what he was doing, or if he was still alive. Her stomach was permanently clenched.

At home on West 113 Street Julia had changed the lock on her apartment and told the super not to let Jack in if he asked. She tried to harden herself against him, she tried to ready herself for the worst. Whatever that was. It was exhausting, being ready. She wanted to hear from Jack; she dreaded hearing from him. The burden of fear was exhausting.

She no longer believed anything Jack told her, although he was her only source and what he said was all she knew about him. He might be lying about everything, she had no way of knowing. Wendell heard nothing from him at all.

The trial was now two weeks away, and she was planning to fly up to Maine with Jack. He'd agreed to do it; he knew about the house. He knew she'd lose it if he didn't come with her. She knew by now she couldn't trust him. She knew this would mean something to him only if he chose it to. She'd told him she'd pay him to go. She didn't call it a bribe; she said she'd pay him for his time, so he wouldn't lose out on salary. It was a bribe. The thought of the trial, the possible loss of the house, sickened Julia.

Someday this would all be over. In twenty years, ten, it would be over; somehow it would be resolved, but how? There were moments when she thought she could not bear it any longer, *she could not bear it,* but she could not stop it. She could not escape it. Jack and heroin made that relentless bass line, that terrible thudding constant in her consciousness. There was nothing else so strong, nothing she could do to stop it. Her cell phone was always on, and each time it rang, her heart lurched with dread.

But the days kept appearing, every morning, in spite of this, as though it were not happening.

Now, in the doorway of the gallery, two friends from Columbia appeared. The opening had begun. Here were Judith and Scott, both artists, both teachers. Judith was tiny, with huge dark eyes, her graying hair in a spiky crew cut. Scott was stocky and intense, with a big nose and short curly hair. Judith waved to Julia and then pointed at the paintings.

"We're going to look first," she called, and they headed for the first one. Julia waved them on. She watched their progress; they moved slowly, stopping at each one, murmuring. Judith was generous and warm-hearted, undervalued, Julia thought, as an artist. Scott was an intellectual, and his work was full of references to international politics. He was fervent and determined, self-absorbed, interesting, challenging.

After their circuit they came back. Judith stood before Julia and took her by the arms and kissed her on both cheeks.

"Congratulations," she said. "It's really beautiful."

Scott nodded. He pushed his glasses up on his nose. "I like the transformations," he said, "the way you're continually asking me to reconsider color theory."

Julia felt a kind of beatific calm settle around her like an aura: this was real. What she was doing was real. There were people who understood it.

The rooms began to fill with bodies and sound. Here was New York, Chelsea, the art world. A tall woman with a mass of blond dreadlocks moved through the crowd, wearing a long skirt and felt boots, and carrying a needlepoint knapsack. Young men in black-rimmed glasses, with stubbled chins, wearing black shirts with the sleeves rolled up, stood about in clumps, holding plastic glasses of wine. The young women wore white shirts and black skirts, skimpy black sweaters.

A fortyish woman with a wide painted face, round red circles on her cheeks like a kewpie doll, talked loudly, laughing and gesturing, with a leash in one hand. A tiny moppy white dog huddled at her feet. Through a gap in the crowd Julia could see him, his front paw raised in supplication. He looked anxiously around, trembling. No one noticed him, and the crowd was thickening. Someone would step on him and hurt him: he was too small for crowds.

Julia wondered if she should say something. She didn't know the woman, and wouldn't it be officious, to tell her how to treat her dog? The woman laughed loudly, leaning her head back. *What should you do, when you saw something going wrong? Sail in and announce your views? Let people run their own lives? How did you decide?* She wondered if her friends had seen things, over the years, that concerned them about the way she'd brought up Jack. Did they talk to each other? Had everyone known she'd been doing a bad job? *Had* she been doing a bad job, or was it bad luck? Was it her fault? How could it not be her fault? She was his mother.

The room was filling with friends and colleagues and students. It was a group that had emerged, from years of having openings, from years and years of New York art. There were artists and art writers, her students and their friends; there were critics and historians, teachers and freelance curators, musicians, editors, dancers, filmmakers, graduate students, gallery interns, art groupies, hangers-on.

And there, she saw, was famous Onie Wexler, with his big thick mop of curly hair, moving through the crowd, with that little smile that he couldn't seem not to wear, nodding at people, noticing everyone noticing him. People who didn't know him watched him out of the corner of their eyes, following his progress through the room, and people who did know him moved at once to speak to him, smiling as though the sun had come out, and why was it that Onie Wexler was so famous and Julia was not? They were contemporaries, they had started out in the same group, they knew the same people, and something about his work had caught fire in the critics' minds, and now he was famous and Julia was not.

There were moments when Julia could not help it, she burned with the pure gemlike flame of envy. Because what was the point of all this, all this groping, year after day, for something hidden and mysterious, this struggle to find the secret harmonies within the music of the world, this struggle to play the great chords of the human soul, if the world were so utterly indifferent to your efforts?

She wouldn't, actually, have minded so much if the world were indifferent to all artists. She could have endured that. What was painful was that the world embraced people like Onie Wexler, that the world took them to its vast, approving, nurturing bosom. It gave them lavish, uncritical praise and respect; it gave them other famous people who sought their friendship. It gave them the belief that what they were doing was important, that their work was respected and recognized as serious. And why did the world not give all this to Julia? There were moments when this was galling and bitter.

But there were also moments, like when Judith grasped her arms and said the word "beautiful," that Julia was simply grateful for the life she had, grateful that she was allowed to do this—make art. She was, miraculously, permitted to make these images, and miraculously, other people recognized what she was trying to do and came to see them and talk about them, and even to buy them.

Julia smiled at them, her friends and students and colleagues. She was introduced to the friends they had brought, and everyone said admiring things, and then they talked about museum shows, and movies, and food, and books, though not about politics, because they all agreed on politics. Simon was not here yet. He was coming later, and would take her on to dinner, with Steven. (Or she *thought* with Steven, they hadn't actually managed to talk person to person to confirm it.)

The gallery was full of bodies, the air humming with talk.

"Julia," someone said, and she turned to see Wendell and Sandra.

"Hello!" she said.

"Congratulations, Julia." Sandra gave her little fox-terrier smile. "What a beautiful show."

"Thank you," Julia said. "Thanks for coming."

Wendell gave a little lift of his chin, instead of a kiss.

"It looks good," he said, serious. "Really good. Anyone come in?"

"The *Times* was here this afternoon."

Wendell nodded encouragingly and held up his crossed fingers. There was a pause. A man behind Wendell caught Julia's eye, and lifted his glass to her. She smiled and nodded, then looked back at Wendell. She saw that he was not through. He came closer to her.

"How are you doing?" he asked, his voice lower. "With everything."

She shrugged cautiously. "All right. What about you?" She didn't want to discuss this here.

Wendell shook his head. "Not so good. I kind of can't shake this." He seemed perplexed, as though the problem were that he couldn't shake it, not the fact that his son was a heroin addict.

Sandra put her hand through his arm. "He can't sleep."

"No," Julia agreed.

"You look tired," he said to her.

She did not answer. She knew how she looked.

"How do you think he sounds?" Wendell asked.

"Wendell," she said.

"You don't want to think about it now," he said.

"There isn't ever a moment I'm not thinking about it," she said.

"I keep wondering if that was the wrong place to send him," Wendell said.

Julia shook her head slightly, irritated. "We have no reason to think that. Why do you think somewhere else would have been better?"

A woman leaned in past him, toward Julia. Her hair was a neat little helmet, going gray.

"Congratulations, Julia," she said.

Julia smiled. "Thank you."

"This is shop talk," the woman said, "but I keep wondering: How do you get those blues?"

"Oh," Julia said vaguely, nodding. "Another time."

She smiled at her and then looked back at Wendell. "All those rehab places say the same thing, you know. Building self-confidence, healthy activities, personal attention, all that stuff. But none of them have good numbers, none of them. They say things like 'Fifty-five percent of our patients are clean for the first year after treatment. Thirty-five percent more substantially reduce their drug use.'" She looked at Wendell. "Only half of them quit. And only for a year. Reducing the use of heroin isn't a cure, it's meaningless. No one offers a cure. The best numbers are for methadone, which is just legalized addiction."

"Yeah," Wendell said. "Maybe we did it wrong."

"Stop it," said Julia. "The chances were always bad. We just didn't want to see it. Anyway, what else was there besides rehab?"

"That was the money for Steven's law school," Wendell said. "And that guy—" He shook his head, mouth tight.

"What's the point of saying this now?" Julia asked. "Carpenter was fine. I mean, Steven was right, he was kind of a jerk, but he was fine. It was something we had to do. It was good for us, and it was the best we could do for Jack."

"Oh yes? What did it do for us? Steven's not speaking to us, and Jack's back on the street."

Angela materialized beside her. "Julia," she said briskly, "there's someone I want you to meet." She gave a brilliant smile. Angela's teeth had been artificially whitened by a process involving custom-made dental trays. She had told Julia about it. "Excuse me, Wendell," Angela said. "Julia, this is James Martin." There was no mistaking Angela's intentions; it was like being suddenly fixed in the glare of a spotlight.

"Excuse me," Julia said to Wendell. She hoped he'd leave. She could not bear going through this, sifting through the husks of their intentions. *What was the point?* It was an endless circle. Someday they'd get through this, someday they'd have their sons back. Someday it would be over. She could not sift endlessly through it, trying to see where they'd gone wrong. They had no options, they'd never had. All they could do was push on until it was over.

"James Martin." The man smiled at her with his mouth closed. "The James Martin Gallery, in Mayfair." His voice shifted, the tone rising. "Mm, I wanted to tell you that I like your work very much."

"Thank you," Julia said.

He told her about his gallery. Julia had never heard of his artists. She leaned politely in toward him.

"I wonder if you could tell me a bit about what you're doing?" he asked.

Julia looked at him. It was difficult, in the middle of this noisy jovial crowd, surrounded by the high dense hum of competitive conversation, to talk suddenly in a different way, using the language of high art. Difficult to move suddenly into another realm, from this jostling, deafening one into the private, solitary one of aspiration. Difficult to explain—right now, at the top of your lungs, standing beside your ex-husband, who is devastated by your son's terrible spiral into despair—that you had a vision.

Was it a vision? Julia wouldn't have described it exactly that way; she wasn't a saint. (Was this something else that was different for men? Did they more readily describe themselves as visionary? Wasn't that grandiose? Were women more modest, more self-effacing?)

What she had was a struggle. She was struggling toward something, some ideal of light and color, some way of locking mass and tone and hue together into something larger than the sum of their parts. Each group of paintings she did moved her further along in that struggle.

And the struggle now had something to do with Jack. There was some connection between the work and that awful thudding bass line, though she could not explain this to James Martin, so sleek and tall and narrow-shouldered, with his beautiful pinstriped suit, beautiful but badly in need of ironing, and his dark blue shirt, his slightly dirty hair and his black-rimmed glasses, his bad teeth and his charming smile.

My son is a heroin addict, and nothing we do will make him stop. Every second I'm afraid I'm going to hear something terrible about him, something I will never recover from. I'm frightened, I'm terrified, all the time.

She talked to James Martin about the long tradition of luminist painting, about the light in Grunewald, La Tour, Fitz Hugh Lane. How the Abstract Expressionists had excluded light as a presence.

"Francis Bacon didn't use light, it wasn't part of his vocabulary," she said. "Neither did Jackson Pollock. The idea of light implies the presence of the natural world, so it violated the idea of abstraction. That really interests me."

She could talk about the way light itself had now changed, how it fell differently on the landscape because of changes in the climate, the shrinking ozone layer. How radiance had become glare, how sunlight as a presence had become destructive instead of benevolent. James Martin might not want to hear that part: he was in Mayfair, after all, not Soho. He might not want ecological statements that challenged the politics of conservative capitalists. He might simply want beautiful landscapes to offer rich newly made baronets.

But light was what informed her work, and she could talk about that. Terror informed her work now, too, it had become a presence, though she could not talk about that. One of the new paintings, mostly red, was full of her terror. Light and terror.

She smiled at James Martin.

He took out a thin, worn, soft-leather wallet and drew out a card.

"I'm at the Mark this week," he said. "Will you call me? I'd love to hear more."

"Absolutely," Julia said, and took the card. James Martin raised his hand, smiling, his head tilted forward in a slightly secretive manner, and slid off into the crowd.

Julia was pleased, but she had few expectations. Nothing might come of this. Even if it did, even if she showed her work in London, the English press would not give her a standing ovation. She was American, she was a woman, she was working in a tradition that others had already mined. It would be good to have a show in London, but it wouldn't be the making of her. She didn't know what would be the making of her; probably there would be no making of her.

"Julia," someone said, and she turned. It was another group from Columbia, her students.

"Hello there." She smiled at them and they smiled back, earnest, hopeful, scruffy.

"This is gorgeous," Anson Weisman declared, shaking his head. He had a big loose mouth and pop eyes, and was her noisiest and most charming student. "Gorgeous."

"Thank you," Julia said. She loved this part of her life, too. She loved her students, and loved being part of something that stretched so steadily out into the future, through these smart, curious, talented people who wanted to learn what she had to say, to better it, to climb onto her shoulders and see into the future, to stand on her shoulders and be the future. "Nice to see you here."

Behind Anson's beaming, cherubic face she saw someone else appear, his face turned partway toward her, his gaze cautious, oblique. It was Eric. As he caught her eye, he lifted his chin warily, a small gesture that she could acknowledge or ignore. Was it Jack's gesture, that little lift of the head?

Suddenly Julia was drenched with rage: it was intolerable that Eric should appear here, flaunting his body, his mannerisms, his DNA. It was intolerable that he might be Jack's father and bear no responsibility for his dreadful life, his ghastly struggle. It was intolerable simply to see Eric here, parading his freedom, his sexual presence, his genetic heredity.

Your son, Eric, if he is your son, is a heroin addict. He's been arrested on felony charges and sent to rehab instead of prison, and then expelled from rehab. Now he's in and out of halfway houses, living in Brooklyn and waiting on tables. Or so he says. Good genes, Eric!

What she would have liked to do was kill Eric, right there. Simply kill him, or have him killed. It should be instantaneous, he should feel no pain, but he should know that she had done it. *Get away from me or I will blow your fucking head off.*

Was that from a movie? Did she think she was holding a gun? It was a wonderful thing to say. She said it again in her head. *I will blow your fucking head off.* She felt herself glowing with hatred and fury. Wisely, Eric turned away; she saw him drifting into the crowd.

"Jules," someone said, right at her elbow. She turned to see Harriet.

"My God," Julia said.

Harriet smiled tentatively. "Here's Allan."

Allan had round eyes, and he wore round tortoise-shell glasses and a striped bow tie. He held up his glass earnestly in a salute.

"To Julia," he said.

"This is a first." Julia wondered if she sounded accusatory.

"Allan had to come to New York on business," Harriet said, wondering if she sounded defensive. "I saw the notice of your show in the *Times*, so we decided to come today."

"That's great." Julia could not remember how she reacted around Harriet—was it cool and wary?—but that wasn't appropriate now. How did she react when her sister did something friendly and generous? It had never happened. And she had never been with her sister at a show like this.

"We've just been walking around," Harriet said. "They're incredibly beautiful. I haven't seen your work in a while."

"We want to buy one," Allan said. "We've chosen it. *Blue Cove III*. Do I talk to that blond girl?"

"I'll tell you who I'm going to talk to, that woman with the cheeks. I'm going to tell her to pick up her dog," Harriet said. "I hope she's not a friend of yours. I'm going to threaten her with a summons from the ASPCA."

"Thank you," Julia said.

Eric had vanished, and Julia felt suddenly at risk. What Julia didn't want was for Harriet to ask about Jack. She couldn't afford to tell about Jack, about how it had all failed, about how she had failed, about how terror had become part of her life; she did not want to break down, right here, in the middle of her own opening.

THIRTY-THREE

"I have the feeling he's right nearby," Julia said. She was looking out the window, watching the people on the sidewalk, "I can feel him."

They were in Wendell's car, cruising through Brooklyn, nearing Jack's old neighborhood. The light was beginning to fade, and the low shabby buildings were turning shadowy. The streetlights had come on.

"Let's try his apartment, the one I saw," Wendell said.

"He shouldn't be there, though, should he?" Julia said. "He has a whole new life. He said he wasn't seeing any of his old friends."

Wendell said nothing.

"I wish Steven were here," Julia said.

"I wish Steven were speaking to us."

"I wish Jack were still at the halfway house," Julia said.

Wendell snorted. "I wish."

On the corner of Jack's street stood a group of heavy young black men in baggy pants and puffy black parkas. Wendell parked halfway down the block, at a hydrant. He locked the car when they got out.

In the foyer they pushed the buzzer for Jack's apartment. "I think this is the name," Wendell said. No one answered. They rang again, and as they stood waiting, a young man opened the door from inside and pushed quickly past them. "Thanks," Wendell said, and caught the door. The man hurried on down the steps without answering.

The hall was dimly lit and smelled of mold. They climbed the stairs to the third floor. Upstairs, the walls were a dirty yellow, the floor gritty and unswept. At the apartment door Wendell knocked loudly. They could hear a television, squeals of a high-speed car chase, the synco-pated rattle of gunfire. Wendell gazed at the door handle, as though he could make it move through concentration.

"Even if he's there, why would he come to the door?" Julia whispered.

Wendell knocked again.

"Maybe we should get a policeman," Julia said.

"You can't just ask for a policeman for an evening," Wendell said. "It's not like hiring a waiter."

"He's jumped bail," Julia said. "Doesn't anyone care?"

"Day after tomorrow, in Maine, they'll care if he's not in court," Wendell said. "But we can't tell a policeman in Brooklyn to go after a bail jumper from Maine."

"We have to find him," Julia said. She felt suddenly mortally ex-hausted, as though she were physically wearing herself out, as though she were rubbing her soul against something solid and abrasive, wearing herself thinner and thinner, using herself up. "We have to find him."

Wendell knocked again. The sound filled the hallway.

They heard footsteps descending slowly down the stairs. A tiny woman came into view, gray-haired and untidy. She moved slowly, us-ing a cane, and setting both feet on each step. She wore a shabby green coat, buttoned wrong, the hem slanting asymmetrically over her heavy black shoes. She pulled her coat tighter when she saw them.

"Don't go in there," she said shrilly, "they're junkies. They'll steal anything you have. They took my cat food last week."

Julia frowned and said nothing. Wendell knocked again. The woman watched them, bright-eyed and accusatory, stepping painstakingly from stair to stair. When she reached the hallway she waved her cane at them.

"I'm telling you," the woman said, her voice rising, "they'll take the fillings from your teeth."

Julia looked at Wendell. He turned the doorknob.

The woman made her way, rocking with each step, across the hall to the top of the stairs.

Julia said quietly, "No one's there."

Wendell said nothing. He knocked again, now with the heel of his fist, loud and authoritative.

The doorknob turned suddenly and the door opened slightly. A man stared at them through the crack.

"What is it?" He was in his thirties, with a wide bald head. His cheeks were unshaven, and the hair on the side of his head was long and unkempt. There were gaps among his teeth.

"We're looking for Jack Lambert," Wendell said.

"We're his parents," Julia said, smiling hard. "He's not in any trouble. We just want to make sure he's okay."

"Don't know him," said the man. He breathed with his mouth open.

"He was living here," Julia said.

"I came to see him last summer," Wendell said.

"Not here now." The man rubbed at his eyes.

"He's in his twenties—" Wendell began.

"Here's a photograph of him." Julia had it ready and held it out.

The picture was from several summers ago, Jack down at the dock with the Whaler. He was tilting his head and grinning, squinting in the sun. Tanned and beaming, the water glittering behind him.

The man glanced down and shook his head. "Never seen him before."

Julia looked at the picture. "He looks different now," she said. "You might not recognize him from this."

"Don't know him," the man said again. His tongue moved among the gaps in his teeth, bulging obscenely.

"Whose apartment is this?" Wendell asked.

The man's eyes narrowed and he tilted his head. "It's none of your business whose apartment this is. I don't let strangers come in and ask questions, okay?" He started to close the door. "I don't know who you're looking for, but he's not here."

Julia slipped her fingers around the frame, so he'd have to crush them to shut the door. "Please," she said, "I'm his mother. Please just listen to us."

The door remained ajar.

Julia looked at Wendell. "What's his name? Jack's friend who lived here? Who was it?" She looked back at the man through the crack. "Russ," she said. "His friend Russ lived here. Is he here now?"

The man shook his head. "Not here."

"But you know him, right? Our son used to play in a band with Russ." Julia hoped that was right. *Please,* she thought, *please, please.* "We just need to see him for a moment. We just need to talk to him. We won't make trouble."

"Not here," said the man. "Look, lady, I can't help you. I don't know your son. Russ isn't here. I'm closing the door, so move your fucking hand."

Julia felt wood against her knuckles, and drew away her hand.

Then the bald man looked past them, down the hall. The old woman had stalled at the top step, staring at them. He shouted, "Get out of here, you old bat, before I rip your legs off!"

"Shut your mouth, you sick piece of trash," the woman muttered, but she kept her voice low. She turned and started laboriously down the stairs, cane first.

When Julia looked at the door again, it was closed. Wendell turned away, heading down the hall.

When they were back in the car, Julia said, "Should we have hired a detective? Maybe that's what we should have done."

"Maybe we should just take all our money and throw it off the Brooklyn Bridge." Wendell turned on the headlights.

"What does Sandra think?"

"Sandra thinks what everyone thinks: we're doing everything that can be done. Christ. We've done the intervention, the rehab, the half-way programs, the outpatient rehabs. What have we missed? A stint at Guantánamo? Rendition?"

He pulled out into the street. A brick warehouse stood on the corner, sealed and shut for the night. A dog hurried across the street, thin and furtive, its whiplike tail tucked between its legs.

"These pit bulls," Julia said. "It's sickening, they use them as weapons. They train them to fight, and if they don't win then they abandon them." The dog disappeared between two parked cars, then emerged to cross the sidewalk and vanish into an alley.

Wendell said nothing.

"Sometimes I think we aren't doing everything," Julia said. "Sometimes I wake up thinking there's something else, something just, you know, right on the tip of my tongue, I can almost get it. I have the feeling there's one more thing I should be doing, something I haven't thought of yet.

"It's like finding something in the last place you look: I'm trying to think of the one thing we haven't tried yet, the thing that will cure him. I chase it around in my mind in circles."

"Sometimes I just want to hire a killer, a hit man, to go and get him," Wendell said. "I just want it to be over. Sometimes I feel as though I'm going crazy: there's no answer to this."

"Sometimes," said Julia, "I feel as though I shouldn't do anything else in my life, anything at all, except try to cure him. I shouldn't go to the movies, or have dinner with Simon, or paint, or teach, or even eat or sleep. I shouldn't do anything at all, nothing except try to find him and help him. Make him stop. That's my task." She gave a tiny snort of helplessness. "But I can't even find him, let alone help him."

There was a pause.

"Another thing," Wendell said. "We have to do something about Steven."

"I can't think about Steven," Julia said. "I can't even think of his name. He has no presence in my mind. I can't even get to the idea of

Steven, because Jack's there first. If I even think about Steven, I feel I'm being disloyal to Jack."

"Yeah," Wendell said. "Sandra says we have to do something about him, though."

"I know," said Julia. "She's right, but I can't."

"I have the feeling we're losing him," Wendell said. "He's kind of drifting away."

Julia shook her head helplessly. "I just can't. I can't do both. I know you're right. He didn't even come to my opening, and the last time I talked to him it was as though we couldn't hear each other. But I can't do it. I have nothing left in me right now." She looked out the window. "Do you remember where the dealer lives?"

"I think I can find it," said Wendell. "I should have gotten that fucking Russian cabdriver to take us, maybe he'd remember."

"I keep thinking I see him," Julia said. "My mind tries to turn every figure I see into his, anyone, even little kids, girls, black people, I sort of mentally force them into being him. It's like that time they were lost out in the boat and we were looking for them. I kept thinking I saw them, I kept making images of the boat and their bodies, out of the mist and the waves." She laughed shortly. "Remember how scary that seemed? My God, it was so simple. It was just a boat out in the dark. All we had to do was find them and they were safe." She sighed. "Jesus."

"I think it's on this block." The shabby storefronts were sealed shut, with corrugated metal shutters drawn down to the sidewalk and padlocked for the night.

"Heavy drug use," Julia said, "that's what those shutters mean."

"What?" Wendell asked.

"Where there's a high rate of drug use, shops use those metal shutters. Junkies break through plate-glass windows."

"We know that." Wendell looked up at a row of dingy brick buildings. "It's one of these. What if we find him and he won't come with us?"

"He has to," Julia said ferociously. "I'm taking him to Maine if I have to carry him on my back."

Wendell turned the wheel hard and began backing into a cramped illegal slot. "Okay," he said. "Get ready."

The foyer was tiny, with scarred gray walls and a floor littered with Chinese restaurant flyers. The lock on the front door was heavily reinforced with metal plates, but the door itself stood slightly ajar. They went inside. There was no light, and they started gingerly upstairs in the dark.

On the third floor Wendell led Julia down the hall. At the back of the building was a heavy door with a peephole. They could hear loud music inside. Wendell knocked hard, and after a moment the music was turned down. Wendell knocked a second time. They heard approaching footsteps, then a rustling sound as someone looked at them through the peephole.

"Who is it?" A low voice, like a man's.

"Hi, I'm Jack Lambert's father," Wendell said, looking ingratiatingly at the peephole. "I came here with him last summer."

"He's not here," the voice said.

"Dana, right? I paid what he owed you," Wendell said. "Remember?"

"He's not here," she said again.

"Please," Julia said, peering at the peephole. "I'm his mother. Please just talk to us. Please."

There was a pause. The music was turned lower and the door opened a crack. A skinny dark-haired woman stared out at them, square-jawed and gimlet-eyed. "He's not here."

"But have you seen him? We need to talk to him," Julia said. "I'm afraid something's happened to him."

"He hasn't been here," the woman said. She stared at them without blinking.

"*Please*," Julia said. "*Please let us in.*" Something was mounting inside her.

"Don't get crazy," the woman said. "He hasn't been here. I can't help you."

"Don't do this," Julia said. "Don't do this to us."

"I'm not doing anything to you," the woman said. Her eyes were narrowed.

"Julia," Wendell said.

"Please," Julia said, "please help us. We have to find him. I know you used to see him, I mean you used—we're not here to make trouble, we just want to find him. Please, please just let us in, please just talk to us. We have nowhere else to go."

"You think if I let you in I'd know where he is, but I'm telling you I don't," the woman said. "I haven't seen him. I can't help you." She shut the door and they heard the locks turning.

"Oh, please," Julia called through the door. "Please help us."

There was no answer, and Julia leaned her face against the heavy door and began to cry, though she had sworn, sworn, sworn to herself that she would not cry on this expedition. She began to cry, very low in her throat, and her whole body began to tremble. Wendell put his hand on her shoulder, and then he put his arms around her. They stood together on the dark landing, holding each other. The music inside was turned up again. It was pounding and loud, like the rumble of tanks.

When they reached the car they got in and shut the doors. Wendell did not turn on the engine. Julia blew her nose and sighed.

"I don't know what to do next," she said. "What shall we do? Drive around? Do you think she was telling the truth?"

Wendell shrugged. "She has nothing to gain by telling us anything. If he'd been there ten minutes ago, why would she tell us? Everything about drugs is illegal. No one will tell us anything. All these people are in their own kind of trouble." He looked out his window. "I don't know how to find him. Nobody knows anything. He hasn't been at the last halfway house in weeks."

They sat in silence. A bodega stood on the corner, and colored lights from its window spilled out onto the sidewalk. The door opened and two Latina girls came out, wearing long wool coats over jeans. They started walking fast, leaning close, their shoulders touching.

"I'm going to lose the house," Julia said.

Wendell said nothing.

"I wouldn't mind if it were in exchange for something—for him. If he'd quit, I'd be glad to give up the house." She shook her head. "It's such a fucking waste to give it up for nothing."

"What part of this is not a fucking waste?" asked Wendell. "What part of this is constructive? What part of it is another aspect of the long, natural, difficult but rewarding task of being a parent? What the fuck is this for? Why did it happen? What good is it? Are we meant to *learn* something from it?" He looked out. A streetlamp stood nearby, haloing the darkness, gleaming on the parked cars beneath it, fading within yards into dimness. "It's not like a disease, or a car accident: random bad luck, part of the natural laws of the universe. This is entirely *volitional*. It could be stopped. This whole situation can be completely reversed, only we can't make that happen." He shook his head. "It's like an exercise in existential torture: our punishment is to sit for eternity and watch our son destroy himself."

"Without eyelids," said Julia, "without blinking. And it's full-time. I keep thinking that if I'm thinking of him, I'm helping him. I have to be always on duty. And I get angry so easily. I can't believe what my friends talk about: a problem student, a sweater the cleaners shrank. I feel enraged. And if anyone's five minutes late, or hasn't done what they said they'd do, I want to tear them apart."

"Yeah. It sucks. All of it." Wendell sighed. "So. It's nearly seven o'clock. We may as well have dinner. Do you want to get something to eat someplace around here, in the off chance we run into him?"

"I want to stay here until I find him," said Julia. "I have to find him to take him to Maine. I can't leave. I want to walk up and down every street."

"We can do that," Wendell said, nodding.

"I have this feeling that he's right nearby," Julia said. "He's just one block over from wherever we are, moving parallel to us. He's within shouting distance. I can feel it."

She opened the car door and leaned out into the darkness. *"Jack!"* she shouted. *"Jack!"*

She stayed motionless, holding on to the door handle, listening. She called his name again. *"Jack Lambert!"*

She remembered the night they were out looking for the boat, calling out across the waves. The call, then the long pause for the answer. She called again, louder, more serious. Wendell, beside her, did not move.

Rounding the corner behind them, Jack stopped at the sound of his name. He saw the small dark car parked at the curb, someone leaning out the open door. He heard his name called again. He recognized the voice.

He drew back into the shadows of the building and turned sideways, hunching his shoulders and ducking his chin beneath the collar of his jacket. He watched Julia leaning against the door, motionless. She called his name again.

The words came at him like weapons. Jack glanced around. A bearded black man with a knitted cap was walking by. He paid no attention. No one noticed the call, no one realized it was his name, that he was Jack. Still, it was like weapons, knives thrown at him. His mother waited, holding on to the door. Jack waited, shifting from foot to foot in the cold. He sniffed largely: doper's drip. Was that his father in the driver's seat? It was. His parents were parked outside his dealer's.

Rage rose up in him: they had no business here. This was his territory, they should get out. The universe was dark enough, filled with his shadows. He could hear footsteps on the sidewalk. He hated that, the pock-pock on the sidewalk, like the horror of an approaching clock. The sound filled up the cavity of his chest. His heart was ready to tear itself from his body, he felt it pounding dangerously in there. No one could come near him, he couldn't risk anyone approaching him. Panic flapped its huge leathery wings about his head and he shut his eyes. The world tipped slowly on its axis, slanting horribly away from under his feet. He could feel its shift: in a moment he'd fall off the curving side of the planet, dropping into black gravityless space. He felt himself losing his balance and opened his eyes. Slowly the planet righted itself. He looked around, in the shadows, but there was no evidence: no slanted buildings, no toppled trash cans. But it was real, he'd felt it in his body, the vertigo, the fear. There was nothing that was safe, nothing. You were on your own. He heard the pock-pock of the footsteps again, approaching him.

Maybe he should walk over to their car and offer to clean their windshield for twenty bucks. Maybe he should just ask his parents for money. But they'd stopped giving him money.

There was something about going up to Maine: it was the fucking trial. That's why they were here. His mother wanted to take him up to Maine for his trial. He'd shoot his foot off first. He'd shoot her foot off. He stood in the shadows and watched them, his chin behind the collar of his jacket. It was getting cold.

They had no right to be here, in Brooklyn. On his own block, one of his blocks, his territory. He was cold. He'd sold his parka, and all he had was this windbreaker he'd found in a bin. He was cold, and he needed dope, and he could feel the world swirling around him. He felt the air fill up with menace. It was in his throat, he felt the choke of it in his throat.

Two young black men, in black parkas and knit caps, walked toward him on the sidewalk. As they neared, one of them glanced at him. His eyes were bulging, the whites liquid and brilliant.

His heart thundered in his chest. Everything now was perilous. The air was full of glittering blades. What he could not see, what was just beyond the corner of his eye, was deadly. How long were they going to sit there in their car, waiting for him to walk by? He should go over and tell them to get out of here. He hated having them here.

"I think he's everywhere," Julia said. She pulled the door closed. "I keep seeing him. I think he's that guy over there on the corner, the one with his back to us, in the windbreaker. He looks like a bum. Jack probably looks like a bum now." She turned to Wendell. "How long do we go on with this? I don't mean looking for him, I mean the whole thing. How long do we just—pursue it?"

Wendell didn't turn. "What choice do we have?"

"Sometimes I just wish it were over, just over, any way. I can't stand this," Julia said. She leaned back against the seat. "I just wish he'd end it."

"I know. I feel like he's taken over our lives as well as his."

"Every day I think about this," Julia said. "While I'm teaching, if the door opens in the middle of class, I look up and think, It's happened. Every time the phone rings I'm afraid to answer. But I can't wait to answer, I have to know right away. I can't stand to be alone, but I don't want to see anyone. I can't concentrate on anything, and I can't sleep. I take a pill and sleep for two or three hours, then I watch TV. I can't even concentrate on that. I'm just waiting. I'm waiting all the time."

Wendell leaned back against his own seat. "It's like that for me, too. But I'm angry all the time. Sandra tells me to calm down." He shook his head. "She has a lot of advice for me. But it's not her son. What does she know? How can I stop thinking about it? I can't take a break." He tapped his thumb against the steering wheel. "We fight about it. I'm angry at her, too. I don't know, we might not make it."

"Because of this?"

"I'm sick of having her tell me how to deal with it. I'm sick of having her there all the time." Wendell tapped the steering wheel again. He glanced at Julia. "She looks like a dog. Did you ever notice that?"

"A dog?" Julia felt guilty, as though she had put this thought into Wendell's head.

"A terrier. The bright eyes, that pointy little nose. I keep wanting to check and see if her nose is damp. Actually, I don't want to touch her."

"Oh God," Julia said. "I'm sorry."

"Yeah," said Wendell moodily. "It's too bad. But you have some new guy, right?"

. She nodded. "I sort of do. Simon. He's very nice, he's great, in fact. But he doesn't understand any of this. He's never even met Jack. I don't want him to see Jack while he's like this, I want to wait until he can meet the real Jack."

The night had darkened around them. The street had turned black. Along the edge of the sidewalk were dirty scraps of frozen slush. On the upper floors dim lights shone from the windows. A drug lord drove past in an SUV, the windows darkened, music blasting and pulsing.

"I want the old Jack back," Julia said. "I keep waiting. I can't get off the ground with Simon. I can't concentrate on that, either. I know he won't wait around forever, but I just can't focus on him. I can't have sex. I feel as though, if I let myself think about Simon, if I let myself fall in love with him, if I stop concentrating for one night, or for one minute, on Jack, I might lose him. Jack has to be in my mind every second, or he'll be lost.

"So I don't know what will happen with Simon," she said. "I don't know what will happen about anything."

"I'm sorry about the house," Wendell said.

"I can't think about the house," Julia said. "The house is the least of it, of everything. And in a weird way it feels like a bargain: if I lose the house, I get him back."

"Goddamn him," Wendell said, his voice low and fervent.

"I know," Julia said.

They sat without speaking. A black woman walked quickly past, wearing a long coat and pushing a stroller. The man on the corner waited, his chin tucked under the collar of his windbreaker, freezing, angry.

The call came at eight in the morning.

It was not an alarming moment of the day, it was not as frightening and heart-thudding as two o'clock in the morning would have been, but still, it was too early for most calls, though what did any of that matter?

Julia went over it afterward, moment by moment, how she had felt when she raised the telephone—faint uneasiness—what she had been looking at—the grimy molding around the kitchen doorway—what she had felt when she heard a strange man's voice say her name—"Is this Julia Lambert?"—terror.

Everything went on high alert, then, heart pounding, chest thudding, as though, by sending out adrenaline, as though by knowing at once what was happening, by giving herself an extra split second of awareness she would somehow be in more control of this, but she was not in control of this, there was no control to be had over this.

"Mrs. Lambert, my name is Terry Shaughnessy, and I'm calling from the Public Examiner's Office. I'm sorry to say that I have some very bad news."

That was how it happened. That was how the rest of your life turned black and empty, like the sky around a tornado. You heard those words, you knew what they meant, and you were powerless to prevent them. You could say, *Don't say anything more,* you could say, *You have the wrong person,* but none of that would help, because what he was telling you was true. It was true and it had happened, no matter whether he told you or not, and it had happened to your son.

She heard him say other things. Where the body had been found, the address. It meant nothing to her. There was identification on the body (the body, the body, she wanted to tell him it was not a body, it was her son), but they needed someone to come and make a positive identification.

Julia was standing in the kitchen. She leaned against the sink, bending over from the waist. "What happened?" she asked. "Tell me what happened." She straightened and put her hand over her eyes, as though that would let her hear better.

"Cause of death has not yet been determined, but it appears to have been an overdose of opiates."

"Yes," she said. "Tell me where he was."

He had been found in an abandoned building; drug paraphernalia had been connected to the body. *The needle still in him.*

A shooting gallery. She thought of his body lying on a filthy mattress, or on the gritty cold floor, in the darkness. He would be in some posture of protest at what was happening, the limbs raised and stiffened, the eyes closed, the features caught up in that last moment, bliss: at least he'd had that. An overdose was said to be the greatest high of your life, though who would know.

As Terry Shaughnessy talked, Julia tried to absorb the idea of his body lying on a mattress on the floor. Not him, but a body, his body. She kept circling back to that. She could not think yet of the word "death." Though that must be what the man had said to her. Had he said that word? She was trying to listen to him while she was trying to remember, trying to circle back and think of the body on the mattress, put that together somehow with Jack.

It had stopped. The body she knew had stopped. Where that life had been, beating on and on, like hers, breasting its way into an unknown future, there was nothing.

She said to Terry Shaughnessy, "What did you say?"

"I said, 'I'm sorry.'"

"Yes." She could not think of how to go on.

When she called Wendell, Sandra answered.

"Hi," Sandra said.

"No," Julia said, struggling upstream, "Wendell."

When he came on, she said, "It's happened," and then she could not say anything more.

They drove over together. As soon as they got off the Brooklyn Bridge, they were lost. They drove among strange boulevards, circles, parkways, plazas. It was nowhere near the area where Jack had lived, and they could make no sense of the landscape. It was as though a last humiliating trick were being played on them.

They found it finally, a tall pale brick building, in the middle of a long low block. They parked in the underground garage below it and took the elevator straight up into the building. The elevator was enormous, battered gray metal. It moved slowly, jerking and halting. Several times it nearly stopped. Julia wondered if it was what they used to bring the bodies up. They would be on those rolling stretchers, the kind in ambulances. Gurneys.

In the lobby upstairs they gave their names to the dour black woman at the desk. She made a call, and a young Hispanic man in an unbuttoned white lab coat came out. Beneath it he wore jeans and a T-shirt. He nodded soberly and asked them to follow him. He walked down the hall, his sneakers squeaking with every step. Julia was afraid of a cold room with bodies in drawers, the ghastly morgue from movies, but he opened the door of an ordinary small room. In the middle of it was a gurney, the body on it draped in white. In the corner were two beige filing cabinets and a metal chair, its back to the wall. Julia wondered if the room was an office at other times. What was in the file cabinets?

Jack took up the whole length of the gurney. His feet, beneath the sheet, were splayed, angled outward. The sheet was pulled all the way up to his chin. Julia wondered if he had been stripped. The thought seemed terrible: the defenseless body. The sheet had fallen slightly away on one side, revealing his neck, pale and beautifully modeled. Julia could not look at his face. The arch of his chest lay lightly under the sheet; she waited for it to rise, for the sheet to rise with his breath. It would not now. She could not bring herself to look at his face, but she could not help it. Her gaze rose to the side of his neck, the long prominent cord, the tender, whorled ear, and then beyond, to the still face.

His eyes were nearly shut. Below the swollen lids was a dull, unsettling glimmer. On one cheekbone was a faint dark smear of dirt. The mouth was slightly open, the chapped lips parted, though not as if he was about to speak. On his chin and cheeks was dark reddish stubble. There were his flat dark eyebrows, the sweep of his hair.

She saw that it was her son, though not. It was sickening. The room seemed full of ozone, too full to breathe. Beyond the gurney were the two file cabinets, the metal chair against the wall. Every detail was both bright and dark, as though seen by lightning. His face was the wrong color, deep blue-gray, and still. It was utterly still. She watched the eyelashes for movement. The skin was like clay, dull and inert, but the hair seemed bright and alive.

Julia reached under the sheet and took his hand, lifting it out toward her. She caught a glimpse of his bare gray hip. His hand was cold and very heavy, impossibly heavy. Along the inner arm were needle tracks, the sores open, dully shining. They would never heal now. This was her son. Something was in her chest, crying to get out.

THIRTY-FOUR

They walked single file through the meadow, down toward the duck. The grass lay in drab brown swathes, thick and beaten flat by the winter. The new growth was not yet started. The sky was dull. It was more like late winter pearl than early spring blue, though it was early spring. The air was cold, the wind fresh.

Julia went first, carrying the box. The undertakers had called it an urn, but it was a box. Bigger than a shoe box, rectangular, surprisingly heavy. It was covered in fake leather, and on the front was a brass plaque with his name on it, his dates. *His dates.*

Wendell was behind her, his parka zipped up to his throat. His shoes were leather, the soles slippery, and he stepped carefully. Behind Wendell, Steven walked on the damp flattened grass, beside Katharine. She was on the path, leaning heavily on her cane and on his arm. They'd borrowed a wheelchair from the Visiting Nurse Association, but it was still in the car. Katharine refused to use it.

Behind them were Harriet and Edward. Harriet had looped her arm inside her father's, as though for her own comfort, but actually she was worried about his footing: the muddy earth was frozen underneath and slick on top. At the end of the line were Simon and Allan, single file, walking carefully.

They had all parked in the driveway and walked around the house to the lower meadow. They had not gone inside. On the front door hung a bright padlock, and nailed above it was a bold black-and-white notice from the State of Maine. Another sign stood out by the road.

It was nearly high tide when they made their way down onto the dock. Julia crouched, balancing on the balls of her feet. She wore jeans and sneakers, a bright blue parka, a red wool scarf. The water lapped restlessly, glinting through the cracks, just beneath the planks.

When she tried to open the box, it stuck slightly. There was no handle on it, no latch; it was held shut by friction. She tugged and it opened with a jerk, spilling a little. The box was nearly full. The ashes inside were grayish, crumbly and grainy, mixed with mineralish bits. *These scumbled bits of cinders were his bones. It was him. His whole life was here. Everything he had ever done had been reduced to this boxful of granular ash. This was all there would ever be of him.*

Julia felt light-headed: the sky turned suddenly bright and spinning. She leaned forward, lowering her head until the blood moved back into it.

She stood up then and offered the open box to her mother.

"Have some," she said. "This is like a cocktail party."

Katharine looked confused. "What do I do with it?"

"We're throwing Jack's ashes into the cove," Edward told her. "Take some in your hand."

The others leaned in around her, scooping it out. Simon stood behind the rest, his hands folded in front of him. He was broad and fair-skinned, with comfortable pouchy cheeks, a lined forehead, thinning dark hair. Julia looked at him questioningly, raising the box, but he shook his head, blinking at her kindly. Allan stood next to him, his face sober.

Edward leaned forward, taking a handful.

These rituals were a way of knowing death. The mind has difficulty with it. It was always a shock, always difficult to absorb. In surgery he'd watched bodies become corpses, he knew the terrible jolt when everything stopped, the magnified heartbeat ceasing, the dentillated line on the screens flattening. Everything shutting down, the frightening intersection between the physical and the metaphysical. The body's decision to do away with the soul. Each time it was terrible, there was never a time it was not. You were losing a soul. Each time it was terrible. He patted Kattie's arm.

"Do we all wait and do it together?" Edward asked. "Or should we each do it separately?"

"I don't think there are rules," Julia said. "I'm going to do it more than once. Everyone do what you want."

Julia stood at the edge of the dock. The water spread out before her, restless and glittering. The smell of salt was strong. She leaned over, holding tightly to her damp fistful. How did you do this? What was she trying to achieve? As she stretched out her arm, the cold wind came up inside her jacket, and she shivered. She opened her fingers and let the ashes drop. They were oddly heavy, slightly moist. They fell in clumps, pitting the surface of the water, some sinking at once, some floating: tiny islands drifting off on the rocking waves.

Harriet took two big handfuls, then stepped to the edge and poured them into the water. Her hands were coated by the greasy ashes, and she dusted them hard against each other. She felt the film still on her skin, clinging, insistent.

Behind her, Julia heard Edward say loudly, "I'm going to see if I can get the house for you, Julia. Buy it back from the state."

Julia turned. "Can you do that?"

"I don't know," Edward said. "But they can't keep all the properties they seize. They must sell them to someone."

Julia's first impulse was to reject his offer, as she'd always done. But now, standing over the moving water beneath an uncertain sky, the cold breeze against her skin, the dark islands floating on the tide, she could not remember why. Why had she always done so? Why did she resist everything her father did, resent everything he said?

All of that seemed burned away from her landscape, which now lay bleached and colorless before her, empty of texture, endless. The briny wind blew steadily against her skin. Why would she oppose her father? The struggle was over. Jack was gone. She was trying to make his absence fit into her mind. The ashes were moving away on the tide, bobbing unevenly, sinking slowly. She could see them descending into the murky water. *The cold green swell.*

"Thank you," Julia said to her father. She turned back toward the water.

She didn't deserve the house: she hadn't saved Jack. But refusing the house would be like refusing to take her body back. It was what she inhabited. If she could have it back she would take it. It was something she needed.

Something about her father had changed, she didn't understand what. Maybe it was she who had changed. Everything about her own life had changed, she understood that, and that she had no power over any of it. She could see that this was how things worked: at speed, without warning, obeying laws that you would never understand. Humility lay over everything like a dense gray mist.

She believed in nothing so simplistic or logical as a natural moral system, no abstract code meting out judgment. She didn't think this was a punishment for adultery, nor for poor mothering, nor for her many sins, accruing over the years to a sum that required, by some terrible accounting, this unthinkable payment. She did not believe this, but she could not put it out of her mind. Because how else did she come to be standing here, under this cold pearl sky, the damp spring wind on her face, watching the burnt bones of her son sink into the moving water?

It was irrevocable, this. She could not now undo it, though she'd done something to make it happen. There was no way to undo it, make reparations, no one to whom she could apologize. Something was required of her, she did not know what. *What is it? What do I do?* But there was no answer, there would never be an answer. She would always be locked into this moment in this place, standing on the warped wooden planks, looking out over that flat, glittering, restless surface, as she had looked out that first night, staring and searching. But there would be nothing, now, for her gaze to light on, no sight that would offer solace. She would not find him again.

It's not my fault, she told herself. It was of course her fault. She was his mother.

Behind her, around her, were the other people in her life. A shift had occurred: Jack was gone, she had been left with these others, for some reason. She felt as though a soft hammer had been beating against her head for days. She could understand none of this. What was required of her? She would never know.

She could feel their presence behind her, these people. They were connected to her by something intimate and fluid, the connection too painful to consider. These were the people to whom she was closest and most painfully distant; the people she most longed to have near, whose touch was unbearable to her. Something in the blood made them kin, kept them apart. She could not bear to meet their eyes; their presence was essential. What was the cost of these connections, the cost of severing them?

Why had she held herself so separate? Her father was an aging man, struggling against the rising tide of mortality; her mother, her mind increasingly adrift, yearned for intimacy. Both of them were failing, losing the steps to life's intricate dance: *why had she insisted on distance?* Julia could not now remember. The breeze quickened, chill, moist.

She still rang with pain. She would carry it with her, high up under her heart, in the place where she had carried Jack, long before he was born, before he was anyone's child, when he was only a dream, swimming through her body. The pain felt like punishment.

She thought of the times when she had wondered where Jack was, sitting on the porch last summer and wondering if he was on some other porch, watching the night sky from there; the time in the boat, searching for the sight of his body; the time in Brooklyn, watching for his shape among the others on the sidewalk; all those times in New York, moving through the day, wondering, not knowing. It was strange to think she would never wonder again where he was. From now on he would be here, he would always be here.

She would not be able to bear it. She felt a sudden towering rage at the people behind her on the dock, all of them alive.

How did you do this? How did you go on?

She was choked by all this, by rage and grief at the loss, but for other things, too. She felt grief for her own cold, unfathered childhood, and rage at herself, for making it last so long, and for holding fast to resentment, and for never becoming better than she was.

All you could do was humble yourself, accept rage, accept grief. You could never be sure this wouldn't happen again. You could only be sure you would never be free of what had happened. This absence: something essential had seeped from the world, leaving it gray and inert. There was now a great silent ringing where the sky had been.

A herring gull flew, low over the water, slowly up to the end of the dock. Lifting and banking its wings, leaning back against the air, it landed gracefully on the last post.

Steven leaned over and took a double fistful of the ashes. It was damp and grainy, and molded to the insides of his fists, little negative casts of his hands, made from his brother's body. *This was like Communion, except real. This was not a wafer, it was the real body of his brother, these soft clenched shapes in his fingers.* All of his brother's knowledge and experience, his ideas and music, his manic humor and wild exuberance, had been reduced to this. *Where was he? He was nowhere in the world.*

He remembered that night in the Whaler, waiting for rescue, how angry he'd been at Jack. His own anger had risen up in him like bile, while the addiction rose up in Jack. He'd let his own small feelings take precedence over something monumental and inexorable. He'd let his brother perish.

He should have done something years ago, he should have gotten help. He'd let him go, he'd let his brother slip away.

He stood with the toes of his muddy sneakers over the edge of the dock, watching the water rocking below. The herring gull stood on the post, stretching out its wings for balance and watching with interest the bits being sprinkled into the water.

He felt wholly separate from the others. Before Jack had died Steven hadn't spoken to his parents in months. Estranged: he had become a stranger. All that time the thought of his parents had enraged him, he had wanted nothing to do with them. Their voices on his answering machine made his heart pound; he punched "Erase" as soon as he heard them, either of them. Everything they said, everything they did, enraged him. Now everything seemed frozen. After the funeral his mother had seized his arm suddenly, pressing her head hard against his shoulder as she wept, but he could feel that she was not asking him for solace. She'd gripped him because he was the nearest solid form.

It was his father who'd seemed to embrace him, to welcome him into a shared grief. During the service Wendell dropped his face into one hand, covering his eyes. As he did so he had reached, with his other hand, for Steven's.

The family was too badly broken now, too shattered, ever to heal. What was left? It was only really himself and his mother, his father had Sandra. What would Christmas be like, Thanksgiving, birthdays? Silence, the awful lifeless rituals, the unspeakable absence. The thought was torture. He wanted no part of it.

The ache he felt toward his mother was like a wound. He could not bear to be near her, but he could not desert her. He saw the two of them limping hideously together, their eyes elsewhere, sharing only this terrible deadening grief.

The water slapped insistently beneath his feet. The gull sidled on the post, spreading its wings, then settling again.

He forgave her, he forgave his mother. Only why had all this happened? How could he forgive anyone?

What lay ahead of him was the rest of his life. He had been accepted at NYU and would study environmental law. The admissions letter arrived the day he'd heard about Jack, splitting his life forever into two halves. What he did from now on would be separate from Jack, his whole life now would be separate from Jack. He would meet new people who had never known he had a brother. The woman he would marry, and the children they had, would not know his brother; they would never know that great central reef in his private sea, his other continent, his other self, himself as Jack. He would go on through his life without his brother.

How was that possible? It was not possible.

Wendell knelt on the edge of the dock. The gray wood was old and porous, saturated with damp. At once his knees were soaked. He leaned over and lowered his full clenched hand into the frigid water. He opened his fist, letting the cindery ashes drift out of his fingers. The water rose in a long heave, taking the sinking clumps from his grasp. He leaned back on his heels, watching, wiping his wet hands on his thighs. They were gone.

Katharine had let go of Steven. She stood with one hand on her cane, the other clenched, full of ashes. She'd seen what the others were doing. She moved toward the side of the float, setting her cane down carefully on the planks, not the cracks. At the water's edge she stretched out her arm.

Were they making wishes? Was that what they were doing, throwing this pale gritty powder into the ocean? Katharine opened her hand and stiffly spread her fingers. The crumbling ash dropped away into the air, and she wished, before she died, to have her daughter back.

ACKNOWLEDGMENTS

I'd like to offer my deepest gratitude to the people who have helped with various aspects of this book.

In doing research, I am indebted to many patient and knowledgeable people. For their very generous gifts of time and attention, I'd like to thank Dr. Lou Cox; Lindsay Ennis; Officer Leigh Guildford, NEHPD; Dr. David McDowell; David Ferriero, Wayne Furman, the Frederick Lewis Allen Room, and the great resources of the New York Public Library.

There is a large body of excellent material written on the subjects dealt with in this book. Particularly useful to me were the following: *Great and Desperate Cures: The Rise and Decline of Psychosurgery and Other Radical Treatments for Mental Illness*, by Elliot S. Valenstein; *Addict in the Family: Stories of Loss, Hope, and Recovery*, by Beverly Conyers; *Substance Abuse: From Principles to Practice*, by David M. McDowell and Henry I. Spitz; *How to Stop Time: Heroin from A to Z*, by Ann Marlowe; *Bad News*, by Edward St. Aubyn; and *The Story of Junk*, by Linda Yablonsky.

For the great gifts of their enthusiasm, support, and direction during the writing of the book, I'd like to thank my friends Susan Burden, Edward Burlingame, Nicole Eisenman, Honor Moore, Paula Sharp, and Andrew Solomon. Also thanks to Robert Pollien, who provided matchless tech support, arriving once within minutes on an emergency call when I had erased the entire manuscript. I am always indebted to my wonderful agent, Lynn Nesbit, and I am newly so to my wonderful editor, Sarah Crichton—to both of them for their wisdom and insight.

I am always, too, grateful for the support of my family, all of you, who make it possible for me to write. And thanks to my beautiful daughter, Roxana Scoville Alger Geffen, for the beautiful painting on the jacket.

A NOTE ABOUT THE AUTHOR

Roxana Robinson is a fiction writer, biographer, and essayist. She is the author of three earlier novels: *Summer Light*, *This Is My Daughter*, and *Sweetwater*; three collections of short stories: *A Glimpse of Scarlet*, *Asking for Love*, and *A Perfect Stranger*; and the biography *Georgia O'Keeffe: A Life*. Four of these were chosen as *New York Times* Notable Books; the most recent, *A Perfect Stranger*, was a *New York Times* Editors' Choice.

Her writing has appeared in *The New Yorker*, *The Atlantic*, *Harper's*, *The American Scholar*, *Best American Short Stories*, *The New York Times*, *Vogue*, *The Wall Street Journal*, *The Washington Post*, and elsewhere.

Robinson is also an environmental, garden, and nature writer. Her novel *Sweetwater* explores environmental issues, while her related nonfiction work has appeared as op-ed pieces in *The Boston Globe*, the *International Herald Tribune*, and *The Philadelphia Inquirer*. As a scholar of American painting, Robinson has written essays for *Artforum*, *ARTnews*, and exhibition catalogs published by the Metropolitan Museum of Art and other institutions.

She has received fellowships from the NEA, the MacDowell Colony, and the Guggenheim Foundation. She was named a Literary Lion by the New York Public Library. Her biography of Georgia O'Keeffe was nominated for the National Book Critics Circle Award. Her story collection *Asking for Love* was named a Book of the Year by the American Library Association.

Robinson has served on the boards of the National Humanities Council and of PEN American Center, and she now serves on the councils of the Authors Guild and the Maine Coast Heritage Trust.

Robinson has taught at the University of Houston and Wesleyan University; she now teaches at the New School. She spends time in New York City, Connecticut, and Maine.

A CONVERSATION
WITH ROXANA ROBINSON

Talk about what inspired you to write Cost.

I began to write *Cost* because I was curious about something rather quiet: the problem of being a good adult child. I was curious about why it is that even when you're a grown-up, and theoretically mature, and when you should have moved beyond all this, the fact is that when you're in the presence of your parents you find yourself tied inextricably to earlier, demanding, immature selves—the needy child, or the rebellious adolescent, or the superior twenty-one-year-old. It seems that all those earlier selves interfere with your attempt to be the mature, reasonable, generous grown-up child you want to be. Why is it that those selves seem often to dominate? When will we be able to disengage, cut ourselves loose from those earlier selves, and be on a level field with our grown-up parents? Why is it so hard to be the person you want to be? I was also interested in what it's like for older parents to be with their grown-up children; how it would feel to have your hold over life begin to fail, fear setting in. Feeling uncertain of your own strengths, frightened of becoming pitiable, trying to negotiate this difficult new territory. I found this interesting. I thought this was the subject of my novel. I thought it would be quiet, interior, meditative, domestic.

Heroin showed up in the story at the same time for the author that it does for the reader—in an early chapter, while Steven is remembering his visit to Jack. Right then it became apparent to me that Jack was a heroin addict. I was horrified both on his behalf, as it was such a dire prospect, so dark and ominous, and on my own behalf, because I saw that I'd have to enter a world I didn't know, one I found deeply daunting. I was daunted, but also fascinated. In fact I found it deeply compelling.

What kind of research did you conduct into the lives of addicts, and how did you get so close to their experiences and those of their families?

I used every method I could to learn about the world of heroin. I read and read and read. I talked to policemen and interventionists, to doctors and psychiatrists and counselors. And of course I talked to the families of addicts, and I talked to addicts themselves.

The novel drifts through multiple characters' points of view; why did you choose to tell the story in this way, and could you discuss the creative challenges of it?

I had written an earlier novel, *This Is My Daughter*, in three voices, but that was also written in three sections, so that each voice spoke alone. I wanted to write something more complex, in which all the internal voices were heard throughout. I wanted the voices to be interlayered, so that you could understand each character's response, what they were thinking as well as what they were saying. Often, what we're saying is different from what we're thinking, and this gap can be the source of deep misunderstandings, particularly within a family. I wanted the narrative to reveal those gaps to the reader. I suppose I was thinking of Wagner, and how he used the music to tell us what the character is thinking, while the libretto tells us what the character is saying. Anyway, I wanted to show the layers of responses that make up any conversation or relationship.

In order to do this without confusion, I wanted the reader to know each character very well before the action began. So I introduced each character slowly, with a lot of background, so the reader would understand the character, and why she feels the way she does, or why he reacts in a particular manner. Once the characters are understood, then, during a scene that involves all of them, we can move easily back and forth from mind to mind.

Cost addresses the social, emotional, psychological, and physical effects of addiction. What do you think addiction truly is, beyond dependence upon a substance?

This is a huge question, because addicition has so many components. But it seems to me that what lies at the heart of addiction is the addict's powerful urge to separate himself from the reality he finds around him. Often this is acted out in other ways, before the drug is finally encountered.

Would you talk about the response that this book has inspired, particularly among those who identify with the Lamberts' struggle to help an addicted family member?

The response to the book has been incredibly moving. I've received many messages from people saying, "This is what happened to me. This is my story, thank you for telling it." Sometimes these were from the addicts themselves, though more often from relatives. People who struggle with addiction often feel they can't talk about it, partly because the subject is so deeply entwined with shame and pain, and partly because most outsiders don't understand it. So these people bear their pain in silence, and pain borne in silence is somehow magnified. Readers told me what a relief it was to have this silence broken. Also, the written word can give a story a kind of legitimacy, and people have told me how grateful they are to see their own experiences articulated, how heartened they feel at being seen and at being given a place in the world. I can hardly express the respect I feel for the people who struggle with addiction. I feel honored to bear witness to their extraordinary compassion and bravery.

There is lately a whole culture of addiction and recovery, especially on television. What do you think accounts for our fascination? Do you find society sympathetic toward the addict or more reproving?

I think people are fascinated by addiction because of its combination of peril and proximity. It's as dangerous as climbing in the Himalayas, but it's right in our backyard. It could be us. How does it happen that one person ends up in the thrall of this demon and another does not?

I think many people feel unconsciously judgmental about addiction, the way they do about serious illness. Judgment works as a form of self-protection: if you believe that the person affected did something to bring this on himself—if you can identify what he did to "deserve" it—then you feel safer yourself. You feel protected. You distance yourself from the affected person, and you feel that in this distance lies your own safety. You think, *I'm not like that.*

When you began writing this novel, did you know already how it would end, or did the characters surprise you?

I did not know how the novel would end when I began it. I don't use plot outlines, nor do I plan the story. I start with characters and a conflict, and let the narrative develop from there. The characters really write the story.

In addition to your novels, you have written a biography of Georgia O'Keeffe, and also have done travel writing and writing about gardening and horticulture. What moves you to break away from fiction to write nonfiction, and on such a range of topics?

I write in so many different forms because there are lots of things that interest me. I can say things in a travel piece—on the writers of St. Petersburg, for example—that I couldn't fit into a novel or a short story. I write often about the natural world—climate and plants and animals—in ways that don't seem right for fiction. And art has always been an important presence to me—I used to work in the art world, and I wrote about American art before I began to publish fiction. Besides, writing a novel is a very slow process for me, and I like to take breaks to do something smaller and faster.

Who are your literary influences, and what are your favorite books?

The biggest influences are from a mostly Anglo-American line: Virginia Woolf, E. M. Forster, Henry Green, Elizabeth Bowen, Elizabeth Taylor, John Updike, William Trevor, Paul Scott, Shirley Hazzard, Isabel Colegate. These are the people who taught me how to write.

Many of my favorite books were written by them, but of course there are others as well: Tolstoy's *War and Peace*, Chekhov's *The Collected Stories*, Flaubert's *Madame Bovary*, Mann's *Buddenbrooks*, di Lampedusa's *The Leopard* (the only book I've ever finished and then, without even closing it, started in on again from the beginning and read straight through), Wharton's *The House of Mirth*. More recent ones: *The Radetzky March*, by Joseph Roth; *Disgrace*, by J. M. Coetzee; *The Rings of Saturn*, by W. G. Sebald; *Runaway*, by Alice Munro;

Whites, by Norman Rush; *Saturday,* by Ian McEwan; *Varieties of Disturbance,* by Lydia Davis.

What are the nuts and bolts of your writing process? What time of day do you write? Pen, quill, typewriter, computer? Do you have any rituals or superstitions about the process?

I use a computer. I start as soon as I get up and write for as long as I can. Fiction in the morning, nonfiction anytime. Coffee first.

DISCUSSION QUESTIONS

Hailed as "one of our best writers" by *The Washington Post*'s Jonathan Yardley, Roxana Robinson writes fiction that deftly explores the limits of human endurance, opening our eyes to the subtle landscape of memory and fate. In *Cost*, she brings us the gripping story of a fragile family tested when a son spirals into addiction.

The novels opens as art professor Julia Lambert, in her beloved summer house in Maine, settles into a visit from her aging parents. Her mother is beginning her descent into Alzheimer's, while her father, who was once a renowned neurosurgeon, copes with his helplessness in the face of her illness. Julia's son Steven arrives with a troubling revelation: his brother, Jack, is showing signs of heroin use. Before the summer is over, Julia will find herself navigating the difficult dual roles of daughter and mother as she tries to restore those she loves to an impossible realm of healing and compassion. Reconnecting with her self-absorbed ex-husband and her estranged sister, Julia slowly discovers the limits of her power as her son's substance abuse begins to permeate their lives. Yet she also discovers her far-reaching capacity for love, weighing her bulwark against a looming tide of loss.

1. Discuss the novel's title. What are the many costs—emotional and material—associated with Jack's addiction? What other circumstances lead the characters to consider their self-worth, or the "worth" of others?

2. How does Julia's relationship with her sister compare to Steven's relationship with his brother? What leads siblings to become estranged despite having been close during childhood?

3. What does the house in Maine represent to Julia at various points in her life? How does the house set the tone for the novel: picturesque, laden with memories, and in need of repair?

4. What does *Cost* tell us about the nature of marriage? What enabled Edward and Katharine to sustain their marriage? How does Wendell justify his affair? Is Harriet wise to avoid marriage, pursuing long-term relationships instead?

5. What are the repercussions of the parenting styles presented in the novel? Was Julia harmed by Edward's judgmental nature? To what extent was Jack's life a response to the way he perceived his parents?

6. Does Carpenter change Julia's family, or are they unaffected by his talk of loving interactions? What is captured in the moment when Edward mentally corrects Carpenter, asserting that addiction is not an illness (chapter 27)? Does Edward have different standards for the ill? Where does he believe self-determination ends and nature begins?

7. Steven is haunted by his parents' infidelity. Why does he blame his mother more easily than his father? How do Julia's memories of Eric shape the way she sees herself?

8. What accounts for the difference between Jack and Steven, who uses his rebellion for noble causes (such as protesting against loggers)? Would Steven have been an achiever if his brother had not been so troubled?

9. What portraits of the mind are offered in *Cost*? How does Edward feel about his memories of being a pioneering surgeon? What remains of Katharine despite her fading memory? What realities does each character create in the face of a disorienting world?

10. In chapter 32, Julia tells Jack that he has to try harder. Is Julia naïve or simply afraid of what lies in store for her son? How do the other members of the family respond to both the psychological and the neurological fallout of his addiction? Why is it easier for Julia to acknowledge her parents' faltering health, while Harriet wants to believe that they are just fine?

11. What aspects of Julia's life emerge during her gallery opening? What is the significance of Harriet's presence there?

12. What were you thinking as you read the novel's closing scenes? Which characters had changed the most, along with your impressions of them?

13. How would you and your family have responded to a situation like Jack's? What do you believe can or should be done to address the needs of those with such severe addictions?

14. What themes are woven throughout this and other novels and stories by Roxana Robinson? What is unique about the approach she uses in bringing Julia's situation to life?

CPSIA information can be obtained
at www.ICGtesting.com
Printed in the USA
LVHW090744080719
623349LV00008B/482/P